Advance praise for

Her
Unexpected
Match

"A beautiful, poignant, and heartwarming story of family, healing, acceptance, and of course, love finding its way. Everyone will want to travel to Crescent Island and never leave!"
—**Naima Simone,** *USA Today* bestselling author

"Lacey Baker writes with the heart our heroine of *Her Unexpected Match* is searching for, with a dash of her sass and layered with humor. She has mentally transported me to Crescent Island and I never want to leave."
—**Bree Hill from The Categorically Romance Podcast**

"A delightful, beachy romance full of heart and hope. Escape to Crescent Island and fall in love!"
—**Teri Wilson,** *USA Today* bestselling author

"A sweet and delightful story with witty and likable characters that give us laugh-out-loud moments and all the small-town feels."
—**Sean D. Young,** author of *Secrets from the Heart*

"A beautiful coastal town, an adorable puppy, a quirky cast of characters, and a slow-burn romance—the perfect feel-good read!"
—**Jennifer Snow,** *USA Today* bestselling author

Her Unexpected Match

Her Unexpected Match

USA TODAY BESTSELLING AUTHOR

LACEY BAKER

Entangled Publishing, LLC
644 Shrewsbury Commons Ave., STE 181
Shrewsbury, PA 17361
Visit our website at www.entangledpublishing.com.

Amara is an imprint of Entangled Publishing, LLC.

Edited by Stacy Abrams
Cover design and art by Elizabeth Turner Stokes
Stock art by Shutterstock/Francesc Juan,
Shutterstock/Timchenko Natalia, ehrlif
Interior design by Toni Kerr

Print ISBN 978-1-64937-350-2
ebook ISBN 978-1-64937-351-9

Manufactured in the United States of America

First Edition March 2023

AMARA

ALSO BY LACEY BAKER

SWEETLAND

Homecoming
Just Like Heaven
Summer's Moon

MORE ROMANCE FROM LACEY BAKER

A Gingerbread Romance
Christmas in Evergreen: Bells are Ringing

CHAPTER ONE

Did the air have a scent? Could she really smell re-laxation and simplicity the moment she stepped off the ferry? The Crescent Island website, along with its corresponding brochure—which she'd stuffed into her purse a few moments ago—said those were the first things she'd notice once her feet hit the island.

Allison Sparks inhaled deeply and released the breath slowly. She was tired and grumpy from travel-ing via plane, car, and then boat to get to this place that she wasn't quite sure was what it proclaimed to be.

Saltwater and…was that fresh bread? No, the smell was sweeter. She sucked in another breath, this time tilting her head back a little and closing her eyes to concentrate. Definitely a sugary aroma. Possibly a cake or cookies. Or maybe she was just hungry since she hadn't eaten in hours—twelve hours, to be exact. Since she'd grabbed the strawberry Pop-Tart the sec-ond it jumped up from the toaster and run out of her condo at five o'clock this morning to make a mad dash to the airport.

You would think that after years of traveling all over the world, she'd be a little more organized when it came to actually getting to the airport, but no, she'd overslept. And when she'd bounced out of bed, curs-ing the alarm on her phone for automatically going into snooze mode, she'd run into the bathroom, blam-ing her boss, Renee, for infusing this newest level of stress into her life.

"Subscription numbers are down," Renee had said four days ago as Allie sat in one of the ivory leather guest chairs in her office. "We have to make a change."

"Are you firing me?" Allie had immediately asked, because losing her job as the lead writer on the See, Eat, Travel blog wasn't exactly on her list of things to do this year.

Renee Timmons, with her close-cut bronze curls, had tilted her head to one side and stared at Allie with those cool, assessing, dusky-blue eyes. Renee and her husband Tyson had created the blog five years ago, and since that time it had morphed into a very lucrative venture.

"No," Renee had replied. "At least not yet."

Allie's stomach plummeted in the way it often did when she was on a roller coaster. She'd sat with one leg crossed over the other, her foot shaking because she'd been anxious to get the meeting over with so she could head out to her next appointment of the day. Not that she longed to visit her dentist, but it was a yearly necessity she'd rather get out of the way. With Renee's words, dental tools suddenly felt preferable, and she focused 100 percent of her attention on Renee. "Are you serious?"

Renee lifted a stack of papers from her desk and shook them in the air. "These numbers are serious, Allie."

"But my column is the most popular on the site," she'd countered.

"It *was* the most popular on the site," Renee corrected. "That was four years ago, when your critical reviews were sprinkled amongst the other content on the site. Now, with the state of the world steeped in one adverse event after another, people are growing weary of the pessimism. And when I say people, I'm mainly talking about some of our sponsors, who no longer want to be linked to so much negativity."

"People always act like they want honesty, then complain when you give it to them," she'd said.

"I'd like it if you found a way to give them a little less honesty. Or at the very least, serve it with heaping spoons full of sugar so it'll be easier for them to digest." Renee had given her a half grin, but Allie knew she was serious when that grin quickly faded and Renee slapped those papers back down on her desk. "Your next article needs to be more positive. Something uplifting and maybe softer."

"But I don't do soft," was Allie's immediate reply. Her lips had clamped shut after the words fell free, as if her body were somehow reminding her brain that shutting up was free.

But it was true. All her life she'd been let down by the concept of positive thoughts, and being soft had never been allowed—although her younger sister Bella would've sworn Allie had that trait perfected. Allie's entire childhood had been disastrous to her mental stability, and in her adult years, she'd fought valiantly to climb that hill to what finally felt like normal.

Changing now seemed daunting.

"I want a heartwarming, family-friendly piece, Allie. One that doesn't include an oversize mouse and his friends." Renee raised her brow and continued, "Find a beautiful vacation spot for parents to take their kids now that school is out for the summer. Tell us all about the fun activities, the delicious, budget-friendly food. Give us pictures of all things wonderful and appealing."

"What if a spot like that doesn't exist?" Because if it had, why hadn't her parents ever taken her and Bella when they were young?

"They do, and you can find them, if you give it a try."

"I find beautiful locations to report on all the time," she'd argued.

"And then you rip them to shreds in your review." Renee shook her head. "After giving some thought to the feedback from the sponsors, I started thinking about how worn out I am, too, by so much negativity. My kids are even coming home from school talking about this argument or that threat of violence they had to be sent home for."

She sighed. "I wish for a kinder, gentler world for them and everyone else. But the only place I really have control over some of that is this blog. So my goal is to soften the tone of the space, add some inspiration and empowering articles. You're among my top three columnists, Allie. And I don't want to lose you; that's why I'm giving you this chance to show me you can find the heart in this new destination and write about that, instead of giving your critical thoughts on the location. Every place has a heart if you're open enough to see it."

Staring through the tinted lens of her sunglasses now, Allie decided she couldn't see anything on Crescent Island that resembled a heart. Not immediately, anyway.

Sure, it was a brilliantly sunny early-June afternoon, and the way the sun's rays glimmered over the surface of the water reminded her of an expertly filtered postcard picture, but looks could be deceiving. Her parents were a perfect example of that.

She walked on four-inch heeled sandals across the wood-planked dock that seemed to stretch forever. Actually, she kinda tip-toed over the planks because the last thing she wanted was a replay of a scene from one of her favorite movies, *The Wedding Planner*. Yes, she loved romcoms—books and/or movies— even though she'd never been brave enough to give love a shot personally. But no, the real reason the movie was her favorite was because of the awesome meet-cute scene, where main lady had the heel of her shoe stuck in a manhole cover and main guy came along and saved her from getting hit by a runaway dumpster.

The writers who'd come up with that had surely earned their pay. It was fiction at its best.

Before she could allow herself to drift into that warm abyss of disappointment mixed with her trademark cynicism, she sighed and took the remaining steps until coming to the part of the dock that split off in three different directions. To her left was more of the thick wood-planked walkway and the red-shingled Ferry Office where she'd have to return at some point during this trip to schedule her ride back to the mainland. To the right was, again, more wood—as if this town had never heard of cement. The brochure boasted no malls and very few streetlights. It didn't say no real streets.

Shaking her head, she tried to rid herself of the

negativity Renee had expressly prohibited in this new article. If it rolled around in her mind, there was a very good chance it would end up on page. So, for the last two days since she'd decided this was the place she needed to be to find the "heart," as Renee had commanded, she'd also been whispering to herself periodically to try and brighten her thoughts.

That shouldn't have been such a difficult task, but after spending the first twenty years of her life holding in every opinion, observation, and accusation she possessed, she'd promised herself that her adult years would be different. Just the thought of her parents and their displeasure with her career choice, her hairstyle—whichever one she had when they saw her—the clothes she wore, her condo—the list could go on and on—had her temples throbbing. She willed the thoughts to cease and sucked in another gulp of the deliciously scented air.

Her stomach churned and her eyes popped open as she recalled she was still hungry.

Turning to her left, she started walking again. If memory served from the brochure, she should've kept going straight toward Main Street where she could attempt to hail an island taxi. That was the only rideshare on Crescent Island. There were also no buses or other forms of local transportation. With her luck, there was probably only one taxi driver and vehicle as well. Sighing and giving herself another mental reprimand about those pesky, dour thoughts, she mumbled, "Look for the heart."

That didn't mean she couldn't find the food in the meantime.

Whatever smelled so good was calling to her, and

she drifted farther down the dock, already deciding that the moment she found it, she was buying and consuming it on sight.

After adjusting the strap of her tote bag on one shoulder, she switched her duffel bag from her right to left hand and looked around as she walked. Beyond the wooden railing was the beach, a few miles' stretch of sand that reached out toward the ocean, waves lapping against the shore with vigor. As she suspected was the norm here during the summer months, the beach was full of chairs, umbrellas, and people. Lots of people.

There had to be an abundance of people on this island for the Written in the Stars author to foster the so-called love matches. Unions that had the blogger pulling in three times the subscribers as Allie's column currently received. Not that she was jealous or anything like that, Allie was confident in what she had and how hard she'd worked for it.

Some might call it coincidence, but Allie didn't believe in those, either. No, finding the popular blog that featured snapshots of this picturesque island off the coast of Maryland's Eastern Shore was a result of Allie's studious research. Imagine her surprise when, in addition to this seemingly beautiful locale, she also uncovered a very intriguing marketing ploy.

Crescent Island had been growing in popularity all because of the anonymous author of the Written in the Stars blog and the promise that love would always find a way for those who visited the island.

There were easily fifty people on the beach at this moment—providing that possibly half of them were already married or in some other type of relationship, the remainder who weren't children were in line to fall in love. But she didn't believe it. No island, nor anyone on that island, could promise such a thing.

Yet, every week—as it had seemed from the archived posts Allie had read online—supposed real-life stories of those love connections were detailed. And from those stories, the author of the blog boasted that tourism on Crescent Island had increased 87 percent in the last two years.

"If there's heart anywhere, it should be here," she whispered. And as long as she had that requested component in the article, surely Renee wouldn't squawk at a juicy tidbit about a debunked matchmaker as well. At least, she prayed her boss would see it that way.

Allie had worked long and hard to build a name for herself in the travel industry. She was proud of that success. She had to be, especially since her parents were still hating that she hadn't become a lawyer like they'd planned. Not achieving all her goals on her terms would only prove that every narcissistic comment the Sparkses had ever made to her were true, and Allie just couldn't accept that. Not anymore.

The fact that the island also happened to be the hometown of her best friend from college, Sofia Parker, wasn't a coincidence, either. It was good fortune, and Allie had wasted no time making her reservations to stay at some place called Lazy Lou's before calling Sofia to let her know she was coming for a visit.

A bell sounded, and Allie turned, just as a man riding a bike breezed by. He touched the bill of his orange-and-black Orioles cap and yelled, "Hi, there!

Welcome to Crescent!" as he rode past.

It was a friendly gesture, one she didn't always see in the city. Of course, she didn't always see someone riding this type of bike in the city either. It was one of those beach cruiser ones in a soft green color. He wore plaid Bermuda shorts and a matching top, and his smile had been one of the most genuine she'd seen in way too long. Belatedly she offered a tentative wave and muttered, "Thank you." But he was already too far away to hear her.

Her attention went to the first of a row of shops on her right, and she picked up her pace, figuring whatever the sweet aroma was that had lured her from the ferry, it had to be coming from one of these places. Strategically located, of course. It was a brilliant idea to have shops within walking distance the moment visitors stepped off the ferry.

Max's Muffin Tops. That's what the sign hanging from the cotton candy pink–painted building read. She was inside the establishment in seconds, but in her haste, she didn't miss the replica of a blueberry muffin doorknob or the rack of T-shirts right inside the doorway.

"There's Nuffin like a Muffin from Max's" and a larger version of the same blueberry muffin top doorknob was printed across the front of each shirt.

Again, clever. Perhaps she'd buy one to take home. But first, she stepped up to the counter and reviewed the menu on the wall. Twenty-two varieties of muffin tops and she went with the obvious choice. Another nod to the smart marketing.

"I'll have a blueberry top, please."

Seven minutes later, that delectable treat had

been consumed and the decision to grab three more for a snack to have later was made. Outside once more, but now with a partially full stomach, Allie picked up another scent—the ocean.

Not that she hadn't found herself admiring the sight of the water while she'd been on the ferry, but it hit differently now as she stood on the dock looking out at the beach. Along the dock were wood ramps at measured intervals. Each ramp cut through calf-high mossy grass that led to the beach. About a half mile down, the stretch of grass met with swells of light-colored sand.

On impulse, she started toward the closest ramp, telling herself she should have her phone in hand to record her thoughts on the first sights she'd encountered on the island. In the distance, a bright blue frisbee soared through the air, and a bikini-clad woman jumped up to catch it. Cutting through the wail of seagulls above, footsteps of people walking along the dock, chatting, and the blare of the ferry's horn calling for passengers to board, the woman's laughter seemed to trickle up to Allie, and something in her stomach clenched. It was an oddly familiar sound that touched on a wound that had throbbed inside Allie's heart for the last ten years.

With a heavy sigh, she reminded herself to focus on the now and perhaps give herself this time to just absorb things without documenting them. Or letting them take her back to a time and events she couldn't change. Maybe if she allowed herself this small stray from her normal work routine, she'd be able to tamp down her forthright inclinations enough to keep her job.

Walking until she stepped onto the grass, she went up on the tips of her toes again, lest she get the heel of her sandals stuck in the soft ground below. It might be time to re-think wearing heels—no matter how cute the strappy, royal-blue sandals were—while on the island. But she wanted to see the beach first.

The sound of the waves rolling and crashing onto shore called to her like she was some sort of mermaid longing for home—which was ridiculous, by the way. Still, she inhaled the glorious scent of saltwater and continued her trek toward it.

She'd been born and raised in Miami, with plenty of pretty beaches, palm trees, and sunny days, so this scene shouldn't have struck her as anything new. Yet there was a reluctant urge to acknowledge the feeling that nothing compared to this place. The water actually smelled saltier here, and the air seemed warmer, but not nearly as sticky as in Miami. And there were so many vibrant colors here, from the natural sky and sealine, to flowers in the huge brown pots along the dock, and the storefronts of each of the shops that gave a cheery allure to the crayon-box scene.

It was June, the start of summer vacation season. Up until earlier this week, she'd had four trips planned through early fall and the remainder of her time would be spent in her condo writing. She was a travel blogger who'd never possessed the need to vacation from a job she loved. Not to mention the fact that she had no one to vacation with. There was no doubt traveling could be done solo, but then, wasn't that just work for her? That was her opinion, and she was sticking with it, so outside of work, the "social" part of her life consisted of sitting on her couch watching romcom movies while enjoying her favorite snacks—just about anything sweet accompanied by orange Crush soda.

A warm breeze lifted the ends of her long, dark brown hair, and she smiled. Perhaps this island view could replace movies and snacks for the next couple of weeks without any complaints from her. She wobbled her way down the slope and giggled when she made it to the flat, sandy surface without taking a nosedive.

Accepting that success as a sign she should quit while she was ahead, Allie figured she should definitely find the B&B and then get some real food into her system. What was the place called again? Lazy Lou's or Lovely Lou's? She reached into her purse in search of the brochure she'd studied just as much as the town's website.

"Oh, come on, I know you're in here somewh—"

Her words were cut off seconds after her legs took a hit and buckled in response. With a yelp that was neither cute nor dignified, Allie felt herself going down, and there was nothing she could do to stop it. The one saving grace was that the sand cushioned her fall in a way the wood planks she'd been on previously wouldn't have. Still, she hit with a thump, her head resting only a second before her eyes adjusted on the huge tongue being dragged across her nose.

And then her cheek, and then…

"Whoa, hold on, Optimus. Sit! Sit!"

That was a man's voice, but Allie was certain that wasn't a man's tongue on her face. At least she prayed it wasn't.

"Sit, Optimus! Sit!"

More yelling from the man, but the dog…yes, she was sure it was a dog now because its big floppy ears swished over her damp face when it decided to turn and listen to who she supposed was its owner.

Her fight-or-flight instinct kicked in at that moment, and Allie lifted her arms to push the dog completely away from her before grabbing her sunglasses that were now half on and half off her face. She could hear the dog panting behind her when she planted her elbows in the sand and attempted to push herself up. The duffel bag and purse were like anchors holding her to that spot, and she grumbled with the next attempt to get up.

"I apologize," the guy blurted out as she continued to struggle. "Is it okay if I take your hand to help you up?"

Asking for consent was always a good thing, but presently she just wanted to get up from what now felt like quicksand and avoid any more of the embarrassment that engulfed her. "I can do it." This time she planted her hands and feet in the sand before trying to push herself up.

It didn't quite work the way she'd expected because of those bags again, but before she could fall all the way back, the guy grabbed her purse and duffel. The bags remained hooked on her arms, but he held them in front of her and took a step back, pulling while she pushed forward.

The action—while successful in getting her in an upright position—was full of momentum, and before either of them had a chance to correct that, they were colliding into each other, her duffel bag and purse the only things keeping their chests from touching.

Nothing stopped her head from tilting back so that she was now looking up into warm brown eyes. There was probably a more distinct name to describe the color of his eyes, but at this moment all she could think was how warm and inviting they appeared.

She stepped away just as he was saying, "Sorry."

"I think it's your dog who should be apologizing." Holding her sunglasses in one hand, she brushed sand from her arms with the other.

As if by mentioning it she'd somehow given it permission to pop up from its sitting position, the spotted gray dog lunged for her again. This time, the owner leaned forward and snapped a leash onto the dog's collar before pulling it back from her.

"Sit, Optimus," the guy directed his dog again.

"Perfect name," she said. "He's a semi-truck just like the leader of the Autobots."

The guy with the warm brown eyes chuckled. "You watch the Transformers?"

She shrugged and looked down to wipe the sand off her jeans. "My neighbor loved them since he was a kid, I guess, and was always quoting something from the movies at our HOA meetings. Eventually, I watched the movie out of curiosity over all his hype."

"Cool. Did you like it? The movie, not the neighbor?"

Her head shot up, and she saw that he was smiling. A really great smile, a perfect spread of his medium-thick lips that also drew her attention to the even line of his low-cut goatee and heavily creamed–coffee complexion. "I did like the movie," she replied abruptly, since her wayward thoughts had gotten the best of her. Then she offered as an aside, "My neighbor's an arrogant jerk."

His smile never wavered. Although she kinda wished it had or maybe that he'd frowned after hearing her negative thoughts about her neighbor. Maybe then his wavy black hair and strong shoulders wouldn't seem so enticing.

Totally off-kilter now by this very unexpected encounter, she frowned down at his dog, attempting to give herself a moment to get control of these ridiculous thoughts.

"You, Optimus, need to learn some manners," she scolded, and the dog sat as if she'd given him the same command his owner had to give multiple times before getting a result. His mouth gaped open, that tongue that she'd unfortunately been personally acquainted with lolling to the side, as his pretty ice-blue eyes stared at her adoringly.

"He's a Great Dane?" Glancing up, she figured it was more polite to look at the guy again and not the dog, who appeared to want something else from her. Because letting him trample her and lick her face obviously wasn't enough.

"Yeah, eight months old."

"Really?" She didn't bother masking the shocked tone in her voice. "He's huge."

"Seventy-one pounds and growing every day. The breed is known for its big, gangly size. But I'm betting you didn't come to Crescent to talk about dogs."

She also hadn't come to Crescent to ogle great-looking guys, but here she was.

"No," she said, glancing again at the dog that was bordering closer to adorable than rude as she'd originally thought. "I'm, uh, I didn't. I should be going."

She never stammered, and the realization had her snapping her attention back to the guy in an attempt to prove that this time she'd have zero reaction to him.

The attempt failed dismally.

"Where're you headed? Maybe I can direct you?"

"No thanks." She shook her head vehemently, then turned to look in the direction from which she'd come. "I'll find it once I get back on the main road."

"Okay, well, let me help you." He stepped close to her again, extending his hand as if he expected her to accept it.

She didn't. Partly because she didn't know him, but mainly because she wasn't sure she wouldn't like his touch. For whatever reason, she was having the weirdest reaction to a total stranger, which was clearly another reason she should be on her way.

"I'll just be going. Bye, Optimus. Have a good evening, sir." She turned and started back toward the slope before he could reply.

She was taking wide, exaggerated steps, being sure to plant her foot soundly in the sand before taking the next step. The last thing she needed was to fall in front of this guy again. And she wasn't taking off her shoes. She should be able to walk in the sand with shoes on.

"Enjoy your time on Crescent Island, ma'am." He yelled the words just as Allie had made it up the slope and came to stand on the grassy turf.

Ma'am? Really?

She almost turned around and yelled she was only thirty-three, which wasn't anywhere near "ma'am" classification, but noted that probably wasn't a good start to the less-critical thought process she was supposed to be adopting. Instead, she just kept walking until she finally made it back to the ramp, shaking her head the moment her heels clicked on the level planks.

That action sent sand flying from her hair, and she sighed, then whispered, "This better be the best story of my career."

CHAPTER TWO

"Ryan Zacharius Parker, you owe me seventy-nine dollars and fifty-seven cents! And I'm gonna kill your dog!"

As if her high-pitched yelling wasn't enough to get his attention, Sofia banged on the bathroom door until the hinges rattled. With a shake of his head, he returned his attention to rubbing a wet paper towel over the spot on his sleeve where Optimus had drooled on him this morning.

"Don't ignore me! You need to train that dog. Teach him that shoes aren't on the breakfast menu."

"I'll get him, Sof. Calm down." It only took a couple seconds for him to realize that was the wrong thing to say.

"Don't tell me to calm down! You get your butt out here and get that moody little pooch in line or I'm callin' animal control. I don't care how cute he is."

Ryan opened the door just in time to see Sofia's fist raised to bang on it once more. When she looked like she would gladly bang on him instead, he frowned. "Where are the shoes? And where's my dog?"

She was alone in the hallway wearing one perfectly fine black shoe with a red-and-white floral design. It looked like the same style of shoe their cousin Mylie Ellis wore when she was on duty at the medical center. Sofia had a few pairs of this particular style, all in different colors and designs, that she

sometimes wore to work at the restaurant. On the
right foot was the clunky medical boot that she'd
cursed at least three times a day in the week since
Doc Hines had diagnosed her acute ankle sprain.

Sofia's glossed lips thinned as she lowered her
arm and narrowed her gaze at him. "Luckily, I had a
second pair with me today, so I didn't have to go back
to the Big House. But my tennis shoes are ruined."

"You mean one of your tennis shoes is ruined?"
he asked, unable to hide the hint of laughter in his
tone.

"Not. Funny." She rolled her eyes and turned to
walk away with as normal a gait as she could manage
with the big black boot running up to rest just beneath her knee.

Guilt edged out the humor he'd tried to use to
handle this situation, and he followed her. He was
careful not to get too close, because Sofia could walk
on her own. She'd told them all that many times in
the past days. Not that any of his family had ever
doubted Sofia Elizabeth Parker could do any- and
everything she put her mind to.

"You're right," he said. "I'm sorry. I'll replace your
shoes. He's just trying to get used to being at the restaurant every morning."

The smirk she gave him when she looked back
over her shoulder was a signature Sofia look, complete with the tilt of her head to go with her practical
vibe. "Then maybe you should leave him at your
place instead of bringing him here to terrorize us."

Younger than Ryan by two years, Sofia had their
mother's expressive gray eyes and soft, tawny complexion. Today, her long locs were piled on top of her

head and held in place by a red-and-white-checkered bandana that matched the tablecloths in the restaurant.

"He's just a puppy, and he's learning his boundaries." Well, Optimus hadn't actually learned much in the three weeks he'd been on the island, but Ryan was optimistic. He also considered himself a good trainer, especially after watching the *Dog Whisperer* twice a week since he'd agreed to adopt Optimus from Fred, the paper goods supply guy.

It would be great if any of those lessons had helped to stop Optimus from jumping on people, namely the pretty tourist who'd been totally ambushed yesterday by his cute, partially trained puppy. The pretty tourist Ryan had also called "ma'am." He didn't groan inwardly at the memory, as he had yesterday after saying it and watching her walk away without looking back. But that didn't mean he'd felt less embarrassed by what was probably an offensive reference to a woman who looked as young as Sofia. Especially since he knew Sofia would've been irritated had he said the same to her.

He could still picture the peachy-colored polish on the tourist's toes, which were visible through the many straps of the ridiculously expensive-looking shoes she'd worn. When they'd finally come face-to-face, he'd been equally mesmerized by her long lashes over whiskey brown eyes and smooth, mocha-hued complexion. And where had all that even come from? There was no good reason he'd lock all those details about a stranger into his mind, and yet it seemed he had.

With a quick blink, he tried to push back the

weirdness of those thoughts and re-focus his attention on his sister, who had paused to clench her fists but was now on the move again.

"He's a menace who trips over his own feet," Sofia continued, referring to his dog. "And right now, he's out back watching Daddy load a second round of brisket into the smokers. That means it's just you and me in front until your brother decides to get his slow butt in here."

Ryan followed her down the hallway where the restrooms were located toward the front of Parker BBQ, the island's oldest and most successful restaurant. Maryland's Eastern Shore was known for its seafood, especially the steamed blue crabs, but Crescent Island was home to the best barbecue in the region. The numerous awards and newspaper clippings framed and hanging on the wall in the dining room could vouch for that.

"Brody called. He forgot to put his phone on the charger last night, it died, and so his alarm didn't go off. He'll be here by eleven thirty."

Sofia wasn't impressed by that comment, which made sense because Brody, their second oldest brother, was famous for giving excuses. "He was supposed to be here at ten. Any other manager would've fired his lazy butt by now." She continued into the main dining area of the restaurant before he could reply. If she was a little out of breath, she'd never admit it, and Ryan wasn't going to mention it. Still, he kept his eye on her just in case he needed to pull the big brother card and force her to sit down and take a break.

Black chairs had already been removed from the

tops of the twenty tables in the center of the space. Along the two side walls were booths with red uphol- stered seats, sporting the same checkered cloths as the other tables. Iron palm tree stands that held salt, pepper, and a bottle of Parker's signature tangy bar- becue sauce were positioned in the center of each. The color scheme and layout of the restaurant hadn't been changed since its inception a hundred years ago, but thanks to Sofia and her obsession with home im- provement shows, it had undergone a complete refurbishing two years prior.

As the sibling who always tried to keep the peace, he continued, "It's fine. We can hold down the fort for two hours. We've done it before."

Sofia grabbed a stack of menus and cloth to wipe them down from the hostess stand. Ryan went the opposite way to the counter, where he turned on the cash register and credit card machine.

"It's Tuesday." Her silence had only lasted a few moments, which for Sofia could be considered a long time. "You know the ferry's gonna be full of tourists wanting to start their rentals during the cheaper days of the week."

She was right about that. They were just entering the first full week of June, and the annual week-long SummerFest would kick off Friday night with a pa- rade and fireworks. As this year was the island's centennial celebration, each of their normal events was being magnified to culminate with a grander- than-ever Christmas Jamboree.

Gael and Baleigh Gibson had supposedly been led to the island by the stars illuminating the sky on the night of the summer solstice one hundred years ago. That was part of the island's history every native was required to know. If they didn't know by the time they started school, it was taught to every kindergarten class via a field trip to the Gibson House/ Museum. The museum was located on the northern end of the island near the only lighthouse and the Baldwin estate.

Many families planned their vacations around SummerFest every year. That meant the island would be packed with tourists who were ready to relax, eat at the great restaurants, diners, or cafes, swim, jet ski, and all the other fun things that the members of the tourist board had come up with to keep revenue flowing to the island.

The mention of the ferry managed to bring Ryan's thoughts right back to pretty toenails and long lashes. Where was she from? Why was she here? More importantly, why was he thinking about a woman he didn't know and who didn't have enough sense not to wear high heels on the beach?

He wasn't, that was the answer, at least not anymore.

"Another year, another SummerFest." He was placing cash in the register drawer when Sofia came up and plopped her elbows on the smooth black countertop.

"It's going to be so busy in here this weekend," she said with a huff.

He glanced up to take a good, long look at his only sister. There was a crinkle in her brow, and her lips were slightly pouty. Sofia had always been spirited and tenacious. She didn't worry or let anything get her down, but today, she seemed off.

"What's up? Why're you acting like Brody being Brody or the thought of crowds on the island this summer is something new?" He left off the part about Optimus eating her shoe. There was no need to get her fixated on getting rid of his dog again.

Sofia sighed. "There's just so much more to do. I've been so bogged down with pulling all those financials together for your presentation. Mama's been accepting more catering jobs with more people coming to Crescent for everything from weddings to family reunions." She shook her head. "That means I'm working back of the house on the books, front of the house when Brody's slacking, and in the kitchen helping Mama. And in between all that, there's Nana going on and on about my biological clock ticking and wanting great-grand-babies."

That was a subject Ryan didn't even want to touch. Exercising extreme caution this time, he remained silent.

"I mean, talk about piling on the stress." She massaged her temples. "Then, going for a long run through the trails at the Springs, the one thing that normally calms me down and centers me, lands me in this ridiculous boot!" As if he didn't already know exactly which boot she was referring to, she pointed down at her foot and frowned.

"Breathe," he told her. "Take a few moments and just breathe."

Her hand stilled over one of the menus, and she inhaled a deep breath, then let it out on a shaky moan. "That's always easier said than done."

"True, but practice makes perfect." One of Nana's tried-and-true statements came naturally even while

Ryan wished there was something more he could do to help his sister.

As the younger two of the Parker siblings, they were closer than Sofia was with either Trevor or Brody. Possibly because the older Parker brothers were determined to keep Sofia in the "little sister" box, while Ryan had been the one to champion her following in his footsteps to leave the island for college.

"You could always try listening to Doc Hines's orders and take a couple weeks off," he added.

"You're only saying that because I've already done all the work you needed for your big presentation," she replied.

There was truth to that statement.

For the past six months, Ryan had been trying to convince his father that it was time for Parker BBQ to branch out, to build on the nationally recognized name on the barbecue circuit by branding and selling their signature sauces. Vernon Parker, however, was firmly set in his ways and the ways the Parker family had run its business in the past. It had only been a month ago that Vernon had finally budged on his position to not fix what wasn't broken. And even that was conditional.

Vernon didn't want their current success interrupted or compromised in any way, so the large infusion of cash that would be needed to build a factory and start production of the sauces wasn't coming solely from the restaurant's profits. Ryan had thirty days to find the financial backing they needed to make this huge move. And Sofia's financial reports and future earnings projections would help seal the deal with a very prominent investment firm in Baltimore.

"And I will be forever grateful for all that you've done to help with this deal. Once the investor arrives on the island and I can show her around, feed her some of our delicious food, basically sell her on the Parker BBQ brand in person, we'll be on our way," he said, optimism soaring through him at the thought.

He had to believe in this expansion. If nobody else in his family did, he knew he had to believe with every fiber of his being. Otherwise, what was the point? *Go big or go home* was more like something Brody would say, but Ryan was okay adopting the mantra as his own for the time being.

"I have no doubt you're going to pull this off, and you know you have my one hundred and ten percent support. But I am not going to lay in bed while Nana and Mama treat me like I'm a six-year-old with the stomach flu again."

She finished wiping down the menus and then walked back over to the hostess stand to slide them in the side holder. The boot was bulky and noticeably slowed Sofia's normally quick strides.

"Maybe you should consider seeing that specialist the doc referred you to over at the medical center," he suggested, knowing it was probably futile to even mention this to her again.

Reeves Medical Center had only been on Crescent for fifteen years. Wilhelmina Reeves, a widowed heiress, had come to the island to live her last weeks in solitude after a metastatic breast cancer diagnosis. After she passed, she'd left a chunk of money to build a state-of-the-art facility on the island, but folks still liked to visit Doc Hines at the clinic he'd operated out of the bottom half of his Victorian-style house for the past thirty years.

Sofia shook her head and moved over to one of the tables. She surprised him by pulling out a chair and plopping onto it. "I don't need a specialist. I came down on the ankle wrong. It's happened before, so I should know better, but that doesn't mean there's anything wrong, other than my carelessness."

"You're never careless when you run," he said. Sofia had been running since she'd been the star of the track team in high school. If their high school had been on the mainland and a part of any divisional sports, she would've certainly received accolades and a scholarship for her achievements. She might've even gone on to compete if the loyalty to the Parker family business hadn't been bred into each of them from the moment they took their first breath in this world.

"Doesn't mean you shouldn't take care of it," he continued. "Take care of you."

She looked over at him and lifted a brow. "You're one to talk. When's the last time you've been out of this restaurant? Or out of that office you turned the second bedroom of your house into?"

Ryan finished with the money and closed the register drawer. "We're not talking about me."

"We are now," she said. "You've been so caught up in planning for the restaurant's future that you never take any time to live in the present. When's the last time you met up with Clay and those other goofballs you went to school with down at the Brew & Grub for beers and pool?"

"We're not teenagers anymore," he reminded her. "And Clay's the sheriff now. He's just as busy as I am."

"You're both full of crap!" She sighed once more and then pushed herself up slowly to stand. "If you want to increase the frown lines growing daily on your forehead from worrying about this expansion and the investor coming to the island, you go right ahead. And I'll continue to limp around for the next few weeks until Doc Hines says I can take this boot off and get on with my life."

The way she turned her back to him and continued to move about the dining room, getting it in order for their eleven o'clock opening, said she was finished with the topic, and Ryan was, too. He'd done his part to try and get her to take better care of her ankle, and he'd done what he could for the time being to get the ball rolling on the business expansion. Sure, there were only two weeks left in the thirty days that his father had given him to secure an investor, but he was certain he was very close to doing just that.

Even though the email he'd received a few days ago from Phoebe Morris, the executive at the Brownstone Group, said she had a family emergency and wasn't sure when she'd be able to make it to the island, he was still hopeful.

He glanced down to ensure he'd closed the cash drawer and was just about to turn away, to head into the kitchen to check on things back there before opening time, when a thought crossed his mind.

In the essence of time, I may have to send one of my associates to the island in my place.

That's what the last line of Phoebe's email had read before her normal sign-off of, Will keep you posted. Best. Phoebe.

Expensive shoes, big leather bag, and orange toenails flashed into his mind once more, and he groaned as he finally connected the dots of the mysterious woman on the beach. "Optimus!"

If his dog had ruined this investment deal for him because he'd just had to run down the pretty associate from Brownstone on the beach yesterday, Ryan might ship him back to Fred on the mainland. And Sofia's chuckle from across the room told him his sister wouldn't mind that at all.

CHAPTER THREE

"Ouch!" Allie yelped as soon as the flat iron tapped the back of her neck.

She'd had to wash the sand out of her hair the moment she checked into Lazy Lou's last night. After she'd dried it and sat on the comfortable bed staring around the attractively decorated room, she'd been too tired to go downstairs for dinner. That hadn't been a problem, as she'd been informed after calling to the front desk and attempting to order room service. Two plates had been brought up to her from the dining room—one with the baked salmon, asparagus, and roasted potatoes option and the other with the grilled chicken breast, seasoned rice, and broccoli selection that had also been on the evening's buffet.

Never shy about eating, Allie had finished half portions from each plate, enjoying all the flavors of the delicious homecooked food while she'd typed in some of her thoughts about the island. Sleep had come a lot sooner than she'd anticipated after such a hefty meal, and she'd lain down to receive the best night's rest she'd had in months.

Of course, that meant one of the first things on her morning agenda was styling her thick tresses. If she'd had the time to properly plan for this trip, she would've gone to her stylist to get a more protective style for the weeks she planned to be in this balmy coastal air. Cornrows, two-strand twists, or goddess braids were her favored summer styles. But for now, she'd have to settle for flat-ironing it straight and then pulling it into a neat ponytail, since yesterday had proven that the elements weren't friendly when she left it hanging free.

But even that plan shouldn't include burning off her skin. She frowned and made a concerted effort to be more careful with the heated hair appliance.

Twenty minutes later, her hair was perfect, her makeup was light and fresh, and she'd rubbed a little bit of Vaseline over the spot on the back of her still-stinging neck. She needed to go over her plan for the day before leaving the B&B, so she pulled out the chair that had been tucked neatly under the antique brown desk.

The desk faced a set of windows and a door, which she'd been told led out to the second-floor deck. She'd opened the frilly sage green curtains earlier this morning and now settled into the chair and pressed the button to power her laptop. Her notes file was at the top of her documents list, and she opened it, quickly reading over the things she'd typed last night.

• *The Docks – functional for the sole method of transportation on and off the island. A bit noisy but that's probably to be expected with the dozen or so boat slips and the traffic from the ferry. It's called The Comet, which is baffling because they'd moved no faster than a snail's pace on the ride over.*

• *The Shops at The Docks – again, functional name for what looks like a strip mall from the '80s. 7 shops painted different colors. Bright. Cheerful. Too cutesy. Max's Muffin Tops = A+ Blueberry muffin tops.*

• *The walk from The Docks to Lazy Lou's on the corner of Main and Cherry Blossom Lane took 20 minutes. *Figure out local transportation and wear tennis shoes or flat sandals.*
• *More cuteness in the yellow Dutch colonial revival house*

That's where she'd stopped because her food had arrived and she'd begun to devote more of her attention to the scrumptious meal.

Now, she put her fingers to the keys and thought about what to type next. The B&B hadn't been that hard to find even though there were five other houses in this block of what she knew was one of the town's main thoroughfares. Lazy Lou's was the only one, however, in the buttery yellow color and flanked by a thriving and colorful garden. Allie wasn't a floral enthusiast, so she had no clue what the names of the varieties of plants and flowers were, but the brilliant violet, powerful pink, oranges, and yellows burst through all the hues of greenery that bordered the house. The walkway and steps were red brick, the columned porch wide enough to hold six rocking chairs and two huge planters full of more flowers. One side of the house was covered in ivy that was a cross between creepy and atmospheric.

She typed the word *charming* because that's what she figured this place would be classified as.

Unlike the dog she'd encountered yesterday, who was firmly in the annoying category. But what about the dog's owner? Her fingers paused over the keys, and she shook her head. What about him? Tall, in good shape—the teal-colored T-shirt he'd worn had fit over his toned chest and upper arms tightly. Great biceps, which she'd noted when he'd been pulling her out of the grips of the quicksand masquerading as a simple part of the beach. Husky voice, not too deep, but just alluring enough to have her sighing as she recalled their brief encounter.

"He was just a guy," she whispered and shrugged when her mind wanted to continue its detailed breakdown of someone who had absolutely nothing to do with her story.

As if she needed another reminder that she'd gotten off track, her phone rang, and she stood from the desk to answer it.

"Hi, Renee."

"Good morning, sunshine! Just wanted to touch base with you and see how your first night on the island went."

Renee never touched base with her when she was on assignment. They were cordial and friendly, but not friends. Allie had only ever had two of those in her life — Bella and Sofia. Which reminded her she needed to call Sofia and let her know she'd arrived on the island.

"If you count falling on the beach and almost being gobbled up by a vicious sand pit the welcome party, I guess I'd say I survived," she replied.

"Oh." Renee sighed. "Well, that's not good. But, hey, everybody takes a tumble sometimes. Today's a new day, and I'm sure you've got big plans to explore the island." Before Allie could tell her she hadn't quite mapped out her plan yet, Renee continued. "I took a peek at the island after you sent your very cryptic email about your travel plans, and I think it's a great choice. There's so much history there, and I'm sure if you dig deep, you'll find that sincere, heart-warming story I need."

Allie walked over to the door by the desk and disengaged the lock before pulling it open. It was almost eleven in the morning, and the air was already thick with humidity. The view of houses across the street could be called picturesque, as much of this island would be, she suspected, but she hadn't yet figured out where the heart was. Instinct said it was with this matchmaker, since this was the person who was messing with matters of the heart. Sure, that may have sounded like a cliché, but this whole place was a big ole cliché.

"I'll get the story, Renee," she said. "I promise."

"That's what I like to hear. Confidence, determination, team spirit. I'm counting on you, Allie."

Oh joy! Another layer of pressure. After disconnecting the call, Allie reminded herself that *she* was counting on her, too. She needed her job; she loved her job. But really, she needed her job. The idea of telling her parents that she was no longer writing for the blog—a job they'd staunchly disapproved of from the start—was less than appealing.

The I-told-you-so look her mother would give flashed in Allie's mind. That would be followed by her father drawing his lips tight, thick frown lines forming on his forehead as he shook his head slowly at her. The disappointment would be palpable but short-lived because Douglas and Claire always had a plan, especially where their daughters were concerned. Which was probably why Bella had run away.

Sometimes, Allie wished she'd been as smart as her sister had seemed to be all those years ago.

"Why do you just go along with whatever they say, even when you know they're wrong?" thirteen-year-old Bella had asked when she'd dropped down onto her bed, face bunched in a frown.

Across the bedroom they'd shared, sixteen-year-old Allie had sat gingerly on her bed. She flattened her palms on her thighs and stared down at the bright pink nail polish she'd let Jordan Rogers apply earlier that afternoon. Jordan planned to attend cosmetology school after graduating from Glendale Academy, the private middle and high school that their parents had enrolled Allie and Bella into.

"Your hair looks cute," Bella had continued. "And that nail color is hot! It would've been really cool if she'd been able to do a pedicure, too. Your toenails are like claws."

"Hey!" Allie had chided. And because she didn't feel like having this conversation with Bella yet again, she reached behind her and grabbed a pillow. When she tossed it in Bella's direction, her agile sister caught it, bunched it in front of her, and leaned forward to continue.

"You just let her tear down everything you do or say. You never fight back," Bella said.

"She's our mother. We're not supposed to fight with her."

"Just because she's our mother doesn't mean she's always right. And besides that, we have minds of our own, opinions, thoughts, feelings." Bella sighed. "She never cares about our feelings. Only what she wants."

Allie had remained silent because her sister wasn't wrong.

"I'm just showing respect. It's what we're supposed to do."

"So you're just gonna take down your hair—which is in a perfect updo, so tell Jordan she's really good. And take all the polish off your nails because Mama said the style is too grown for you and the polish looks gawdy."

Their mother had actually said a little more than that, with her signature frown and haughty tone. Recalling it still had Allie's heart pounding with ire and hurt, but she didn't say that to Bella. Her little sister was already worked up enough.

"She didn't even put a lot of gel in my hair, so it wasn't going to stay like this long anyway. You know how wild I sleep. My scarf would surely slip off and tomorrow I'd wake up with my hair looking like a bird's nest." She shrugged. "I might as well just wash it out tonight."

Bella shook her head. "You mean you might as well do what she wants without ever pushing back."

When Allie didn't respond, Bella fell back on her bed and groaned. "I can't wait 'til I'm grown and I can get away from them. They won't be able to tell me anything then. None of Mama's mean comments or opinions, or Daddy's stern looks and yelling, will matter to me anymore."

In the years to follow, Bella had pushed back against their parents more times than Allie could count, until finally, just as she'd said she would, Bella had left.

And Allie had stayed, shouldering their parents' disappointment in Bella along with their continued critical assessment of her.

But that was neither here nor there. It was a part

of her past that couldn't be undone. Her best bet—as she'd told herself so many times before—was to keep moving forward.

And today, forward was on Crescent Island.

She stepped out onto the porch, tentatively, because she wasn't certain of the condition this old house was in. Looking down the street, she saw a huge yellow ball with circles and smaller orbs around it. The sight reminded her of a science project, and she grinned with the memory, noting that her first stop today would be visiting the Galaxy Emporium.

Ten minutes later, she'd packed her laptop, phone, and charger into her tote, pushed sunglasses onto her face, and headed downstairs. Thoughts of the room she'd left behind floated in her mind.

Those soft green curtains were at every window, and the honey-colored hardwood floor gleamed from beneath floral area rugs. The walls were papered in a striped design with tiny pink roses and the four-post bed with its matching fluffy green, beige, and pink comforter was the perfect piece to complement the space. It occurred to her then that it felt homey here—in the bedroom and now, walking into the brightly lit lobby area with burgundy papered walls, there was a sense of comfort. If she allowed herself, she might just get lost in the simplicity of this moment.

Simple had never really been her thing, not in terms of the way she lived her life. Her professional success had been hard won; the degree in journalism she'd planned to use to write the next literary Pulitzer piece had dwindled after she'd been let go from her first two magazine jobs.

But then she'd finally found her niche at See, Eat, Travel, and her salary had slowly crept up to the high five figures. There was some buzz about her entering the influencer realm, which would bring more notoriety and money that would continue to pay the mortgage on her ocean-view apartment and the BMW she drove. Yet the quaint little room in an island B&B with the full-size bed and antique radiator in the corner had held more appeal than she'd expected.

With a sigh she wasn't sure was full of regret or exhaustion, she reached into her tote and pulled out her phone. She'd forgotten to call Sofia when she was in the room, so she was doing it now before her thoughts became even more scattered.

"Hi, Sofia. It's Allie," she said when the familiar voice answered.

"Hey, Allie! Are you here? Please don't tell me you're calling to cancel. I was really looking forward to us having some girl time together. It's been way too long."

Sofia Parker was the talker of the friendship— much as Bella had been in their house when she and Allie were younger. The thought had that light feeling the B&B had produced spreading in Allie's chest, and she grinned as she replied, "No. I'm not calling to cancel." The words "this time" hung on the line between them. "I'm here at the B&B. I figured I'd do a little exploring first and then you and I could meet up for lunch or something."

"Oh, sure, I wish I could go exploring with you," Sofia said, and the way her tone had gone from excited to sullen alarmed Allie.

"Are you okay? If this isn't a good time for a visit, I can entertain myself." Even though she'd been counting on Sofia for the insider scoop on the island and the identity of the infamous Written in the Stars blogger.

"Yeah. I'm fine. Just fine," Sofia said and cleared her throat. "Just come over to the restaurant when you're done. I'm working, but by the time you get here, we can have lunch and talk."

"That sounds good, but only if you're sure I'm not intruding."

"Nonsense. You're like family," Sofia said. "I'm so excited you're here. I'll text you the address."

"Great. I'll see you later."

Allie disconnected the call and dropped the phone back into her tote. It had been years since she'd spent any time with someone on a personal basis. Her mother was too busy running her law firm and her father practically lived at the hospital where he was chief of neurology. And Bella…the heavy sadness that oftentimes came like a tidal wave when she thought of her younger sister settled like a rock in her gut. Allie hadn't seen or heard from Bella in thirteen years, since the day she'd found Bella's packed bags in their bedroom closet.

"How'd you sleep, Miz Sparks?" Lindy, short for Malinda Coleman, daughter of Lou, namesake for Lazy Lou's, asked.

Allie had met Lindy ten minutes after staring at the similar smile of her daughter Lucy, who'd greeted Allie the moment she came into the B&B last night. Both women were very cheerful and polite, and Allie found herself liking them instantly, even though she feared the overuse of "L" names would confuse her sooner or later.

"Wonderful," she admitted. "I don't know what's in that mattress, but it's heaven."

"Well, that's good to hear. Are you here for business or pleasure?" Lindy's strawberry-blond hair was pulled back into a ponytail, her hot-pink eyeliner matching the color of the perfectly fitting T-shirt she wore.

"I have a friend on the island," she said. It had been her experience that telling people she was a travel blogger either put them on high alert and led to very stilted treatment from that point on, or made them go overboard with niceness, both of which worked Allie's nerves.

Lucy tilted her head. "Really? I'm surprised you aren't staying with your friends, then. I mean, everyone in Crescent treats everybody they know like family. Well, unless your last name is Baldwin or Parker. Then you're enemies by default, but that's another story."

"Another story you won't be telling," Lindy interrupted while tossing her daughter a warning glare.

Sofia's last name was Parker, and if Allie wasn't mistaken, she'd heard a few stories about the Baldwin family when they were in school. But "enemies by default" was definitely intriguing.

Allie had missed this morning's breakfast but listened as Lindy ran down tonight's dinner menu and promised to see the mother-daughter duo later. Then she walked outside, where she immediately inhaled deeply. The ocean air definitely hit different on this island. It wasn't tinted with the sweetness she'd immediately picked up down at The Docks yesterday, but it was certainly a more subtle scent of the sea, the balmy breeze, the…

"Mornin'!"

She turned at the sound of a voice and locked gazes with an older gentleman with thinning white hair on his head, a full Santa-looking beard, and a wide grin. He rocked slowly in one of the chairs that gave her flashbacks of old-time shows like *The Waltons* and *Little House on the Prairie.*

"Good morning," she replied and attempted to mimic his brilliant smile.

"It's a great day for sightseeing," he continued after a nod in her direction. "The Springs are just a ways over there. You could walk, but it'd be smarter to call the taxi and have Eddie drop you off over there."

"No, she should get The Coaster. It'll be comin' along soon. Stops right over there on the corner."

She turned to look toward the second set of rockers on the other side of the B&B's front porch. Another gentleman with a bald head and pecan complexion sat in the chair, one leg crossed at the ankle over the other. His denim overalls were frayed at the edges, striped shirt pressed to perfection. He hadn't been looking at her but instead squinted as he stared across the street where he pointed to the corner.

Allie followed his gaze to the indigo-painted bench. Beside the bench was a black lamppost similar to the ones she'd seen when she'd walked down Main Street yesterday. Rectangular banners with a laughing cartoon sun and flowers that spelled out

"SummerFest" hung on each post.

"The Coaster will take you all around the island and give you a little bit of the history for everything you see. It don't cost too much, either. A good price if you ask me, you know, for what you get out of the ride," he told her.

"How much?" she asked, curious what the man thought was a good price.

"Nineteen ninety-five," the first man said. "Eddie will only charge five dollars to take you over to The Springs, then you could walk down Crescent Row from there, see some sights at your leisure."

The second man grumbled, and Allie turned her attention back to them.

"You just tryin' to get your son some work," the second man told the first one. "He'll get other people calling him for rides. Let this pretty young lady get the full view of the island. That's what she came here for anyway. Ain't that right, darlin'?"

Amused by the exchange between the two lively gentlemen, Allie dismissed the overly familiar "darlin'" he'd used, noting that if she were back in the city, she would've quickly corrected any man for calling her such.

"You don't know what she came here for, Cyrus. Always thinkin' you know everything about everybody," the first man accused the other.

Cyrus shrugged. "I know most things about most of the people on this island, that's for sure. And I always know more than you, Barney, and that's a fact."

"I was going to walk down to the Galaxy Emporium," she interrupted them.

Barney and Cyrus looked up at her as if just

remembering she was there. She wondered if this was what they did all day, every day—sit on this porch arguing over whichever topic arose. She could probably take a seat in one of the rockers and be thoroughly entertained by them for hours.

"That's a good idea. The Sinclair Sisters own that place. They've got lots of great stuff there, too. Any souvenirs you want you can find them at the Emporium," Barney said.

"You like cinnamon rolls?" Cyrus asked but continued before she could respond. "The biggest, gooiest, most delicious buns you ever tasted. Go on down there and get yourself one."

"I thought it was a gift shop," she said.

"Got a little bit of everything down there," Barney said.

"Alka-Seltzer," Cyrus added. "The only place on the island you can ever find the stuff."

Barney nodded. "Like I said, a little bit of everything."

"If you get on across the street, The Coaster should be comin' along in a few minutes." Cyrus pointed again as if she still needed directions.

Taking the hint this time, Allie offered the men another smile. "Thanks so much," she said. "I'll just go over here and wait for The Coaster."

She walked down the steps as their conversation shifted to a bird that flew by. Cyrus gave the name of the bird while Barney insisted he was wrong. A smile ghosted her face as she continued down the walkway and crossed the street. The dark blue bench was sprinkled with tiny yellow stars, and she took a seat.

This town and its homage to the whole cosmic

gimmick was either over the top or just the right amount of quirky. She hadn't decided which yet.

At least not until a few minutes later—just as Cyrus had predicted—when what looked like a school bus that had been painted light blue on one side and dark blue on the other came down the street. From what she could see, the light side of the bus was daylight with a huge sun on the side of the bus, the sandy beach along the lower half. It was a guess, but she suspected the other side of the bus would resemble the bench she just stood from with its twinkling stars.

Over-the-top cosmic gimmick for the win.

A ride that probably should've taken roughly seven to eight minutes stretched on as the bus proceeded at the lowest speed limit Allie had ever experienced while the driver talked about this colonial home and that Victorian on the other side of the street. She hadn't paid particular attention to the driver's commentary, but she had pulled her phone out to take pictures of the houses to go along with her story. At some point the topic of conversation shifted to the driver launching into a story about a girl named Sybil, her calico cat, a candy apple, and the fire hydrant at one of the corners he'd turned.

Allie moved on from taking pictures to checking her email messages on her personal account. Nothing from PointBlank Investigations. How long had it been since she'd received a response from the private investigator she'd finally decided to hire to find Bella? Three weeks. And before then, Guy the PI's monthly update had been short and sweet: Following a lead. Will be in touch with confirmation.

Of course, seconds after reading that message, Allie had fired off a response with a litany of questions: What lead? Is it concrete? Do you have pictures of her? Location? But he hadn't responded.

To get her mind off her personal issues and back on the matter at hand, Allie exited out of her inbox and returned to a familiar website—the Written in the Stars blog. This morning's post began with the usual not-so-subtle advertisement:

JoEllen's got java! It's not one of my favorite drinks as you know I prefer my energy to come naturally. But as I've decided to kick off the summer highlighting the best beverages of the island, today's is JoEllen's java at the Readerly Bookshop on Moonlight Drive.

The article was five paragraphs—which seemed like a terribly long time to discuss coffee, and not even flavored coffee. It also included pictures of the outside and inside of the bookstore and one of a mug filled with what she suspected was JoEllen's java sitting on top of a black bistro table. Allie wasn't a big coffee drinker, either, preferring tea as her hot beverage of choice.

She scrolled further down until she found what she was looking for, the column titled: *Finding Love.*

Welcome to Crescent peachesncream1 and goodguy1973! If you were doubting the power of love radiating on this island, these two will surely change your mind. They were one of our #CrescentMatched last year and are back to celebrate their engagement at this year's SummerFest. Some might think it's in the water, or perhaps just luck, but I know that the best love matches are written in the stars. Let love find its

way to you via Crescent Island, of course.
Creschamofcommerce.isl.com

Again, subtlety was out the window. This was where the author used the suggestion of finding true love to get people on the island. It was like a tourist dating app, and Allie hated dating apps. Sure, she'd read about success stories from the apps as well, but since she'd never had anything but bad luck the few times she'd attempted to use them, she was firm in her belief that it was all a hoax. Just like this blogger's ploy to get lonely tourists to this island.

Reluctantly, she admitted the blogger was clever. What better way to talk about all the wonderful aspects of what had grown to be a generally successful tourist attraction than to wrap it in a mystical package filled with the fantasy of falling in love? It was expert marketing, something Allie had become keenly aware of while selecting places to visit and then critiquing every aspect of what she'd been sold on in the first place.

By the time she'd left the Emporium—forty-five minutes later because the place was huge and as interesting as the brochure and Cyrus and Barney had explained—hunger had been the next thing on her mind instead of the story she was here to research and write. Luckily, Brenda Sinclair, the oldest of the sisters as Allie had learned after chatting with the duo in the store, had given her Eddie's number. So, once she'd left the store, Allie called and requested a pickup.

"Be there in five," Eddie had replied before disconnecting the call.

She'd stared at her phone a few seconds, thinking

that back in the city, she would've either driven her car to wherever she needed to be or if it was to the airport or train station she would've contacted a rideshare service via the app on her phone. That reminded her to open her voice text messaging again to record her thoughts on the Galaxy Emporium with its ceiling that was painted to look like an actual galaxy and the retro Motown tunes that blasted through the speakers. How the Temptations or Smokey Robinson related to Pluto no longer being considered a planet or the woman sitting at a card table tucked into a corner reading tarot cards, she had no idea and had been afraid to ask.

CHAPTER FOUR

Ryan couldn't get her out of his mind. Not *her* specifically, but the associate he suspected Phoebe had sent to the island to inspect and evaluate the restaurant.

They'd been swamped in the two hours since they'd opened this morning, so he hadn't gotten a moment to call Phoebe and ask if she'd sent a replacement. Yet the more he'd thought about Ms. High Heels and Pedicured Toes, the more he believed she was the one.

The associate.

She could also just be a tourist. With schools on the mainland out for the next few months and the festival kicking off at the end of the week, summer was the beginning of their biggest tourist season. Even though she hadn't quite been dressed for vacation, those pretty toenails could've been freshly pedicured for a week of lounging on the beach.

But something about her had struck him as more than just an average tourist. It could've been her quick wit as she'd surveyed Optimus, or the independent streak that had quickly appeared each time he'd offered to help her, or maybe it was the spark of humor he'd seen in her eyes when his dog had dutifully disobeyed him. Whatever it was, she wasn't lingering in his thoughts like any other tourist he'd ever seen on the island.

"Orders in the window," his mother announced,

and Ryan jumped into action.

He hadn't stood still for hours, and the second he did, she'd caught him. Just like whenever Brody and Trevor used to track sand and mud through the kitchen, they were never caught. The moment Ryan had tried to run through the kitchen to his bedroom after being on the beach, his mother was sitting at the kitchen table with her cup of coffee, giving him that "I knew it was you all along" look. The childhood memory had him shaking his head.

Sarah Parker was a stickler for honesty, hard work, excellent customer service, and a giving heart. The second born of three daughters raised on a farm in North Carolina, she could be bossy but loved with just as much spirit as she ran her kitchen. She was the spark to Vernon's flame, as his father had said more times than Ryan could count.

"Got it!" he replied when she'd circled back to slide two more plates into the window and offered him another glare.

They were short a server since Mikayla, who'd spent her summers working in the restaurant since she was sixteen, was spending the week on the mainland to attend her father's third wedding.

Sofia had been helping their other server, Gwen, until Nana had come in and ordered her off her feet. Just in time, too, because Ryan had noticed her moving slower than she had been earlier when she'd also been threatening his dog.

"Hurry back and get the lemonades for Nana and her Diamond Club before Ms. Reba starts her litany of complaints. I swear that woman only agrees to have their little club meeting here every other month so she can run back to the Baldwins and give them updates on what we're doing."

Ryan took a plate in each hand and stared through the opening in the wall to his mother.

She was easily the most beautiful woman he'd ever known with her high cheekbones and sandy brown hair. At sixty, her mind and spirit were as astute as if she were in her early twenties. She was and would always be his first true love, even when she was trying really hard not to be a part of the messiness that was the age-old Baldwin/Parker feud.

"She's just a widower like Nana. She's not a spy, Mama," he said.

Sarah sucked her teeth. "I know exactly what that mean-spirited pain-in-the-butt is."

With a grin and a shake of his head, Ryan delivered the food to table number six and was just about to return to the window for the four glasses of lemonade with fresh slices of lemon and sprigs of mint when he saw her.

The associate. Or the tourist.

Whatever her title, she appeared even prettier than he'd decided she was yesterday. The thought capturing his attention as soundly as the flash of her smile when she settled her sights on something to her left. She was standing just inside the front entrance, looking around with a curious expression on her face. Her eyes had narrowed and then widened, her lips going from a slight smirk to a tentative smile as she took a few steps forward, stopping when Gwen moved past her carrying a full tray of drinks. The same tote bag she'd carried yesterday hung on her left shoulder while she gripped her phone in her right hand.

She wore a dress today, or something that looked like an oversize denim shirt, its edges brushing over her thighs. He swallowed as he did a double take. Yeah, it was her thighs and not her knees. It would've been so much better if the dress were long enough to touch her knees, if it showed less of her lovely long legs with all of that glorious deep brown skin than had been offered yesterday. That would've been so much less distracting.

He couldn't afford distractions. Not now. Everything he'd been working toward in the last three years was about to come to fruition. Just because the person who would be making the decision that would determine the trajectory of his part in his family's business was quite possibly this extremely attractive woman didn't mean he was on the brink of messing up again. It couldn't mean that.

He hadn't even realized he'd been weaving his way through customers standing to leave or being seated, had simply kept his gaze focused on her. But she'd turned around as he'd been moving across the room, so that now he had a side view of her as she lifted her phone close to her face.

"A country western vibe with a distinct soul food aroma." He heard her speak as he came to a stop just a few steps away from her.

She paused, lifted her phone a little higher, pressed a button on the screen to open the camera, and snapped a picture. Then she turned until her back was facing him, this time snapping a picture of the outside dining area visible through another set of open windows to her right.

A slight ping of disappointment settled in his chest as he took in the sight of her and concluded that she was definitely surveying the place. Tourists also did a version of this, taking pictures of the great water view just through the patio or the open windows on the left side of the dining room. But they rarely took recorded notes of what they thought of the place, something he heard her doing again as he stood directly behind her now.

"Staff seems friendly. Comfortable vibe. Clean from what I can see so far. Music isn't too loud, and wait…I know this song."

She actually sang the next line of Stevie Wonder's "Isn't She Lovely," and Ryan wished he hadn't liked the sound of that as much as he had.

"I can give you a tour," he said, reminding himself he had no business liking how she looked in that dress or the sound of her singing.

Either his words or his presence—most likely both—startled her, and when she attempted to turn around to face him, she lost her footing. He grabbed her arms to steady her.

"You," she whispered and narrowed her eyes as she stared back at him. "You and your dog seem to prefer me lying flat on my back," she continued and then snapped her lips shut as if she'd cursed in church.

The quick visual of her on her back in his bed came and went as he cleared his throat. "If you'd like to see the restaurant, I can give you a tour. I'm Ryan."

"And you're supposed to be delivering these drinks," his mother said as she came up behind him

and gave him a playful slap against the back of his
neck.

Embarrassed and grateful that his mother's tone
was light instead of annoyed, he said, "Sorry 'bout
that."

"Mmmhmmm," Sarah mumbled and continued
walking to the booth on the left side of the dining
room, by the patio doors, where his grandmother's
club always sat.

Returning his gaze to the associate—because he
was fairly certain that's who she was now—he noticed the mortified look on her face.

"That. Did. Not. Come out right," she whispered.

The possibility that his mother had overheard her
comment about being flat on her back had apparently embarrassed the associate. He could tell by the
lift of her brows and the tightness of her tone. His
previous thought about her being prettier was also
confirmed now that he was afforded a close-up
look—her hair pulled up into a high ponytail and her
pert lips coated with a gloss that almost matched the
tone of her skin.

"No worries," he said. "It's noisy in here. I doubt
she heard you." Even though his mother had that
extra-sensory hearing he knew all mothers possessed.

When she looked as if she were about to speak
again, a rumbling sound erupted, and her eyes widened. The hand holding her phone flew to her
stomach as the other covered her mouth. Again, her
eyes widened.

Ryan grinned. "Maybe we'll do the tour after we
get you something to eat."

Easing her hand away from her mouth, she shook

her head. "I can't win for losing with you, can I?"

He chuckled. "It's all good. Hunger is as natural as breathing, and it just so happens that you're in the best place to calm your stomach's current revolt. Here, let's get you settled in this booth and I'll get you a menu."

She followed him almost to the back of the restaurant where double doors opened up to the outside seating area. Ceiling fans whirled overhead, keeping the dining room cool as the balmy ocean breeze filtered inside. He pulled out the chair and waited while she sat before pushing it closer to the table. Her ponytail swished behind her, and he was just close enough to catch a whiff of honey and vanilla. The urge to touch the silky strands burned his fingers, and he eased his hands back from the chair to stand up straight without speaking. Not only did he have a sister, mother, and grandmother, but Ryan had been around enough Black women in his lifetime to understand the boundary that was their hair.

He even recalled a day when he and his brothers were just hitting their teens. Nana had sat them down and explained so many things about girls/women—one of them being how their hairstyles were often a personal expression of who they were and a visual of the evolution of their culture over time. It had taken him a while, but it was times like these that he appreciated the women in his family for filling him with just as much relevant knowledge as the Crescent public school system had.

"I don't need a menu," she said, interrupting his thoughts, which he hadn't realized had strayed so much in such a quick span of time.

"We have some really good specials for today, but there're a few favorites I'd like to go over with you before you order." He came to stand at the side of the table as if he were the server assigned to this area instead of the manager who wanted to broker this deal with her.

She was shaking her head again, and he made a concerted effort not to stare at the movement of her hair or the way her mouth had softened as she looked up at him now.

"I studied the online menu on the ride over," she said. "At least, I did after I told the driver I needed to focus on my work email so he'd stop talking."

Ryan grinned at that. "Let me guess, you got a ride with Eddie?"

She dropped her bag on the empty chair next to her and set her phone on the table. "Yes. He came highly recommended, and since there's no other rideshares on this island, I guess I had no choice." She shrugged.

"Well, that's only partially true. We have The Coaster."

Holding up a hand to stop him, she interrupted, "Rehabbed school bus that looks like it should be in a children's cartoon. Yeah, I've had the pleasure of riding that this morning, too."

And she didn't sound overly excited about either. "Well, there are other vehicles on Crescent. So if you need a ride someplace else, let me know. I'd be happy to take you."

"In your car?" she asked. "With your dog? Who I'm surprised is not running around this place at the moment."

Ryan shook his head quickly. "Nah, he's out back in the pen my dad built to keep him out of trouble."

"Your dad's a saint," she said and then smiled.

His breath caught, and a punch of something he hadn't felt in far too long landed in his gut.

"I'll have the pulled pork sandwich, extra spicy coleslaw, with a side of mac 'n cheese, string beans, and a large sweet tea," she said.

He blinked and cleared his throat to cover the fact that her smile had left him momentarily speechless. Then he nodded. "Okay. I guess you have studied the menu. I'll be right back with your drink, and I'll put that order in for you."

"Thanks," she replied and looked away.

Ryan didn't move but continued to stare at her and felt like an awkward fifteen-year-old when she turned back to him with a quizzical gaze. "Uhhh, I'll also bring you the dessert menu." Although after all the food she'd ordered he wasn't sure she'd have room for anything else.

But when he finally walked away from the table, he realized she was probably just trying a variety of things on the menu to get a taste for what they offered. Yeah, that made sense. Certainly, more sense than what he knew was an interest that went well beyond business where she was concerned. Mentally shaking free of those thoughts, he scribbled the order on the top sheet of the pad at the hostess stand and walked it back to the kitchen himself.

Then he kept on moving to the farthest end of the restaurant, where a few offices and the private staff bathrooms were. His parents shared the biggest of the three offices while he and Sofia each had a

smaller—closet-like—one at the very end of the hall.
Brody and Trevor presented an ongoing argument
about why they didn't have offices as well during
their Monday family brunch meetings. Nana always
claimed she didn't need an office, she ran the show
from whichever room she was in, and that was certainly the truth.

Going quickly behind his desk, Ryan found the
large folder full of copies of his presentation, Sofia's
financial reports, pictures, and sales projections for
the signature sauces he wanted to market and sell.
With the file in one hand, he used his free hand, to
riffle through those papers, not really to read them,
but to give himself a few seconds to find his focus.
This was the moment he'd been waiting for. It was
the culmination of the last three years of research
and development, and it meant more to him than
anything else he'd ever done in his life.

Closing his eyes to the magnitude of that thought,
he whispered a silent prayer for this to be whatever it
was meant to be. At this point, that was all he wanted.
If his purpose in life was to expand the family's legacy by selling their signature barbecue sauces
worldwide—and he sincerely believed it was—then
that's what would happen.

That woman sitting out there waiting for him to
bring her food would be just as wowed by the taste of
the sauces, the atmosphere of the restaurant, the
beauty of Crescent, as Ryan and the thousands of
others who'd visited Parker BBQ had. And because
she'd be wowed, she'd advise Phoebe that this was a
solid investment. Then the check would come, he
could buy that stretch of land that old Sanford

Grambling owned down by the Docks and build the warehouse. If they had a light winter on the island, production could start as early as February, late spring if the blustery winds and snow blew their way instead. At any rate, there was a complete and perfect plan that couldn't go to the next steps until the associate gave the green light.

With a sigh, he tucked the file under his arm and headed out of the office. Every step he took was full of purpose, anticipation, and hope. His father was a stickler for the old, the legacy that had made the Parker BBQ name, and Ryan wasn't against any of that. He wholeheartedly believed in everything his great-grandfather had started when he'd been asked to be one of the founding members of this island. And everything that had been built in the Parker name since that moment was a source of pride for Ryan. But what he was doing now was about forward movement. It was about finally finding *his* place within the legacy.

He gritted his teeth as he entered the dining room in time to see Gwen delivering the food to the associate's table and Sofia sitting across from her laughing. Wait, why exactly was Sofia sitting across from someone she didn't even know?

He started for the table, only to get stopped by a couple just leaving their booth.

"Everything was great," the man, who'd introduced himself earlier as Paul Grimes, said and Ryan paused to smile.

Paul was with his fiancée, Teri. They were here to celebrate their engagement at SummerFest.

"Thanks," Ryan replied. "Glad you enjoyed it.

Hope you come back before you leave the island," he said.

The woman grinned. "Oh, we'll be back all right. But for now, I've got enough desserts in this bag to cure my sweet tooth," she said, holding up a black bag with the restaurant name arched over the smoker logo on the front. "I've even got a couple of those cinnamon rolls. The lady over there wouldn't let me leave without them."

She'd nodded toward the table where Nana and her Diamonds sat. Ms. Annabelle was one of the four members of his grandmother's group of friends. She made the best cinnamon rolls on the island, and she wanted everyone to know it. Which was why she delivered a fresh batch to the restaurant and a few other places around town she called her special spots every day.

"You're going to love them," Ryan said. "And Ms. Annabelle would love to hear how much when you see her around the island again."

"They smell divine," she said.

"Which is code for she's going to eat them all," her fiancé chimed in.

Normally, Ryan enjoyed talking with customers. Today, he really wanted this chatting to end. And when it finally did, he moved faster to get to the table with the associate and Sofia. They were laughing too hard, and warning bells were ringing loudly in his ears. If Sofia was messing this up for him, he was going to let Optimus chew *all* of her shoes...

"Well, that'll teach you to kiss 'n tell," Sofia was saying as he approached the table.

The associate covered her face with her hands as

she laughed and shook her head. "You're a horrible person," she joked and dropped her hands.

"I might have to agree," he interrupted.

The associate sobered and gasped as she stared up at him. "How long have you been standing there?"

Sofia waved a hand. "Oh, don't worry about him. Remember, I used to tell you about how Ryan hated parties? He still does, so I don't bother him with those stories of our crazy college years."

"This is Ryan?" the associate asked as she turned to stare at Sofia once more.

Sofia nodded while something inside Ryan shifted.

"Yep! This is my strait-laced brother. The one who graduated tops in his business class at Columbia, giving me the idea to escape to New York and go there as well."

"Wait a minute," he said, thoroughly confused by what was going on yet acknowledging the burn of dread settling in his gut. "You two know each other from college?"

Sofia gave him a "duh" expression and huffed. "Ryan Parker, this is my best friend—even if she's never visited me here on the island before—Allison Sparks."

"You can call me Allie," she said and extended her hand to him as if this were the first time they'd met.

Still trying to figure out what was going on, he was a couple seconds delayed in reaching out to accept her hand. But when he did, there was a jolt of something that matched that previous shifting inside him perfectly. Like a message had been received loud and clear, but he had no idea what that message was. The surprise he saw light her eyes at their touch meant she'd felt it, too. Which was even more ridiculous, since this really wasn't the first time they'd met, or even touched for that matter. The memory of how soft her skin had been when he'd taken her arms to keep her from falling a little while ago was still seared into his mind.

"It's very nice to meet you, Allie. What a coincidence that your work would bring you here after all the time you've known Sofia."

She pulled her hand from his grasp. "My work?"

"Yeah," he said. "At the Brownstone Group. Phoebe said she might need to send her associate down here to look things over before she makes the final decision about the investment. I wish I'd known it was you yesterday. I could've given you a tour around the island before you came into the restaurant. But I can still give you the tour later today."

Sofia shook her head. "What are you talking about? Allie doesn't work for Brownstone. She's a writer, and she's spending her summer vacation here with me."

That dread that had been stirring rose to the surface, and he cleared his throat. "You're not the associate?"

Allie shook her head and spoke in a slow and deliberate tone, as if to make her words easier to understand. "No. I'm Allie."

"She's the BFF," Sofia added for further clarification. "And her food's getting cold while you stand there ogling her."

• • •

Had he been ogling her?

Ryan Parker. Sofia's brother.

The guy who liked her flat on her back. Wait, no, that still wasn't right.

Allie picked up her glass and gulped the iced tea as Ryan made his excuses and left. The tea was delicious, sweet, lemony, and refreshing. She definitely needed that refresh. Her growling stomach—which had so rudely introduced itself to Ryan a little while ago—and seeing her longtime friend had been the main reasons she'd interrupted her research to come to this restaurant. Of course, everything she did on this island would be research to an extent, but she'd never heard Sofia sound the way she had when she'd spoken to her over the phone this morning, and she'd wanted to make sure her friend was okay. She hadn't considered she'd run into the guy from the beach again, and certainly not in such a literal sense.

The skin on her arms still tingled from where he'd held on to her to keep her from hitting the floor the way she had the sand yesterday. Not to mention the warmth that continued to radiate in her palm where their hands had just met for a cordial shake. She pressed that palm against the cool of her glass after she'd sipped and held on.

"You okay?" Sofia asked from across the table.

"Huh?" Allie blinked, her friend's face once again coming into focus, replacing the memories of the beach and the last few moments. "Oh. Yeah," she continued and cleared her throat. "I'm good. Just thirsty." She took another quick sip of tea before setting the glass down. "But tell me about you. How'd you hurt yourself? What's the prognosis and recuperation time?"

Allie never lacked questions. She'd always been the inquisitive one of the Sparks daughters. The one most likely to spot a problem, figure out and implement a solution. That's why her mother had wanted her to become a lawyer and her father had been convinced that her future was in medicine.

Sofia sat back in the chair and pointed at the plates in front of Allie. "Eat. I wasn't kidding when I said your food was getting cold. Mac 'n cheese is much better when it's hot and the cheese is all melty. Mama makes it the best, but Nana's got a good recipe, too, that she uses when she cooks over at the Big House."

Allie picked up her fork and dug into the mac 'n cheese first. "The Big House?" she asked before putting a forkful into her mouth and moaning at the cheesy deliciousness that exploded on contact. "Oh my, this is ahhmazing."

Sofia smiled proudly, a really pretty smile that always reached her eyes and added to her exuberant personality. "Told ya," she said. "And the Big House is where my family lives. It's just a few minutes to the left of here but closer to the water."

"That's right," Allie said when she'd finished chewing. "I remember you telling me that your family had owned land here since the island's inception." If memory also served, there were other founding families on this island, which meant even more people who knew everything there was to know about this place and most likely the people who resided here. All of that meant somebody was bound to know who was writing the ridiculous blog.

"Four," Sofia said as she reached for one of the paper napkins at the center of the table and twisted it between her fingers. "They actually call them the First Four," she continued with a shrug. "The Gibsons, Parkers, Baldwins, and Rivas. Four families who invested in this place and created a home that still stands for four thousand two hundred and ninety-eight permanent residents. Four thousand two hundred and ninety-nine in a couple weeks when Laney Mitchum is scheduled to deliver her second baby girl."

She made a mental note to look into those names when she returned to the B&B, but the last comment had her raising a brow. "You know offhand who's pregnant and their due date? That's kinda taking small town to an extreme."

Sofia chuckled and shook her head. "Laney does my hair," she said. "And sometimes her four-year-old, Jasmine, brings her baby dolls in the room to keep me company. The new baby will be named Lavender, because Laney loves her floral scents."

Oh, so Laney was Sofia's friend. The unexpected jolt of jealousy came fast, and Allie ate more mac 'n cheese, hoping she'd swallow the ridiculous emotion.

"But Crescent does live up to the small-town stereotype of everybody knowing everything about everybody else." Sofia shrugged. "It's just life, I guess."

A life Allie wasn't certain her friend was enjoying at the moment, and that was unlike Sofia. In college, she'd been boisterous and energetic, ready to explore every inch of New York City. But there'd never been any doubt that Sofia would return to her little island off the Eastern Shore. She'd spoken so highly of the place, its ocean views and amazing people. It occurred to Allie at that moment that she didn't recall Sofia talking as much about what she planned to do with her degree once she returned here.

"You always were good at controlling the conversation," she said and picked up the pork sandwich this time. "But, as you may recall, I love asking questions, so I'll return to the one you're obviously trying to avoid. What happened to your ankle?"

She took a bite of the sandwich and chewed.

"The Parker house sauce has a sweeter base. Brown sugar and molasses are key ingredients. Daddy's got a sweet tooth," Sofia said.

"As I mentioned to Ryan earlier, your dad's a saint and a man after my sweet-addicted heart. I've always preferred my BBQ on the sweeter side. Were you running?"

Sofia grimaced and rolled her eyes. "Yes. I was running on a very familiar trail by the Springs, and it's just a sprain. Two to four weeks in this boot and I'll be good as new."

Her friend's adamant tone and the way she'd clearly wanted to avoid this topic confirmed there was more going on than Sofia wanted to say. Allie could push, ask more questions, insist on more answers, but she knew from experience that wasn't the route to take with Sofia. They'd spent countless nights lying awake in their dorm room talking about any- and everything, both of them sharing parts of themselves Allie had been certain they'd never shared with anyone else before. And over the years, since they'd gone about their adult lives, they'd still managed to share more close moments, but Allie had obviously missed something lately. Something she felt guilty about not catching until now.

"What can I do to help?" she asked. "I'll be here for at least two weeks. I can go to therapy with you. Help with any exercises they prescribe. Run some errands. Just tell me what you need." She could work all of that around writing her story with no problem. If Sofia needed her, then Allie wanted to be here for her. Especially since she couldn't offer her blood sister that same support at this time.

"You're on vacation," Sofia said. "And you're a guest on my island. I should be showing you around, introducing you to all the things I love most about Crescent."

Which was exactly what Allie had presumed would happen when she'd called Sofia to let her know she was coming. But that part of her plan would obviously have to change. Allie was nothing if not adaptable; she'd had to be to survive growing up with controlling parents and traveling the world for a living.

"I'm also your BFF. Isn't that what you just told Ryan?" This was the second time she'd said his name and the billionth time she'd tried not to think about him as anything other than just some guy. A guy that after two brief encounters had somehow made her feel things that she'd never thought existed for her.

Sofia's eyes widened, and Allie prayed her friend couldn't read her thoughts.

"That's it!" Sofia said, leaning forward and slapping her hands on top of the table. "Ryan will show you around the island."

"What?"

Sofia didn't answer her question because she was already waving to someone she could see behind Allie. That someone was him, Allie knew it without even turning around, and she wanted to argue that she didn't need a tour guide. Especially not that very attractive one whose dog had slobbered all over her.

"Ready for dessert?" Ryan said as he came over to stand beside their table again.

She wasn't going to look up at him. Not when she was pretty sure looking at him would lead to recalling that electrifying touch they'd shared. Reaching for her glass to take another drink seemed like a much better idea.

"I need you to show Allie around the island since I'm apparently going to be hobbling around the house for the next couple of weeks." Sofia sent a glare toward a table of older women and sighed. "Nana called Doc Hines, and he told her I should be elevating my ankle at least six hours a day, so she's banned me from coming into the restaurant after today."

Allie finished her drink and watched as Ryan followed his sister's gaze. When he turned back to them, he nodded. "Hate to say it, but that last part's a good idea. You need to make sure you're healing correctly, Sof."

His tone had softened, and so had his eyes—almond-brown eyes. When she'd first seen him on the beach, she'd known his eyes were more descript, and now she'd just found the right words. The way he looked at his sister was full of caring and love. In that moment Allie could tell he'd do anything for Sofia, and that just about melted her heart.

Her friend obviously wasn't feeling the sentiment, because she waved her brother's words away and continued. "I'll be stuck in the Big House, but there's no reason why Allie shouldn't see all the sights of the island. So I need you to show her around. I can't ask Trevor or Brody because they'd be too busy hitting on her."

Allie coughed up that last sip of tea, and Ryan raised a brow.

"I…ah…" She cleared her throat. "I told you I don't need a tour guide, Sofia."

"Nonsense. I want you to see everything I love about this place, and nobody knows that better than Ryan. And you don't have to stay at the B&B. There's plenty of room at the Big House. Right, Ryan?"

"Uh, yeah, sure. The Big House has six bedrooms, and since I moved out a couple years ago, mine is empty."

Sleep in Ryan's room. Allie was already shaking her head.

"Since I offered you a tour of the restaurant earlier, I can take you to Sof's favorite places around the island, too. It's the least I can do for my rude dog and mistaking you for a business associate," he said.

She did wonder how he'd made that mistake. Surely, it didn't involve her, but Ryan didn't strike her as a guy who didn't have all the answers.

"Come on, Allie," Sofia said. "You asked how you could help me. This is how. You come stay at my house. Let Ryan show you around during the day, and at night you'll be at my beck and call to stop me from dying of boredom."

Did she really have a choice? She felt like she had

that morning in Renee's office when her boss had told her to get the right story or lose her job.

"Sure," she said. "I'd love for Ryan to be my tour guide."

And nothing more, she reminded herself when her gaze met his again. *Absolutely nothing more.*

CHAPTER FIVE

"SummerFest starts in just a few days," Reba said. "Now's not the time to bring this up."

Shirleen Parker, lovingly known by her family as Nana, shook her head and pushed her black tortoise frames up on her nose. "For once, I have to agree with Reba." She'd wash the distaste out of her mouth later. "Nobody needs to know about this until after the festival. This is our centennial year, after all. We don't need this type of stress looming over the island."

"Bad vibrations," Annabelle Gibson chimed in. "We've experienced them before and we've survived."

The fourth member of their group, Margie Kimpton, better known as the worrisome one, tore the last shreds of a napkin she'd been twisting in her fingers for the past fifteen minutes. "Secrets always come to light."

Shirleen looked around the table at the women who'd been as close to her as sisters for most of her life. She and Annabelle had played in the sandbox together and continued on as friends throughout their school and adult years. Margie's family had moved to the island when she was in middle school, and Reba was originally from Boston, but after her parents died in a car crash when she was sixteen, she'd come to the island to live with her aunt and uncle. It wasn't until after she'd married Arnold Ray, who worked for the Baldwins, that Reba had begun trying to impress Crescent's royal family.

By that time, Reba had already been a member of the Diamonds and they couldn't put her out just because she'd decided to align herself with the high-and-mighty ideals of the Baldwin family.

"It's just another week, Margie. Nothing's going to happen in that time," Reba said, her thin lips turning up in a smirk.

"I just don't like it." Margie sighed.

"Nobody likes it," Shirleen stated. "But we can't change it, either. All we can do is bring it up when the time is right."

"And that's not during SummerFest," Annabelle said. "We're in agreement, three to one, about that."

Annabelle was a direct descendent of Gael and Baleigh Gibson. She even lived in the big blue Victorian house that doubled as the Gibson Museum.

"Fine," Margie snapped and pushed the mountain of shredded napkin toward the center of the table. She grabbed her empty glass of lemonade and fished out the lemon. "But let the record show that I don't like it."

At seventy-seven years old, Margie was the second oldest of their group. Shirleen was a year older than her and had started the Diamonds when she was a junior in high school. Annabelle and then Reba were the youngest members. But Margie had always been the timid one of their bunch, full of complaints and hesitation when they were together but quiet as a mouse in public. She very rarely won any of the disagreements within the group, partially because her arguments usually boiled down to something that she was afraid of, and the Diamonds as a collective were strong, resilient and tops in their class, without any doubt. They'd also never voted a member out of their small group, not for any reason. The majority simply refused to vote with Margie and her negative thoughts.

"You don't like anything," Annabelle quipped.

"Not true," Reba added. "She likes when old Cyrus smiles at her—that's why she's always taking her morning walks past the B&B even though she lives all the way over past Crescent Row."

Margie's cheeks went red seconds before she looked away from Reba and put the lemon into her mouth. Shirleen chuckled. "Ain't nothin' wrong with liking a man," she said. "Lookin' can be fun even at our age."

Annabelle didn't comment. She never did when they talked about men, love, marriage, or anything relating to all of the above. Shirleen knew why, and she respected her friend's privacy in that regard. But both Shirleen and Margie were widows. They'd loved hard and grieved the same way. Now, as far as Shirleen was concerned, looking was a glorious pastime, but her heart would forever belong to Teddy Parker and the family they'd built together.

"Well, let's go over what we're going to have at our booth at the carnival. We won't have much time to set up because I have to help Vernon and Sarah with the food. But we don't want to forget anything," Shirleen continued, bringing their meeting back into focus.

They ironed out the details and ate some of Annabelle's cinnamon rolls, which they'd unanimously dubbed the best dessert on the island. Even though Shirleen and her daughter-in-law made some pretty tasty apple pies and peach cobbler for the restaurant. The meeting ended just ten minutes over their allotted hour timeframe, and when they parted, none of them spoke about the secret again.

As Shirleen had told them, it could wait another week.

· · ·

Ryan almost knocked down the stack of trays sitting on the counter.

"Hey, man, watch what you're doing." Brody was louder than he needed to be with his warning, and the couple at the table closest to that end of the counter looked over at him.

Ryan gave them a smile and a nod, then elbowed Brody as he moved around him. "Keep it down."

"Sure will. When you start paying attention to something other than that woman Sofia's talking to."

"She's not a woman, she's a writer." With gorgeous, deep-brown skin and pert lips. And she was his sister's best friend, not the associate who would be making or breaking this deal. A fact that made her off-limits for even more reasons.

First and foremost, he didn't date Sofia's friends. Just like he'd banned her from ever looking twice at any of his friends in that way. Because if dating ever went wrong—which it inevitably did—then he'd have a serious problem with his friend for hurting his sister. On the other hand, the last thing he ever wanted to hear was all the grief he knew Sofia would give him if he ever hurt one of her friends. On top of all that drama that he just didn't have time for in his life, Allie didn't live here. And long-distance relationships were another no-no in Ryan's life, for more reasons than he cared to examine right now. Gritting his teeth wasn't going to erase any of those facts. Neither was turning to lean against the wall so that he could see past Brody into the dining room.

They were still sitting at the table, Allie finishing up her food and Sofia talking with the animated look on her face Ryan noted he hadn't seen in a while. Even before she'd hurt her ankle again, to be exact. He'd considered himself close to all his siblings, they had a very tight-knit family, but he and Sofia always had a special bond, perhaps because they were the youngest. Yet he hadn't known anything about this best friend of hers who was a writer and an imposter. Although the latter hadn't been her fault. That big mistake had been all his.

Brody's brow furrowed as he looked from Ryan to the table where Sofia was sitting and then back to Ryan. "Bruh, she's definitely a woman first."

Walking past Brody because he didn't need his brother pointing out the obvious, Ryan pushed through swinging double doors and arrived in the kitchen. Unfortunately, Brody was right behind him, carrying the dirty trays Ryan had almost toppled onto the floor.

"What's eatin' you? Is it Sof?" Brody continued when Ryan didn't respond fast enough. "Yeah, Nana seems pretty worried about her injury and how Sof's not taking good care of it. Trevor mentioned her needing to be more careful, too, but you know she's not tryin' to hear a thing he says."

No, taking advice wasn't one of Sofia's strong points. And being tactful or compassionate wasn't Trevor's. The two of them were like oil and water sometimes, butting heads about everything from the weather to whoever Sofia was dating at the moment. To be fair, none of the brothers went lightly on the guys who dated their sister. But only Trevor had threatened to break a guy's jaw before.

"She said she's going to be on house arrest for the next week or so," he said because if he didn't join in Brody's conversation, it would never end. He was the most talkative of the three Parker brothers, a fact that easily made him the most annoying.

"Yeah? What's Mama gonna do, tie her to the bed?" Brody asked and then chuckled. "Sofia's the stubbornest of all of us."

Another fact. Just like the fact that Allie Sparks had caused something to shift in Ryan's world. He looked down at his hand, the one that had held hers briefly for a shake. He'd filed away that smile she'd given him half an hour ago, stuffing it securely in the place where he put all things that were a waste of his time. Still, the memory of her touch was lingering, just as the urge to go over to their table to see if she needed anything else.

"We should take bets on how long she actually stays in the house. I'm going with one day." Brody was still talking, and Ryan had forgotten why he'd come into the kitchen in the first place. It couldn't have been just to get away from her. He'd never run from a woman or a problem in his life.

"Her friend's gonna be staying there with her, so

she might last longer than that," he added. Then with
a snap of his fingers as his memory decided to func-
tion again, he moved to the refrigerator to get a
count of how many desserts they had on deck for the
upcoming dinner crowd.

"Really?" Brody paused and looked over his
shoulder. "That woman out there is gonna be sleeping under the same roof as me?"

Jealousy bubbled in the pit of Ryan's stomach,
and he gritted his teeth again. "She's Sofia's friend,
man. Give your hormones a rest."

"What? She's a grown woman capable of making
her own decisions, I'm sure. And once I lay on the
charm, you know what she'll decide." The rise and fall
of Brody's brows together with what he often called
his money-makin' smile only pressed the panic button in Ryan's gut a little harder.

It was a totally ridiculous reaction. He'd only paid
so much attention to her because he'd thought she
was the associate he needed to impress to close the
deal. "She's off-limits. The same way we used to tell
Sofia our friends were off-limits to her."

Brody shrugged and returned his attention to the
trays. "That's what you told Sofia. I told my buddies
I'd gut them like a fish if they even looked her way."

Ryan sighed. Brody and Trevor should've been
twins. Their athletic builds, charisma, and penchant
toward physical violence were identical.

"Don't mess with her, Brody," he said, his tone
much stonier than he'd intended. "Let her help Sofia
through whatever's going on with her."

"I hear you," Brody replied. "But if she falls for
me, I'm not backing down."

Ryan hoped she didn't fall for Brody. He hoped that almost as fervently as he'd been praying on this deal closing.

"Plus, you don't know, she might like it here so much, she decides to stay. I mean, the Big House is a great place to live," Brody added. "You know it's true. You lived there the majority of your life."

"I moved out of the Big House two years ago," he reminded his brother and refused to ponder any scenario where Allie would decide to stay on the island.

Brody washed and rinsed a tray before setting it on the wire shelf to his left. "And Dad gives you hell about that every chance he gets."

"I'm a grown man," Ryan countered. "Besides, I decided to build on part of our land so nobody would feel like I was abandoning our legacy." Nana had given him that suggestion after Ryan and his father had one of their monumental arguments. Nobody could get under Ryan's skin like Vernon Parker and vice versa. Now, if any of the Parkers didn't mix all the time, it was the two of them.

Ryan loved and respected his father, and he had no doubt his father loved him, too. But at thirty-five years old, he'd hoped his father would've learned to trust him. Vernon had scoffed at him moving out and argued almost as vehemently about that as he had Ryan's idea to sell their sauces.

Ryan pulled the refrigerator door open and counted the apple pies on the top shelf.

"Hey, I totally understand," Brody said. "But after you returned from college, I don't know why you thought rattling Dad's cage every chance you got was the smart thing to do."

"None of us were raised to go along with the status quo," Ryan said, even though, where his two older brothers were concerned, he wasn't sure that statement was true.

It wasn't that Trevor and Brody did everything their father wanted on purpose. Ryan was certain they both loved sports and smoking barbecue just as much as their father. The Parker legacy was different where the men were concerned. Ernest Parker, his great-great-grandfather, had been a pioneer in the barbecue arena, creating everything from the Parker signature house sauce to special cuts of meat he deemed good enough for his sauce to grace. Whenever talk of barbecue arose, Ernest Parker's name was at the forefront. And once his name was mentioned, his sons and their sons came after. Vernon was all about that legacy, which meant Trevor, Brody, and Ryan were expected to be all about it as well.

It was just Ryan's luck that he dreamed bigger than cooking and serving succulent meats and sides to the masses. He wanted the Parker name to soar as high as the heavens. He'd wanted that since the first time he'd watched his father accept a grand prize trophy on the competition circuit. Ryan had been fourteen then, and he'd known without a doubt that there was more success ahead for the Parkers.

"Is that what you think we do around here? Go along with whatever we're told?" Brody asked.

The tightness in his brother's tone put Ryan on alert. "That's not what I'm sayin'," he replied. "You know I believe everybody has the right to walk their own path. I just wish Dad would think along those same lines."

"He does. He just loves his family. I guess one day when we each have our little branch of the Parker family, we'll feel that way, too."

Brody's words made sense. Ryan was just in a peculiar mood. He knew why, and that only irritated him a little more.

Satisfied they weren't going to run out of desserts before the dinner shift, Ryan closed the refrigerator and turned to look at Brody. "The ferry's got three more runs before we close up tonight. Crowd's only gonna get bigger, so let's make sure we're fully stocked with everything."

That was Ryan's way of ending the uncomfortable conversation he'd inadvertently broached with his brother. Brody finished the trays and wiped his hands on the black apron tied around his waist.

"I got it," Brody replied with a nod. "Trevor's out back unloading the latest batch of chickens and ribs. And Mama's got potatoes and macaroni boiling to make more sides. We'll be fine."

"Cool. I'll head back out here to help serving. But if you need me, I can do double duty." There wasn't a day that he hadn't worn more than one hat at the restaurant. They all had for that matter, only none of them touched the books except Sofia.

"Nah, we'll keep the back of the house running smoothly," Brody told him as he moved close enough to hand Ryan the stack of now clean and dried trays. "You just go on up front and keep smiling at the customers. Especially our new house guest."

Brody winked, and his big grin spread. The Parker brothers shared their mother's lighter complexion, but each had the same wavy black hair that had graced their father's head before Vernon went bald and his deep brown eyes. Brody's often held more laughter than Ryan's or Trevor's, and today was no different. He was getting a kick out of the fact that Allie's presence had thrown Ryan off-kilter. The siblings were too close not to notice these things about each other, and Ryan knew it was pointless to try and deny it.

"I'm the focused Parker brother, remember?" he said as lightly as he could manage with the stress from today's developments still bubbling just beneath the surface. "Sofia's visit with her friend has nothing to do with the running of this restaurant."

He took the trays from his brother and turned to walk out of the kitchen.

"Yeah, but last time I checked, none of the Parker brothers could ignore a good-looking woman," Brody joked.

Ryan kept on walking, remembering a time when he'd had no other choice than to let a woman walk out of his life. He'd told himself then that he'd never travel down that path again, not with a woman who didn't want the same type of life he did.

Everything about Allie Sparks said big city. He'd noticed that the moment Optimus had run into her on the beach. When he'd seen her for the first time today, she'd even had her cell phone in hand, taking pictures like a tourist. Most days, Ryan forgot his cell phone was tucked in the back pocket of his jeans, and a good portion of the older members on the island didn't even have one.

No, the pretty and sophisticated writer still sitting across from his sister when he entered the dining

room again was as out of place on Crescent as Ryan
had been when he'd gone to school in the city. Even if
that weren't the case, she'd still be off-limits, just like
he'd told Brody.

Now, all he had to do was remind himself of that
fact each time he saw her and he'd be just fine. She
was still bound to be a distraction while she was here,
but Ryan could handle that; he didn't have much
choice, especially since he'd agreed to be her tour
guide. He'd kick himself later for going along with
that, but for now, duty called, and nothing came before Parker BBQ.

Not even the city woman with great-smelling hair
and a big appetite.

CHAPTER SIX

- *Parker BBQ*
- *Delicious food – mac 'n cheese was phenome-nal, pork was tender, but the sauce was definitely the money-maker. More varieties listed on the menu, try them all.*
- *Ambiance – country western vibe, ocean-view*
- *Service – Cordial staff*

Was cordial the correct word to describe Ryan Parker?

Allie sat back against the sturdy black headboard. Her fingers were poised over the keyboard of her laptop that she'd positioned on top of the pillow on her lap.

He was tall. Possibly six feet, or a little over that, she'd guess, since she was five feet five inches and she'd had to tilt her head back to meet his gaze.

"Attentive" was another word that described him. That hadn't been concluded solely because he'd helped her up yesterday on the beach. He should've done that, considering it was his dog's fault she'd taken a tumble. But today, he'd been right there to help her to her seat, had even taken her order when she'd sensed an air of authority in him as they'd stood in the middle of the busy restaurant.

Later, after he'd mistaken her for a colleague and then agreed to be her tour guide, she'd covertly watched him talking to other customers. He'd seemed to know a good many of them, but even the new ones he gave the same pleasant smile and knowledgeable advice about the menu, the island, and just about whatever else they asked him. Sofia called him a people-person and fun to be around. Of course, Allie had acted uninterested the moment her friend shifted their conversation to him. Ryan Parker wasn't the topic she'd come here to research.

Clearing her throat, she looked at her screen and prepared to continue typing her notes for today.

It was eleven thirty at night now, and instead of the homey, sweetly decorated room she'd stayed in last night at Lou's, she was sitting in the center of a full-size bed in a room with mahogany wood floors and a wall of windows with views of the sprawling green grass of the Parker property. In the not-too-far distance was the beach and the rippling waves of the ocean. Earlier this evening, she'd stood at those windows for about twenty minutes. During that time, she'd been blissfully unaware of Sofia's grand-mother—who insisted Allie also call her Nana—unpacking her duffel bag and putting all her clothes in the dresser drawers. Her toiletries were neatly lined on the dresser, and Nana had been about to tackle Allie's tote before Allie had realized she was there and was able to rescue it.

The dinner of meatloaf, mashed potatoes, and corn had been served promptly at six thirty. The people in Crescent seemed to be pretty punctual when it came to their dinner time. Ms. Sarah, Sofia's mother, had done the cooking, and the food had been just as tasty here as it had been in their restaurant.

But now, Allie had to work. She'd gotten her first glimpse of some of the permanent residents of the island, and she needed to start her list of possibilities for the one who authored the blog.

Who is it? she typed in bold.

• *Has to be an islander (that's what Sofia called them). Someone with in-depth knowledge of the island and a vested interest in the tourism*

• *Man or woman?*

• *Active part of the community or a recluse? Active part of the community, how else would they know about the tourists who came to town?*

That question ran through her mind, and she paused to consider it further. The Ferry Office and the Chamber of Commerce would most likely be good places to start her search tomorrow. Anyone visiting the island would need to book a ferry ride. She nixed the idea of the Chamber of Commerce because other than visiting their website, she rarely actually went to the office of anyplace she'd ever visited. But tourists would need a place to stay, so she'd circle back to Lazy Lou's and chat with Lindy and Lucy some more. Lucy was young and most likely tech-savvy. Perhaps she'd started the blog to get more people into their family's establishment?

But was Lucy a matchmaker?

Allie shrugged. "Could be," she said, answering her own question. But what would be the point? What satisfaction did Lucy, or whoever this person writing about these mysterious love connections, get from doing this? Blogs generally made money via advertisements and subscriptions, so it made sense that if as many people who signed up for dating sites believed the stories being told on the blog, they might subscribe and possibly head to the island.

She lay her head back on the pillow. Would she pack her bags and travel to a coastal island just to meet a guy?

If the guy smiled like Ryan Parker while serving her a delicious pork BBQ sandwich, yes. Absolutely yes!

First, she frowned at how quick and unequivocally that answer popped into her mind, then she sighed with the truth of every word.

Ryan Parker.

His name blinked in her mind like a neon sign. She wasn't going to deny it, not in the privacy of this room—the room that she was trying desperately not to recall had once been his. She liked him. It had taken tremendous strength on her part not to wonder about which clothing items he'd stacked in the dresser drawers or hung in the closet. Or how annoyed she became each time she wondered if he'd ever snuck a girl (or *girls*) into this room.

On an impatient sigh—impatient because she didn't have these types of thoughts about men—she lifted a hand to rub her eyes. She liked his voice and the way he'd looked so natural and at home in the pictures with his family. Pictures she'd glimpsed on the mantel in the family room and the walls of the hallway leading to the living room in the brick-front ranch-style home the Parkers called the Big House. It was a logical description considering there were six bedrooms, four bathrooms, a family room, study, living room, dining room, and professional kitchen that looked like it had been ripped straight from the pages of a *Good Housekeeping* magazine.

Graduations, family dinners, playing on the beach,

Christmas morning, were all featured in the pictures where members of this family smiled happily for the camera. She'd heard Sofia talk about her parents and siblings before, but seeing these special moments of their life in snapshots had scraped against the rawest parts of Allie's soul. The parts that she'd told herself she wasn't responsible for and that needed to be buried for her peace of mind. Yet now there was Ryan's face in the center of most of those pictures.

She was delusional. She had to be. It had only been two days. Well, one full day and a quarter of a day since she'd first laid eyes on this man, and here she was thinking about him like he'd been her long-lost love.

It was beyond weird, and she needed it to stop immediately.

Closing the laptop, she set it and the pillow aside and then climbed off the bed. She plugged her phone into the charger and was about to make one last trip to the bathroom before changing into her pajamas and going to bed when she paused and looked out the window. The water in the distance glistened like a shimmering black sheet. No moon was visible tonight as clouds had moved in later that afternoon. It was an ominous kind of quiet that called to her until she was pushing her bare feet into a pair of flip-flops and heading out the door.

The walk from the Big House to the beach took about five minutes with the night air fanning across her face and the lulling sound of crashing waves echoing in the distance. This place was simply beautiful, even in the dark, and as the sand tickled her toes, she wrapped her arms around her chest because there was a light breeze down closer to the water.

Looking back at the house, the illumination flowing from the windows cast a soft golden glow against the dim landscape. Memories had been made there; she knew because Sofia had talked about some of them, whenever she hadn't been talking about her plans to rule the world. Allie grinned at the thought. They'd both had big plans for their lives back in college, but Sofia had her family's support in pursuing her accounting career.

That memory had her imagining what it would've been like to grow up in a place like the Big House. The Sparkses had lived in a two-level penthouse in Miami with Allie and Bella's bedroom on the lower floor. Their unit faced the beach, but because her mother detested sand and the idea of it being tracked into the house on their pristine white floors, it was a look-but-don't-touch arrangement for the girls.

Well, tonight, Allie was going to touch.

Kicking off her flip-flops, she waded down to the water, grinning when her feet made first contact with the coolness. That grin turned to full-scale laughter as she walked in farther, hearing the sound of her mother's shrill voice telling her, "Stop playing around, Allison. Focus on your work."

Allie continued her jaunt in the water, walking around and kicking her feet up so that splashes of water landed on her arms and the tip of her nose. She did a little dance in a circle, water lapping around her legs, getting the lower half of them wet in the process. Why hadn't she done this before? Like in her adult years, after she'd bought her condo on the beach?

Excitement bubbled in the pit of her stomach,

circling and traveling until she erupted in giggles. The thought of playing in the water seemed so silly, and yet it felt exhilarating. She'd opened her arms by then, swinging them in the air as she moved, enjoying this freedom.

It was a moment in time she'd never forget.

Especially not when water began to slap against her face, arms, and chest at a rapid pace as man and dog swished through the ocean headed directly toward her.

"Not this time!" Ryan yelled as he reached out and grabbed Optimus up in his arms.

But he was too late, sort of. Allie was already sputtering and wiping the water Optimus's exuberance had splashed into her eyes.

"At least I caught him before he could jump on you again," Ryan continued as Allie struggled to find her words.

He was standing about two feet away from her now, dog tucked under his arm, with a smile on his face while she frowned. They'd messed up her moment.

"Gee, thanks," she snapped. "How about catching him before he gets anywhere near me next time?"

In answer to her suggestion, Optimus shook the water from his coat, once again sending sprinkles into Allie's face.

"All right, stop that." Ryan took a step back with the dog that was still flailing in his arms.

"He really doesn't listen to you." She started walking toward the shore, sober now from her "freedom" experience. When she was clear of the water, she looked down with a huff as thick globs of sand now coated her feet and ankles.

"We're just getting used to each other." He'd come out of the water, too, and was now standing beside her. "You know, like you'll get used to the island while you're here. I mean, you're gonna be here awhile, right? At least until Sofia's better?"

Allie found her shoes, pushed her toes between the straps, and resisted the urge to frown at the knowledge that now her flip-flops were full of sand, too. Maybe her mother had a point about the beach being too messy.

"Yes. I mean, I plan to do what I can to help Sofia recuperate. I'm scheduled to be here for at least two weeks."

She started walking again, heading back toward the house with the warm golden light pouring from the windows. Where she should've stayed before, especially if she'd known Ryan and his dog liked taking midnight walks along the beach.

"It was really nice of you to come here for Sofia," he said.

Optimus ran in a big circle around her and yes, Ryan, who had fallen into step beside her.

"I didn't know she was hurt when I called to tell her I was visiting. But she's the closest friend I've ever had, so helping her during this time is no problem for me."

"But you're not really into island life, are you?" There was a hint of humor in his tone, and when she looked over at him, he pointed down to her feet. "You should've just carried your flip-flops in your hand and walked back to the house barefoot. That would save you from having to drop the flops in the sink when you get inside."

Restaurant manager, tour guide, and flip flop expert? This guy was too much.

And he was standing too close to her.

"I live in Miami so, you know, beaches are everywhere." He didn't need to know she rarely walked on them with bare feet and traipsed into the water happily, the way she'd just done a few minutes ago. Nor did she think it mattered to tell him that as part of her job, she'd traveled to more islands than he probably knew existed.

"But Miami's a big city, and Crescent is just a small island. We're not really into all the fancy stuff you have in the city."

"I happen to like what I've seen of this small island so far." A little more than she'd anticipated.

"That's good to know." He paused, staring at her for a few seconds like he was thinking of what to say next. "Do you like your room at the Big House? I'm sure it's not as fancy as the houses in Miami."

Was he being sarcastic? She was picking up on a tone, or perhaps she was looking for one. Searching for something, anything to make her not think about him as fondly as she had been earlier tonight. "You know very well it's a nice room, since you used to live in it."

He grinned. "It was cool for a guy's room, but that doesn't mean it works for you."

But it did work for her, and not just because it had been his room. She liked how relaxing it had felt in that house tonight. Similar to the way she'd felt last night at Lazy Lou's, but different. It didn't make sense to her at the moment, but that was the only way she could explain it.

"It was really nice of Sofia to offer to let me stay and of your parents for agreeing."

"You're Sofia's BFF. That means you're like family," he said.

Their gazes held for a moment. A very still and quiet moment during which time a sadness seemed to wash over her. Maybe not quite sad, but definitely disappointing. His words were similar to what Lucy had said yesterday, which made this reaction even weirder, because if Sofia was her family, then so was Ryan. Even if the way she'd been thinking about him tonight had been the farthest thing from a familial feeling.

"It was really nice of her to offer, and nobody says BFF anymore," she replied, her throat suddenly dry.

"Sofia does," he replied. "That's where I got it from."

Allie shook her head because Sofia had her using the same acronym earlier. "Sofia doesn't count. She's always walked and talked her own way." It was one of the first things she'd learned and had admired about Sofia. There was a strength in her, a determination to do whatever she wanted in the way she wanted, regardless of what anyone said or did. Allie had always been jealous at how easily that type of conviction came to Sofia, while she'd had to fight for every ounce of independence she claimed from her parents during her adult years.

The Big House wasn't that far away now.

Optimus had run ahead of them and was rolling on the grass in the distance as if he hadn't a care in the world. She almost chuckled at his silly and carefree antics. "Why did you move away from your family?" The question tumbled free before she could consider whether it was something she really needed to know.

It was certainly none of her business. What he or anyone else in this family did was of no concern to her. At least it shouldn't be. She didn't know them, and they didn't know her. Despite what he'd just said, being Sofia's friend didn't really make her one of them.

"I didn't go that far," he replied and turned a little as they walked to point behind him. "I've got a house straight down the beach. Close enough to get here quickly if I'm needed, but far enough to have some privacy."

She nodded as if she understood, but privacy hadn't been something she'd sought where her family was concerned. To the contrary, she'd longed for a closeness to her parents and her sister that she supposed was never meant to be. "But you were homesick, so you decided to come by for a late-night visit?" She purposely lightened her tone, tired of the melancholy thoughts of a past she couldn't change seeping in.

"Nah." He nodded ahead of them this time. "House training that guy."

The dog yipped and played as if he didn't have a care in the world. "Oh. Does that guy usually have to pee at midnight?"

She was treated to Ryan's robust laughter again, and this time she tried not to enjoy it as much as she had before. It would be better if she didn't enjoy it at all. He was Sofia's brother, and she was Sofia's best friend. Admittedly, that didn't make them related, but it did create another boundary, one that might threaten her friendship with Sofia if something between her and Ryan didn't end well. Romantic thoughts and the relationships that usually came with them were only for the movies. They weren't for people like her who didn't have the capacity to exist in a healthy relationship. How could she after growing up the way she had?

"That guy always has to pee." And, as if to prove his owner's point and effectively drag her thoughts back to the present, Optimus stopped rolling around and squatted where he was to relieve himself.

Before she could catch herself, she chuckled. "Well, I guess when you gotta go, you gotta go. But wait, I thought boy dogs raised their legs to go."

He shrugged. "Not this one, and when I asked Fred, the guy I got him from, that same question, he said he might start to do that when he gets older or sees other dogs doing it, but then again, he might not. I don't really care as long as he learns *where* to do it." It was his turn to laugh. "I've only had him a few weeks, so we're working on some other things in addition to the house training. But he's a good little guy."

"Who likes to bring me and the sand a lot closer." She looked down at her feet again and realized he was right; she shouldn't have put her flip-flops back on.

"Optimus loves the beach, and since it seems you're drawn to it as well, I'd say you two have something in common."

They'd come to the set of wooden stairs that

would lead to a stone pathway, and she stopped. "Never thought I'd have anything in common with a dog. But I guess I'm cool with it."

It seemed Optimus was, too, because the moment she'd stopped walking, he'd bounded over to her and was now running circles around her, pausing to jump up on her legs when she didn't give any form of acknowledgment.

Allie never had a dog, or any pet for that matter. Her mother didn't like dirt or messiness, which meant pets were a no-no in their penthouse. And the families her parents associated with who had children, weren't pet people. Now, as she gave in to a foreign urge and knelt down to drop a hand on Optimus's head, she wondered if she may have missed something.

The dog leaned into her, twisting his head until he could lick her fingers, then going for broke and jumping up to rest two big paws on her thigh.

"He really likes you," Ryan said.

"I think I like him, too."

The dog, not the guy. Oh please, for all that was holy and right in this world, don't let her start liking this guy.

CHAPTER SEVEN

It's gonna be a hot one here on Crescent today, but beautiful. Summers are always beautiful on the island. Gorgeous time of year to fall in love. Not so much for the Gemini, as they sometimes take a longer route to love. You wouldn't guess it at first as they're pretty social creatures who generally like meeting new people. But once you capture their heart, you'll see what a real "gem" they can be.

A few minutes ago, Allie would've sworn she'd just received the weirdest text ever. It had to have been spam, since the sender's identification was a series of five numbers, not ten or eleven, which would represent a telephone number and area code. She'd read it twice as she walked out of her room and down the wide hallway toward the center of the Big House. It was Thursday, and she'd just spent her second night with the very generous Parker family, but she already had half the house memorized.

It wasn't until she stepped into the kitchen that the weirdness of the message switched to a vague sense of familiarity. She moved quickly to the oval-shaped wood-topped table and pulled out a chair with white spindles and a daisy-covered seat cushion. Dropping down into the seat, she swiped her finger quickly over the screen of her phone. The site she'd been reading last night while she'd been sitting on the back porch with Nana and Sofia was still in her browser, and she refreshed the screen before scrolling midway down. And there it was, the same message she'd received on her phone, listed here under the *Finding Love* column.

"Mornin's are the most perfect time of day."

Allie's head shot up at the sound of Nana's voice, and she stared across the room to see her standing at the counter.

"Oh, sorry. I didn't know anybody was in here," she said. "Good morning, Nana."

"The kitchen is the heart of the house. Most times if people are at home, there's someone in the kitchen," Nana said.

Well, wasn't that a peculiar thing for her to say? There was no way this woman knew that Renee had all but demanded Allie produce a story with some heart to save her job.

"Left you some breakfast," Nana continued while Allie sat torn between the ingrained urge to be cordial and wanting to continue scrolling to get to the bottom of the unexpected text message.

"Thank you," she replied and gave in to using her manners over her investigative skills. She set her phone on the table and stood. "Coffee smells wonderful."

Nana was dressed in black slacks and a white T-shirt today. She wore unattractive black rubber-sole shoes that Allie suspected were skid-resistant for the hours she spent in the restaurant. Her snowy-white hair was in tight curls tucked neatly under the hairnet she always wore at the restaurant as well. It was a little after ten in the morning, so part of the reason Allie hadn't expected anyone to be in the kitchen was that she assumed everyone would be at the restaurant getting ready to open.

"I like my tea in the morning. Earl Grey with a tablespoon of honey," Nana said and reached into the microwave above the stove to pull out the plate she'd saved for Allie. "But I've got you some waffles and sausage here."

"Thanks," Allie said as she found a mug in the third cabinet from the window where she'd been told yesterday they were kept. "I'm a tea drinker, too, but I think I'll try this great-smelling coffee. And you didn't have to go to all the trouble of saving me breakfast."

Nana was already unwrapping the plate and setting it back inside the microwave. She closed the door soundly and pressed a few buttons to warm the food. "Nonsense. Everybody needs breakfast in the morning. Even those of us who try to sleep the early hours away."

Allie found the sugar and creamer and mixed them into her mug until the coffee looked more like beige milk—which in her book was perfection. "I'm usually an early riser, but I've just been sleeping so well here," she admitted. It was the truth. Initially, she'd thought it must've been something in the mattress at Lou's, but then the first night she'd climbed into the bed down the hall, she'd slept just as soundly. Despite the fact that it was Ryan's old bed and the moment she'd closed her eyes that night, his face had appeared in her mind.

"It's the island air," Nana said, turning to Allie. "It's good for your soul." The woman lifted her arms then, holding her hands out as if she were giving praise for the air she spoke of.

Allie leaned her backside against the counter and took a slow sip of her coffee. "My condo faces the water in Miami." She didn't know why she mentioned that, but the thought had occurred to her that sleeping with the scent of the water wafting through the windows wasn't new to her. Then again, more often than not she had the air conditioner blasting in her apartment to ward off the sweltering Miami heat. Here, a cool breeze rolled off the water and snuck through the open window in the room where she was sleeping. She was certain the sound of the waves and the delicious scent of the sea air helped to lull her into the blissful slumber.

"How often do you get out there and enjoy it?" Nana asked. She folded her arms across her chest and tilted her head as she stared at Allie.

The resemblance between Mr. Vernon and his mother was obvious in the depths of their umber complexion and their deep, assessing gaze. Allie had yet to share a meal with all of the Parkers at one table because of their schedules at the restaurant, but Sofia had assured her their Monday brunches were a lively affair.

"Sometimes," she lied and shrugged. Then she took another sip of coffee in the hope that the act would keep Nana from seeing through her veil of dishonesty. "I work a lot."

"Balance," Nana said and reached out a hand to pat Allie's arm. "A happy life means finding balance between the work you enjoy and spending time doing the things you love or with the people you love."

"I don't love anyone." The words fell from her lips before she could stop them. The thudding echo of "and nobody loves me" sounded in her mind, and her temples throbbed.

"Good morning!" Sofia said, easing her way into the kitchen. She'd started physical therapy yesterday, and the therapist had said she might be a little sore this morning. From the way she seemed to be dragging her right leg along beside her, Allie suspected that despite her cheerful tone, she might be in pain.

"Another late riser," Nana said as she moved away from Allie. "But you've got an excuse, so I'll let you slide. Sit on down and I'll get your fruit out of the refrigerator."

Allie opened the microwave and retrieved her plate. She carried it and her coffee to the table and sat in the seat where she'd left her phone.

"How're you feeling?" she asked Sofia.

"Oh, I'm just jolly," Sofia snapped. "I felt better before therapy. Now, it feels like the swelling is back, and any weight I try to put on it has my eyes tearing. But yeah, I'm just jolly."

"Don't be sassy, Sofia. Healing takes time." Nana came to the table and set a bowl of fruit and a fork in front of her.

"Thank you," Sofia managed but then frowned when her grandmother walked away. "I hate being stuck in this house, not doing anything."

"Well, what do you want to do?" Allie asked after taking a bite of her sausage. "I've got Eddie on my speed dial now, so I can give him a call and see if he can pick us up. I'd planned to visit the bookstore today, but you and I could do something else, maybe go to the beach." Allie glanced at Nana, who gave her a tentative smile.

"The utensils need to be packed and the new travel menus folded so they'll be ready for us to take to the carnival tomorrow night," Nana said. "You could sit out on the back porch and do that today. Listen to the waves, smell the fresh air, and keep your ankle elevated."

Sofia forked a piece of cantaloupe into her mouth and groaned. "Going out on the porch isn't really leaving the house," she said. "But I'm gonna agree with you today, Nana. I don't really feel like moving around a lot."

Allie nodded. "Then I'll set up my laptop on the porch and I can sit outside with you." She could also ask her more questions about the people on the island. Her list of possibilities for the blogger was ominous with only traits and clues but few real people to match them to.

She hadn't made it to Lou's yesterday to chat with Lucy. And after Sofia's therapy appointment, they'd sat in the living room watching movies. It'd felt just like old times. So much so that by the time Allie had climbed into bed, she was missing her college years and praying even harder that the private investigator could find Bella. It'd been way too long since she'd felt that type of closeness with anyone, and she longed to feel it again with her sister. But for now, she'd focus on this time with Sofia.

"Nope," Sofia said and hunted down a grape with her fork. "I already called Ryan and he's on his way over here now. You're getting out of this house today."

"I got out of this house yesterday," Allie said. "With you, when we went to your appointment."

Sofia shook her head. "That doesn't count. Trevor and Brody went to the restaurant with Daddy at the crack of dawn this morning, and so did Mama. They've got a full staff of servers on schedule for today, so Ryan doesn't need to be there every second. He's available to take you around town."

Allie knew that was part of the agreement for Sofia to allow them to help her during her recuperation, so she didn't argue her friend's suggestion. Besides, Ryan might be just the person she needed to ask who on this island could've gotten her cell phone number and given it to a blogger to spam her with unsolicited horoscopes.

• • •

"If I fall—"

"You're not gonna fall," Ryan interrupted and put a hand on each side of her waist.

Like that was going to keep her steady. Ryan's hands on her were notorious for doing the exact opposite, although she'd been doing a fantastic job at ignoring thoughts like that for the past couple of hours they'd been together.

"I don't know why I let you talk me into this," she continued, taking a tentative step forward.

She'd wisely worn tennis shoes with her jean capri pants and purple halter top today. After Sofia had announced Ryan was coming to take her out sightseeing, she'd gone back into the bedroom, changed her shoes, and pulled her hair back into a ponytail once more. At the time, she'd had no clue where they were going, but she'd wanted to be ready for anything.

But even wearing smarter shoes didn't prepare her for this.

She placed another foot in front of the first and felt her legs shaking beneath her. Arms stretched out straight, she attempted to calm her thoughts, hoping that would resonate with her body and get her safely across this log. Toppling over into the water was going to be embarrassing—and wet.

"Talk you into what? Being adventurous?" he asked from behind her.

Right behind her, just as he'd been only a step or two away from her everywhere they'd gone. Those places had included taking some of the leftover boxes from the restaurant and dropping them off at the community center where Ryan told her they were separating all the prizes for the games that would be featured at the carnival. It was their kickoff to the SummerFest activities and had been the talk of the Parker household since she'd been there.

"This is foolish, not adventurous," she replied. "There was a perfectly good path right down that hill. Why we had to walk across this wobbly old log, I'll never know." And as if that log hadn't liked how she described it, the thing twisted and her feet moved in double-time to stay upright.

"Whoa, there. You tryin' to take us both down?" He chuckled and released his hands from her waist.

She didn't look back but suspected he was now holding his arms out, too, figuring he needed to fend for himself at this point.

"Well, there's no point in me swimming alone."

He laughed, a rich, deep sound that echoed through the trees and settled in her chest with a thud.

"You wouldn't be alone. Optimus is tied to that tree over there enjoying himself in the water he's able to reach."

She frowned. "He's at the lower end of the river," she said. "You purposely put him over there, out of harm's way. But then led me up here to do some daredevil act."

"Sofia and I used to wear blindfolds and bet on who could get across here the quickest," he said.

They were at the Springs, apparently one of Sofia's favorite places on the island. Allie could see why. The place was gorgeous. She'd seen waterfalls in Fiji and rainforests in South America and Tanzania, but neither of them compared to this. Here, the river had cut through the mountain, eroding the bedrock down its side panel until it snaked along in a fierce stream, creating this frosty flush through the dark-colored rock and vivid greenery. The water spilled into the lower river where more clefts had formed, probably because of more erosion in the area. The beauty of nature never ceased to amaze her, especially when it was untouched, as she suspected this area had been.

But this ridiculous log they were trekking over was unnecessary. Or perhaps it was just to add to the beauty of the area? Whatever the reason, she wanted off it right now.

She took faster steps.

"Oh, so now we're racing?" he asked, amusement lacing his tone.

"No. Not racing, just hurrying up before I fall and break my neck on one of those river rocks."

"I won't let you fall."

"You won't be able to stop me," she countered. "Your efforts would likely only take us both down."

He laughed again.

"Really? That's funny, too? Both of us falling into the water."

"Well," he said between guffaws, "we *are* on an island. I mean, it seems natural that at some point in every day we'd end up in the water."

She could see the river's bank — a lush carpet of grass sprinkled with white flowers. "When I'm ready for a swim, I'll put on my bathing suit and head to the beach," she said and then leaped the short distance from where she stood to ground.

Her arms flailed as she landed, and she prayed silently that she could stick the landing like she often watched the trained gymnasts do during the Olympics.

"Yeah!" Ryan yelled. "That's what I'm talkin' 'bout! See how you took that chance?"

He was right behind her as she leaned over, her hands on her knees as she tried to get her bearings. "You're a goof," she mumbled between breaths.

"Nah, I just like having fun. And taking chances. Are you afraid to take chances, Allie?"

Allie looked up at him, mouth gaping as no answer to his question came. How could she be afraid to take chances when he'd just told her she'd taken a chance jumping off that log? And besides that, she wasn't afraid of anything. She couldn't afford to be. "Was this fun?" she asked instead of repeating any of what had just rolled through her mind.

He sat down on the grass and leaned back to rest on his elbows. "Yeah, it was." Optimus came running over, stretching his long leash until he could snuggle against his owner. Ryan immediately reached out a hand to rub the top of his head and then unhooked the leash from his collar.

Allie sat, too, crossing her legs in front of her. "This is not my idea of fun," she said and then looked around. "But it is gorgeous here. I can see why Sofia loves it."

"Any places you love in Miami?"

Why did the sun's beams have to snake through the trees and fall on him in golden slashes that made him seem like some perfectly crafted cover model?

She blinked away the thought and cleared her throat. "There's a park I like to go to when I have free time. I can sit there and read for hours. Providing I have the right snacks."

"Snacks?"

"Yeah, snacks," she said and must have said the magic word for Optimus, because he came over to her then, climbing up on her thighs. She stared down at him for a few moments before she gave in and cupped his adorable face with her hands. "You like snacks, don't you, Optimus? We have to have the right ones to go along with what we're reading."

Ryan arched a brow curiously. "Which snacks go with reading?"

"Ideally something that comes in pieces. Like Junior Mints, Skittles, honey roasted almonds if you're going the healthier route. That way you can pop a few in your mouth and keep turning pages—or swiping if you're on an ereader—and snacking at the same time."

The sound of his laughter once again had her

looking over at him. "I'm glad I've been able to entertain you today."

He shook his head. "I just think it's cute that you have snacking down to a science. I mean, it's also a little weird, but it's still cute."

"So I'm weird and cute?"

He stared silently for a second. "You're more cute than weird."

It was her turn to laugh because the butterflies that now danced in her stomach shouldn't be addressed. "Well, gee, thanks. I think."

No, what she thought was that this was too easy. Being with Ryan in this very casual, low-key way was much easier than any date she'd ever gone on. After years of being forced to simply go along with her parents' rules and expectations, she'd found it hard to be comfortable enough in any relationship—other than the friendship she'd managed to forge with Sofia—to let go of all her reservations and pretenses to simply laugh and enjoy the moment.

She was enjoying this moment with Ryan, though. Now that her heart had stopped its attempt to thump right out of her chest when she walked along that log, that was. He was easy to be around with his quick laughter and affable demeanor, and she'd decided the dog only added to his overall allure, but none of this was the green light it could've been if circumstances were different.

She just had to keep reminding herself of that fact.

"What else do you do in Miami? Party with friends? Go out on dates?"

His rapid-fire questions yanked her away from

thoughts she shouldn't have been entertaining anyway, and she paused to consider her response. Would he think she was pathetic or, worse, take pity on her if she said no to both? The familiar tendrils of worry eased along the base of her neck, and she resisted the urge to squirm, hating every second she let what someone thought of her matter in any way. How many times had she replayed some of Bella's last words to her in her mind?

"The only person you need to please is yourself. If they don't like your choices or who you are outside of who they think you should be, to hell with them!"

Of course, her sister had been speaking about their parents in particular, but Allie had soon learned it was a message she could apply to all aspects of her life. It was something she had to remind herself of way more frequently than she liked to admit.

And really, as it pertained to her current situation, why was she even talking to Ryan about her personal life? Or even sitting by this lovely river with him on a pretty summer's day? This wasn't what she was on this island to do.

She mentally shook herself free of all those heavy, conflicting thoughts and cleared her throat. "Does the Crescent Chamber of Commerce collect information on tourists?" She blurted out the question and watched as confusion covered his face.

• • •

Ryan was just kicking himself for asking her about her dating life when her response sent a curve ball soaring in his direction.

Not just because it was totally off topic from what they'd been talking about, but also because of the way her brow had furrowed seconds before she asked the question. For just that quick moment, she'd looked as if she were irritated. With him or with herself?

It also wasn't lost on him that she'd dodged his earlier questions about taking chances, the same look he'd just seen flitting across her face then, too. He'd be lying if he said he didn't wonder what that look meant. Or what he could do to make it go away. Resisting the urge to groan out loud or do a face palm that any emoji would rival because what the hell was he thinking—he tamped down on his thoughts and took a deep breath. After a thorough inhale of the light scent of flowers mixed with the earthy nature aroma, the unusual prick of nerves he'd been experiencing in the last few minutes began to settle.

Allie was still there as he released a pent-up breath, sitting on the grass with her legs tucked under her, face free of any makeup, hair that looked so soft his fingers itched to touch, held away from her face by a black band. In this moment, it was hard to believe she belonged in the city. With the Springs as a backdrop, the denim shorts and peach tank top she wore, she looked like any other islander. Except she wasn't really like any other woman he'd ever seen in Crescent or when he'd been at school in New York.

And none of that really mattered, did it?

Of course it didn't. This wasn't some romantic hookup. He was doing his sister a favor by showing her the sights. And now, he realized, he was actually enjoying himself. But what was the harm in that?

There was none, and he refused to overthink this…this, whatever he'd fleetingly felt about being here with her. Besides, he had so many other things to think about. Yesterday had been extremely busy at the restaurant. So much so he hadn't gotten an opportunity to reach out to Phoebe again to ask who, in fact, would be coming to the island on behalf of the company. He'd had enough surprises in that regard and wasn't in the mood for any more.

It occurred to him then that this was the first time he'd thought about the deal since he'd been with Allie today.

"Earth to Ryan. Come in, Ryan," she said and waved a hand as if to remind him that she was there.

Her presence wasn't something he could forget. Not when his dog had seemingly fallen in love with her.

"You want to visit the Chamber of Commerce?" he asked. "Are you writing a book about the island? If so, you'd do better to talk to Nana and her Diamonds club. They know everything there is to know about Crescent."

"No, no. I'm not writing a book," she answered quickly.

Too quickly. And there was that look again. Her eyes had widened slightly, then her nose and brow crinkled. It was almost a frustrated look, but it came and went so fast he couldn't actually pinpoint it. But there was no doubt he wanted to know what was causing it.

"Okay, so you're not writing a book, but Sofia said you were a writer."

She nodded. "Yes. I am. Mostly articles and stuff. I mean, I write for a travel blog. So, I was just wondering…" Her words trailed off as she reached back and pulled her phone from her pocket.

"About Crescent's Chamber of Commerce? Are you writing an article about the island?" If there was a hint of excitement in his tone, she didn't seem to notice. Instead she stared at him, blinking once and then twice before sighing. An article about the island could only boost tourism, which in turn would look great whenever the rep from Brownstone did arrive.

"Uh, yeah, I am," she replied. "I'm writing an article about the heart of Crescent Island." Another quick nod and she moved to ease Optimus off her lap.

His dog, of course, protested, and she ended up cradling his bulky body in front of her like he was a baby, while she walked toward where Ryan still sat. It took some finesse, since Optimus was no lightweight and she was still trying to hold her phone in her hand without dropping it.

"See, I received this message," she said, thrusting her phone in his face.

He didn't actually want to take his attention away from how much he liked the sight of her holding his dog so close to her, but she obviously had something else she wanted him to see. And he wanted to hear what else she had to say. He read the first few lines and then grinned.

"Remember the other night when I said you were one of us?" he asked. He'd been recalling those words so much himself that they were becoming a mantra or an incantation to warn him against impending danger. The danger that was enjoying her presence way too much.

"Yes," she said. "Even though I'm not convinced a college friendship classifies me for such a connection. After all, this is the first time I've been on this island or have ever met your family."

"And why is that?" he asked as he looked up at her. "Why haven't you visited Sofia before?"

She rubbed a hand absently over Optimus's head and shrugged. "I travel a lot for work, so it keeps me busy. But Sofia and I've seen each other a few times over the years. Just last year we met up in New York when one of our dormmates was in a Broadway play."

"And now you're finally here to write about our little island. Well, I've gotta tell you that seems like a pretty great idea."

"Really?" she asked, again looking unsure. "I mean, usually most people aren't totally sure they want to see a story about their hometown online."

"I'm not most people," he said.

"No, you certainly are not," she mumbled and then cleared her throat. "Anyway, I don't know who sent this text. It could be like one of those spy apps that tracks when you go to a mall and then sends you emails from the stores in that mall."

"Or the ones that track which websites you shop on and then ads for that site begin to pop up in your inbox," he added.

"Right!" She nodded. "But I try not to think I'm being watched that closely by bots or some secret government agency, so I thought maybe the Chamber of Commerce collects data on tourists and somehow the person who sends these weird horoscopes got ahold of that information."

It was his turn to frown as he came to his feet. She took a step back, putting some space between them. It was a cautionary gesture, one that could mean she was reacting to their proximity in the same way he had been all day. He was drawn to her, had been he supposed from that moment on the beach. But whenever she was near, he wanted to be closer, to talk longer, to listen more closely.

Wow. That wasn't weird at all.

He reached for her phone, and she let him slip it from her hand. Reading the text again, he sighed. "It's the town horoscope hotline. Everybody on the island who has a phone gets them at some point."

"Wait, you mean like those sites where you sign up for daily horoscopes, except these come straight to your phone?"

"Yep," he replied. "Sometimes they come every day, sometimes once a week." With a shrug, he looked at her again. "You don't believe in astrology?"

She frowned. "Not really. But I guess it's on brand for this island."

"Ha! You picked up on our island theme, huh?"

"It's kind of hard not to when the island is shaped like a crescent moon, and there are streets called Moonlight and Sunset Drive. The huge solar system on top of the Galaxy Emporium. You're not exactly subtle around here."

He had to laugh at that because she wasn't wrong. "It's our thing," he told her. "Some people take it to the extreme while others just acknowledge our history and move about their lives. But this is harmless," he said and handed her phone back to her.

"It's not harmless to give out someone's personal information without their permission. That's illegal."

"Whoa. That's a little serious. It's just a horoscope, and there're instructions right below it that tell you how to unsubscribe."

"I didn't subscribe in the first place," she countered.

"That's fair," he said and then nodded toward his dog, who was now squirming in her arms. "You'd better put him down. I think he has to go."

She almost dropped Optimus on the spot at his words.

"Oh. Oh. Okay." She lowered the dog's now-flailing body to the ground, and Ryan grinned.

"Look," he said when she stood up straight again and frowned down at her phone. "I doubt it came from the Chamber of Commerce. Willie Rand runs that office. He's about a hundred years old, give or take ten or twenty years. His two granddaughters work there with him, but they're more focused on trying to get Hollywood to take notice of the island and start filming movies out here so they can be discovered than they are about reading any moon charts to tell somebody's horoscope."

"Then how would somebody get my cell phone number? The only place I've been on this island besides your family's house and the restaurant is Lazy Lou's." She looked thoughtful. "Lucy and Lindy seemed really nice. And I doubt it was those two bickering men on the front porch."

"Nah, it definitely wasn't Cyrus or Barney. I doubt either of them even have a cell phone. Well, wait,

Cyrus might, since his niece works at Tiberius."

"What's Tiberius?" she asked and brushed a few wisps of hair from her eyes.

There was a light breeze today, cool enough to bring the humidity down and persistent enough to wreak havoc with what had started out as a neat hairstyle on her.

"It's the telecommunications company that was built here about ten years ago. We used to have satellites, but then some big corporate guy came to the island for a visit and figured he could save us from our primitive ways by providing more stable telecommunications connections."

"The wifi is great here," she replied. "I was surprised. But I guess now I'm not."

She would be surprised that their small island had something as sophisticated as good wifi. The reminder that she wasn't from here struck him hard, but instead of letting his thoughts drift to yet another reason why this woman wasn't for him, he decided to help her write the best article about Crescent Island as he could by showing her all the things to love about the place he called home.

"Still," he continued. "I'm certain it's not anybody at Lou's. Lindy and her family have always been nice, upstanding people. Maybe you signed a mailing list or something when you were doing your sightseeing before you came to the restaurant."

"How'd you know I did some sightseeing that day?"

"I'm sure you already know our dearly beloved island isn't that big," he told her. "Word travels fast, especially about city women wearing sexy high heels when they step off the ferry."

Which was exactly how Trevor had described her when he'd stopped by Ryan's yesterday morning.

She looked down at her tennis shoes and then back up at him.

"Smart choice today," he replied. "Come on, I've got another errand to run, and then I'll drop you off at the house. I'm sure Sofia's bored out of her mind by now and eager for some company."

At least he hoped she was.

It had taken Herculean strength to keep from reaching out to tuck those wayward curls that had escaped from her ponytail, back behind her ear. To do so would've possibly had his fingers skimming along the line of her jaw, touching what looked to be smooth, soft skin. But she was a *look, but don't touch* type of woman. At least in his mind, that's what he'd declared her. There was too much at stake otherwise.

CHAPTER EIGHT

Eddie Lukes drove what Allie figured was the world's oldest minivan. The vehicle was unlike any model she'd seen in her lifetime, a rust-colored boxy edition that produced a surprisingly smooth ride, no air-conditioning included. Her ponytail blew in the balmy wind as the front windows on the driver's and passenger sides were fully open. The seat belt hugged her tightly—a plus she figured if the van ever went over thirty-three miles per hour—and the interior smelled like fruity candy courtesy of the rainbow air freshener that dangled from the rearview mirror. She could recall experiencing worse rideshare aromas and counted this one as a win.

"How you likin' our island so far?" Eddie asked as he turned onto Crescent Row.

The Big House was located at the very end of this street, around a bend that bordered close to the shore. In a few minutes the restaurant would appear on her left, the outside seating area undoubtedly full as it drew close to five o'clock in the evening. Ryan had dropped her off at the house about half an hour ago, and after finding Sofia asleep in her bedroom, Allie had decided to make another trip back to town.

"It's nice," she replied, mentally reminding herself to resist words like "painstakingly slow-paced." "I had the opportunity to visit the community center and the hospital so far." Neither were places she'd ever been to in Miami.

Well, except for a trip to the hospital emergency room the morning after she'd returned from Cozumel covered in hives.

"Oh yeah," he replied and tapped his fingers on the steering wheel. "Lots of fun things go on down at the community center. Good programs to support lots of the folks on the island, you know."

She didn't know, but Allie nodded in agreement anyway. Eddie looked to be somewhere in his early to mid-fifties, his close-cropped gray hair receding. A faded blue polo shirt stretched over a medium-size paunch at his midsection, a big-faced silver watch on his right wrist.

"Wait 'til tomorrow," he continued. "SummerFest is a week full of fun, and it gets started with the carnival."

Now, she did know about that. "Right. Tomorrow night. I've heard it's a big deal." Aware that she sounded less than enthused, she shifted in the seat, reminding herself that she was keeping cynical-Allie on a tight leash during this trip.

While she'd waited for Eddie to arrive, she'd checked her work email. There hadn't been any messages from Renee, but Renee's assistant had sent a link to a series of comments that had been posted beneath Allie's story on the Winterbourne Resort in Aspen.

Sunshinesally: *Are you being paid to trash the places you write about? If so, I'll bet you're rollin' in dough by now. :-(*

Eggscited4u: *Do you like anything @AlliTravelz? You act like a year-round Scrooge*

5491starsky: *Maybe you need a travel buddy.*

Rrjensons1: *I stayed here last week and the views were phenomenal, the slopes top notch. Sometimes you have to focus on the positive @AlliTravelz*

She'd frowned down into her phone, knowing that Renee had probably instructed her assistant to send her these comments to hammer home her point about Allie needing to write something softer. But it wasn't her fault the food at the Winterbourne had been far too unrecognizable to be considered family-friendly and the wait for the ski lift had exceeded forty minutes each way for three days straight, was it? Yet apparently, based on those comments, she either needed a travel buddy or to be visited by the ghosts of Christmas past, present, and future in order to write a flattering review.

Her thought process had always been that destinations shouldn't be rewarded for their subpar presentation to guests. After all, her mother had frequently reminded her of always putting her best foot forward.

"You're going to be a Black woman, Allison. And as such, you're always going to be expected to work harder, be smarter, do better, just to get the same treatment as everyone else," Claire had said more times than Allie could count.

Well, despite knowing—and despising—why those higher expectations had been placed on her shoulders from birth, Allie refused to accept that it should only apply to her. If she were going to push for perfection in her life, then she wanted the same thing from her mechanic, the homeowner's association she wrote a check to every month, and any other place or person she did business with, including every resort, hotel, or destination she was assigned to evaluate.

And wasn't that the information she should be giving her readers? Letting them know which destinations were the best to visit, for the best prices. Another comment suggested she wasn't doing that, either:

Willvecna: *Do you have a list of places you like to visit anywhere on this page?*

No, she didn't have a list like that, nor had she ever thought of producing one. Now, she sighed as those thoughts had continued to play through her mind and she stared out the window as Eddie drove.

It wasn't lost on her that it'd seemed easier not to critique every part of this island when she was at the Big House or the restaurant or with Ryan. She'd actually written about the views and the great food in her notes. This time she'd make sure she included those points in her story.

"Oh, it's something," Eddie continued talking, although she'd only been half listening to him. "You just wait and see. I can come and pick you up if you want. Things'll get started after the parade around Starry Circle around this time tomorrow. Carnival is being set up right there in the park across from City Hall."

Starry Circle was the epicenter of Crescent Island. Their City Hall building with the huge star in the center of its domed top occupied the middle of the circle. While Main Street and Crescent Row were the main thoroughfares to wrap around the space, more shops and a few municipal buildings occupied both streets along the circle, but the park and its magnificent trees and shrubberies grouped near benches and

a gazebo lined most of the area. She'd admired it
when Ryan had driven by earlier this afternoon on
their way to the hospital. It had been the first time
she was on what they called the other side of the island.

Unlike Miami, where moving in and out of different neighborhoods could produce a drastic change in
building structure and community atmosphere, all the
areas she'd seen of Crescent Island so far were a picture of impeccably maintained landscapes, well-kept
buildings with architecture from another time in history, and people moving about with a leisurely
attitude.

"Do you have things like this often? Carnivals, I
mean," she said as she looked out the window to the
shops coming up.

A bright yellow sign that read "Sunny's Bridal"
sat atop a rose-colored painted storefront with a ruf-
fled wedding gown in the window. The exterior was
surrounded by bushes with cheerful, hot-pink flowers
that put her in mind of a bridal bouquet. Shops like
this popped up all along the lower ends of Main
Street and Crescent Row as well.

"We like to celebrate here in Crescent. My granny
used to say it's what set us apart from across the water
to Ocean City. People went there to party and drink,
but over here we like to appreciate and acknowledge
all that we've been blessed with." He pressed on the
brake long before they'd come to another intersection
to let a woman pushing a stroller and a toddler holding her other hand cross the street.

"Just about every holiday you see on the calendar
we've got something planned for it. Willie and his

granddaughters down at the Chamber work along with the Island Council to make sure all the events are full of fun and unique ideas. We've got a bonfire with fireworks coming up in a couple more weeks at the beginning of July."

"That sounds nice," she said. They passed a tall structure that looked more like the buildings she was used to in the city, and she wasn't surprised to see the name "Tiberius" in silver block letters across the top. That and the satellites on top of the building told her this was the communications company Ryan had told her about earlier.

"You can let me out right up here at the corner, Eddie. I'm going to run into the Emporium again." She wanted to get a closer look at that mailing list she'd filled out and ask the Sinclair Sisters exactly what they were doing with that information.

Of course, she'd find a nice, polite way of making her inquiries, being careful not to tip anyone off that she was perturbed by the fact that her information was given out just yet. From the way Ryan had reacted when she'd mentioned something illegal going on, she figured the other citizens of this town might become alarmed in the same way. Not that committing a crime shouldn't be alarming, but she wasn't quite ready to ruffle their feathers.

"Need to pick up a few things, huh?" he asked and ignored her directive by turning the corner. "Yeah, this is the place to get 'em. Brenda and Wanda have everything in there."

From the outside, the Emporium looked to be the size of a Walgreens in the city. But it was a two-story structure with white stucco siding. Shutters, the same indigo blue of the benches at every stop for the Coaster and around Starry Circle, flanked each window. That solar system she'd spotted her first morning on the island was perched on the roof to overlook the island. The store occupied this block, taking up the corner of Crescent Row and Main Street, its double doors facing a generous group of trees across the street.

"I remember," she said and pulled the straps of her tote onto her shoulder as she prepared to get out of the van.

Eddie came to a slow stop at the curb. "You give me a call when you're ready to head back to the Big House."

"I will," she said, not bothering to tell him she was considering hopping on the Coaster or walking down to Lou's when she was finished here. Eddie would only offer to come and take her there, too. The man acted as if he didn't have anybody else to drive around the island but her. She didn't complain, just gave him the five-dollar bill she'd been holding in her hand for his fare.

"Happy shopping!" he replied with a big grin after accepting her money.

Allie climbed out of the van, closed the door, and stepped up onto the sidewalk. She moved to the glass-front doors and entered.

The sound of whimsical chimes above the door announced her arrival. As a backdrop to the chimes, a familiar song about sunshine on a cloudy day blasted through wall speakers as her tennis shoes moved quietly over the worn hardwood floor. There was no suppressing a grin as she looked around the open space once again, wondering what would possess someone to paint all the walls navy blue and sprinkle glitter over them and why in the world such an odd design choice seemed to work. Well, she knew the answer to that last part: it worked because this was Crescent Island.

Ryan had mentioned earlier that this island and its cosmic roots were just who the people around here were, and Allie wondered how true that was. The first time she'd been in here, she'd taken everything she saw as a gimmick. From the walls covered with shelves and everything from salt-and-pepper shakers to crystal balls marked "Welcome to Crescent Island" stuffed onto them, to the racks of T-shirts in a rainbow of colors—some plain and others with the zodiac symbols or the Crescent Island logo on front—this place looked like the perfect tourist shop.

But the music that played through the speakers gave an intentionally comforting feel, to someone who was familiar with that era of R&B music, of course. Allie was, because she and Bella had spent a lot of time alone in their bedroom when they were younger. Music blotted out the unnerving quiet that always blanketed their home. It also made her and Bella feel like they were different people, normal people, they used to say to each other. When they were in their room dancing and acting like they were singing, they felt like the young girls they saw in television shows. They did each other's hair the way they'd seen on magazine covers in the store, and they pretended that outside their bedroom door wasn't the carefully maintained prison that their parents called a home.

"Well, hello there. You're back to visit us so soon," a slender woman wearing huge gold hoop earrings said.

This was Brenda Sinclair. Her bronze-streaked hair was cut in a chin-length bob, deep-set eyes accented with lashes too long, curly, and perfect to be real.

"Yes," Allie replied. "I wanted to pick up a couple of souvenirs for my coworkers." She really didn't have coworkers, since she either worked out of the second bedroom that doubled as an office and closet in her condo, or in whichever hotel room she was occupying at the time. But she always bought souvenirs from her travels because it made her feel like she had other people in her life.

"Oh." Brenda's pert lips formed a perfect circle as she stared at Allie. "So you're leaving us soon?"

"No, no. I'll be here on the island for a while longer. I just didn't want to wait 'til the last minute to get these things. Wanted to make sure I don't forget." She offered a smile with that statement. The citizens of Crescent loved to smile. A stark change from the people she saw in the city. A pleasant change.

Brenda didn't disappoint as her brilliant white teeth came into view. "Well, you're in the right place, my dear. Let me show you around."

Allie had walked the entire first floor of the store when she was here the other day, but she wanted to keep Brenda talking.

"Do you sell a lot of these shirts with the zodiac signs on them?" she asked when they passed a rack full of pastel-colored T-shirts.

"Yes, indeed," Brenda replied. "It's like having your name on your shirt but a little more personal. You know your zodiac sign says a lot about who you are and your purpose in life."

Really? Allie had listened to plenty of podcasts claiming to help reveal one's purpose, but she didn't recall any of them mentioning a zodiac sign. "I always thought zodiac signs, horoscopes, and all that astrology stuff ranked right up there with believing in one's destiny or existing on some type of spiritual plane."

That was true. Anytime she'd seen a commercial for a psychic hotline on television or passed a quirky-looking shop on the street with a sign that advertised tarot readings, it freaked her out because she'd been raised to believe in the things you could see. The tangible things that you worked hard to receive and maintain.

"Oh, honey, that's the media doing what they do best—sensationalizing everything to make a buck." Brenda shook her head, and those big earrings smacked against her cheeks. "No, we *feel* things here on Crescent."

Allie stopped to see Brenda with her palm planted over her chest and a wistful look on her face. "Feel things like what?" If Brenda was about to start talking like one of those characters on *Stranger Things* or *Supernatural*, Allie was running out of here.

"We're not freaks or anything like that," Brenda told her. "We just believe in what the universe is happy to tell anyone who wants to listen. Now, how about a T-shirt for you? Turquoise is your color."

Allie watched her move to a rack a few steps ahead and pull a turquoise shirt out for her.

"How do you know that's my color? Did the universe tell you that?" The questions slipped out before Allie could tell her skeptical half to shut her trap.

Brenda offered another smile, but something in her eyes said she might snap back the next time Allie gave a sarcastic remark.

"That purple top you're wearing is a great choice," Brenda said. "And the other day when you were in here you wore turquoise earrings to match your blue dress. Jewel tones look nice on you."

Allie looked down, heat fusing her cheeks as embarrassment spread. She looked up again and took a step closer to reach for the shirt. But she stopped when she read the word printed in small silver studs along the front of it.

"How did you know I was a Sagittarius?" Allie asked, the question coming slowly as suspicion bubbled back to the surface.

Brenda shrugged. "I just grabbed the first turquoise shirt on the rack."

"Allie? What are you doing here? I thought you were hangin' with Ryan today?"

Allie turned at the sound of Nana's voice. The hairnet from this morning was gone, but the older woman still wore her same outfit.

"Oh, hi, Nana. He said the tour was finished for the day and wanted to get to the restaurant, so he dropped me off at the house," she replied, hoping her voice was returning to its normal tone. She'd been ready to start firing off questions at Brenda.

"That boy just can't take a break," she said. "None of them can, and I blame Vernon for that nonsense." Nana waved a hand when she finished that sentence as if to wipe the words away altogether. "Anyway, you shopping?"

"Actually," Allie said and then looked over to see that Brenda had come to stand beside her. "Brenda was kind enough to select the perfect shirt for me."

"Oh, that's a beautiful color on you," the woman standing next to Nana said.

Allie had been so thrown off by Brenda's shirt selection and then Nana appearing that she hadn't paid any attention to this third woman. Now, as the woman took the shirt from Brenda and moved to put it up to Allie's chest, she couldn't help but notice her.

Skin the same deep tone as Allie's, wide expression-filled brown eyes and a mass of curly brown hair surrounded her face. She wore a misty gray blouse with wide sleeves, and what seemed like hundreds of silver bangles on each wrist jangled as she moved.

"Isn't it, Shirleen? Her skin just glows with this brilliant color," the woman continued.

She smelled like sugar and rain, an odd combination and not any perfume Allie could recall.

"It does," Nana replied, coming to stand a bit closer to Allie.

Obviously, the women of Crescent knew nothing about respecting someone's personal bubble because the trio of them were super close and Allie felt like bolting again.

"And it's your size, too," the woman continued. "You should buy this one."

Nana nodded. "I agree, this is a good choice."

"I wasn't here to buy a shirt for me," Allie said quietly. "I was shopping for my coworkers."

The woman laughed. "Girl, please. You don't buy

a thing for another soul until you've bought something for yourself. That's my first rule of shopping." There was a twang to her words, a mixture of a Southern accent and something else Allie couldn't place.

"Annabelle, you're a mess," Brenda said and reached for the shirt. "I'll just take this up to the counter, Allie. You keep right on shopping."

Annabelle pursed her lips and glanced at Brenda. "I'm not lyin'," she said.

Nana grinned. "No, she's not. I've gone shopping with this one here for many a year and she always buys herself something first. And in every store we go in, too."

"That's right. The rule applies to each individual store," Annabelle added.

The women laughed, and Allie took a relieving step back to watch them. Outwardly they seemed different, but there was no mistaking the bond or familiarity that simmered between them. It was recognizable to Allie because it reminded her of the way she and Bella used to be.

"Now, come on here," Annabelle said, moving to lace her arm through Allie's. "Let's get some more stuff for your peoples back home."

When Allie looked to Nana for help, the woman simply shook her head. "Ain't no stopping her once you say shopping."

And that was the truth. For the next hour, Nana and Annabelle walked Allie around every inch of the Emporium, even up to the top level where there were books crammed onto uneven shelves, a huge selection of crystals, and a display of mason jars filled with potpourri that seemed oddly out of place. When Allie finally made it to the counter to pay for her purchases, she glimpsed the canary yellow notepad bound to a clipboard on the counter.

"Oh, you already filled that out, honey," Wanda, the other Sinclair sister, said from behind the cash register.

Wanda was a few inches shorter than Brenda, and she wore her gray hair in stylish bantu knots. Her lips were a little fuller than her sister's, her earrings a much smaller circle of gold.

Allie read the title of each column, noting that beside email and phone number was a space for birth date. So that's how Brenda knew her sign and her number to send that text. "You're right," Allie said as she looked back up to Wanda. "I did."

Wanda gave her a total, which was way more than Allie had intended to spend in this store, but Allie handed her a credit card and tried to figure out if she was going to record this as a business expense. "Do you send out newsletters or sales alerts?" she asked. "I mean, if you have online ordering, I definitely want to know when you have new items in the store that I can purchase." That sounded a lot better than the "hey, did you send me that silly horoscope this morning?" she really wanted to say.

Finishing up the transaction, Wanda shook her head and handed Allie her card. "No, we don't do anything online," she said. "You want something from the Galaxy, you've got to come to the island."

Then they didn't need her email address or her cell phone number, for that matter. So what were the Sinclair Sisters up to here in this cosmic gift shop?

The answer to that question would have to wait, because the moment Allie had her card tucked in her purse, Nana grabbed her hand and ushered her out of the store.

"We've already missed dinner, but if we hurry on back to the house, we'll be just in time for dessert," she said as she led Allie outside to see a golf cart and a lilac-painted pickup truck parked at the curb.

Annabelle came out of the store behind them. "I'll see you in the mornin', Shirleen. I've got a lot of dough left over, so I'll be bringin' extra cinnamon rolls to sell at the restaurant."

"You know we do make our own desserts, too, Annabelle. We'd like to make a profit on them sometimes," Nana said with an edge to her tone.

Annabelle kept right on walking until she opened the door of the pickup truck. "My cinnamon rolls are the best thing on this island and you know it. Lucky for you we've been friends since the Ice Age and I like you enough to share my glorious creation with your family's restaurant." She climbed into the truck without waiting for Nana's response and waved through the window. "See ya later, Allie!"

Allie waved in return and mumbled, "See ya later, Ms. Annabelle."

One thing Allie had always been taught was to put a Ms. or Mr. in front of her elder's names when speaking to them as a sign of respect.

Nana moved to the golf cart and eased onto the seat behind the steering wheel. "She's always been a conceited one," Nana said. "Get in and let's get home."

Allie put her bags on the backseat of the cart and

walked around to the passenger side to climb in. She'd never rode on normal streets in a golf cart before. She'd also never had anyone say, "Let's go home," to her before.

Later, she would realize how much she enjoyed both.

. . .

After dropping her bags off in her room and making a quick stop in the bathroom, Allie followed the voices through the Big House. There was deep laughter from a couple different people but still a very heartfelt and relatively unfamiliar sound to her. She thought they were in the kitchen—where Nana said people were bound to always be in a house—but this time, they were just beyond that room, through the screened patio doors, on the back porch.

The light was dimmer in here than it had been this morning, but the space was still cheerful and inviting with a homey blend of chic and country design. With its dark Spanish tile floor that added a splash of rustic elegance, pine wood cabinets that along with the wide windows added the softness, and chunky wood-based island at its center, this was clearly the meeting place of the Parker household. The table tucked into a nook of more windows where she'd sat with Sofia that morning was on the other side of the room but still worked to form the whole of this love-filled area.

A part of her wanted to turn around and head back into the bedroom. This wasn't her space. She was the outsider.

That apparently wasn't as big of a deal as she

wanted to believe as her feet led her to stand at the patio door, though. Peering through the screen, she could see them all.

The Parkers. A family.

Nana, who'd come into the house with her about fifteen minutes ago, had claimed one of the rocking chairs in the corner of the wide, screened porch. She looked relaxed as she leaned back in the chair, her legs crossed at the ankle, hands folded over her mid-section. In another rocking chair a few feet away from Nana's, Vernon sat with his hands resting on the arms of the chair. He was a tall, bulky man, rich umber complexion, bald head, and a diamond stud in his left ear. Across from him was his wife, Sarah, who had the prettiest smile that lit up her light-hued eyes.

Sofia sat in an Adirondack chair, her booted leg propped up on a plaid ottoman. Optimus lay on the porch beneath her leg as if guarding her. It was the sweetest thing Allie had ever seen. Ryan was talking, saying something she wasn't really focused on because the sound of his voice touched something else deep inside her. Simply put, she felt odd standing here watching them. She felt weird each time she reacted to something Ryan said or did.

She felt…she just felt so much when she was around all of them.

On either side of Ryan were the other Parker men—Brody and Trevor. The trio were tall, easily over six feet, each with the same lighter complexion as their mother and sister, dark eyes and startling good looks. Like really, model-ready handsomeness that she was sure had roused many, if not all, of the single ladies on this island. Collectively, they were the epitome of the word *foine*, but Allie's gaze circled back to Ryan.

Brody, the younger of the trio who winked at her each time he'd seen her around the house but followed that wink with a goofy grin that only made her chuckle instead of the desired allure she figured he thought he was soliciting, stood and elbowed Ryan, telling him to remember something or other. Trevor, the more muscularly built of the trio who wore a burgundy T-shirt that hugged every sculpted part of his upper body, used a hand to cover his grin and rub along the low-cut beard along his jaw.

Sofia cut in with her comments, and everyone in the family laughed. That laughter rang in Allie's ears until her heart ached. There'd never been laughter like that in the Sparks home. Not between the parents and their children. And the laughter she and Bella shared was always behind the closed door of their bedroom. That realization wasn't new, and yet it still stung.

Allie was just about to turn and walk away when she heard her name.

"Allie! Come on out and pull up a chair. You can help me against these people who like ganging up on me all the time," Sofia said.

Wishing she hadn't been noticed at all, Allie slowly turned her gaze back to the screened door, where just on the other side, every member of the Parker family now stared at her.

"Uh, I was just going to get a snack and head back to my room to get some writing done before I go to sleep," she said, knowing instinctively that they were never going to let that stand.

Ryan walked over to the door, sliding it open before extending his hand to her. "Nah, the workday is over. Sit out here and relax with us."

She accepted his hand because there were too many eyes on her to turn and walk away. They would think she was rude and probably kick her out of their house. The thought of the latter shouldn't bother her as much as it did. She hadn't come here to stay in this big house or to bond with this loving family. Yet, here she was, being welcomed in as if her plans had never mattered.

Ryan gripped her hand and pulled her gently through the doorway. It was a good thing, too, since just because she took his hand didn't mean her feet got the message that they should move. Brody retrieved one of the empty chairs from the other side of the porch and positioned it next to Sofia. Ryan led her to that chair and didn't release her hand until she was sitting down.

Sofia reached over and rubbed her arm. "Now, settle an argument for us, or at least add some weight to my argument. Which duo sang the best version of 'Endless Love'? Luther and Mariah or Lionel and Diana?"

"Lionel and Diana win this argument every time," Sarah said with a shake of her head.

Vernon nodded. "Hands down."

"I don't even know why we keep having this argument," Brody added. "Who even cares about love songs?"

"Says the guy who has a date with a different woman every weekend?" Trevor added. "You'd think you would pay attention to some sort of romance.

Then again, if you did, you wouldn't be with a different woman all the time."

"Ooooohhh," Nana said with a chuckle. "He's hittin' below the belt tonight."

Allie smiled, and her gaze met Ryan's.

"So, what's your choice, Allie?" Sofia asked.

"Umm," she said, turning away from him to look at Sofia. "I like both versions, but I guess if I had to, I'd go with the more recent version of Luther and Mariah."

"Yes!" Sofia yelled and lifted her arms in the air. "Another vote for my fav."

"You still lose," Trevor said. "Five to three."

Again, her gaze went to Ryan's. "You like the Luther and Mariah version?" Allie asked unable to hide the surprise from her tone.

He'd been leaning back against the railing, his arms folded across his chest. "It's the version I've heard the most."

"But love songs aren't really our thing," Brody interjected. "We're the hip-hop and R&B of the early 2000s generation."

That was partially true for Allie, too, but she was marveling at how the topic of this family's conversation was music, one of the very things that had saved a portion of her childhood. The duration of the night only got better as that conversation moved into another, and the time passed until they'd been sitting out there past eight o'clock, when the elder Parkers decided it was time for them to head off to bed.

On her way to the door, Nana had reminded Sofia that she'd sat up long enough today and getting some rest in bed would help prepare her for the stress of being up and about all day tomorrow and most of the night at the carnival.

"I'll help you to your room," Allie said and hopped up from her chair.

"That's okay," Trevor said, moving around her to stand in front of the chair where Sofia sat. "I've got her. Come on, big head, let's get you to bed."

Allie watched as Trevor lifted his sister under her arms and pulled her up to stand. Sofia playfully swatted at his shoulder when she was standing. "I got my big head from you, *big* brother," she quipped.

"You and me, breakfast early tomorrow," Sofia said to Allie as she passed her.

"Deal," she replied.

"Can I come?" Brody asked. "I'll bring the orange juice?"

Sofia looked over her shoulder to roll her eyes at her brother. "Me and Allie, you goofball. Set your alarm tonight so you'll make it to work on time."

Ryan chuckled as Brody continued the argument walking behind Trevor and Sofia into the house.

"You goin' to sleep or are you going to your room to write?" he asked when they were alone on the porch.

There was so much moving through her mind right now, none of which fell in line with the story she wanted to write. In fact, she was starting to think this island and the people on it were working in conjunction with Renee, giving her way more soft and positive things to write about than she usually encountered. Still, she did feel the urge to get her thoughts from today out of her head and onto paper.

"I might write for a bit, but I'm kinda tired after somebody had me hiking around the Springs and running all his errands today."

He grinned like she knew he would, and she enjoyed the sight.

"Just wait 'til tomorrow," he said and snapped his fingers so Optimus stood and ran to him. He and his dog started walking toward the door, and Allie fell into step behind them.

"What's happening tomorrow? I mean, other than the carnival? Is there more log walking or whatever you called that outing today?"

"Nope," he said, entering the house. "We're talking rides on the Ferris wheel and the swings, pie-eating contests, and games that I'm pretty sure I'll beat you playing."

It was her turn to mimic Sofia's move and slap Ryan's shoulder. "Don't start sellin' wolf tickets. I'm pretty good at games." And she seemed to be even better at taking these changes to her plans in stride. Not that she was going to give the credit for that to Ryan, because he didn't have that type of effect on her. Not him or his enigmatic smile, definitely did not have any effect on her. At all.

Until he stopped and turned back to face her, staring for a few silent beats. She'd stopped walking, too, wondering where their conversation was going to go next. And oddly enough, not wanting it to end.

"I bet you're good at a lot of things, Allie," he said, his voice suddenly softer. "More things than you probably know."

How was she supposed to respond to that when her stomach had done this odd flip at his words, leaving her breathless as she stared at him?

"See ya tomorrow," he told her before turning and walking away.

Allie stood there for a few seconds longer, still not sure how she could've responded to him. Surely running over and wrapping her arms around his neck, planting her lips on his, wasn't an option.

CHAPTER NINE

Why was she so cute when she laughed? What was up with that distant look she sometimes got in her eyes? Or the way her brow furrowed when she thought she may've said or done something wrong?

And why did he even care?

Ryan lifted his face to the spray of the shower, closing his eyes as the warm water washed over him.

Because he liked her.

He scrubbed a hand over his face and cursed.

He liked a woman who wasn't from the island and had no plans to stay here. "Glutton for punishment" in no way described what that meant to him. Not to toot his own horn, but he considered himself a relatively smart guy in business and in personal dealings. That made this realization even more concerning. If he knew what was good for him, which he definitely did, he'd steer clear of Allison Sparks. She wasn't good for him, no matter how amazing it felt to see her smile.

Unfortunately, he'd already lost a relationship to the lure of city life. That wasn't a path he wanted to travel down again.

And as if that weren't a big enough warning, she was still his sister's best friend. And, as of last night, a new addition to his family. His parents and grandmother were friendly people — to everyone whose last name wasn't Baldwin, anyway — so it didn't really come as a shock to him the way they'd immediately embraced Allie. What had surprised him last night was how easily Allie fit in with their clan. But he was sure she didn't notice that. The way she'd tried to stand apart from them last night, when he could see clearly in her eyes that she wanted to be there.

The moment he'd seen her standing in that doorway, he'd known. Her discomfort had seemed to radiate from her in thick waves as he'd walked closer to the screened door. And when he'd taken her hand, for a split second he'd thought she was going to pull away.

But Allie wasn't a runner. He'd seen that in her eyes when she'd climbed onto that log even though the thought of falling off and into the water had scared her. He liked that spunk in her, the confidence that sometimes hid behind her nonchalance and burst on the scene when necessary.

He flattened his palms on the tiles in front of him and lowered his head. What was he doing? Thinking about a woman who was out of his reach for reasons he knew very well and reasons he wanted to keep buried.

With a burst of energy, he finished his shower and went to his room to get dressed. Optimus had already been out for his morning walk and now ran around the house, chasing one of the noisiest toys ever created. Ryan made a mental note to dispose of that bright orange rubber pig the moment Optimus abandoned it for something else to chew on. He had just finished brushing his hair when there was a knock at the door.

Ryan liked his little house. Two bedrooms, a living

room–dining room combo, a big kitchen because he needed room to try out new sauce recipes and to fix meals when he wasn't bringing home food from the restaurant or eating at the Big House, and two bathrooms just because it made sense to not have a guest using his.

Optimus was already at the door, sitting and then bouncing up to run in a circle and bark because Ryan was obviously taking too long to come and answer it.

"You could learn how to open the door yourself," he said to the dog and reached for the door handle.

"What took you so long? You in here getting all prettied up just to see me?"

Trevor walked in without a formal welcome. He was mildly out of breath, the front of his gray tank top darkened by the sweat that ran down his face and neck.

"I don't usually get crack-of-dawn visitors," Ryan replied and closed the door. His comment wasn't totally true—of his two brothers, Trevor was the early bird and sometimes dropped by before or after his morning run. But that was only when he had something on his mind, like he had a couple days ago. That meant today was too fast for Trevor to have something else he needed to talk about.

His brother had gone straight to the kitchen, and Optimus had followed. Ryan did the same as he watched Trevor open the refrigerator and grab a bottled water. With two long gulps the water was finished, and Trevor dropped down onto one of the stools positioned at the island in the center of the kitchen.

Ryan crossed the room to the counter, where he

removed two slices of bread from the loaf and dropped them into the toaster. "You do have a house with bottled water just about five minutes away from here."

"But there's no little brother who needs to be talked to there, and technically I don't live in the house five minutes away."

With a shake of his head, Ryan decided it was much easier to go with the last part of his brother's statement. "You haven't officially moved out," he said. "Even though you've been spending more nights at Taylor's house than Mama is comfortable with."

Trevor grabbed some paper towels and wiped his face, then around the back of his neck. "I'm a grown man."

"Correction, you're a thirty-eight-year-old man who's too much of a coward to tell his parents that he's ready to move out of their family home."

"Nope," Trevor replied. "I have too much respect for my family to rock the boat when it's not necessary. Living with Taylor full time isn't high on my list of things to do, either."

The toast popped up, and Ryan reached into one of the cabinets for a plate. "And how does Taylor feel about that? Ms. Annabelle told Nana she saw Taylor and her sister in Sunny's Bridal shop last week."

Trevor froze, a frown marring his otherwise pretty face, and Ryan chuckled. "Man, you're the one who needs to be talked to. You're making a mess that's about to explode in your face."

"And you're not?" Trevor asked.

Ryan smeared butter on one slice of his toast, then shot Trevor another look. "Me? I'm not the one leading a woman to believe I'm ready to make a bigger commitment to her while at the same time trying to keep my family from going ballistic about me leaving."

"No, but you're the one falling for your sister's best friend."

It was Ryan's turn to go still, the top to the butter container in one hand.

"Uh-huh, you thought nobody noticed, didn't you?" Trevor continued as Ryan knew he would. "Brody told me you couldn't keep your eyes off her in the restaurant the other day, but we both figured it was because she was new in town. But this agreement with Sofia to be her tour guide while she's here…" Trevor smirked. "That's a genius move, little bro. Still a problem with movin' in on your sister's friend because you know Sofia will totally flip if you hurt her girl, but an excellent way to get close to her."

Ryan pressed the top down on the butter and walked to put it back in the refrigerator. He took a bottled water out before closing the door and went back to stand at the opposite counter with his toast.

"I didn't plan to be her guide. Sofia asked me to."

"And you can't figure out why Sof would ask something like that?" Trevor laughed. "Come on, Ryan, you're the college graduate here. You gotta be smarter than that."

Ryan and Trevor's relationship had always been the big brother–little brother type. Where Trevor told Ryan what to do and how to do it because he figured he knew best being the oldest. Except there were parts of Trevor that did acknowledge Ryan's expertise in his field. The Parker children were good at identifying each other's strengths and letting one another walk in that lane. And there was no competition between them, just love and the occasional overprotectiveness, which Ryan figured was Trevor's sole purpose in being here.

"You think she's purposely trying to hook me up with Allie?" Ryan asked, letting that thought float around in his mind.

They'd never done that before—Sofia finding him a date or vice versa. And if anybody knew well Ryan's reservations toward dating someone who didn't live in Crescent, Sofia knew.

So, no, that wasn't what was going on here.

But Trevor nodded. "It kinda makes sense."

Ryan shook his head. "No. It doesn't." Then, before his brother could reply, he continued, "You run the full five miles this morning?"

Trevor nodded tightly. "Don't try to change the subject."

"There's no subject to change."

"Whether there's a coordinated hookup planned or not, you like her," Trevor said.

"*Her* name is Allie," he countered.

"So, you admit it?"

Ryan sighed.

Lying wasn't something the siblings did to each other, either. They'd grown up with the belief that if they couldn't count on anyone else in this world to be honest and true, they could definitely count on each other. Ryan couldn't bring himself to make this his first time going against that mantra.

"She's nice," he said by way of admission.

Trevor didn't smile or laugh with triumph. Instead,

his brother leaned forward to rest his elbows on the island top. "You know it won't work, right?"

Ryan folded a piece of toast like a half sandwich and took a bite. He chewed even though he didn't taste the bread. Swallowed because it was necessary and sighed because it was inevitable.

"I know all the reasons it's a bad idea," he said slowly. "And I'm not gonna deny there's something brewing. But I can handle it."

Trevor raised a brow.

"I'm a grown man, too, Trevor," Ryan continued.

"True. But you're always gonna be my little brother, and that means I'm always gonna look out for you. She's only here for a couple of weeks. Like her all you want until then and then let her go. Plain and simple."

Unfortunately, for Ryan, that was easier said than done.

• • •

The Big House was bustling with activity by eight o'clock on Friday morning. Allie had heard noises the minute she'd rolled out of bed an hour earlier. And as she moved about the room getting her clothes out for the day, doing a quick check of work and personal email, and then heading into the bathroom to shower, she'd thought about her time on the island so far.

She'd met some pretty interesting people. Creating a separate document with their names and her impressions of them had seemed like a good idea. That list had grown longer than her memory of all the people she'd interacted with in any meaningful way in the past fifteen years of her life. The thought had made her a bit melancholy, and feelings of incompleteness pricked at her.

It was something she'd felt many times before, one she'd told herself she'd have to live with, but this morning when she walked out of that bedroom fully dressed and inhaling the smell of fresh-brewed coffee, she'd wondered if maybe something on this island was filling those small, abandoned cracks in her soul.

Turning into the kitchen, she collided with a broad chest, and long arms wrapped around her while the scent of soap mixed with a strong cologne and coffee aroma.

"Oh, sorry," she said immediately and pulled out of Brody's loose grasp.

"No worries, little lady. Everybody's on the move this mornin'." His grin was slow to spread, but that glint of humor she always noted in his eyes was still there. He hadn't bothered to shave this morning. The shadow of a beard and the inch or so of uncombed curls on top of his head gave him a rugged appearance.

"So I've heard," she said and looked around him to the empty kitchen. "I was supposed to meet Sofia for breakfast. Have you seen her?"

"I don't think she's come out of her room yet," he said. "Heard Mama talking to her through her door when I came out of my room."

"Oh, then I guess she's running late. I'll go see if there's anything I can help her with."

She was about to turn and walk away when Brody spoke again.

"You and Sofia are pretty close, huh?"

"Uh, yes, we lived together for four years," she explained.

"College roommates." He nodded. "Ryan mentioned that. But it's kind of odd that Sofia hadn't told us anything about you before you popped up."

Well, she hadn't had a real Q&A session with any of the Parker clan yet. Ryan wasn't included since he was doubling as her tour guide and she was spending more time with him than the others, but even his questions hadn't been as many as she would've expected.

"I can't explain why Sofia did or didn't talk about me, but we've kept in touch since college. Seeing each other a few times here and there, FaceTime calls and email. Stuff like that," she said.

"Where're you from?" he asked as he leaned back against the island.

"Miami," she replied. "It's not as quaint as Crescent, but the water's beautiful." In that moment she promised herself she'd pay more attention to that water and the loveliness of the beaches in her home city when she returned.

"You got family there, too?"

"Yes, my parents." She didn't say that her maternal grandparents who she only vaguely remembered lived in the Hamptons and her paternal grandfather had relocated to Seattle with his third wife a few years ago.

"No siblings?"

She should've known that question was next and prepared herself for it so the hurt wouldn't bubble to the surface so fast, but she hadn't, and she opened and closed her mouth without responding. Brody tilted his head slightly, already reading into her pause. Allie cleared her throat and shook her head. "My sister travels a lot."

A slow nod took the place of Brody's next question, and Allie decided she'd been patient enough with this conversation.

"I'd better go see what's keeping Sofia," she told him and left the kitchen without waiting for his response.

If he found her departure abrupt and quizzical, she didn't really care. Talking about Bella to people she wasn't likely going to see again after she left Crescent wasn't necessary.

Allie paused at Sofia's door and knocked gently, waiting a few moments before hearing Sofia's soft response, "I'll be out in a bit."

"It's me, Allie," she said. "I thought we were going to have breakfast. Are you feeling okay?"

"Come in, Allie."

She opened the door and entered the room, closing it behind her. Sofia's room was larger than the one Allie was in, a queen-size bed in its center. Deep purple circle-shaped rugs in a few sizes covered parts of the light wood-planked floors, while pillows in that same intense color along with a gentler cream tone flanked a lounge chair across the room. Sofia sat in the center of the bed, her back against the beige upholstered tufted headboard, her legs stretched out in front of her. She wore white shorts and a green-and-white-striped halter top. Her dreadlocks were pulled up to the top of her head in a messy bun.

"I'm not having a good morning," Sofia said, her

voice still quiet, her somber eyes meeting Allie's gaze.

Crossing the room, Allie eased onto the bed beside her and took one of Sofia's hands. "What's going on? Are you in pain?"

Sofia shook her head. "Not really. I mean, my ankle's always a little stiff when I get up in the morning, but I moved around okay as I was getting dressed."

Allie noted Sofia hadn't put the boot on yet, her white-painted toenails staring back at them as Allie glanced over her shoulder. She wore a gold ankle bracelet on the left side, a crescent-shaped charm dangling from it.

"That's probably normal," Allie said, returning her gaze to her friend. "Aside from your injury, we're getting older and our bones don't always feel their best when we first get out of bed in the morning. I know mine don't."

"Excuse you," Sofia said with a lift of one thick and expertly arched brow. "I'm only thirty-three. That's not hardly old."

Allie grinned. They were the same age, with Allie being three weeks older than Sofia, whose birthday was a few days before Christmas. In fact, Sofia was also a Sagittarius, an odd thought that only popped into Allie's mind because of the turquoise shirt now folded and tucked into one of the drawers in her room down the hall.

"I always thought thirty was old," Allie admitted. "When Bella and I were younger, we talked about needing to have our lives together by the time we turned thirty because after that it was all downhill." A chuckle escaped, but the sadness that had burst forth when Brody had asked about her siblings a few moments ago pooled in the center of her chest.

Sofia covered their joined hands with her free one. "Has that PI you hired found anything?"

On their last call before she'd reached out to tell Sofia she was coming to Crescent, Allie had mentioned wanting to find Bella. Sofia had been the one to suggest the PI.

"He said he had a lead, but I haven't heard from him in over a week. I'm trying not to worry." Or get too excited about the possibility of seeing her sister again. The heartbreak of failure would take a tremendous toll on her, and Allie wasn't looking forward to the ordeal. "Anyway, that's not the most pressing issue. Tell me what's going on with you. I know you've been a little off since I arrived, but I can't tell if this mood has been going on before then."

That was her failure as a friend. She wished she'd been paying more attention during their calls, so she could've picked up on something bothering Sofia. Would she have come to Crescent sooner if she had? As it was, she was really here for work right now, not to take care of her friend. That thought only added to the guilt Allie already felt where Sofia was concerned.

Sofia let her head fall back against the headboard. "It's nothing and then it's everything. You know what I mean?"

On a very strange level, Allie knew exactly what Sofia meant. She'd felt that way more often than not in her lifetime. "Yeah," she managed to say without going into detail.

"It's like I have it all—at least all that I planned to have," Sofia said, staring up at the ceiling. "I'm doing the work I love in the family business that I cherish. I've found my place in the Parker legacy, and that means so much to me." She sighed. "But then, there's this emptiness." The hand that covered their entwined ones moved and went to Sofia's chest.

Allie felt the mild thump as if she'd put her own hand over her chest.

"It started out as like this little spot of something, but then it's been growing and growing, and for the life of me, I can't figure out what it is or how to get rid of it." Sofia lifted her head again and glanced at Allie imploringly.

Unfortunately, Allie didn't like the answer she was about to give. "Discontent," she said somberly. "I know it well."

"But I don't have a reason to be discontent," Sofia argued.

"Don't you?" Allie asked. "I remember when we were in school you said you wanted to see the world. That you loved this island with every ounce of your heart, but you wanted to see more. To experience everything there was in the world before you settled down and built your own branch of the Parker clan in Crescent."

Allie recalled that conversation specifically because she hadn't possessed a similar goal. While Sofia had longed for the husband, kids, and a gorgeous family home, Allie had accepted that she'd most likely never have those things. Mostly because she'd never seen the happiness in that type of life and so she doubted she could pull it off.

Sofia nodded. "I did say that."

"So really, you're only half doing what you always

wanted to do. Perhaps you're feeling discontent because you're still longing to do the other stuff." Why
was it so easy to give others advice and simultaneously the most difficult task to take that same advice?
"What's stopping you, Sofia? Why haven't you traveled the world the way you wanted to?"

"Duty. Loyalty." Sofia used a knuckle to catch the
tear before it fell. "My family needed me more than I
needed to run around the world doing who knows
what."

"Did you tell them that you wanted to go?" The
Parkers had struck her as loving and supporting parents, and the way Vernon looked at Sofia said his
daughter was still the apple of his eye. So Allie had a
hard time believing they would deny Sofia anything
she wanted.

"No," she admitted. "I was afraid to. Afraid I'd let
them down."

Now that surprised Allie. Sofia was the most fear-
less person Allie had ever met and, on some level,
Allie had always longed to be like her. "You don't
really believe that, do you? That you could ever let
your parents down."

"You don't know my family, Allie. Not like I do.
There are expectations."

Oh boy did Allie know about expectations. "Girl,
you know you're preachin' to the choir there."

Sofia nodded. "Yeah, that's right. Your parents
were pretty tough on you. But at least they didn't su-
garcoat it. They stated what they expected of you and
demanded you give it. My family's so caring and loving, the expectation is wrapped in this thin layer of
guilt that my dad quickly drops over you the second

he even thinks you're going to stray. Why do you
think we're all still living under his roof?"

"Ryan's not," she said and then wished she hadn't
mentioned him at all.

Last night she'd tossed and turned with thoughts
of him plaguing her mind. Thoughts of how badly
she'd wanted to kiss him in the kitchen last night and
how thankful she was that he'd had the sense to walk
away when she'd been so desperately close to destroying the only friendship she'd ever had.

While there'd never been a discussion about this
before—mainly because Allie hadn't met any of
Sofia's family until now—and it wasn't like she had
prior experience with dating a friend's sibling, Allie
had watched enough movies and read plenty of
books to realize how badly that particular scenario
could go.

What if she kissed Ryan and he kissed her right
back, then they went on to have some torrid affair
that Allie would eventually mess up because she
didn't know what a healthy relationship looked like
off-screen? Sure, she could imagine a whole relationship in her mind, but implementing the emotional tap
dance that she was certain might come with a romantic entanglement wasn't something she thought she
could handle. That would inevitably lead to her
breaking up with Ryan, or him breaking up with her,
and then what? How would Sofia feel about that?
Would she take her brother's side?

Of course she would, and then Allie would really
be alone in this world.

"Yeah, but he's not that far, and he and my dad
argued the entire time Ryan was building that little

house down the hill," Sofia continued, thankfully snatching Allie from her distressing thoughts. "Mama was heartbroken, and Nana was grouchy. Me, Brody, and Trevor supported Ryan's decision but knew not to voice those opinions too vehemently for fear that Daddy would shift his ire to us."

"Your father really doesn't strike me as that type of man. I mean, not after growing up with my father, who practically yelled down the entire building we lived in over a C- I received in chemistry." That memory made her shiver, the fear she'd felt in those moments Douglas Sparks had raged about her possibly not getting into Yale and going on to the prestigious medical school he'd already decided she would attend because of one mediocre grade still breathing inside of her.

"No, my dad doesn't yell or berate," Sofia said softly. "But the quiet logic, the weight of a legacy resting on your shoulders can be just as heavy and intimidating."

"I'm sorry," was all Allie could say in that moment.

"And I'm sorry for you, too." Sofia scooted over until she could wrap her arms around Allie.

For endless moments, they held on to each other, not speaking but reveling in the love and understanding that cocooned them in that moment.

When they finally broke apart, Sofia wiped her eyes with the backs of her hands and gave a heavy sigh. "You're the stronger one, Allie," she began. "Stronger and smarter. So, when I tell you I'm disappointed in you, I want you to take that with all the love I have for you, my sister by choice."

Allie blinked at the abrupt shift in topic. "Wait, what did you just say? Before the loving your sister by choice part."

Sofia grinned and dropped her hands to her lap. "You're not doing what you always said you wanted to do, either. Where's the book? The story of your heart you were yearning to tell all through college? The reason you studied harder than any other student at Columbia and graduated with honors to prove it."

Nobody, not even Allie's parents, could land a blow like Sofia. The woman was blunt and could be relentless when she felt strongly about something. It was strange how they both possessed these great traits that should've shielded them from the hurt and pressure they'd endured in their lives, but that old saying that nobody could hurt you like family was the absolute truth.

"But I am a writer," Allie replied. "Just like I always planned to be." Yet the words sounded hollow, even to her.

Sofia's lips twisted and her head tilted as she gave Allie a "really?" look.

"What?" Allie sighed. "Well, I am writing. I have a story due in a couple of weeks to prove it."

"A story for that blog you've been wasting your time and talent on."

Allie narrowed her eyes. "You know that I write for a blog?"

Sofia waved a hand. "Of course I know. Did you think I wouldn't make it my business to know what my best friend was doing with her time when she obviously wasn't giving me a bestselling book to read and praise?"

"Have you…" Allie swallowed. "Have you read any of my stories?"

"Yes, I have," Sofia replied. "And I feel the pain and unhappiness in every word of your reviews. All while being hopelessly jealous of the fact that you're out there traipsing the globe and finding every single thing wrong with it in the process."

Allie chuckled and then sighed. "It's good work if you can get it," she only half joked. "I mean, it pays the bills and it's entertaining."

"But it's not what you want to be doing? And for the record, I know for a fact you won't find anything critical to write about Crescent, because we're just pleasantly regular here and the island itself is too gorgeous not to love. So good luck with this one."

Only Sofia could make Allie smile when she was facing the most important story of her career. "I'm going to lose my job if I don't write a story with more heart and less critique," she blurted out.

For a second they were both quiet, then Sofia lifted Allie's hand in hers. "If you really want this job, you'll write the best story you've ever written." A slow smile spread across her face, and the light that had been missing in her eyes gave a little shine. "But if you reach down deep and decide to take your own advice and do the thing you've always wanted to do, I'm available to read that book before it's published."

This time when Sofia hugged her, Allie held on tight. Tighter than she'd ever held on to anyone before, because hearing that not-so-subtle challenge her friend had just issued scared Allie more than anything else she'd ever encountered in her life.

CHAPTER TEN

Allie screamed as her body was jerked from one side of the seat to the other, where she crashed right into Ryan's waiting arms.

He'd done the teenage guy thing and dropped his arm across the back of the seat once the door to the car they were riding in had closed. There'd been enough space for another person between them, but his fingers had still brushed along her bare skin. The white top that crisscrossed and tied at her back left a lot exposed, and he'd thanked the heavens for scantily designed summer clothes.

Now, his hands were on even more of her as she held on to the safety bar in front of them and he held on to her.

"This ride goes faster than I imagined," she said as the car tilted and swerved, all while the entire ride went in circles. Her hair, which was an array of curls this evening, blew in the wind, the sweet honey scent of her shampoo sifting through the air.

"I love it!" he said, hoping she didn't pick up any undertones in his words.

Not that there were any. Ryan wasn't in love with Allie.

But he did like her a whole lot.

After his chat with Trevor this morning, he'd attempted to drown the thoughts of Allie out of his mind. Because the more he thought about her and the reasons why he shouldn't pursue anything with her, the more memories of Kerry and the massive misjudgment he'd made where she was concerned tried to bubble to the surface. And that was the last thing he needed after all this time.

There'd been a supply issue at the restaurant, one that kept him barricaded in his office and on the phone for an hour and a half with one of the farmers on the mainland who provided a good deal of their vegetables and produce. Prices were skyrocketing, but Ryan understood the rule of supply and demand, so he'd paid them without much of a squabble. But when their shipments were shorted, that was a problem, and he hadn't held back an ounce of his indignation during the phone call.

Still, the moment that fire had been put out, his thoughts had returned to Allie. There were so many similarities and just as many differences between her and Kerry. One woman had been born and raised on this island but had a need to leave it, and the other was just visiting and had no desire to stay. The result for him was the same.

Yet Allie's laugh was different, the way his heart stuttered and paused when she smiled at him unlike anything he'd ever experienced. He could talk to her for hours, he knew, even if so far their talks had been restricted by time or circumstances. Something about her seemed to resonate with something inside him, and that was the most confusing part because he hadn't yet been able to pinpoint what that something was. All he knew was that it was strong, pulling and tugging at him even though he knew the smart thing would be to keep a safe distance or retreat altogether.

The ride jolted them again, and they both slid into one corner of the seat, laughing and trying to catch their breaths from the exhilaration. Well, for him, it was from the way everything about her seemed to take his breath away.

Minutes later, when the ride finally came to a stop, they were still laughing. Allie scooted to the other side of the seat, hands patting down her hair. "That was a bumpy ride," she said. "Fast and whirling and totally out of control."

A buzzer sounded, signaling the safety bar was now unlocked, and Ryan pushed it back away from them. He couldn't tell from her tone if "out of control" was a good or bad thing.

"Let's do it again!" she announced when he was about to reach around her and open the car door.

In that moment, it wasn't just the broad grin covering her face, it was also the sparkle it brought to her eyes, the fist that tightened around his heart at the sound of pure joy in her voice. The combination had him sinking deeper, and the bigger part of him didn't even want to reach for help.

They rode the scrambler ride two more times before climbing off with wobbly legs. When she bumped into him, he took her hand and guided them toward the Ferris wheel.

"C'mon, the line's shorter now," he said. He'd wanted to ride this one first since he'd brought it up last night in his parents' kitchen, but when they'd first walked to it, the line was snaking around to the other side of the path.

"Is this one going to scramble my limbs like the last one?" She asked the question but kept right on walking beside him.

"No, this one is nice and slow," he told her. Like he wished he could convince himself to go with her. Slow and steady, he'd told himself the moment they arrived.

Just continue to be her tour guide. Stay focused on showing her a good time while she's here. Don't think about how soft her fingers are each time you take her hand in yours. Or how good she'd felt pressed up against you, laughing hysterically.

He'd replayed those words in his mind over and over, and still, the moment they slipped into the car of the Ferris wheel, he'd wrapped an arm around her again, pulling her close to him even though this ride didn't usually result in people being smushed together. Besides, how bad could having her sit close to him be? It was just a ride anyway, and once they got off, they'd go back to the booth and work the rest of the night beside his family.

So, yeah, this wasn't a problem, and it didn't mean anything.

The voice in the back of his mind screamed he was doing a horrible job of fooling himself. Luckily for him, Allie's mind seemed far from his battle over what was friendly and what was beyond the boundaries.

"It's so peaceful here," she said with a huff as she relaxed against him.

The ride had begun to move at its nice and slow pace, lifting them into the air.

"The city's pretty vibrant, especially certain areas of South Beach," she continued. "Not that I have time to go there often, but even in my neighborhood people are always on the go. Heading to work, to the gym, to this party, or on that date."

He didn't really know where this conversation was going but decided to go along with the comparison. "Crescent can get pretty exciting around certain holidays or celebrations. Fireworks later next week, the seafood festival in September, Harvest Homecoming."

"That all sounds so lovely," she added with another sigh. "I didn't think I'd like it here."

"Because it's not the city?" he asked, hating how those words sounded because for him there had never been a competition.

"Because I didn't think there'd be so many great people here," she replied. "I mean, the island is beautiful, there's no doubt about that. But I feel like it's really the people who're making me see things a little differently."

He didn't realize what he was doing until he'd reached down with his free hand to take hers in his. Lacing his fingers through hers, he stared down at the connection he'd just made, loving the feel of her soft skin against his. "Any specific people?" he asked, again without thinking.

"Fishing for compliments, Mr. Parker?"

He grinned. "Not at all, Ms. Sparks. Just wondering who I need to thank for making you like this island more than you anticipated."

She shifted, and he turned his gaze to her just as she looked up at him.

"Well, I can admit that you're partially responsible," she said, her voice notably softer. "I mean, I never thought I'd do a log race and win, because you know, I did get to the end before you."

Now, he laughed. "Okay, that's partially true. Even though I wasn't really trying to race you."

"So you're saying you let me win?" Her lips had spread into a huge smile, eyes alight with humor.

"I'm saying I wasn't racing."

"Fine. I'll give you a rematch."

"Competitive, aren't you?" he asked with another chuckle.

She shrugged. "I just like to do my best. So if you insist you weren't racing, then we'll have a rematch where the intention is clear, and then I'll win." She sat up then, squaring her shoulders and looking away as if what she'd said was set in stone.

He wasn't going to argue with her. Another day with Allie at The Springs seemed like a win to him.

"What's that?"

"What's what?" he asked, following her gaze. They were at the top of the Ferris wheel now, and the ride had stopped to let some people off and new people on.

He tilted his head back to look up at the sky like she was.

"That cluster of stars? Don't they have names or something?"

"Constellations," he told her. "Yeah, they have names. But I don't know what this one is. Or if it's one in the first place."

Her head turned quickly in his direction. "What? You call yourself a Crescent Islander and you don't know all the constellations? Shame on you." The huge grin that followed her words had him laughing, and warmth spreading across his chest. He really liked her smile.

"Ha ha, very funny," he replied. "I told you we're not all into that cosmic thing. Some of us just go with the flow."

The ride had started to move again but this time with a jolt that had his arm protectively tightening around her, pulling her even closer.

She continued to stare up at him, her face suddenly only inches from his. "You don't strike me as the kind of guy who just goes with the flow," she said in an almost whisper.

Their gazes were locked, her face so near to his, her breath a warm flush against his skin. "Really? What kind of guy do I strike you as?"

He wasn't going to wait for an answer because the urge to close that small distance between their mouths was overwhelming. Warning bells sounded in the distance, and he ignored them, wanting just one quick touch. But that wasn't meant to be as the ride came to a sudden stop this time, jerking them again.

Instead of coming even closer—most likely ending up in his lap—she slid back across the seat. "I thought you said this was the nice and slow ride."

With the mood effectively broken, they both chuckled as the ride continued until they could finally get off.

She'd started talking about some of the games they could see up ahead, but he led them to a bench, deciding he needed a moment to recover from that interrupted kiss and the way it had left him feeling like he'd lost something valuable.

"This is so much fun," she said with a chuckle as they sat.

The bench was positioned under some trees and out of the path where people were either going toward more rides or heading in the direction of the food and game setup.

"We have to ride everything here." Her eyes were alight as she looked around. "How many rides are there? Ten, twelve, not including the kiddie ones even though some of them are really cute."

They'd been there for an hour, after Ryan had left Trevor at the restaurant with a slim evening crew. He'd gone to the Big House to pick up Sofia and Allie and the boxes of stuff for the Parker BBQ booth located along the row of the other food vendors. Nana and the Diamonds had their own table and had been here much earlier doing whatever it was that they did during these celebrations, while his parents had packed up most of the food they planned to sell at the restaurant truck.

"When's the last time you've been to a carnival?" Excitement was clear in her tone and the way she looked around at everything as if it were her first time.

"I've been to Carnival in Trinidad and Tobago, and also in Rio," she said and shook her head. "Of course, they're nothing like this."

"No," he agreed that there was clearly no comparison even though he'd never experienced either of those events. "Amusement parks?"

"Not until college. One spring break, me, Sofia, and a couple other girls from our dorm drove down to Virginia. We went to Busch Gardens and Kings Dominion and stayed two nights in Virginia Beach. It was a busy and amazing week."

He'd only been to Kings Dominion, also during college with friends, so he nodded. "Small-town carnivals are a little different. They're a special blend of nostalgia and community."

"Nah, they're *a lot* different," she said. "More fun, I think because it's smaller so you can enjoy rides more than once without super-long lines, and I'm certain it's cheaper. That funnel cake Sofia and I shared when we first arrived would've cost double the price in a big amusement park."

He nodded. "True."

She pointed and gave a quick clap. "Oh, look, balloons!"

Ryan frowned before chuckling. "You're not going to tell me you've never had a balloon before." It would break his heart if she did.

"No," she said and leaned in to jab a playful elbow into his ribs. "I just like them. They're so cheerful. One time when I was ten and I went to my weekly piano lessons, my instructor surprised me with cupcakes and a huge bouquet of balloons. Pink, purple, and white ones. I loved the sound they made as they bumped together and how pretty the colors were—like a burst of smiles."

She sounded almost animated as she spoke, and Ryan couldn't keep his eyes off of her. That's how he saw that lightning-fast flash that clouded her eyes. Her lips tightened as she looked to be physically stopping herself from saying or feeling more, and he instinctively squeezed the hand he still held.

"My parents didn't do big birthdays." Her voice was quieter this time, so quiet if he wasn't sitting so close to her, he wouldn't have heard her over the noise of the rides and the people mulling about. "A card, a dinner of our favorite foods—the ones they approved of—and maybe a movie. If it didn't interfere with our studies or extracurricular activities."

In that instant, he knew he didn't care for her parents.

"So when I got home with the balloons, I gave half of them to Bella. I split them equally because we shared everything."

Even the sorrow. She didn't say that part, but Ryan felt it in the rage that burned in the pit of his stomach.

"How old was your sister?" he asked.

"Seven," she replied. "We're three years apart."

She looked down at their hands now, as if she were examining their intertwined fingers. Her fingernails were manicured and painted the same lively orange as her toes. His hands were thicker, the faint scar along his left thumb from the time when he was twelve and had laughed at something Brody said while slicing brisket and nearly cut it off. Well, it hadn't been that dour, but Mama and Nana had acted like it.

With her free hand, she traced a finger along that scar.

"Kitchen accident," he said.

"While you were helping them cook, right?"

"Yeah."

"We didn't help my parents do anything. They were the best at what they did. Mom won every case she tried because she was smarter and more prepared than any of the other lawyers. And Dad was the head of his department at the hospital because he had the steadiest hands and performed the most delicate neurosurgeries." She continued rubbing her finger along his scar, staring down at it as if it were now the most important sight. "If Bella and I studied hard enough, if we got the best grades and excelled in piano—not dance—we'd be good enough. Bella loved to dance, but when she asked if she could take formal lessons, Mom told her it was whimsical and therefore foolish. That her career would never be in dance so she needed to focus on doing the things that would get her into Stanford. Dad wanted me to go to Yale."

"What did you want?" he asked and wondered if it was the first time anyone had ever asked her that question.

"One Christmas, when she was nine, they gave Bella a camera. It was one of the fun gifts. We were allowed three of them, but only if our grades that semester were worthy." She looked away then.

Following her gaze, he saw a group of young girls, probably middle school age, each of them holding cotton candy in one hand. They laughed and giggled, and Ryan wanted to gather Allie into his arms and tell her she could have all the cotton candy she wanted and anything else tonight. If only for tonight, he wanted her to have all the fun and laughs and genuine happiness she could find, because from the sound of it, her childhood hadn't contained nearly enough.

"Bella loved that camera, almost as much as she loved to dance." A hint of light touched her tone. "She danced really well, but only in our bedroom and one time in high school when she joined the modern dance club. But Mom found out and put an end to that."

He gently tugged on her hand until she turned her face to look at him. "What about you?" he asked again. "What did you want to do?"

She gave him a bleak smile. "I had a journal," she said. "I had a lot of them, actually. I loved to get ones with different designs on the cover—colorful designs like paint splashes or rainbows. One time I found one with balloons and I used my entire allowance to buy it." She inhaled deeply, and Ryan used his free hand to trace a finger along her jaw.

Before this night was over, he was going to buy her all the balloons she could carry back to the Big House.

"I used to write in them," she continued. "In the morning when I woke up—I always got up half hour earlier than the alarm. Bella said waking up early on my own was unnatural." She chuckled but cut it off abruptly. "I'd write all my plans for the day—mostly the things I wished I could do as opposed to the strict schedule my parents had us follow. And at night before I went to sleep, I'd write about all the things I did. Only they were the things I wished I'd done. I was in the eighth grade before I realized I was writing fiction. I'd created a whole life in those journals, one I wished I'd been leading."

"And when you became an adult, you decided on a career in writing." He didn't think he'd ever felt prouder of anyone than he did her in this moment.

The smile she gave him then was genuine and wide, and the joy he'd seen in her eyes on both the rides reappeared. "Yeah," she said. "I decided where I wanted to go to college, and it didn't matter if my parents threatened not to pay if I didn't go where they wanted. I had a full scholarship to Columbia. I'd had to sneak in the application, but I got it."

Sofia had also received a scholarship. While the schools on Crescent weren't under any of the mainland districts and so didn't get the heavy sports scouting like most high schools in the States—which had been unfortunate for Sofia and Trevor—there were academic opportunities available.

"You're amazing," he said.

"You don't really know that," she replied. "I just told you I grew up writing fiction. For all you know, everything I just said was made up." Her upbeat tone had returned along with the sassy tilt of her head when she spoke.

But she wasn't fooling him.

"Then you'd still be amazing for telling such an impromptu, yet heartfelt, story." If it made her feel better to act like that hurt little girl didn't really exist, at least for the moment, then he'd let her have that.

"What else are we gonna ride?" she asked. "I want to get all my rides in before we have to return to your family booth. Sofia's threats to kidnap Optimus and put sand in your bed were serious, so I don't want us to be late getting back over there to help out."

He laughed. "Sofia's all talk," he said and then thought better of it. "But yeah, let's get going."

They'd just stood and taken a few steps when a bell rang. It sounded like a dinnertime call, but Ryan knew it was signaling that it was time for the speeches.

"Mayor Nat's gonna talk and probably Willie from the Chamber, or Bethany, the Island Council

President," he told her as he led her toward the gazebo where the podium and microphone had been
set up.

"Oh," she said and followed his lead.

"This is the kickoff to our centennial celebration,
so there'll be a lot more pomp and circumstance this
year. Hopefully, if Bethany's gonna speak, Mayor Nat
will let her go first and then cut her off if she tries to
go too long." He looked over at her. "Bethany always
tries to talk for too long."

They made it to the gazebo just as Mayor Nat
stepped up to the podium. Natalie Devenshire was
two years older than Ryan and had won the last elec-
tion three years ago. Some on the island were still a
little salty about having a mayor under forty, while
others—which turned out to be the majority—had
thought it was time for some fresh, young leadership
on Crescent.

Of course, Nat had gone into the office with another strike against her besides her age: her family
had a very close relationship with the Parkers. So
close, that for a while everyone had thought Trevor
and Nat would join the two families in holy matri-
mony. Trevor and Nat obviously had a different plan.
But Bethany, being Caleb Baldwin's cousin, had
brought new light to the age-old Parker/Baldwin
feud.

A ridiculous discourse that was rooted in classism
as Harvey Baldwin and his wife had brought their old
money and affluent lifestyle to the island upon special request from Gael Gibson. It hadn't mattered
that Gael had also invited Ryan's great grandfather,
Ernest Parker, who'd already had a little pit beef

stand in Ohio at the time. Ernest obviously wasn't as successful as Harvey Baldwin, and the two men butted heads on how the island should be run. Luckily, Gael and Mahalia Rivas, the dressmaker he'd also invited to come and start this island community with them, had ideas for a more congenial lifestyle.

"We have some very special guests here to help us celebrate this auspicious occasion," Nat was speaking as they came to a stop behind a crowd of people.

Ryan recognized the couple from the restaurant earlier this week, Paul and Teri.

"As you all may know, our little island has been getting some notoriety via a popular blog called Written in the Stars. Now, I have no idea who writes this blog, but I'm hoping they're here tonight to see what a magnificent job their writing is doing for our community."

Beside him, he felt Allie's hand stiffen in his.

There were some murmurs in the crowd, but Nat continued.

"Thanks to the attention the blog has been receiving, our tourism has been boosted, and we all know that's fantastic for our economy," she said.

Some minor applause came.

"But what I think is most important about this blog is its dedication to love and happiness. It's what the Founding Four built this island on, and every post celebrates those factors."

"The Founding Four," Allie whispered.

Ryan glanced over at her. "Yeah, the Gibsons, Parkers, Baldwins, and Rivas. They founded the island."

When she returned his gaze, she offered a tentative smile and nodded.

Nat kept talking. "And tonight, we're excited to have not one, but three couples that were brought together by the blog and subsequent visits to our island. Ladies and gentlemen of Crescent Island, let's give a warm welcome to Paul and Teri, Webster and Nora, and Jessica and Angela."

Applause rang out, and Ryan released Allie's hand to clap along with the crowd. The boost in tourism had been another nudge for him to start pushing his father a little harder on the idea of expanding the family business, so he proudly supported the town's success in whichever form it came.

He noticed that Allie wasn't clapping but figured it was because she didn't belong to Crescent. Or at least that's probably how she felt. He, on the other hand, was beginning to feel like she'd come here for a reason. That maybe she'd come here to find the happiness she'd missed most of her life. And if in doing so, that also brought her to him for however long he'd have her around, then he definitely wasn't mad at their boost in tourism.

In fact, he liked it even more.

CHAPTER ELEVEN

The combination of funnel cake, pulled chicken sliders drenched in Parker's Sweet Maple Glory sauce, a huge slice of Nana's apple pie, and one of Ms. Annabelle's prized cinnamon rolls were a sure recipe for a stomach ache.

Allie groaned as she continued to type her notes from tonight. They'd arrived back at the Big House a little after ten, and she'd come straight to her room and changed into the shorts and tank top she planned to sleep in and pulled out her laptop. Her stomach was still full, her mind whirling with the events of the night.

The events and the feelings they evoked in her, that was the bigger part, but she was trying to leave those off the page. This story wasn't supposed to be about her. It was about the island and the blogger who was making it so popular. At least that was the spin she'd wanted to put on the article Renee had requested.

Mayor Natalie Devenshire doesn't know who the blogger is. The three couples thanked the blogger publicly and issued an invite to them to attend their weddings. Was the blogger at the carnival?

Allie had looked around while the mayor had been speaking. Her gaze falling on so many faces, a very few that she knew, but more that she didn't. How would she know who the infamous matchmaker was? And did it really matter? Admittedly this wasn't part of the article Renee wanted, but from the moment Allie had learned of the blog, she'd known this blogger was an important part of the island. Mayor Nat had confirmed that tonight. So how could she write about Crescent Island without including its star matchmaker? The answer was, she couldn't.

When Ryan had grabbed her hand and pulled her toward the gazebo, she'd followed, thinking that perhaps they were going to head to more rides. That had been a fun-filled distraction from her work.

Attend more carnivals in the future.

She added that as a reminder to herself.

Ryan had chatted with each one of the couples, and Allie had joined in, believing it was a perfect time to surreptitiously dig for answers.

"The vivid descriptions of the island drew me here for a fall vacation last year," Angela had said. "The last thing I was expecting was to meet someone."

"Me either," Jessica had replied and lifted Angela's hand to kiss the back of it. "She arrived on the island two days after I did. We met on the hayride during the Harvest Homecoming, and the rest is history."

Two people decided to visit the same island and ended up meeting and falling in love. Could it be coincidence? Once maybe, but three times? And that was only looking at the couples that had been standing on that stage. How many more were there and how did the matchmaker know who was coming to the island and when?

"This trip is doubling as an engagement announcement and planning session. We want to get married on the island, too," Teri had said enthusiastically when Ryan asked when her and Paul would be heading back to their home in Maryland. They'd both been from different cities in the state but after meeting last year had moved in together.

That was another thing that Allie had found unrealistic. Who picked up their life and moved to a different city or state just to be in a relationship? Sure, she'd seen this type of happy-ever-after in tons of romcoms she watched, but her thought after each one had been that she'd never uproot her life to be with a man. What would happen when that relationship failed? Would she then have to pack up and head back to Miami? It all seemed so counterproductive and exhausting.

A tie-dyed balloon drifted across the ceiling, its long, twirly string brushing over her arm, and she jumped. She'd forgotten about them—all twelve of them. At one point when there'd been a long line at the Parker booth, Ryan had vanished. Sofia had cursed and Sarah had reminded them both that customer service was the number-one priority. When he'd returned with the balloons, she'd been flabbergasted—and touched beyond words.

She hadn't intended to tell him about the best birthday present she'd ever received and wasn't sure what to say about the fact that he'd not only listened, but had thought enough of her to buy her another balloon bouquet. Moving a hand from the keyboard, she reached up to twine the string around her finger. The act pulled the balloon down until it was eye level, and she grinned.

Ryan had given her balloons. He'd also walked her around the carnival, climbing on whichever ride she'd wanted to get on. Which was all of them; she'd wanted the opportunity to ride every one of them for fear she'd never get the chance to do so again. Her gaze went back to her screen where she'd typed the note to visit more carnivals. But would they be the same without Ryan? Who would she fall into when the moving floor in the fun house took her off guard? And who would be so lousy at pointing out constellations to her while they sat at the top of the Ferris wheel?

Another smile ghosted her lips as she recalled sitting close to him and him holding her hand. He'd done that a good portion of the night, and she hadn't bothered to stop him. Because she'd liked it. On a heavy sigh, she realized she'd liked it way too much.

And it wasn't just Ryan and the balloons that had touched a long-dormant part of her. Working the Parker booth alongside the family had been exciting and fun, especially since she'd been tasting a good portion of the food they'd served.

"I like this one," Vernon had said to nobody in particular when he'd clapped a hand on her shoulder and pulled her against his burly side for a hug. "She's got a good appetite. Not walkin' around here hollerin' 'bout being on some type of diet."

Allie hadn't been able to respond since her mouth had been full of chicken, or the brisket which was the most tender piece of meat she'd ever experienced.

"Yep, she's a keeper!" Sofia had replied and winked at Allie. "My best friend for life."

Her heart had swelled with Sofia's words, and she'd given her friend a smile and a thumbs-up. But when her gaze landed on Ryan, he'd been nodding and grinning, too. "I agree," he'd said.

And Allie had been speechless—and not just because of the food she'd been chewing.

Is matchmaking such a bad thing?

She forced herself to start typing and stop remembering. Making memories could be good, but it was when those memories came back to haunt that things became tricky. What was she going to do with all these fond memories of Ryan once she was back in Miami?

Is wanting love a bad idea?

For her it was, and that was the bottom line. She couldn't afford to want what she couldn't sustain.

Could a person fall in love with a place? The Springs? The carnival at Starry Circle? The Big House?

No was the answer. At least not for her. There'd never, in all her travels, been a place she'd fallen in love with. A place she'd longed to visit again and again because she just couldn't stay away from it. Crescent Island—even with its very nice people and picturesque views—wasn't that place, either. It couldn't be.

Or was the answer more like, she wouldn't let it be?

That question brought back another memory, a painful one this time, and she closed her eyes as the scene from long ago replayed in her mind.

"What is this?" twenty-year-old Allie had asked Bella after she'd noticed two suitcases and a duffel bag in their bedroom closet.

They'd just returned from an excruciating dinner at some five-star restaurant with their parents. The next day was Bella's high school graduation, but their father would be on-call, which meant he'd likely miss the entire ceremony and end up at the hospital. So the celebratory dinner had been the night before.

Bella shrugged in response, then dropped down onto her bed to remove the strappy sandals she'd worn.

Allie had come home for a long weekend to be here for her sister's big day and to spend a couple of days with her since the last time they'd seen each other was five months ago at Christmas.

"Are you going somewhere?" she'd asked because as far as she knew, Bella had yet to settle on a college she wanted to attend.

She'd of course been accepted to Stanford and Yale, thanks to their parents' connections and Bella's grades. But Bella had also insisted on applying to other colleges, and their parents' only compromise on that was the other colleges also needed to be Ivy League.

"Yes," was Bella's simple answer as she'd unbuttoned her blouse.

"Where?" Allie asked and then, because she was tired of this clipped, basically one-sided conversation, went to sit on the bed beside Bella. "Have you chosen a school? Where are you going that you've already packed your bags?"

Bella dropped her hands to her lap, the blouse she'd removed bunched between her fingers. "I'm not going to college," she said flatly and stared into Allie's eyes.

"Okay." Allie had said that one word very slowly. "So what are your plans?"

She wasn't terribly surprised by Bella's announcement because of the two of them, her sister had always been the one to buck against whatever their parents wanted for them. It had always been that way, and on some days Allie had admired Bella for her confidence and tenacity.

Bella turned on the bed, tucking one leg under her as she now faced Allie. "I'm just leaving," she'd said. "I've got a plane ticket to L.A. that Pete bought for me. From there, I'm just gonna see how things go."

Allie shook her head, heart hammering in her chest. "What? You can't just run off. Mom and Dad will totally freak out!"

Bella sighed. "I don't care what they do. I've waited all my life for this moment. I'll be eighteen in six months…"

"Then leave when you're eighteen," Allie had implored, hoping her sister would come to her senses in those six months. "If you go now, they could send the police after you and bring you back. You're still considered a minor."

Bella shook her head. "They're not gonna do that," she said with a rueful turn of her lips. "They're never gonna admit to anyone, especially not the police, that their child was so eager to get away from them that she ran away instead of taking the thousands of dollars in tuition they were so willing to pay."

"Bell…"

"No," her sister had said, holding up a hand. "They'd rather spend those thousands of dollars sending me to a school I don't want to attend, to learn how to do something I don't want to do, than simply have a normal dinner with me and listen to *my* ideas and goals for *my* life."

They'd had a similar conversation to this one when Allie was graduating from high school. Bella had only been marginally happy about Allie going to a school of her choice, but her sister had been beyond upset at that argument their parents had still put up at Allie's decision. And the fact that Allie had been forced to apply to the college she wanted to attend in secret. "I understand what you're saying, but…"

"But what?" Bella had interrupted again. "But I should just do what they say because it's easier that way? Is that what you're going to tell me? Oh, yeah, of course you are, because that's exactly what you do."

"Wait a minute, don't make this about me," Allie argued.

"But this is about you, Allie. It's about how they've treated both of us all of our lives. We've never been able to make our own decisions or follow our own dreams. Everything from the clothes we wear to the color of the bands on my braces for three years was what they wanted. I'm sick of it!"

"I know, but it gets better."

"How? Should I have snuck and applied to a school they didn't approve of and then pray they'd finally agree like you did?"

Allie gasped. "That's not what I did."

"That's exactly what you did," Bella told her. "You didn't even have the guts to just tell them you didn't want to go to an Ivy League college, that you didn't want to be a doctor. You just went behind their backs to find your own path."

"Okay. Fine, that's what I did, but it put me on the track to my dreams. Not theirs. Bella, you can do that without running away."

Bella shook her head. "I'm not running away from anything, Allie. I'm running toward my life, my freedom. Don't you want to do that?"

"I have done that. And really, you're doing the same thing I did, just to a different extent because you applied to all those schools they wanted you to attend, knowing you had no intention of going there, too."

"No," Bella said and sighed. "You're still not free of them. You may go to school in New York, but you're coming back here. You've already gotten an internship to come back here and work."

"Well, sure, but I'm coming back here to start my career as a writer, not as a doctor like Mom wanted." Because Allie had eventually put her foot down about what her career was going to be regardless of what her parents thought. Bella didn't seem to be giving her credit for taking that step on her own. That both hurt and infuriated her.

"You could've started your career as a writer in New York, but Mom already picked out a condo building where you can rent a place until you're ready to buy. And you know that just means she's keeping you close so she can continue to work on changing your mind about your future. They love steering us in the way they want us to go." Bella had rolled her eyes and folded her arms over her chest.

Their mother finding the condo for Allie had been a huge help since Allie's part-time earnings from the bookstore weren't going to get her a very nice place.

"You don't even have a career in mind, Bella. You're just running away to do what?"

"To live," her sister had snapped. "On my own terms, by my own rules. Do you ever see yourself doing that, Allie? Or will you continue to dangle on their strings to some degree for the rest of your life?"

That question still resonated in her mind as Allie's eyes popped open. It took a few seconds of deep breaths to bring her firmly back to the present and another soul-searching question. Was she refusing to entertain the idea that Crescent was a place she could belong because she was afraid to leave Miami? To cut those final strings that attached her to appeasing her parents on at least that one level as Bella had suggested.

With a heavy sigh, she shook her head. None of this was what she should've been thinking about right now. It was fine that she didn't want to stay on Crescent Island; her purpose for coming here was for her job, not to find a new home. Why her mind had somehow tried to connect the two, she had no idea, but she wasn't going to entertain it.

She closed the laptop a bit harder than she'd intended and frowned, because the last thing she needed was to break her equipment and have to replace it. Another sigh had her closing her eyes and mentally warning herself to get it together. All she had to do was write this story and get back to Miami. That's it. Then all would be right in her world once more.

The throbbing that began in her temples had her wondering if all was ever right in her world before now. Putting the laptop aside, she eased slowly off the bed. She needed to move, to stretch her muscles, clear her mind. Lifting her arms above her head, she leaned back and felt the elongating of muscles she feared she'd forgotten about. The groan that followed was proof that neither she nor her muscles were happy with her right now. She pushed her feet into her flip-flops and walked out the patio door. Maybe some fresh air would do the trick.

She didn't stop walking when wispy strands of mossy grass tickled the bare skin of her legs. In the mornings she watched as the breeze blew against these brown stalks so that they looked as if they were performing some synchronized dance, swaying in one direction or the other. At night, the color was barely perceptible here, and beyond there was the stretch of sand before the rolling waves of water crashed and faded. Her steps continued, her gaze focused on that water.

With her head tilted back against the night breeze, she wrapped her arms around her chest and felt the soft sand seeping between her toes despite the flip-flops she wore. Her breaths came easier here, in and out, deeper and deeper, pushing the scent of the sea through her nostrils and into her body as a sort of cleanser. The sound of the waves came to wash away the confusing thoughts, to leave her mind free of conflict.

"Write the story," she whispered. "Find the heart." *Don't think about the past because it couldn't be changed.*

A tiny gasp escaped at that last thought. The past couldn't be changed. Bella had left, and Allie hadn't spoken to her since. She missed her sister terribly, probably more so because a small part of her believed that Bella had been right. That no matter how much Allie had thought she was breaking free of their parents' unhealthy hold on them, she was still placating them by staying so close, taking their calls and the slices of time they allotted her, listening to their criticisms and internalizing them.

She stopped when she felt the cool water covering her feet, then retreating.

How was she supposed to find the heart of any story when she'd never felt the heart in any other aspect of her life? "Just write the story," she told herself again. "Write it and get on with your life."

"Talking to yourself?"

She jumped at the sound of his voice, then had just enough time to turn around before Optimus came charging at her. Now she knew how to receive him without being knocked on her butt. Bending her knees until she was in a squatting position, she opened her arms to him, and he crashed into them as if he hadn't just seen her yesterday.

"Hey there, buddy," she said as her hands moved over his head and under his chin. He loved when she rubbed under his chin and on his stomach. He would look up at her with such an adoring gaze, as if she—or rather her hands—were the answers to his doggie dreams. "You out for another midnight stroll?"

"Seems he wasn't the only one that needed some air tonight," Ryan said as he came to stand closer to her.

Allie continued to stare into Optimus's blue eyes. "There's nothing like the sea air, is there, boy? You like running along the beach, don't you? He thinks you've gotta go, but really, you just want to be out by the water." He seemed to nod in agreement, and she chuckled.

"You wanna walk with us?"

She looked up at Ryan then. He'd changed clothes, too. Instead of the khaki shorts and navy-blue T-shirt he'd worn earlier, he now wore light-gray basketball shorts and a black sleeveless shirt. She wondered if that was his sleeping attire as well.

When she stood, her reply was a shrug, and she fell into step beside him. They walked a few minutes in silence, but for Optimus's heavy breathing as he ran between and around them, looping back and forth before trotting a couple of feet in front of them.

"You wanna share what's on your mind?"

"No," she answered immediately. She didn't want to tell him that he was confusing her. That this island and his family were throwing her off-kilter.

"That's cool," he said. "But I've had something on my mind all day today, and since you were out here at the same time I'm out here, I'm gonna take that as a sign."

"A sign of what?"

"That this isn't something we can ignore."

There was an intensity to his softly spoken words, a seriousness to the set of his jaw and piercing way in which he'd looked at her. Glancing away, she tried to ignore it. "I don't know what you're talking about," she said.

"Don't you?" She could feel his gaze on her even though she continued to look straight ahead.

She shook her head in response.

He reached for her hand, easing his fingers slowly between hers just like they'd done at the carnival. She should pull away; touching him didn't make the thoughts running through her mind any clearer. It didn't make them worse, either. In fact, his touch brought an undeniable calm to her stressed-out mind.

"At first I thought, she's Sofia's friend."

"I am," she replied. "My friendship with her is very important. I would never do anything to jeopardize that."

"I know," he said and pulled a treat out of his pocket with his free hand before tossing it to Optimus. The dog jumped up to catch it before bobbing along happily once more. "But then I considered that of all my siblings, Sofia probably knows me the best. And if she's your best friend, that means she knows you, too."

"She's very perceptive," Allie replied, thinking of how on the mark Sofia had been this morning when she'd called Allie on not writing that book.

"That she is," he said. "Which is why I think she knew there was something brewing between us the minute I walked up to that table a few days ago."

It didn't take long for his words to sink in and for her to stop walking and ease her hand out of his. "You think she meant to set us up. Like on a date or something?"

Or like a matchmaker?

"When's your birthday?" she asked abruptly.

He frowned. "May 22nd, why?"

She shook her head, realizing that wasn't a helpful answer, not for her anyway. "What's your sign?"

"Gemini. You letting this island get to you now?" His tone was light, and he even smiled as he asked, but Allie's mind was whirling with possibilities.

Sofia already had her phone number. She could've easily sent her that cryptic horoscope text about capturing a Gemini's heart.

"Just wondering if my best friend is playing matchmaker," she said, slowly digesting how she felt about that possibility.

He closed the small space between them. "Would that be so bad if she was?"

Tilting her head back so she could hold his gaze, she had to swallow before she could speak. Ryan knew she was here to write an article about the island, but he had no idea she planned to incorporate the matchmaker into that story. And since he liked downplaying the cosmic nature and other gimmicky parts of this island, she hadn't thought it necessary to give him that detail. But now he was standing close, asking if it was a bad thing that the matchmaker was trying to fix them up.

He'd been invading her personal bubble so much today that she hadn't thought anything of it, until now. Mostly because she'd enjoyed him being so close, so ready to touch her without knowing how good those simple touches made her feel. His biceps appeared bigger now that they were totally bare. The broad expanse of his chest more muscled, the scent of his earthy cologne a little more prominent.

"I don't like to be manipulated." It was the only response she could muster, since the logical path her mind was taking toward the matchmaker's identity was now being muddled by the flip-flopping of her stomach caused by Ryan's sultry glare.

He nodded. "Neither do I," he replied. "Nor do I think that's possible. Look, people can set other people up on blind dates, but if there's no chemistry between those two, nothing happens."

"So you don't believe in matchmaking?"

"I believe in connections. Sometimes we may want to ignore them; other times we may act on them and they fail, leaving us raw and ragged. But they exist for better or worse."

"This would be for worse." She swallowed hard as he lifted a hand to push some strands of her hair back behind her ear. "I didn't come here to be matched with anyone. I came here to write a story and to visit with my friend."

"And I didn't wake up one morning and say to Optimus, 'Let's head down to the beach and run into a beautiful woman,'" he said.

His fingertips brushed along her jaw, and she shivered. "Then we're on the same page."

He nodded slowly. "I believe we are."

"Good," she whispered.

He cupped her face with one hand, tilting her chin as he leaned in closer.

"Good," he repeated.

"So we understand each other." She licked her suddenly dry lips.

"Completely." He whispered the single word two seconds before his lips touched hers.

CHAPTER TWELVE

Soft, sweet, slow, needy.

She was a writer; she should've been able to come up with a better description of this kiss, the feelings it evoked, the hunger it sparked. But really, all Allie could do was clasp one hand to Ryan's biceps and the other to mold against the back of his head and hold on.

He'd snaked an arm around her waist, pulling her against him, while the hand that had cupped her face eased down to cradle her neck in a move so gentle and yet so seductive, her legs trembled. The sound of the ocean roared around them as he took the kiss deeper, threatening to drown them both in this unexpected pleasure.

So many thoughts danced around in her head as she closed her eyes and sank faster. Interludes with a man were nowhere on the list of things she'd come to Crescent to do. Nor was greedily moaning into the mouth of her best friend's brother.

And yet, here she was.

Here *they* were, doing the unpredicted and, from her point of view, enjoying it immensely.

When he pulled away just enough to rest his forehead on hers, she sucked in a breath and prayed for something coherent to fall from her lips when it was time for her to speak. Blabbering like an inexperienced teenager wasn't an option, even if she'd never been kissed like that before.

"I should apologize if that was inappropriate," he said, his eyes still closed, hands still touching her.

"I don't want an apology," she replied.

It was dark down by the water, but they were so close she could see the struggle in the tenseness of his jaw. The way he almost squeezed his eyes to keep them shut, as if opening them might shatter the memory of the kiss. Her lips still tingled, so she doubted that would be happening for her anytime soon, but she couldn't close her eyes again. Couldn't stop staring at this man she'd wondered about being this close to.

Now it was her turn to cup his face. Maneuvering her arms so that her hands could slide between them and her fingers could feel the warmth of his cheeks, she nudged his head back slightly, and he opened his eyes slowly to find her gaze. From the moment she'd met him, she'd known there was something different about his eyes. Instinct had her believing that varia-tion was the color, but no, the darker shade of brown, whatever name it was given, wasn't what struck her as distinct now. It was the untold story behind them, the depth that swam in them that held her in his arms now, wavering under his alluring spell.

"How could I be sorry about such a lovely kiss?" she said softly and stroked her thumbs over the soft-ness of his skin.

He blinked and turned his face slightly into one of her hands. Closing his eyes again briefly, he inhaled a deep breath like he wanted to suck in every nuance of this moment and then released it slowly as he looked at her again. "It was…uh, much more than I'd anticipated."

Her lips trembled into a small smile. "Yeah, same here. I've been thinking about this for a couple days now," she freely admitted.

After a quick sigh, he grinned. "So, it wasn't just me?" He shook his head. "I was thinking it wasn't possible to be this all-in so soon. Plus, there was the whole Sofia's BFF thing looming in the air." He reached up and grasped her wrists as if he didn't want her to take her hands from his face.

She nodded. "Yes, there's that," she said. "But there's also this. I think we're all mature enough to adjust to the current situation and whatever may come later." As in, when whatever this was ended. It seemed weird to think of the ending so soon after the beginning, but Allie was nothing if not practical.

No, this wasn't intended, and for the past few days she'd even told herself it was out of the question. A pointless urge since she wasn't in the business of relationships. But she was a woman with wants and needs, some of which she'd denied herself for far too long. Obviously, that thought didn't pertain to just this situation with Ryan, but it was the pertinent one at this moment. Was there really a reason she shouldn't have enjoyed this kiss? It's not like it was a marriage proposal or anything as serious. It was just a kiss.

"We're definitely going to have to adjust, because I'm certain that won't be the last time I kiss you," he stated.

• • •

Ryan stood on his front porch at a little after seven the next morning. Optimus was stretched out in the middle of the living room fast asleep after his walk and breakfast. With a half-empty bottled water in one hand, he pressed the other into the front pocket of his black jeans and stared out at the land before him.

Mayor Nat's older brother Kevin owned the best realty company on the island and had been happy to negotiate a fair deal with Vernon for this part of the Parker land. Ryan and his father hadn't been able to come to amenable terms on their own, probably because Vernon had been still irritable about Ryan's desire to leave the Big House. But eventually, an agreement had been met, and Ryan had used his inheritance from Papa Teddy to make the purchase and build this house. While Nana and his father had received the most from Papa Teddy's estate, their grandfather had also provided a generous check for Ryan and his siblings. It wasn't lost on Ryan that if he hadn't insisted on buying this land and building this house himself, he'd have the money to fund the expansion he had planned for the family business. Still, he'd tried not to dwell on that too much.

Every man's got his own path to follow.

It was one of the most contradicting statements his grandfather had ever made considering Papa Teddy was all about the Parker BBQ legacy and every member of the family doing their part to keep that legacy thriving. Even if it meant sometimes that family member had to forego their own dreams in the process. So far, Ryan didn't believe any of his siblings had done that. Trevor had loved playing football, but the car accident he'd been in a month before his senior prom had put an end to that. Even without the accident, though, Trevor had never expressed a desire to play professionally. He'd been in the kitchen at the Big House or out back on the smokers cooking all his life, right alongside the rest of them. And Brody, he was so busy chasing women and getting into any other trouble he could find, the safest place for him *was* the kitchen.

That thought brought a wry grin to Ryan's face. Man, he loved his family. He loved being here on this island with them and sharing all their ups and downs. But a part of him wanted more. A big part of him, he admitted and took another swallow of his water.

He wanted to take Parker BBQ into a new direction, and when that dream came to fruition, he wanted to build his own family. That part right there was the one he'd pushed so far to the back of his mind he'd been shocked when it first began to prick his senses again—somewhere between the time of seeing Allie sitting on his parents' back porch and listening to Trevor candidly put Ryan's feelings for her on blast. And were they really feelings? Or was it just an interest in a woman? He hadn't experienced that in so long, he wasn't sure how to tell the difference.

So why had his thoughts been circling around seeing Allie in this house all night long? That kiss was the answer. Closing his eyes briefly to the warmth of the morning sun fanning over his face, he recalled the second his lips had touched hers.

Time had stood still. It had to because every part of his body and mind had done the same. He'd been afraid that if he'd moved, the contact would be broken and that was unacceptable. He supposed that kiss had been coming for the past few days, since he'd helped her up on the beach earlier this week. That tugging he'd felt in the pit of his stomach as he'd watched her walk away that afternoon had only increased. The desire to be closer to her, to hear her laugh, touch her hand, or enjoy the scent of her shampoo had only grown more intense the longer she stayed on this island. After they'd kissed, he'd asked her to go on a real date with him tonight, and she'd agreed.

Last night had been like a door opening. A door that he'd closed and bolted so very long ago when Kerry left. Not that he'd never intended to open it again, but he'd been there and done that, and while he also didn't like comparison, preferring to give everyone and every situation a fair shot, he hadn't been able to deny one simple truth where Allie was concerned...

She was from the city, had a whole life there, one that as far as he knew—despite her childhood—she had no problems with and planned to get back to at the end of this trip. That was a big deal, an obstacle that put more than just thousands of miles between them.

His home was here in Crescent. The career and personal life he'd planned for himself was here. He couldn't, no, he wouldn't ever again expect anyone to choose the same just to be with him. Yet knowing all that, she'd plagued his thoughts every waking second last night and into this morning. By the time he'd stepped out of the shower and began to dress, thoughts of how he could build an addition onto the back of the house to make an office for her to write were taking form. A wall of windows facing the water could be inspiring and relaxing. And at night they could come out here and sit with Optimus lounging on the floor between them.

She liked his dog well enough. Actually, he was fairly certain Optimus was growing on her. And she enjoyed being with his family, another huge selling point. There was no mistaking the joy he saw in her when they were at the booth together last night. The way she and Sofia joked and how attentively she listened to whatever his mother told her about the food and how best to serve it… For that matter, she'd even gotten along with his father. Not that Vernon was a hard man, he was just a man set in his ways and, in addition to that pertaining to the family business, it was even more true when it came to his children. Vernon wanted them all to settle down and build a family but with someone he deemed worthy of entering the Parker fold.

Setting the bottle of water on the railing, Ryan lifted a hand to squeeze the bridge of his nose. How had he gotten so off track so quickly? These types of thoughts were happening way too soon, and they were probably far from reality. Allie wasn't staying in Crescent, and he needed to focus on getting his business plan off the ground before he could imagine any type of personal happy-ever-after.

That thought reminded him he still needed to send an email to Phoebe.

He pulled out his phone and opened his inbox to do that right now. It was a quick message—a simple greeting and then the question: Can you provide a status on whether you will be visiting the restaurant or if I should seek other options?

He hit send and slipped the phone back into his pocket. The negotiations with Phoebe had been going on for the last three months, and he'd provided her with every shred of information she could possibly need to make this decision. At this point, it was down to a yes or a no, and while that may've seemed impatient or impetuous, he needed to keep moving forward. He was down to the last week of his father's four-week timeframe to get this deal done, and he hated the idea of possibly having to start all over again, but he would if necessary.

With that in mind, he grabbed the water bottle and headed back into the house. He wanted to get to the restaurant and go over his proposal again just to see if he'd left any stone unturned. That was unlikely, but he also needed to start thinking of a plan B. All of which would hopefully keep his mind from straying too far into a future with Allie.

He was heading toward his bedroom to grab his phone charger when—speak of the devil—his phone buzzed. Hoping it was an email notification and Phoebe was getting back to him with good news, he hurriedly pulled the phone from his pocket and looked at the screen.

Circumstances can be discouraging. But there was no mistaking the stars as they aligned above while you sat on the bench last night. The Sagittarius will be noncommittal to love, and the Gemini will be intrigued to learn more. Only time will tell how this will end, but there's a vibrant energy in the salty sea air and good news is on the horizon.

He read the text again. Slowing down on the "while you sat on the bench last night" part. This wasn't the first time he'd received text horoscope messages. It was just one of the things that happened on Crescent, one of those astrological things. He frowned because those were his father's words. Vernon didn't buy into all that stuff, and as such, Ryan and his siblings didn't put much stock in it, either.

At least not until it seemed to be as on the nose as this one was. A part of him figured this had to happen from time to time. A random horoscope resonating with a particular person—whether that person believed in astrology or not—probably occurred more often than he actually knew.

But not to him.

His brow was still furrowed, his mind trying desperately to get a grip on this message and what it could possibly mean, when there was a knock at his door.

With a heavy sigh, he pushed his phone back into his pocket and hurried over to his nightstand to grab his charger. Then he headed back out to the living room, where Optimus was barking wildly at the door. Ryan sincerely hoped it wasn't Trevor again. The last thing he felt like right now was hearing his brother's unsolicited advice about love and dating on the heels of a horoscope hinting at an uphill battle to matters of the heart.

But when Ryan opened the door, he received another shock, one that had him rocking back on his heels and the breath whooshing out of his lungs. "Kerry?"

CHAPTER THIRTEEN

Kerry Lennon stepped inside Ryan's living room, and Optimus danced around her, waiting for a touch, a word of greeting, anything that would acknowledge him in some way. While Ryan closed the door with a resounding click and turned to look at her, confirming that she was indeed here, alive and well, on Crescent Island once again.

"It's so good to see you, Ryan," she said when she stopped to stand in front of his couch.

She wore a coral pantsuit, a beige blouse beneath the jacket, and beige high-heeled shoes. Her coal-black hair was longer than he recalled, falling in bone-straight strands past her shoulders. The face that had once been so familiar to him was now layered with makeup—long lashes, coppery eyeshadow, and red lips.

"It's a surprise to see you, Kerry." He couldn't think of another response, not one that didn't run the line of rude or salty. And he didn't want to be either.

She slipped the matching tote bag from her shoulder and set it on the couch. The sleeves of her jacket had been rolled up to her elbow, and she pushed a curtain of hair back from her face as she lowered herself to sit.

"I know I was the last person you expected to see today," she said.

That was an understatement. Just as seeing her, in this very personal space he'd built for himself, wasn't quite right.

He moved farther into the living room, not taking a seat but standing a few feet away from her near the leather recliner he liked to lounge in when he was watching television in this room. Optimus followed him, as unsure about Kerry, who still hadn't acknowledged him at this point, as Ryan was.

"Why are you here?" Candid wasn't the same as being rude. Nana had told him that when he was younger.

She crossed one leg over the other and sat back. "I'm here to make your life better."

He couldn't help it—he chuckled. "You? The person who all but destroyed my life five years ago is now here to make it all better? Do tell how you plan to make that happen."

Old emotions—rage, hurt, betrayal—bubbled in the pit of his stomach, and he fisted his hands by his sides.

"Okay," she said with a sigh. "I guess we need to get this out of the way first." She cleared her throat. "You're still upset that I chose my life over living the one you had planned out for me."

Ryan shook his head. "Correction. I'm still baffled that the future we planned together was so easily dismissed the moment you received a job offer in the city. A job, I might add, that you actively pursued without even telling me."

Which had been a special kind of hurt all in itself. They'd dated on and off for the first two years after he'd finished undergrad, then became more serious once he'd received his master's degree and officially assumed his role as the manager at Parker BBQ.

She'd graduated from college by then, too, with a degree in finance that she'd planned to use working at the island's only bank, Seabreeze Savings & Loan, which her uncle owned.

"I had a right to be happy, Ryan. You're still so rigid in your small-town thinking." She pursed her lips. "I wanted more, and I asked you to come with me."

And he'd immediately told her no. The city life wasn't for him. He loved Crescent and its close-knit community, and he was 100 percent devoted to his family and their legacy. Nothing, not even what he'd thought was the love of his life, could change that.

"My life is here," he said, the words echoing what he'd told her the day she'd walked away.

"And my career, the life I wanted for myself, was in the city."

They stared at each other in silence for endless moments, until he finally sighed.

"Now that we've covered that old familiar ground, I'll ask you again, why are you here?" There was no good reason for her to be sitting in his living room at this moment, none at all. She'd made her choice, and he'd lived with it. He'd tried like hell not to resent her for it and had thought he'd been successful until they'd come face-to-face again.

She let her hands fall into her lap and took a quick breath before saying, "I'm from Brownstone Investments. I'm here to perform an in-person evaluation of you and the restaurant and to decide whether we will be authorizing funding."

Ryan was stunned, could barely breathe as he digested her words.

This wasn't happening. After all the work he'd done, all the planning and praying, the most important business move in his life couldn't come down to *Kerry's* decision. The universe wouldn't possibly be that cruel.

• • •

Allie couldn't stay in her room all morning, touching her lips and grinning at the memory of the sweet 'n spicy kiss she and Ryan had shared last night. Sofia had sent a text around six saying she was hitching a ride with Nana to her crack-of-dawn physical therapy session at the hospital. So Allie had taken that opportunity to sleep in.

Well, she hadn't slept. She'd gotten an early shower, then came back into her room to dress and sit on the bed with her laptop. Type a few sentences, look up and stare out the patio door to the shore for a few moments, then type some more. That's how the first few hours of her morning had progressed.

Early mornings on the island are unlike anything I've ever seen. The sun bursting amidst a brilliant blue sky, sprinkling drops of golden light onto the crystalline water. There's a serenity in the scene, a quiet lulling that gives just enough optimism to start the day.

How would it feel to wake up to this scene every morning? To see the stalky grass blowing in the breeze and inhale the salty sea air mixed with the undeniable smokiness of Vernon and his sons preparing their first batches of smoked meats for the restaurant?

The Parkers are hosting a game night at the restaurant tonight. It's part of the ongoing SummerFest celebration. I don't know when the last time I played a game was and have no clue what type of games will be played. But I'll be there. I told Ms. Sarah I'd help serve while Sofia acts as the MC for the night. I enjoyed working in the booth with them last night, so this should be fun, too.

Her fingers paused over the keys, and she stared toward the patio door once more. She hadn't missed that her notes had taken a noticeably softer tone. Yeah, Renee had her using that word now.

A little chuckle escaped at the thought, but she couldn't deny the truth. This island was growing on her. Last night had been more than a little fun. And she wasn't just talking about the time at the carnival, while that had been memorable as well.

It was just through that door and down the beach that she'd walked until Ryan had joined her. As if he'd somehow known she would be there. Or perhaps she'd gone out there hoping to see him? Optimus was still being housebroken, and it seemed that around midnight was one of the times his bladder scheduled a release. She was positive she hadn't been thinking that when she'd gone out last night, but what if subconsciously she'd known? What if she'd sought him out—Ryan, not the dog—expecting that kiss?

She willed her hand not to move this time, to keep her fingers from touching her lips again. She'd awakened this morning, and it'd seemed so surreal, that one kiss could leave such a lasting impression on her. That one man could so quickly—in just about a week—break through her no-serious-dating stance.

To be fair, she was still considering this a vacation fling. Repeatedly reminding herself of that had probably been the only reason she'd been able to sleep at all last night.

But now that she was fully awake, she figured it was better to focus on work instead of the unexpected pleasure of Ryan Parker. She wrapped up her notes, saved the document, and closed the laptop. In the next few minutes, she'd put on a pair of natural-colored flat sandals to go with the denim shorts and black tank-top she wore. Then she left her room, heading to the kitchen where the scent of fresh-brewed coffee beckoned.

"Good mornin', Ms. Sarah," she said upon entering the room awash with sunlight.

This space had definitely become one of her favorites in the Big House. The large windows that in the evenings had sheer curtains drawn, during the day were usually open to the sea breeze, those same curtains pushed to the side and out of the way. The sunlight bounced off every surface from the marble countertops to the concrete farmhouse sink.

And this morning, it also cast an ethereal sheen over Sarah's golden-brown skin tone. Her sandy-brown, shoulder-length hair was pulled into a messy ponytail, and she wore a beige apron that read "my kitchen, my rules" over gray capri pants and a peach-colored T-shirt.

"Good morning, Allie," Sarah replied. "I didn't make any breakfast. Tryin' to get the dough rolled for the pot pies we're having tonight. But there's coffee and some donuts Brody picked up. I swear that boy is just like his daddy. The first tooth he grew in was a sweet one."

Allie chuckled. "It's fine. I'll just take coffee." Even though she eyed the box of donuts on the counter as she made her way to the coffeepot.

They were much bigger than the ones she was used to seeing at the Dunkin' in the city. And covered with a variety of toppings that had her mouth watering.

"Nonsense," Sarah prodded. "Get yourself a donut and have a seat. Sofia's already at her doctor's appointment, so you can take a minute to keep me company."

Keep her company.

Those words had Allie pausing momentarily, her gaze resting on Sarah's back as she moved around the island to grab a bowl of flour.

Had her mother ever requested Allie keep her company? The answer to that came quick and clear—no.

For starters, Claire Sparks barely had a moment to spare, let alone enough moments to think she'd need someone to share them with. Allie figured that had to have been different at some point in her mother's life, otherwise how did she and Bella come to be? But for all the time that Allie had known her, Claire had been on the move.

Allie fixed her coffee and selected a donut that looked and smelled strongly of cinnamon. She considered crossing the room to the table tucked in the breakfast nook but acted on instinct instead and sat on one of the stools positioned at the end of the island.

Allie picked up the donut and took a bite. Heaven had arrived here on earth. "This is soooooo good," she murmured as she chewed and cinnamony sweetness burst into her mouth.

Sarah chuckled and nodded. "Yes, indeed it is. That's the cinnamon crumb one," she said. "Tara Kincaid went over to the mainland for culinary school, came back a talented pastry chef. Used every dime she saved from working as a server at the restaurant to buy a little shop over on Wishful Drive. Now, we've got Meg's tasty muffin tops down at the Docks and Tara's delicious donuts and other baked treats a little farther into town."

"I've had the pleasure of those muffin tops, too," Allie replied. "I can safely say that Crescent has some of the most delicious food and desserts I've ever tasted in my travels." She had to be sure to add that to her story. A compliment, not a critique. Coupled with her softening toward the island overall, she was certain Renee would be satisfied with her final story—even with the additional matchmaker angle.

"Oh, really now?" Sarah nodded and pushed the rolling pin over one of those balls of dough. "That's good to hear. You been traveling to a lot of places?"

Allie finished chewing her second bite of the donut. "It's what I do for a living," she said.

In general, she rarely had to disclose her purpose in any location. Tourist was as good a title as any other. But she was quickly learning that the Parkers were full of questions. They were also together a lot and thus talked to each other all the time. Yet it was apparent that neither Ryan nor Sofia had told Ms. Sarah why she was here or anything else about her job.

"So, you just travel around the world? How do

you make the money for all that traveling?" Unaware of Allie's slight confusion, or purposely overlooking it, Sarah continued with more questions. "And doesn't your family miss you while you're away?"

"I'm a writer," Allie said. "I get paid for my articles. It's just me and my parents in Miami, and we aren't really close, so they rarely notice when I'm out of town." That was true enough. And there was really no need to get into so many details when everything—besides her relationship with Sofia—about this trip was temporary.

Her budding friendship with Ryan, the obsession she was developing for the brisket at Parker BBQ, her growing affection for Optimus, and her interactions with the rest of the Parker family were all just temporary. A piece of the donut lodged in her throat, and she reached for her mug to take a few sips of the heavily creamed and sugared coffee.

"Oh, yes, I think Sofia did say you were a writer. I don't know why I thought that meant you wrote books or something like that." Sarah's hands moved deftly, and the dough quickly flattened on the countertop. "Well, we do like to feed people here on the island. You should check out the Brew & Grub, too. They've got a terrific fried catfish platter, and Polk's Seafood has the best steamed crabs. Well, when Vernon and the boys don't go over to Ocean City's bayside to catch some live ones. That's when we really have a feast, you know, after they've steamed them up right out back."

The older woman looked up from her work and glanced down the island to where Allie sat cradling that mug in her hand.

"You should have Ryan take you down there to-morrow night. He's not scheduled to be at the restaurant, and Nana and I have got to take dinner over to Betsy Carrollton's house. Betsy plays the organ at the church, but she broke her foot a week ago, so the members of the Women's Guild and Nana's Diamonds are taking turns feeding her until she's up and running again."

"That's a very nice thing to do," Allie said, trying to ignore the fact that Ryan's mother was planning a date for them.

She also wasn't about to tell Sarah that she and Ryan had already agreed last night to go on a date. But she would probably ask him if they could go to one of those places Sarah had just suggested. With that small tidbit of satisfaction, Allie relaxed a little more.

"Are you very active in your church?" she asked. "I mean, how do you even find the time? From what I can see you're at the restaurant most of the day, then you're here cooking for your family and Sofia said you also do some catering."

Sarah nodded again and smiled. "I just do all the things I love," she replied. "That's how I was raised. I do the things that make me feel happy and complete, then I take care of the family that I helped to create. Makes a full circle life, the only kind of life I'd ever want to live."

Allie took another sip of coffee and continued to stare at the sheets of dough Sarah was now using a bowl to cut into uniform disks. "I was raised to work hard and be successful. I guess that's kind of the same," she said.

"Not if that's all you do," Sarah countered. "Or if you're working so much that you don't even notice when your child is out of town." There were a few seconds of silence when Allie didn't know how to respond to Sarah's soft jab at her parents.

"The thing about a circle is it can be filled," Sarah continued. "You can put all the things you love into it to make your life complete. Work and success, those are just a couple of things, and they rarely complete that circle on their own."

Of all the things Allie had heard her mother say, all the lessons she'd been primed to learn from her mother's career path and subsequent prestige in Miami's legal community, none of them had ever pricked Allie's senses the way Ms. Sarah's words just had.

Was her life an incomplete circle?

Had she been so focused on leading a life totally different from the one her parents had planned for her that she'd built another type of fortress?

The weight that settled in her chest at that thought was intense, and she may've gasped. She wasn't quite sure. It was hard enough trying to focus on breathing through the immediate burden of the possibility that she'd done herself more harm than good. Her pulse quickened, her vision going a little blurry as she considered she might be heading toward a monumental panic attack.

"Stop thinking so hard and come help me with this dough," Sarah said, successfully pulling Allie from her thoughts.

She cleared her throat and then eased off the stool. "I don't know how to make dough."

"Nonsense," Sarah replied with a shake of her head. "You can do whatever you're taught to do. Now, just take this here."

When Allie came around to the side of the island where Sarah stood, Sarah pushed the rolling pin in front of her.

"Get some flour on your hands and the pin so the dough doesn't stick."

Not waiting for Allie to follow directions, Sarah reached into the bowl of flour and dropped a handful over Allie's hands and the rolling pin. Allie choked on the white cloud of flour dust and then laughed when Sarah nudged her with her shoulder.

"Nothing wrong with getting your hands a little dirty. Cooking can be fun and soothing," Sarah said. "Just bring your worries on into the kitchen and work 'em out here."

"The kitchen is both the heart of the house and its therapeutic epicenter," she quipped.

Sarah laughed. "I guess that's a way to put it."

Allie dipped her fingers into the flour and this time sprinkled it over the ball of dough just like she'd seen Sarah do. Then she put the rolling pin on it and pushed forward. The activity didn't go quite as planned, and the pin ended up slipping right out of her hands, crashing into the flour bowl and turning it over so that flour dust once again filled the air, this time falling in sprinkles over Allie's face and black shirt.

"I said a *little* dirty!" Sarah laughed again, this time so hard she held her stomach, and Allie, she laughed, too. Longer and harder than she had in years.

. . .

Thirty minutes later, Allie wore a new shirt and she'd
decided to call Eddie for a ride into town. Sarah was
taking the dough over to the restaurant where Nana
had been making the filling for the pot pies, while
also getting together the sides to be sold at the restaurant today. Sofia had sent Allie a text saying she
would be at therapy a little longer because at the last
minute her doctor had wanted to perform another
test, so that had left Allie alone. But not without
things to do.

She wanted to visit the Sinclair twins again and
also go back down to the Docks to grab a couple of
muffin tops, since Sarah had brought them up a while
ago. With her phone in hand, her purse hanging from
one shoulder, Allie stepped out of the Big House
onto the front porch. She had just activated the
screen on her phone and was about to pull up Eddie's
number so she could dial it when the text message
came through.

*Circumstances can be discouraging. But there
was no mistaking the stars as they aligned above
while you sat on the bench last night. The
Sagittarius will be noncommittal to love, and the
Gemini will be intrigued to learn more. Only time will
tell how this will end, but there's a vibrant energy in
the salty sea air and good news is on the horizon.*

"What?" she whispered. "No. No. Noooooooo."

Was this about them? Her and Ryan? Of course it
was.

She paced the front porch. Weren't they sitting on

the bench in Starry Square last night? When she'd inadvertently told him about the dysfunction that was her childhood. They'd held hands while they walked over to the bench and then again when Ryan stood and led them over to the gazebo where the mayor gave her presentation.

I have no idea who writes this blog, but I'm hoping they're here tonight to see what a magnificent job their writing is doing for our community.

That's what Mayor Nat had said. Was she there? At the carnival last night, had the author of that blog, aka the Crescent Matchmaker, been walking about amongst the clusters of people she'd seen while sitting on that bench with Ryan? Had she been standing there in the crowd looking at those three couples with pride? During the speech, Allie had looked around trying to place a face with the words she'd read on the blog. It had been a futile effort, she'd known it then, but she'd had to try. Especially since she'd received that first text. The one that Ryan had brushed aside, but that Allie had felt a tingling of a connection to.

Was it Sofia?

Her friend wasn't here right now so she couldn't just march up to her and ask, but she could do something even better. She was going to ask Ryan what this all meant. Surely, he'd see that this was way too much of a coincidence, considering she was a Sagittarius and he was a Gemini.

Before she could talk herself out of it, she stomped down the front steps and walked halfway down the walkway before cutting over onto the grass. Ryan's house could be seen in the distance to the left just as the restaurant was in walking distance to the right. If she'd gone out to the road, she could've walked along the gravely path to get to his house, but she wanted to get there faster. So she moved through the grass, thinking with every step how foolish this all was.

Whoever sent this text didn't know her, and they had no idea what had been going on between her and Ryan on that bench last night. Could there have been someone else sitting on another bench somewhere along the seven-mile radius that was Starry Circle? That was a definite possibility, but something—probably the heat that had swirled in the pit of her stomach the moment she'd read those words on her phone—had told her it was them. She knew that these text messages referred to her and Ryan as surely as she knew her name.

And she didn't like it one bit.

Her arms were swinging at her sides, cool blades of grass tickling her toes through the flat sandals she wore, as she continued her trek toward the cute little gray house with black window shutters. If she wasn't on a mission, this might be construed as great exercise as her heart began pumping faster. She was moving so quickly the straps from her purse slipped off her shoulder, and she had to use her free hand to catch them. Her phone fell when she saved the purse, and she cursed before kneeling down to pick it up.

If that hadn't irritated her enough, as Allie lifted her head and began to stand, her gaze caught movement on Ryan's porch. A woman came out his front door and stopped just short of the steps. Ryan followed her out. Allie gasped.

There were certain emotions she'd never imagined she would feel. One was romantic jealousy. And sure, it wasn't like Ryan was touching the woman or standing unreasonably close to her. But there was no denying the clenching of her teeth as she watched them on that porch. A part of her screamed she was being unreasonable. She'd only known Ryan for a week and they had kissed exactly one time. This reaction was totally irrational.

And yet, the twisting that had begun in the pit of her stomach at the sight of that text message had morphed into a full-blown firestorm that left her temples throbbing. The combination of both incidents had her pushing forward, fully determined to approach Ryan and whoever Ms. Pretty Coral Pantsuit was.

Optimus must've seen her the moment she came close enough to the house because he bolted off the porch, running straight for her. If she'd had a change of heart and wanted to turn around and leave Ryan to this—whatever this was? A morning-after goodbye?—it was too late.

CHAPTER FOURTEEN

"I got another text, and I think we need to figure out who's sending them and tell them to stop it. I didn't come to Crescent to be matched with anybody."

Allie had stomped up onto his porch just as Kerry had backed out of his driveway and turned down the road.

Two women, two unexpected visits, and a headache that threatened to break him.

"What?" he asked when he forced his gaze from the fancy car Kerry obviously had the *Lucky Seven*— the vehicle and equipment transport ferry—bring over for her.

"The text message," she said, thrusting her phone out for him to see.

But Ryan didn't look at the phone. Instead, he looked at the way she held Optimus in one arm like he was a baby instead of a thirty-two-pound merle Great Dane.

"I got this about fifteen minutes ago. Did you get one?"

He dragged a hand down his face and prayed that when he dropped his hand everything would be as it was when he woke up this morning. He'd be still recalling the kiss they'd shared last night, and Optimus would be sleeping on the floor content that his stomach was full and his bladder was empty. Sure, there'd still be the confusion of what this thing was with Allie and how far it could go, but that was a welcome issue compared to what now plagued his mind.

"Check your phone," she said. "Maybe the text came while you were…entertaining…Ms. Pretty Coral Pantsuit."

He narrowed his gaze. "Who?"

What was even happening right now? Why had she walked over to his house and why was his dog cuddled up in her arms as if she were the only woman he had ever loved? And why, in the name of all that was holy and right in this world, had Kerry returned to the island?

He didn't wait for an answer from himself or Allie but walked around her to go back into the house. She followed him and closed the door.

"Are you all right?" she asked when he'd stopped at the back of the chair in the living room and held on.

If he let go, his knees might give out and he'd fall on his face. The same face that Kerry had closed the door on five years ago. And if he fell, he'd crumble like a pile of discarded rocks, the same way he'd done on the worst day of his life. The memory made him feel weak, even though he didn't normally subscribe to men feeling or showing emotion being less than normal. He had feelings, and generally he owned them, regardless of what anyone else said or thought.

Today, however, he wanted all those feelings to stay locked inside. To not rear their ugly head, putting him in a place he'd crawled long and steadily to get out of.

"Ryan." Her tone was softer now, and she touched his shoulder. "Are you okay?"

"Yeah." He ground the word out in one rough

syllable. "I will be."

And he would. He'd survived Kerry before and he would do so again. This time because there was no love left, only ire and now utter shock that she was the one who held his family's legacy in the palm of her hand.

"Do you need something to drink?" she said. "Or maybe you should just sit down for a few minutes."

He heard Optimus bark and then scatter across the floor. The dog would circle between the couch and this chair waiting for one of them to sit so he could park his butt either on or right next to their feet. That's what he did when he wanted to be close to someone, to stake his claim on them. Odd that the dog had kept his distance from Kerry. Something Ryan wished he had the good sense to do all those years ago.

"No. I'm good. Really," he said and then turned around to face her. "I just needed to get my head cleared."

"From what? Ms. Pretty Coral—"

He held up a hand to stop her next word. Allie's agitated state hadn't been lost on him. It had, in fact, rested on top of the pile of other issues that taunted him this morning. "Her name is Kerry Lennon, and she's here to evaluate the restaurant to decide if her company will invest in my idea."

With her brows arched, she asked, "Your idea for what?"

Tilting his head, he watched the question flit across her face. Her eyes widened slightly with interest as she waited for his response. He couldn't believe he'd been with her almost every day this past week and hadn't told her about his plans for the restaurant. Then again, why would he have? She wasn't staying here, and it had never come up. If they were really dating, like truly trying to get to know each other, he certainly would've shared his hopes and dreams with her. Right?

He cleared his throat and moved to the couch before dropping down onto it. Allie followed him, sitting sideways on the couch beside him, folding one leg beneath her. She looked amazing today. The jean shorts were very short, and the white top she wore left a few inches of her midriff bare. Her hair was a wild mass of natural curls haloing her face, and large hoop earrings dangled from her ears.

"My great-grandfather created the Parker House Sauce that sits on each table at the restaurant. But on the menu, there are six other sauces that can be requested to accent the smoky flavor of our meats."

"Cajun Fire, Simply Sweet, Blazin' Blues, Sweet Maple Glory, Happy Pineapple Peace, and Honey Haven," she recited with a nod. "The House Sauce and Sweet Maple Glory are my favorites."

Ryan looked over at her and couldn't resist the urge to grin. She'd practically memorized the restaurant's menu. He'd marveled at that fact last night at the booth when she'd known exactly what people wanted to order before they'd even gotten it out completely. Each day he was around Allie, he found something else to adore about her, a look, a scent, her voice, her mind. He was mesmerized by her and at the same time haunted by the fact that she wasn't staying here on this island. Or with him. Having the other woman who'd chosen city life over him show up on his doorstep unexpectedly only exacerbated that painful reality.

"Sweet Maple Glory is Brody's favorite," he said.

She smiled. "I think your dad, Brody, and I share a love of sweets."

It was such an ordinary statement and yet it had touched Ryan in an unfamiliar place, bringing some sort of odd calm to his irritated soul. This woman whom he'd just met and had an unexplainable connection with also had a connection to a few of the people who meant the most to him.

"I want to bottle the sauces and sell them online. The restaurant may be the only place you can get our signature tender and delectable smoked meats, but if we could get the sauces out worldwide, we'd make a ton of money and our name would go beyond the pit master circuit. We'd be on the playing field with real manufacturers."

"Wow," she said and blinked as if just seeing him for the first time. "I never would've imagined you planned that way."

"What does that mean?" he asked for clarification, because it seemed as if she was saying he wasn't capable of thinking along those lines. But that could just be the lingering irritation still trying to dominate his current mood. Still, the urge to give his credentials was strong. "I mean, I know I'm just a small-town guy, but I do have a master's in business. I know how to market and sell what's been in my family for four generations. I can make this happen and take my family's legacy into the next century."

She reached out and put a hand on his thigh. A motion that was again calming and simultaneously

LACEY BAKER   219

arousing. After last night's kiss, there was no denying
that he wanted Allie. The question was how much did
he want from her, or better yet, how much could he
expect?

"I don't doubt you can," she said softly. "I apologize if you thought I meant something else. It's just
that since I've been here, all you've talked about are
the sights around Crescent, checking inventory at the
restaurant, what your mother or Nana's cooking for
dinner, or—"

"Kissing you," he interrupted her.

Now, she blushed, and it was the prettiest thing
he'd ever seen. If he could just sit and stare at her for
the rest of the day, he was certain the bad vibes he
was getting from Kerry's appearance would disap-
pear. Or at the very least subside until he could think
of a professional way to deal with her. Staring into
Allie's eyes right at this moment had him welcoming
her as a distraction this morning and, honestly, for
however long he could have her.

"Yeah, that too." She cleared her throat. "I guess
what I'm saying is I would've liked to hear about
your goals and plans, too."

He took her hand in his. "I'll make a deal with
you," he said. "When we go to dinner tomorrow, I'll
tell you all about my hopes and dreams, and you can
tell me about yours, too."

There was a flash of shock. That crinkle on the
bridge of her nose appeared and then vanished. But
he didn't release her hand. Instead, he squeezed it
tighter, hoping that act reassured her that whatever
concerned her about what he'd just said was unnecessary. All he wanted was to show her a good time, to

let her see that everything didn't have to be serious or as bad as whatever she might be imagining. That wasn't the easiest feat, especially not considering how his morning was going, but he figured it was what they both needed right about now.

"Sure. Oh, and I want to go to Polk's Seafood for some steamed crabs. Your mom said they're the best except for when your father takes you and your brothers to the Bay to catch your own."

"Wow, okay. Mama told you all that, huh?"

"Yeah. While we made dough for the pot pies they're serving tonight." She shrugged. "Well, she made the dough. I made a mess."

He chuckled. "Been there and done that."

Silence fell as they sat there holding hands, both of them looking down at the way their fingers were intertwined.

"I don't like feeling jealous," she said suddenly. And then a little louder, "But I'm going to ask who she was and what she was doing here so early in the morning. You can tell me it's none of my business. That since this thing between us is only temporary. You don't have to explain yourself to me. And that'll probably be true. But I'll regret it later if I don't ask the question." She sighed heavily. "So, who was she and what was she doing here so early in the morning?"

Still reeling from the admission that she was jealous and the reminder of the temporary status of their relationship, Ryan wondered how best to reply. There was no doubt he wanted to tell her everything about the Kerry situation if for no other reason than to assure her that her feelings of uneasiness were totally unwarranted. But he'd be lying if he said the situation wasn't still a sore spot for him.

"Kerry is my ex," he said and huffed out a breath. "We dated for a total of three-and-a-half years. I thought we were going to get married, but she took a job in the city and moved away." That was it. He let the words linger in the air, wondering if Allie would let it rest at that or push further. It occurred to him in that second that he hadn't completely answered her question and that's what she was waiting for.

"I never asked what company she was going to work for in the city because I didn't care. All I knew was that she was destroying all the plans we'd made to fulfill a dream I hadn't even known she'd had."

That had been part of the kicker during their breakup. If Kerry had once told him she wanted to move to the city to work, Ryan knew he would've addressed their relationship differently. Just as he was being forced to address what was happening between him and Allie differently.

A big part of him urged to just be happy with what he could get for the time he could have it. While another—growing—part of him was starting to wonder if that was such a smart idea, considering how much he was starting to like her. What he knew for certain was that no matter how much he'd cared for Kerry, he'd never asked her to stay just because of him. And he wouldn't ask that of Allie, either. He couldn't.

"I need an investor to build the plant and warehouse for the sauces and then to start distribution. Kerry's here to make the final decision on the deal."

Allie nodded. "She's the associate," she said, using

the title that he'd assumed she was when she'd arrived on the island. "But isn't the fact that she was involved with you and once lived on the island a huge conflict of interest?"

"Yes," he said and sighed. "And I don't know how that works. I wonder if I should reach out to Phoebe, the executive I've been dealing with all this time, to ask about that." He dragged his free hand down his face and gave her a wry smile. "What I do know is that now I wish my original assumption had been correct and that you were the associate who'd come to decide my future." Those last words lingered in the air while he was afraid to decipher them, and for an instant Allie looked like she didn't even want to hear them.

"If it were me," she replied, her lips spreading into a wide grin, "you would've had me at the Sweet Maple Glory sauce."

They both laughed then, and Ryan felt better. He felt a lot better just sitting here and laughing with her. No, he didn't feel amazing or even like going to the restaurant now. But he also didn't feel irritated all over again the way he'd felt when Kerry had been there.

Now, with Allie sitting beside him, her hand in his, her smile and laughter just for him, he felt lighter. His mood marginally easing. Later he'd analyze why it was her who'd been able to make him feel this way and what he was going to do about that. But for now, he sat back on the couch, patted his thigh until Optimus jumped up onto his lap, and continued to marvel at this moment.

The moment that resembled his thoughts from earlier, of Allie in his house and as part of his family.

• • •

"I did get that text," Ryan said after they'd been sitting on his couch in silence for what felt like eons.

There was a comfort to them sitting there, a weird sensation of normal as she crossed her legs at the ankle and relaxed against the back of the cushiony couch. This room was nice and cozy. Think planked wood floors and chunky furniture that made her envision a cabin in the wilderness, one owned by a man, of course. The heavy furniture, dark browns, and earth tones throughout the space felt masculine. But the huge fireplace across the room with its stone ledge bench in front added a warm touch that brought to mind chilly winter nights and a crackling blaze.

With Optimus curled up between them now, she could also imagine them sitting like this in the evenings after dinner. Sharing details from their day, discussing what would happen in their future. The thoughts had quickened her breathing, and when he spoke, his words only added to the building anxiety.

"Uh, you did?" She realized she'd actually forgotten about it for a minute, but the text messages had been the sole reason she'd come over here to see him this morning.

Even though he'd been on her mind all through the night, she hadn't planned to purposely see him so soon. Certainly, they would see each other at the game night later, but they'd be at the restaurant, which was bound to be full of people. There'd been no need to feel any discomfort at their first conversation after the kiss. Now, circumstances had changed, and she found herself juggling multiple feelings surrounding this one man.

"Yeah," he replied. "I got it just before Kerry arrived, so I didn't have much time to digest it." Then he reached into his pocket and pulled out his phone.

She watched his fingers move over the phone's screen as he retrieved the message. When he read it aloud, her skin tingled like it often did when she was embarrassed or nervous. She rubbed her palms up and down her thighs.

"I take it you're a Sagittarius," he said when he finished reading. "When you asked my birthday the other day, it hadn't occurred to me to ask yours."

"Because you weren't doing Astro cartography, looking at cardinal houses, the moon's nodes, or whatever else," she teased.

"No," he said with a wry chuckle. "I wasn't. And I'm a little shocked you even know those terms."

She didn't, not really. Being surrounded by all the things astrological on this island, she'd reluctantly added it into her research. If she was going to tell the story of this eccentric matchmaker, then she had to have some background. If a tiny part of her found the intricate studies of astrology interesting, she wasn't owning up to it, especially not right now.

"I did some research," she admitted.

Optimus shifted his head so that it was tucked more firmly under her arm, and she glanced down to his adorable face. She could so get used to seeing this little guy every day.

"For your story." It was a statement and not a question, and Allie slowly lifted her gaze to his.

There was no way she was going to lie to him, not

after their kiss and certainly not after his mother had so blatantly suggested a date for the two of them.

"Yes," she said and nodded just in case he didn't hear how softly she'd spoken the one word. "Remember I told you I was a travel blogger and that I'm writing a story about the island? Well, my plan is for the Crescent Matchmaker to be a big part of that story."

It was the first time she'd said it out loud to anybody. Not even Renee knew the angle Allie planned to add. Her boss had been so taken with the quaint beauty of the island as it appeared on the website Allie had given her in the email proposal that she'd instantly launched into that "find the heart of the story" dialogue that still baffled Allie.

Ryan stared at her with more curiosity than she'd ever seen him toss her way before. She knew he wanted to know all the things about her, and she had, in fact, told him much more than she'd intended to. But her job hadn't been a topic that he'd circled back to often. Well, until last night when she'd let slip that she'd once fancied herself a fiction writer.

He stared down at his phone now, either re-reading that text again or wondering what to say to her next. She could fix that.

"I don't believe in it, you know. All this matchmaking stuff." She shrugged even though he wasn't looking at her. "It's just a sham to get tourists on the island. There's no way this person can know all these things about someone they've never met. Or predict who that person will fall in love with. It just doesn't make sense."

"So it can't possibly be true that two people could

meet on an island and fall in love?" he asked.

There was a tone to his question, a touch of wonder mixed with a heavy dose of offense. He'd told her he wasn't into all that astrology stuff so she wasn't sure where either of those reactions was coming from.

"Listen, I watch and read a ton of romcoms," she began. "In fact, they're my favorite type of movie. So I know all about the meet cute, the conflict, black moment, and eventual happy-ever-after of a love story. There are some I've really enjoyed and others I've had a few questions for, so don't get me wrong, I do believe in people falling in love."

"You just don't believe in *you* falling in love?"

Okay, now this conversation was shifting in a direction she did not want to venture into. She extended a hand to pet Optimus on the head because she needed something else to do, something to re-focus her mind so she wouldn't be tempted to tell Ryan why she didn't believe in love for herself. It didn't matter to their situation anyway, since this was just a vacation fling.

"Again, it's not that I don't believe in a couple finding their happy. I just don't believe there's one person who can predict that happy for them. Finding love is more about fate and circumstances that uniquely align."

"Like the stars?" he asked and began petting Optimus as well. Of course, he kept his hand at the opposite end of the dog's body, but Optimus didn't care. He made a guttural sound of pure bliss as he rolled over onto his stomach, a move meant to encourage the humans to continue with the delightful contact.

Allie sighed. "I don't believe the stars were aligned when we sat on that bench last night," she said evenly. "What I do believe is that this matchmaker person was at the carnival, walking around and spying on people so they could get this text out this morning."

"And specifically send this text to us? Because they saw us and think we're the next Crescent Island match to be made."

"See! Even hearing you say it sounds incredulous, right? Like it's something out of a book."

"But you love romance books."

Again with the calm statements that twisted her words. Or did they? Well, they certainly made her uncomfortable. The reason why, she didn't want to deal with right now.

"I've got a few ideas about who I think it is, and I'm going to follow up today," she announced and got to her feet. "You don't have to help me if you don't want to. I totally understand if you feel conflicted, since you live here, but I need to know."

"So you can tell everyone this matchmaker is a fake?" He didn't wait for her response but stood so they were now facing each other. "Is there really something so wrong with wanting people to be happy in love? Because the couples I've met that have fallen in love here, this was the best thing to ever happen to them. They're elated."

"It's not real," she replied quietly. "Loving someone so completely and having them love you back, it's not real. It only happens in books. Look at what you went through with Kerry. You loved her and thought the two of you were going to share a future

together, but then she had other plans." Allie lifted
her arms and let them drop to her side, exasperation
sifting through her.

She saw the moment her words changed Ryan's
whole demeanor. The straightening of his shoulders,
the slight widening of his eyes.

"I'm sorry," she added immediately. "I didn't
mean to push that button. I just don't believe the
things you do."

He gave a curt nod. "Understood. And you don't
want anyone else to believe either. Is that right?"

"People can do what they want, but they should at
least know the truth," she said. A big part of the way
she'd always written her stories centered around being honest with people, giving them all the
information—good or bad—and letting them decide
what to do with it. Softening this story didn't mean
keeping out any truths, to her way of thinking.
Obviously, Ryan didn't know that part of her assignment, but she hoped he could understand where she
was coming from anyway.

"This is a phenomenal marketing plan to boost
tourism on the island," she continued, being sure to
keep her tone light. "And hey, maybe you should
think about advertising your new sauces on the blog.
It's getting millions of views per day and has a huge
subscription following. Surely, it could help boost
sales for Parker Sauces as well."

It occurred to her then that she could probably do
some type of story on the restaurant and the signature sauces, too. In the past year she'd received a few
offers from brands looking for influencers to represent their products. She hadn't really considered

herself an influencer, wanting instead to focus on her writing, but she definitely wouldn't have a problem getting behind the Parker products.

"I'd have to land that investment deal first," he replied with a sigh. "Which reminds me, I need to get to the restaurant. Kerry's coming by later to do some taste testing and talk to some of the customers."

"She won't be disappointed," Allie replied, more relieved than she'd imagined she could be that they'd shifted their conversation from the matchmaker.

Not that it meant she wasn't going to continue with her job, just that she wasn't going to talk to Ryan about it anymore since he apparently had different feelings about it than she did.

"If it'll make you feel better, I'll see what I can do about stopping the text messages," he said.

"What? How can you do that? Do you know who's sending them?"

He shook his head. "No. But one of my closest friends is the sheriff, and he can probably go over to Tiberius and do some digging to see where they're originating from. Just enough to issue a cease and desist where you and I are concerned. Because Allie, despite my failure at love and whatever hang-up you have against it personally appearing in your life, people deserve whatever happiness they can find. Even if it comes from someone who charts birth dates and moon signs."

He was speaking in that same tone he'd used when he'd been trying to convince her to take a chance and walk over that log at The Springs. And looking at her earnestly, like maybe his words had some other meaning. She wanted to question him, but she'd just told herself not to continue the match-maker conversation with him.

Apparently, Optimus agreed the conversation was over as he jumped off the couch and bolted for the door. Allie grinned. "I guess he's ready for me to leave, too."

She walked to the door without responding to Ryan's last comments. She didn't know what to say—rebut or admit to the biggest fear she'd ever had in her life—so she chose to move on instead.

"Hey, boy. You wanna hang out with me today?" The offer came spontaneously as she made her way to the door and looked down at the exuberant pup. "You should focus on impressing Kerry," she said when Ryan came closer and she stared up at him. "I can take Optimus around town with me and bring him to the restaurant when I come over for game night."

The slow smile that spread on Ryan's face was the first genuine one she'd seen since she'd arrived, and she liked it. She liked it a whole lot.

"Then I guess I'll see the two of you later," he said and reached out to toy with her earring.

It was a simple touch, one that didn't have any meaning besides maybe he liked silver hoop earrings. Yet it sent a trickle of warmth down Allie's spine and incited a buzz of energy that was both foreign and invigorating. It wasn't until she and Optimus were back at the Big House, sitting on the front steps waiting for Eddie to pick them up, that she recalled some of the words from that text.

Only time will tell how this will end, but there's a vibrant energy in the salty sea air and good news is on the horizon.

CHAPTER FIFTEEN

Surgery wasn't an option.

Sofia didn't care what Dr. Johansen, the orthopedic specialist Doc Hines had referred her to, had to say. He was a surgeon, after all, one who obviously wasn't opposed to working on Saturdays. What was he expected to say? With all those degrees hanging in perfect symmetry on the wall in his office, and the accolades ranging from plaques, trophies, and other crystal statue thingies she'd seen lined up like soldiers on the black lacquer file cabinets, he was a very decorated one. And with all those decorations most likely came a huge paycheck. One he'd no doubt want to keep rolling in, especially since he'd had his Mercedes SUV brought over on the *Lucky Seven* last month when he arrived.

Not that any of that mattered, because she still wasn't having surgery.

Trevor had gone through three surgeries after his accident, and he'd never played football again. Not only that, he'd never been the same, not mentally or physically. If she had this surgery, would she ever run again? The same question could be asked if she *didn't* have the surgery, but she refused to think of it that way. Her body had always healed—it wouldn't let her down this time. No matter what Dr. Degrees and Fancy Car said.

"Hey, Sofia, honey! You need a ride?"

She'd just stepped up on the curb and spun

around cautiously so as not to topple over to see Ivy Lawson bringing her delivery truck to a stop in the middle of the street.

"Hey, Ivy," Sofia said and gave a wave. "No. I need the fresh air and exercise."

Ivy and her mother, Ellen, ran the Flowers 'R Us florist. Sofia and Ivy had gone to school together and had been pretty close until Sofia went away to college. Ivy had married her high school sweetheart Delvin the week before Sofia left for New York, and the two now had three beautiful children and a pet pig named Cleveland.

"You're gonna walk all the way back to the restaurant? That's over twenty miles," Ivy said, her pert little nose crinkling.

She wore sunglasses so Sofia couldn't see her eyes, but she knew they were scrutinizing her.

"Not all the way. I'll call Ryan or somebody for a ride in a bit. I just felt like walking for a while." Actually, she felt like running. The urge had been beating at the back of her skull like a drum, the tension and stress in her mind and body since the accident steadily building until she wanted to scream out in rage.

"I have a delivery at the restaurant, though. Your grandmother ordered dozens of daisies in small arrangements for the tables tonight," Ivy continued and pointed a thumb toward the back of her truck.

"Nobody's gonna be looking at the flowers when there's good food and Uno tournaments happening on the premises," Sofia said.

Ivy chuckled. "You're right about that. My mom says she's looking for Ms. Margie, who she's certain cheated in their last game."

Sofia shook her head. "Ms. Margie's never gonna admit to cheating, and besides that, she's gonna park herself at that Diamonds' table and hide behind the rest of the women of that little clique to refuse a re-match."

"Yeah, you're probably right. I should warn Mom now." A truck circled around Ivy, beeping its horn as it did. Ivy gave the driver her middle finger and shouted, "Tourist!"

"Um, our economy sort of likes tourists," Sofia said but grinned at the glimpse of the feisty Ivy she'd known in high school. It had been hard to see that girl in the woman who was now a mother, wife, and business owner.

Turning her attention back to Sofia, Ivy shook her head. "Not the rude ones," she said. "We don't go speeding around the streets at ten in the morning here on Crescent."

"No. We much prefer limping down the street on an endless trek at a pace slow enough that the Crawley twins passed me on their bike ride around the Circle."

"Well, don't be so down on yourself. It's a big cir-cle."

"They passed me six times already," Sofia said drily. She'd been walking since she'd left the medical center just up the road, and she did need to take a seat for a while, but she wasn't getting inside Ivy's truck. The mood she was in wasn't conducive to see-ing pictures of the kids on Ivy's phone, hearing about whatever sweet thing Delvin had done for her, or inhaling the sickeningly sweet scent of a bunch of flowers.

"That's why you should hop on in here with me. Besides, the humidity's already starting to rise. You're gonna be sweating and cranky in a few."

She was already cranky, but Sofia didn't say that.

"I'll just keep going for a little while longer, and then I'll call Ryan to pick me up."

Ivy finally gave up and with a shrug said her good-byes before pulling away. Sofia let out a huge sigh of relief before she started to walk again.

A few minutes later, she spotted a bench. Speeding up her walk at the thought of getting a little rest, she made it to the bench just in time to hear a scream. This time when she spun around, it wasn't with as much care because she'd thought someone was in danger. Her good leg bumped against the bench, forcing her down onto it with a thump just seconds before a blur of gray and black came barreling her way.

Before she could mimic the scream she'd just heard, that blur of gray and black was jumping onto her lap, dropping yellow and violet pansies and a mountain of dirt onto her shirt and jeans.

"Oh no! Oh no! Optimus!" a familiar voice yelled.

Sofia blinked and looked from the dog now, pressing his big goofy paws on her chest and sniffing her chin, to Allie running with the leash in one hand and a small bright orange bag of dog poo in the other.

"He got away from me," Allie said, coming to a stop at the bench. "I was cleaning up after him and he just took off."

She was out of breath, the blush-colored tunic she wore over the crop top and shorts flying behind her like a cape.

"And now somebody's gonna have to clean me up," Sofia said drily. "Get off me, you little pain in the butt." She pushed Optimus away, but without picking the pooch up and tossing him over her shoulder, he just leaned to one side and stuck his face into her crossbody purse instead.

"He's a runner," Allie admitted. "Especially after he's done something he knows he's not supposed to do. Little rascal."

She couldn't resist, she scrubbed her fingers over the top of his head and watched as he stared up at her lovingly. "You know exactly what you're doing, too," she told him and rolled her eyes.

"He's giving me a heart attack. That's what he's been doing all morning." Allie dropped down onto the bench beside Sofia. "And that's all I need is to kill this guy's dog."

There was something odd about the way she'd just said that, but there was also something stinky about the bag she'd just set on the bench between them.

"Ew, no, put that over there," she said, pointing to the other side of the bench.

Allie looked up at her and then down to the bag. "Right." She picked it up and set it on the ground beside the bench. "Don't let me forget that. I don't want to get some type of fine for not cleaning up after this dog."

"Is that what they do in Miami? Fine you if you leave the dog poo on the sidewalk?"

"Absolutely," she said. "I've seen the signs warning of just that thing in dog parks and around some neighborhoods. My condo building allows pets, so there's signs in the building, and it's outlined in our HOA agreement."

"Wow, that's pretty serious," Sofia said. "I guess that just doesn't happen here as much so we don't have to resort to signs. It's like a known fact, your dog, your clean-up." She shrugged. "But what do I know? I don't own a dog."

"No. This little guy is all Ryan's. And I can't wait to deliver him to his owner tonight."

There it was again, just a little difference in her tone as she spoke about, damn, about her brother. All the pain and stress Sofia had been under didn't make her oblivious to how chummy Ryan and Allie had become. Trevor bringing up the same topic last night when he'd come home from the restaurant and she'd been in the kitchen inhaling mint chocolate chip ice cream had also come to mind. Her comment to her older brother then had been that she'd roped Ryan into showing Allie around town, but Trevor thought there was more going on than just a chaperone service. Now, Sofia wondered the same.

"So what're you doing, dog-sitting?" she asked since that certainly wasn't part of the deal she'd suggested.

"Yep! Ryan needed to focus on some stuff at the restaurant today. The associate is here, so he has to impress her." Allie looked across the street. "He has to impress his ex-girlfriend."

And there it was for a third time. That little change in Allie's voice. The one that hinted at something out of the ordinary for her.

"Whoa, wait, what did you just say?" Because along with the out-of-the-ordinary summation, Allie's last comment was filled with speculation and irritation. Of which Sofia had an abundance as well.

"Oh." Allie looked over at her, regret clear in the way her forehead scrunched. "I don't know if that was something I was supposed to say or not."

Nice try, but Sofia certainly wasn't letting her off that easily.

"If it pertains to my brother and the ex I think you're referring to, you definitely need to say something." Sofia prayed it wasn't *that* ex, but Ryan didn't have that many. Unlike Brody, he wasn't collecting ex-girlfriends like stamps or baseball cards. And this one had done a real number on Ryan. If she was back in Crescent for whatever reason, it wasn't going to be good.

Allie sighed. "Okay, I guess you'll find out as soon as you get to the restaurant anyway, so." She pushed the sunglasses she wore up until they settled inside the nest of curls on top of her head. "Remember when I first got here and Ryan said he thought I was the associate? Well, of course, that wasn't me. And at first, I didn't know who or what an associate was and I didn't think to ask. I mean, I guess I figured it was his business. And I was here to carry out my business."

She paused briefly, took a breath, and continued. "But today I saw this woman leaving his house. And her pantsuit was so pretty. I should've known it was expensive. I mean, if she's some bigtime associate at an investment firm, then of course she'd wear great clothes. But anyway, Ryan was pretty pissed that she turned out to be the associate and now holds the key to him expanding the family business. Which I didn't even know he wanted to do, but it's a great idea."

Because her head was whirling by now—a mixture of the headache that had been brewing since she'd left Johansen's office and the anxiety stoked by the possibility that her brother was about to go through some emotional warfare—she reached out a hand to touch Allie's shoulder. Then she shook it hard enough for Allie to stop talking and look at her.

"What?" Allie asked. "Oh. Was I babbling?"

Sofia nodded and pinched her thumb and pointer finger together to symbolize her next words. "A little bit."

"Sorry."

Allie only babbled when she was unsure about something and that something she was unsure about was a big deal. Now, Sofia's curiosity was definitely piqued.

"What's the associate's name?"

"Kerry Lennon."

Sofia sighed heavily. "That bitch."

"Whoa," Allie said.

"Well, that's what she is," Sofia replied. "She broke Ryan's heart, then trampled on it as she packed up and left town."

"So, he really loved her, huh?"

"He was thinking about marrying her." Which was something her brother hadn't told anyone else in their family. "She's working for Brownstone, and she's here to decide whether he gets the funding or not?"

"Yup, that's the deal."

Now they both sat back and sighed.

"Do you like Ryan?" Sofia asked, because that

seemed like the obvious next question. After all, there was nothing she could do about Kerry's job or the role it was now playing in Ryan's life. That was some pretty terrible karma, and she hated that Ryan had to go through it, but she'd stand by him as she always did. Just as soon as she got back to the restaurant.

But right now, there was something else going on here.

"Of course I like Ryan. I like all of your brothers and your parents and your grandmother."

Silence.

Which seemed like the better option, considering she knew Allie was smart enough to know that's not what Sofia meant by that question. But what Allie said next did shock the piercing pain out of Sofia's temples.

"Are you the Crescent Matchmaker?"

If the words hadn't halted the headache, the quick way she'd turned her neck to stare at her friend probably would have. Or increased it until she yelled out in agony. "What?"

Allie stared back. "You heard me. Are you the one writing that blog, claiming to be a matchmaker so you can get people to come to the island?"

Sofia blinked and tried to wrap her mind around how this conversation had gone quickly from the rowdy dog who'd dropped dirt and flowers in her lap to her playing matchmaker for what? Profit?

"First, you're the writer, not me. I know you recall how much I hated my English courses in college. Why would I ever take on a task like writing a blog?"

Allie's lips twisted as if she were considering

Sofia's response.

"Second, I crunch numbers for a living. But I'm not the one responsible for Crescent Island's fiscal status. And I'd never want to be." She rolled her eyes to signify that fact. "And finally, the only person I've been trying to get to come to Crescent is you."

Allie narrowed her gaze. "Why?"

"Uh, because you're my best friend."

"And not because you wanted to set me up with your brother?"

"If I wanted to set you up with Ryan, I would've just said, *Hey, Allie, I want to hook you up with my brother*." Sofia shrugged and blinked at Allie, waiting for her friend to get a clue. This line of questioning was strange but sort of confirmed what she was beginning to suspect.

Allie huffed. "But you have my cell number. You know my birthday, so you'd obviously know my zodiac sign. The person sending these text messages knows all of that. And they know that I was sitting on this very bench with Ryan last night."

"Huh," Sofia said and then stared across the street in the same direction Allie was.

They were sitting right across from the City Hall building, with its big gold star at the top like it was a Christmas tree instead of a municipal building.

"So this matchmaker has set her sights on you and Ryan?" Sofia asked.

"I guess," Allie said. "But that's just so ridiculous. I mean, why would anyone even think—"

Sofia held up a hand. "Stop. I was just thinking the same thing."

"What? But why? I've only been here a week, and

the time Ryan and I have spent together has been at your directive. Nothing personal or our idea, I mean at least not until…"

Sofia glanced over at her. "Oh no, don't you clam up now. Spill it."

Letting her head loll back, Allie groaned. "Okay. We kissed, and we're going on a date tomorrow. But it's not a big deal. It's just a date and one kiss, and then I'll be gone."

There were so many things Sofia could say at this moment.

For one, she loved Allie like she was a sister, and if there was anyone she'd want to see Ryan with, it would be her. They were like-minded, focused, tenacious, talented, and smart. But what she definitely did not want was for her brother to have to mourn the loss of another woman going off to the city. That's the only reason she gave Allie this warning: "Don't hurt him."

Allie looked over at her and nodded. "I'd never do that. It's why I'm being so up front with him about what this is and what it's definitely not."

"But the way you sat down talking about Kerry seemed like you might be a little threatened that his ex is in town."

"You didn't see that pantsuit," Allie said and huffed again.

Sofia grinned. "But he kissed *you* last night, and today you're picking up his dog's poo."

Allie chuckled. "That might be the most unromantic thing I've ever heard," she said. "You're such a goof. And I don't know what I'd do without you."

When Allie reached out to take her hand, Sofia

intwined her fingers with hers. "Ditto," she said.

She didn't know what she'd do without her best friend, especially now that she was facing the possibility of never being able to fulfill her own dreams.

. . .

Clipboard in hand, one hour before the game night was set to begin, Ryan walked out the back door of the restaurant and down the stone pathway to the row of charcoal smokers his father had been using since before Ryan was born. Across from the smokers was a table with benches and coolers stacked in threes. On the table were aluminum pans, meat hooks and claws, mops, bags of hickory, apple, and mesquite wood chips, some of the things needed to create the most tender, mouthwatering chicken, beef, and pork in the country. It was what they were known for, after all, what his father, grandfather, and great-grandfather had won numerous awards for.

If he was still raw from the fact that his goal of bringing yet another reputable title to the Parker BBQ franchise was on the line, he was trying valiantly to push that aside. Had been doing so all day.

"Hey, son," Vernon called to him as he came closer to the table.

"Hey, Dad. Just doing a last check for the night." Game Night would begin at seven thirty and run until the restaurant closed at ten. But the smokers would be on until eight forty-five, giving them the last hour and a half of the night to cool down before everyone left.

Vernon nodded, sweat beading over his brow and

bald head. He wore a red T-shirt today with some slogan from one of the sci-fi movies he loved so much. Ryan had never been a movie buff—a thought that had him thinking of Allie again. She'd said she loved romcoms. He wondered which ones. Not that he wanted to watch them, though. He shook his head to clear the thought.

"We're looking good. This last round of briskets is about to come out. Pork butts will follow in the next half hour. Just put those chickens in a little while ago, so they've got about another forty-five minutes."

Vernon used a towel to wipe his head.

"What's the count on each?" Ryan asked, looking down at his inventory sheet. He'd checked with his mother and Nana, and they were good on all the usual sides. Plus, they'd made those pot pies—chicken and turkey—that smelled so delicious Ryan had been tempted to confiscate one and go hide in his office.

He'd spent the first two hours of his morning at the restaurant in his office poring over his proposal. There wasn't a word or number he hadn't memorized, and he'd waited all day for Kerry to show up to start her evaluation, but he hadn't seen or heard from her yet. And he didn't want to be closed up in the office when she did appear.

"Twenty birds," Vernon said. "Eight briskets and butts. We're good, son."

They also had hot wings, smoked sausage, a small vegan menu, and a host of salad variations. All items that he'd checked on while he was in the kitchen.

"I just don't want to run out," he replied.

"We never run out."

"Tonight's gonna be a bigger crowd. And people

will want to keep eating as long as they're here playing."

"Yup," Vernon added. "Business is gonna be good."

Ryan nodded. He needed business to be *great* and for Kerry to see that. Of course, she already knew how their food tasted, save for a couple of the newer sauces, but Ryan still felt like he had to convince her to believe in the product and their ability to sell nationwide, or she'd never advise Phoebe to invest.

Vernon clapped a beefy hand on Ryan's shoulder. "You all right, son?"

Ryan startled at the touch and the question. "I'm fine," he snapped and turned away from his father.

He walked over to the smokers himself, then circled back to the table and set his clipboard down to put on the oven gloves.

"So you don't believe your old man now? Is that it?"

Ryan clapped his hands together. "I just want to see for myself."

Vernon didn't say another word, and Ryan continued, counting, coughing as a cloud of succulent-smelling smoke blasted his face, and then going back to the table to write down the numbers. As he was removing the gloves, he heard the crack and hiss of a can being opened and glanced up to see his father taking a drag from a beer.

"Drinking on the job?"

A wry chuckle sounded. "Been taking in a beer every night while I run these smokers since I was fifteen years old."

"Papa Teddy let you drink at fifteen?"

"He didn't know back then, at least I don't think he did. But that was probably just my teenage ego talkin'. Parents always know what their children are doing or feeling."

Vernon let the last word linger, and Ryan dropped the pen onto the clipboard. He turned away from his father and clasped his hands behind the back of his head.

"You can talk about it or brood about it. One's liable to get you some progress, the other's probably gonna lead to a headache or, worse, an ulcer." Vernon paused and Ryan heard shuffling behind him. "Take a seat," his father said.

Ryan turned slowly to see his father had already done so, sitting on the opposite side of the bench from where Ryan stood. He took a seat, placing his elbows on the table and dropping his head.

"That bad, huh?"

"I don't want to hear 'I told you so,'" Ryan said. If he did, he'd definitely lose it, right here and right now.

"Wanna give me more credit than that?"

Ryan looked up at his father. "Seriously? You've been against this idea of me selling the sauces ever since I first mentioned it."

Nodding slowly, Vernon propped his elbows on the table, too. The two Parker men mimicked each other's position while their minds were probably worlds apart.

"Tell me what's going on," his father said.

Ryan scrubbed his eyes. "Kerry's back. And she's the one who makes the final decision for the investors."

Vernon let out a low whistle. "Now, that's a tough

pill to swallow."

Everyone in his family knew just how hard it had been for him when Kerry left and they'd supported him in any way that they could. Nana had even offered to join Sofia on a trip to kick Kerry's butt if that would make Ryan feel better. Obviously, that wasn't going to help, but the measures to which his family had gone and were willing to go to stand up for him and be there for him had touched his heart.

Now, tonight, after the day Ryan just experienced, he really needed his father to be on his side again. Arguing with Vernon about this business deal wasn't going to make Ryan feel any better. In fact, he feared that just might make things worse.

"Let me ask you this," Vernon began. "If she wasn't here to interrupt your business plan, how would you feel about seeing her again?"

Smoke filled the humid air as the sun began to set. Across the yard, on the stoned platform they'd had built twenty years ago, every table was full of guests. The low hum of their chatter as well as the music coming from inside the restaurant mingled with the sound of the surf rolling in.

"I'm not in love with her anymore, if that's what you're asking me." He'd stopped loving Kerry, or the idea of loving Kerry, a long time ago.

"I asked how you felt about seeing her again," Vernon re-stated.

"I never wanted to see her again," Ryan replied. "I never thought I'd see her again. And now that she's here to decide my business fate, I just wish she'd stayed gone."

"That's fair," his father told him. "There's no rule

stating we have to like the people who hurt us."

"I'm not worried about that, Dad. I'm worried about her not approving this deal."

"Okay, that's also fair. But think about this: if she doesn't approve the deal, is it still a good deal?"

Ryan held his father's gaze for endless seconds. "Yeah," he said and nodded. "It is."

"Then that's that." Vernon stood and moved back to the smokers. "With or without her, you've still got an idea and a good plan. All you've lost is some time."

"Time I don't have thanks to your deadline," he said, still incredulous at his father's reaction.

He'd expected the "I told you so" he'd warned his father not to give. Perhaps more telling him to be grateful for what he had, something he'd been saying to Ryan for a few years. But this cool nonchalance about the situation was a little odd.

"Special circumstances," Vernon said. "That's what we'll call it. If Kerry hasn't developed some good sense in the time she's been away from this island, then you'll move on without her. Parkers don't quit, son. We rise."

CHAPTER SIXTEEN

Every table in the restaurant was filled. An old Earth, Wind, and Fire song played, and a handful of people danced in the far corner near the opening to the patio. They were older people enjoying the classic tune while two tables away, a younger cluster of folks giggled and commented about how outdated the song was and how the music of that generation compared to today's.

After enjoying her experience helping at the carnival, Allie had offered to assist the servers tonight since the restaurant was so crowded. It had come as a surprise how much she liked learning more about the business the Parkers had built. Tasting the items on the menu was also a perk, but watching the customers appreciate the food and being a part of the inner workings of the establishment had sparked a sense of reward in her. So much so that she'd found herself contemplating what else she could do to be a part of this historic legacy. Her earlier comment about featuring Ryan's sauces in a story came to mind.

But fleshing out the details for that would have to wait as she walked quickly past the table of older singers after delivering their desserts. Then she moved on to the table with the young gigglers to drop off a stack of napkins they would surely need since they'd ordered hot wings and cheese-covered french fries. On her way back to the window to see what other orders were ready, she was stopped by a hand to her arm.

"Slow down there, darlin'. You're goin' a mile a minute."

She turned back to see Mr. Cyrus's smiling face. "Oh, hi," she replied. "I'm sorry, did I miss your table? Did you need to order something?"

"He don't need a thing, Allison," Barney chimed in from the other side of the table. "Just wanted a reason to stop you and start gibbering. You know how he likes to hear himself talk."

"That's because I always have something to say, unlike some folk around here," Cyrus added. He'd released her arm but continued to smile at her.

"Well, you might as well talk. You've eaten up just about everything in the place tonight. Well, except for those milkshakes, on account of your lack of tolerance."

Cyrus shot an exasperated glare at Barney. "It's lactose intolerance, old man."

Barney shrugged. "Well now, that's your issue not mine." He chuckled as if his goal had been to get that point out about Cyrus. "You know they sell those pills you need to take before you eat anything you have a lack of tolerance for down at the Emporium."

Cyrus nodded. "Got a little bit of everything at the Emporium," he said, reminding Allie of her first encounter with these two back at the B&B.

"Did you need me to get you something else, Mr. Barney?" she asked because as much as she enjoyed these two, she couldn't stand at their table listening to their banter all night.

"Not a thing," he replied, sitting back in his chair and sticking a toothpick between his teeth. He wasn't picking his teeth, just twirling that toothpick around like she'd seen people do in the movies. "Had the ribs, collards, and cornbread, so I'm stuffed to the brim. Just gonna sit here and continue whuppin' old Cyrus's beehind in pinochle."

He slapped his hand down on the deck of cards between them, and Cyrus grumbled.

"This man's got his head up there with the stars just like ole Annabelle over there," Cyrus said.

Barney turned in his seat and glanced at the table across the room. "Oh, you mean Annabelle who's sitting next to Margie whose rear end you like to watch when she takes her morning walks by the B&B?"

Allie was certain that remark was meant to get a rise out of Cyrus, but the other older gentleman simply grinned and rubbed a hand down the back of his bald head. "Told you I know most things about most people on this island and one of those things is that Margie Kimpton is a good-looking woman."

When Allie's eyes widened in surprise, Cyrus winked at her.

Barney grumbled something incomprehensible and then said, "Shuffle the cards, old man."

Cyrus gave a deep belly laugh as he reached for the cards, and Allie said, "I'll leave you two alone. Let me know if you need something else from the kitchen."

When she moved away from them, she bumped right into Gwen, one of the other servers.

"Sorry, didn't see you," she mumbled.

Gwen shook her head and touched Allie's arm to steady her. "No worries. Girl, it is wild in here tonight."

They'd been introduced two hours ago, when Ms. Sarah had led Allie to the back to get an apron and order booklet. Both Gwen and Mikayla had been great and extremely patient with Allie, who'd never been a server in a restaurant before. In college, she'd worked at a bookstore, which never saw this much or this type of traffic.

"You're gonna be dead on your feet tomorrow," Gwen said as they both walked back toward the kitchen.

"I hope not," Allie replied, thinking about the date she and Ryan were scheduled to have.

The date that had been on her mind nonstop today. Well, in between the time she'd spent chasing after Optimus and talking to Sofia. That last part had also been a turning point in her day.

Not only had Allie not been expecting to see Sofia while she was in town this morning, but she certainly hadn't expected Sofia to ask the questions she did. Or to sort of give her approval of Allie dating Ryan, with the warning that she not hurt him.

Do you like Ryan? Sofia had asked.

What kind of question was that anyway? Probably a question that a sister would ask a woman whom she thought was interested in her brother. If Allie had a brother, she suspected she'd want to know a potential love interest's intentions toward him. Or was that just a position that brothers took about their sisters? Well, obviously that wasn't true. She gave herself a quick shake at the ridiculous thoughts.

Of course, a sibling had a right to be concerned about the other sibling. Especially when a woman her brother just met came to town and kissed him.

It'd been hours, coming up on twenty-four to be exact, since they'd shared that kiss, and Allie could admit she was looking forward to another one. Was that wanton? Was it being too eager for any type of affection? She'd always wondered if she'd ever reach that point. Because up until now, she hadn't. And yes, that was pretty pathetic for a woman her age. So much so, she pushed the thought to the back of her mind.

"You're doing great, though," Gwen said. "For someone who's never done this before."

They were close to the hostess stand now, both of them turning to face the liveliness of the full dining room. There had to be at least eighty people inside and another forty to fifty in the outside eating area. At each table there'd been a board game or some type of card game. The only electronic games were the ones that required batteries to operate. No computers, tablets, or other type of technology. It was an old-fashioned game night, as Vernon had described to her when she'd walked around the back of the restaurant earlier with Optimus in tow.

He'd helped her get the still boisterous after all day long of running around and getting into mischief dog into the pen and had put a small bowl with a few chunks of brisket in her hand. She'd eaten it standing up she'd been so hungry, and Vernon had chuckled. While their physical similarities weren't immediately noticeable, there were subtle things that Allie had picked up that Ryan and his father shared. The way their shoulders squared when they stood, the way their jaws tightened when they gave a command to Optimus. The slow lifting of the left side of their mouth as it broke into a smile.

A hand on her shoulder had her jumping right out of her thoughts once more.

"Sorry," Gwen said and let her hand slip away. "You looked like you were in another place there for a second. I was asking what you did for a living in your hometown."

Uncomfortable at being caught with her mind wandering, Allie shook her head and smoothed her hands down the front of her thighs. "Girl, I was caught up in this music and this entire scene. It's like something out of a movie I've watched."

"Yeah, it reminds me of get-togethers my family has had over the years. Especially in the summer when my mother and her sisters have their big cookouts. We have tables packed into the backyard. Speakers blaring this same music because the old heads love themselves some good '60s and '70s tunes. And we'd be going all night. Playing Spades or Tonk. I even remember me and my cousins sneaking sips of the beer that was plentiful in the big coolers."

Gwen chuckled, and Allie laughed along with her. Even though Allie had no memories like this. There'd never been any summer nights filled with family, food, and good times. That thought sparked a pang of loneliness even as she stood surrounded by so many people.

Her chest felt heavy with a nostalgia that she could only share via some movies she'd seen and that she was experiencing now only because of this story she'd decided to write.

"You don't like to talk about yourself, do you?"

Gwen was still pushing the conversation that Allie

seemed to drift in and out of. All day she'd been talking to people; even when Sofia had offered to come
along with her to visit the Sinclair sisters and Lindy
at the B&B again, there'd been conversations going
on. But she had to admit that tonight, she'd felt a little more contemplative.

"Well, I don't really get out to a lot of gatherings
like this," she admitted. "And my family isn't close."
The more times she'd said that while here on this island, the less polarizing it'd felt. Sure, she caught the
way people looked at her when she said it, a toss-up
between pity and confusion, like no one on this island could relate to not having a relationship with
anyone in their family. But admitting the dysfunction
she'd grown up around was oddly relieving.

Even the friendships here seemed so tight and
committed. She glanced across the room to the table
which Sofia had dubbed "the Diamonds' spot," where
Nana dropped by intermittently to sit with the three
older women, including Ms. Annabelle, throughout
the night.

"They look so close," she mumbled and was a bit
startled when Gwen commented.

"Oh yeah, the Diamonds. They've been around
forever, and that's not just a crack on their age." She
elbowed Allie playfully. "My mother said that Ms.
Shirleen and Ms. Annabelle have been friends since
they were little girls, and Ms. Margie and Ms. Reba
joined the group in their late teens."

"Really? That's a long-lasting friendship. And
they look so happy." They were all laughing now.
Nana stood at the end of the table, a glass of something Allie knew wasn't just lemonade in one hand.

She'd seen a bottle covered by a paper bag on the table and had watched a short while ago as each woman poured a little out of it into their glass. She only hoped whatever it was didn't have the women drunk in the next hour or so.

"They are. Have been thick as thieves forever, my mama said. But they do good around the island. You know Annabelle's relatives were the ones who found this place."

"Oh yeah, that's right." Allie had read about the Gibson family online even though she hadn't immediately connected Ms. Annabelle to them. Not until she'd met the woman face-to-face at the Emporium a few days ago.

She was just about to ask Gwen if she were related to any of the First Four when Brody came along and grabbed her by the waist. It was a quick-and-easy motion of him lacing his arm around her and pulling her into a dancing stance.

"C'mon, let's hit the dance floor," he said with his usual jovial tone.

Allie had laughed, dropping her hands on his shoulders and hurrying to step along with him so she wouldn't be dragged onto the so-called dance floor. "This isn't a dance party," she said but couldn't help the quick grin.

There was just something about Brody's friendly eyes and his upbeat personality that relaxed her. Even when he'd done his bout of Q&A with her the other day, she hadn't picked up on any tense vibes or dislike from him. Just an affable demeanor sewn into a guy with a great face.

"We make it what we want," he told her. "I know

the owners, and I'm sure they won't mind."

She laughed along with him again as he broke into a hand dance while a Donna Summers song started to play. Remembering the steps to this particular dance from something Bella had taught her, Allie easily slipped into the moves with him. Before she knew what was happening, Brody was holding her by one hand while she danced a little away from him, then pulled her back in close while they carried out the orchestrated steps together.

"Ah, shucks, city girl's got some moves," he said once when they were close again.

She only responded with more laughter as exhilaration soared through her along with the lyrics of the old song. A quick look around as she and Brody did the next moves showed that they'd actually made it to one of the bigger openings between the tables and were now the center of attention.

Brody apparently loved the attention, because he continued the dance, holding her hands in his as they both shuffled their feet, did the twists and turns, and returned to face each other with huge grins on their faces. When the song was finally over, they continued to hold hands, chuckling at the applause that exploded throughout the room.

"I think we might've just made this a dance party," Brody said when she started to walk back toward the hostess stand and he'd fallen into step beside her.

"You're a mess, Brody," she told him, still a little winded from the unexpected exertion. "I'm supposed to be working tonight."

"Me too!" He laughed some more. His smile so genuine it not only reached his eyes but seemed to extend to whoever was in his immediate vicinity. Which in the next moment was Kerry Lennon.

"Well, well, well, Brody Parker. I see you're still sweeping all the women off their feet," Kerry said.

Allie felt like the air had just been sucked from her lungs as she looked at the woman who tonight wore a very short yellow dress with thin straps at her shoulders. Her hair that had been left to hang long and free early this morning was now styled in loose bump curls that fell over her shoulders.

"Kerry Lennon," Brody said, sobering just a bit. "I heard you were back on the island."

Kerry raised a perfectly arched brow. "Don't sound so happy about the news."

"As I recall, you didn't have a very happy departure, so I don't know that you should've expected a welcome party," Brody replied in a tone that was shockingly different from what Allie had come to expect from him.

"Well, I don't know," Kerry said and lifted an arm to flourish out toward the tables. "Looks like a party to me."

"It's SummerFest," Allie blurted out, and Kerry's gaze landed on her.

Great, announcing the obvious to someone who'd been born on the island was the perfect way to enter this conversation. But it was clearly too late to take back.

Now that her attention was fully on Allie, Kerry tilted her head slightly. Her eyes were a lighter shade of brown, her makeup expertly applied. There was no doubt she was a pretty woman, but the jury was still out on her personality. So far, Allie had picked up on a haughty air, one that didn't quite fit with the people she'd met on the island so far.

"I know what SummerFest is and when it takes place on the island. But I'm assuming this might be new to you, Miss…"

Kerry let the word linger as her way of asking Allie's name, and Brody answered for her. "This is Allie Sparks. She's Sofia's best friend and a close friend of our family's."

He'd moved closer to her as he spoke. Not putting his hands on her again but filling the space near her in the same way that Optimus did when he was being protective.

"Oh, a close family friend. Well, I guess that explains why you were at Ryan's place this morning," Kerry said.

"I didn't know I needed to explain that," Allie replied and realized that this was turning into some weird sort of confrontation between her and a woman she didn't even know.

Honestly, it was enough to know Kerry had broken Ryan's heart to have her on Allie's list of skepticals. And the fact that she had a power that extended to Ryan and his family's business in her hands didn't help, either.

"You don't," Ryan said as he joined them.

His presence and the tight look on his face confirmed that this was a tense situation.

"Hello, Ryan. I was hoping we would get a chance to chat tonight. But since I've just arrived, I'd like to grab something to eat first. Is Mr. Vernon still making those overstuffed pulled pork sandwiches?" She rubbed a hand over her very flat stomach and closed her eyes momentarily. "I remember rushing over here each day after school to get one. Lunch in the cafeteria had nothing on a hot pulled pork sandwich with your daddy's house sauce slathered all over it."

"Then let's get you one," Brody said and stepped toward Kerry. "You can sit over here at the counter."

Kerry looked at Ryan, their gazes holding. "Thanks, Brody. So hospitable of you. Ryan, we'll chat before the night's over."

"Looking forward to it," Ryan said. "Enjoy your dinner."

A few uncomfortable moments passed as they stood there. Allie wondering if she should speak again or walk away and Ryan looking like he wanted to say something more to Kerry but was wisely holding his tongue. His stance was tense, his legs slightly parted, hands fisted at his sides.

He wore black slacks and a white button-front shirt with the sleeves rolled up to his elbows. A muscle twitched in his jaw, and he turned quickly to catch her staring at him.

"Let's get some air," he said tightly and then reached for her hand.

She followed him out, ignoring the eyes she could feel on them as they moved past the tables and out to the patio. It was a full house there, too, so Ryan guided them toward the end of the concrete area and over the pavers in the grass. They kept going until they were a distance from the restaurant, flanked in the evening and the waning glow from the string lights that ran along the railing of the patio space, then away from the restaurant altogether. They didn't stop until they came to a line of trees and a cluster of huge rocks tucked into an alcove.

He led her over to one of the largest rocks and released her hand. There was enough space for a booty to sit even though upon first glance she'd doubted that. Ryan sat on the other side and leaned forward to rest his elbows on his knees.

"I hope she doesn't make this harder than it needs to be on purpose," he said after a few more moments of silence. "All her life Kerry's gotten her way, except for when I didn't go to the city with her."

"Don't let her," Allie replied.

"That's easier said than done." He shook his head and stared toward the trees.

She suspected that statement was accurate. Having never been in love before, she had no idea how it felt to lose that love but assumed it was a painful ordeal. It occurred to her that maybe this was just another reason why she'd never tried her hand at love. Another protective mechanism she'd put in place to keep the sting of disappointment and love-lessness her parents had cultivated from bleeding over into her adult life.

"Did you decide to contact the executive you were originally working with about Kerry's involve-ment? I know you mentioned it earlier today but wasn't sure if you'd acted on it." Thinking about it now, she was certain that should be an option he considered. If Kerry being back in town and involved in this deal was agitating him as much as it seemed, there was definite friction that could affect this deal. "I mean, it certainly feels like a big conflict to me."

He nodded. "I've been thinking about that, too. I'm almost positive she couldn't have told Phoebe about our past relationship. As obvious as it is for us to see the conflict, I'm sure Phoebe would've noted it right away, too."

"So you're going to call her?"

Now, he shrugged. "Her involvement now could also be seen as an advantage. Kerry knows this restaurant. She's been here countless times to eat, not to mention the times she'd been at the Big House for dinner. I know she's been away for a few years so she might still need to be convinced that we're doing as well as we were back then—even better, actually— but otherwise, this could be a slam dunk."

"But you don't really think it'll go that way, do you?"

"I can't tell. I mean, she wanted to clear the air as soon as she showed up at my place, and so far, I don't see that she has any plans to sabotage me. But then I haven't had a chance to sit and talk to her about her thoughts or motives."

She could understand what he was saying. It was definitely a precarious situation he was dealing with, one she hoped would have the resolution he wanted.

"Well, then let's just not talk about the situation when it's not absolutely necessary. It's really nice out here," she said.

Allie breathed in the air, picked up the hints of the salty scent she'd come to love and the smoky goodness she knew was within the walls of the restaurant.

"I was out here a little earlier when I brought Optimus back, but I didn't see this."

"You can't see it from the main pathway," he said, following her lead with the shift in topic. "Nana calls this the Parker courting rock."

"Oh." She couldn't hide the shock or the tiny trickle of awareness that laced her spine at his words.

He looked over his shoulder and grinned. "Yeah, that was my exact reaction when she told me that. I think I was maybe nine or ten."

"And she said the word courting to you?" Allie couldn't imagine her mother ever using that word to her or implying it in any way for that matter.

"Yeah, Nana's not one for mincing words."

"I can see that," Allie said.

"I didn't get a chance to ask you earlier. It got super busy around here the moment game night started. But how was your day with Optimus?" He sat back then, letting his hands fall into his lap as he gazed over at her.

"If I had to give it one word, I'd say adventurous," she replied and then grinned. "That dog sure does pull every bit of energy out of you."

Ryan nodded. "That he does. And imagine he's only three months old. I don't know what I'm going to do when he's full grown and getting into even more trouble."

"I know! But I bet he's going to be gorgeous. I looked up merle Great Danes online and fell right down a rabbit hole." She admitted. "They're a beautiful breed and so gentle. I guess Optimus will get to that part sooner or later."

"I sure do hope so," Ryan added. "Do you go online and look up everything?"

She shrugged. "I like research. Digging to find the answers, then ruminating on the answers I find."

"You always want the answers, huh?"

"How will you ever know anything if you don't look for the answers?"

"Ever thought of just experiencing things?"

And by "things" she was fairly positive Ryan wasn't talking about Great Danes anymore. Plus, he reached out and took her hand, rubbing his thumb along skin she'd never known was so sensitive as more of those interesting trickles eased up her arm.

"I experienced your dog ripping through a garden, eating one of my shoes when I thought he was sleeping in my room while I worked, and trying to eat the muffin tops I had stashed for later."

Ryan threw back his head and laughed. She could see all of his teeth and felt the booming laughter straight through to her soul. Her smile was huge, probably a million watts if she had a mirror to look just now. But it was also genuine. The happiness she felt in this moment was new, but awesome just the same. How could it be that she'd traveled so far and for so long, only to find this right here and right now?

"He really likes you," Ryan said when he'd finally gotten his guffaws under control.

"Well, he has a strange way of showing it," she said and glanced down at their intertwined hands.

Ryan's thumb was still moving over the back of her hand, as if he liked the feel of it as much as she did. He held her hand tightly, and she wondered if he thought she might run away if he let it go. She'd certainly thought that. If they released their hands, would this moment slip away? Would she have to go back into that restaurant and in another week, to her life, and leave this behind? That was a powerful thought, one that had something shifting deep inside her, but she didn't have time to examine it because Ryan was touching her again.

He turned his body slightly and, with his other hand, cupped the side of her neck, easing her face closer to his.

"I think I can do better at showing you how much I like you," he said, his voice soft as he lowered his mouth to hers.

A soft, feathery touch that seemed appropriate for the island life. A slow, casual beauty that snuck up and grabbed her with its potency. The gentle swipe of his tongue along her lips when he pulled back just a little. Enough to whisper, "I like you a lot."

She trembled. From the base of her neck down to her toes, her body reacted to those words as her mind fought to decipher, dissect, accept. His tongue moved over her lips again before slipping easily inside. She drank him in.

She lifted a hand to cup the back of his head, easing another around his waist to hold on to him tightly. He tilted his head, taking the kiss deeper, and she felt herself falling. Easing effortlessly into the sweetness that he so eagerly gave, sinking deeper like she'd done in the sand her first day on the island.

· · ·

"Don't you do it," Shirleen said as she came to stand behind Annabelle.

She'd watched as her longtime friend had gotten up from the table and made her way out to the patio, stopping to speak to people on her way, but with a definite destination in mind. Annabelle's steps had been sure, one of her hands tucked into the deep pockets of the baggy purple jumpsuit she wore.

Annabelle's footing was sure as she navigated the familiar pavers and when she veered off them just a few feet before her true destination appeared. Shirleen followed a safe distance behind, knowing instinctively what was going on and determined to stop it. Something they'd all contemplated doing before.

"I'm not doing anything," Annabelle replied when she spun around to face Shirleen.

"You can't lie worth a damn, Annabelle. Never could," Shirleen snapped.

Annabelle pursed her lips, the sparkly lilac-hued gloss she'd slathered on glittering in the moonlight. "I know millions of people who'd disagree with you."

Shirleen folded her arms over her ample breasts. "That's exactly why I followed you out here. To tell you not this one."

Her friend's eyes widened as she shook her head slowly. "Oh no, *we* don't choose. You know that, Shirleen. The stars have the last say."

Shirleen had subscribed to that notion for as long as it had provided a way for them to preserve what they each loved so dearly—Crescent Island.

Annabelle, on the other hand, had lived and breathed every ounce of the teachings her great-grandparents had passed down. She'd become the island's eccentric historian by the time she was seventeen and her parents had died in that horrific accident, leaving the entire Gibson legacy to her. Her penchant for the color purple—her truck, the majority of her clothes and makeup obviously, everything but the pale blue of the old Victorian where she and all the members of her family had lived for centuries—was another signature. And her mind was always fixated on love. Had been for a very long time despite the fact that she'd never married.

"I don't want you foolin' with my family," Shirleen continued. "There's over a hundred people in the restaurant tonight, and even more were at the carnival last night. The Chamber's done a ton of advertising for this and all the summer events in an effort to pull in as much money as possible."

Even though none of them really knew why. It had been Annabelle who'd found the old land deeds in the basement of her home, and when she had, she'd brought them directly to the Diamonds with shaking hands and fear in her voice.

"It's not my choice," Annabelle said. "You know that. I've showed you the charts before and you've always agreed."

"I've always agreed because it was never any of mine."

"Just because he's yours doesn't make it any less true."

"He's not ready for this, and neither is she," Shirleen protested. "I won't have you toying with them."

Annabelle narrowed her eyes and took a step toward Shirleen. "Now you take that back right this minute. You know I don't toy with anybody. Never have."

That was true, Annabelle believed wholeheartedly in what she was doing, which was why the idea to start that blog and use the matchmaking to lure singles to the island had been a good one, in the beginning. Not everybody had believed it would work. Reba had pushed back for weeks, saying it was a ridiculous scheme that they were all too old to pull off. And Margie had wanted to go to the mayor and the Island Council immediately. If ownership of Crescent Island was in danger of falling into the hands of the federal government of the United States, then the leadership of their small community had a right to know.

But the vote had been clear, the Diamonds, as a few of the oldest members of this town and their inexplicable ties to three of the First Four, had to do this for all that their ancestors had worked hard to create.

"I'm telling you to find someone else, Annabelle."

"And I'm telling you that's not how it works, Shirleen."

"If you cause my grandchild to be hurt…"

Her words trailed off, and Annabelle lifted her chin. "I didn't tell her to come here. She came because she likely saw my blog. She writes for one herself, you know."

Shirleen did know. She'd gone over to the library the morning after Allie had showed up in the restaurant smiling prettily at Ryan and eager to take care of Sofia. They'd never heard of this friend before, but that didn't mean she hadn't trusted Sofia's judgment. If that wasn't the case, she'd have squawked about Allie staying at the Big House. Vernon and Sarah's names may have been put on the deed after Teddy's death, but as long as Shirleen breathed, that was still her house, and she would always know what was going on in it.

"Besides, it's too late." Annabelle stepped to the side and peered through the trees. "It's already started," she whispered and waved a hand for Shirleen to follow her.

Shirleen did, leaning over Annabelle's shoulder and staring in the same direction to see Ryan kissing Allie.

Annabelle was right. It had started, and Nana was determined not to let it end in heartache, for her grandson or for Allie.

CHAPTER SEVENTEEN

"When will he get over this midnight bathroom rendezvous?" Allie asked Ryan late Saturday night as they walked the familiar trek along the beach.

"Experts say around the six-month mark, but I'm not sure Optimus will adhere to those guidelines," he replied. "He seems to love the beach."

"Who wouldn't?" she asked and then wrapped the lapels of her tunic around her front to ward off the cool breeze. "I wish I'd taken the time to experience it a little more at home."

"You live in Miami and you don't go to the beach?"

She didn't bother to look at him. The confused look on his face would be the same as she'd seen it before. His lips pursed at the ends and his eyes narrowed as if he were trying to decipher if whatever was said was true.

"Like I told you before, I work," she said. "I go to the park and read or I sit in the house and have movie nights."

"By yourself?"

"Is that your way of asking if I have a boyfriend? Because my reply would be, 'Really, aren't you a little late with that question?' seeing as you've kissed me a couple of times now."

There was a chuckle as he kicked at the sand. They'd both removed their shoes and left them on his back porch, so his toes were digging deep into the wet grittiness, just as hers were.

"Next time, *you're* gonna kiss *me*," he said.

Now she did look at him. "Really?"

"Yes. Really," he told her and then winked. "And I wasn't trying to ask if you had a boyfriend. I knew you didn't, otherwise you never would've let me kiss you twice."

That made sense. It also meant that he was paying just as much attention to her as she was to him. They knew things about each other now, like family or lovers would. The latter had her coughing, and he instantly moved in to pat her back.

"Okay?"

"Yeah," she said, waving him away. "It's the salty air, or the sand, I don't know. Something just got lodged in my throat."

He moved a few steps away from her, but he turned around so that he was now walking backward and he could look directly at her.

"What's your favorite color?" he asked.

She hesitated. "What are you doing?"

"Getting to know you better."

Better than knowing the meaning behind each other's facial expressions or whether someone was being upfront or not?

"Blue," she replied, still skeptical about what was happening here. "What's yours?"

"Green," he answered. "Favorite food?"

"Baked mac 'n cheese. Yours?"

"Smoked sausage and peppers." He groaned. "Nana makes a huge Crock-Pot of it that simmers all day long before she spoons it over a plate of wild rice. So delicious."

"It sounds like it. None of you are ever at a loss for a good meal around here," she said.

"We're a cooking and eating family."

"No. You're just a great family." Why had she said that? For the second time tonight, words had fallen from her lips that she couldn't take back, and now she had to say something to stop him from looking at her with pity. Or possibly contemplating buying her another bouquet of balloons to put her in a better mood.

"It's just that I never experienced a family like this," she told him.

"You mean a nosy, sometimes interfering, and overprotective family?"

"That's not all they are and you know it," she replied.

Optimus ran between them, trekking into the water to splash around at the shallow part. When Ryan yelled, "Optimus. Come!" the dog looked at the water, then back to Ryan, and then repeated those steps again. He finally decided to go with listening to the guy who always seemed to have dog treats in his pockets and ran back in their direction. As soon as he was close enough, he did one of those full body shakes where his ears flapped over his face and sprinkled water all over her and Ryan.

"Thanks a lot, buddy," she said and wiped at her face.

"You're right," he said, "my family means a lot to me. The business my ancestors built here, their reputation. It's all very important to who I am and what I do."

She could tell that by the way he worked in the restaurant, how he paid attention to every detail while also being attentive to his family and their customers' needs.

"You're very good at your job, and your family's built a great business. I actually think you should look into more online marketing. I mean, even aside from selling the sauces."

"I thought about that, but with only this one location and the ads we run on the island's website, I figured that was enough."

She shook her head. "I really think it'd be a good idea for you to tap into the influencer space, not just website ads." She thought about those ads on the Written in the Stars site but didn't mention that again. For whatever reason, she didn't want to talk about the matchmaker tonight. Not about the fact that after questioning the sisters at the Emporium about their mailing list, asking Sofia if she were the culprit, and visiting the B&B to ask Lindy and Lucy if they knew anything about the matchmaker's identity, she still had no idea who was behind the text messages and wasn't sure she'd actually find out before it was time for her to leave.

"Influencers?"

"It's when somebody has a social media platform, like a movie star who has millions of followers. If that movie star says, 'When I'm on Crescent Island, I enjoy a fantastic meal at Parker BBQ,' then their followers eventually book a trip to the island just to eat at your restaurant, that movie star is considered an influencer."

"Got it." He knelt down then to check Optimus's mouth since the dog liked to sniff and eat just about anything.

When he stood again, he was closer to where she'd stopped walking.

"So if you wrote an article about the restaurant on your blog, your followers might see it and come to the island."

Her first instinct was to tell him that's not typically the kind of story she wrote, but since she'd been considering that exact thing, something totally different fell from her lips. "I was actually thinking about doing that. And my words would be honest, since I love your dad's smoked meats, and your mother and Nana's cooking is phenomenal. If I weren't totally settled in my life in Miami, I would move here just so I could eat their cooking every day."

Ryan stopped again, this time taking her hand and pulling her close. "You'd move to Crescent just to eat my family's food? That's a huge endorsement."

That had been a huge, unanticipated statement as well.

"Uh, yeah, I mean, if I didn't already own a condo there and have a job there, I'd certainly consider it. For the food." The words came out in a choppy rush, and she didn't think he was buying any of it.

He was staring at her in that way he did again. The way that said he saw her, all of her, and he knew exactly what she wanted even though she hadn't admitted those facts to herself. It was a disconcerting look, but simultaneously one that made her feel desired in a way she'd never experienced before.

In a way she'd never imagined she could be.

With his free hand, he brushed the back of his knuckles over her cheek. A small smile tilted his lips. "I can't figure out what this is or why it's happening so quickly," he said. "But I know I don't want it to stop."

And wow. Speak of things she imagined happening in her life. If she were writing a love story, she would've crafted this exact scene. A slither of the moon peeking through the clouds, the sound of the waves rising and crashing, sand gushing between their toes. Okay, maybe not that last part. But definitely everything else.

Especially the part where the barest touch from him had her stomach flip-flopping just like those waves, her mind going fuzzy like one of those love songs that had played in the restaurant tonight.

"Say something, Allie." His voice had lowered to a whisper. "Tell me I'm not dreaming this, that you aren't just appearing on these midnight walks with my dog because you enjoy my dog. Please tell me that's not true."

It was her turn to grin, and she did, just before she leaned into the touch of his fingers. He dragged his hand back then, pushing those fingers through her hair.

"I hope it's not true that I only appear when it's time to walk your dog." Her tone was light, her voice a little shaky. She felt unsteady, like she was treading water, but unsure of when the depth of the ocean would shift and she'd be completely sucked under.

His smile spread. "But you are feeling this, aren't you? I mean, I'm not imagining this pull between us?"

She shook her head. "Nope. If you're dreaming, I'm skating along in that dream with you."

That's it, keep making light of a situation that in

reality scares you to death.

"But I hope you're not worrying that I'll want something more because I won't," she said hastily. "Or rather I can't."

For a second his hand stilled in her hair. "Can't or won't?"

He made it sound so black and white, in or out, do or don't.

But for Allie, the only thing that had ever been that simple, or rather blatant, was what her parents wanted her to do and eventually be. It had taken her so long to figure out what she wanted and how she could get it, at least part of it, that now she doubted she could have taken any other steps. Hesitated because to want more would require so much more courage and strength. Both things that Bella had in spades, but Allie...

Forcing herself to stay in this moment, she replied, "I'm good with whatever we can have right at this moment." Encouraged by those words, she stepped closer to him. "I won't expect anything more of you as long as you don't ask more of me."

He resumed massaging her scalp with his blunt-tipped fingers, an action that should not have been as arousing as it was, but actually had her moving even closer, until their bodies touched. "I know how to remain present," he said.

"Good," she whispered. "Because that's exactly where I want you to be. Here, in the present with me, so I can do this."

She gripped his shirt at his sides and tilted her head up until he met her halfway and her lips touched his. Hers wasn't a soft kiss. There was no gentle stroking of her tongue over his lips or a tentative delving into his mouth. She went all in immediately and whimpered when he tumbled right along with her.

• • •

Wrangling Optimus up and getting back to his house had never taken so long, but they'd finally made it.

Ryan locked the front door and made a quick sweep of the house for all of Optimus's toys that once he gathered, he dropped onto the dog bed in the corner of the living room. With an arm gesture and a "go to bed" directive, he waited while the now tuckered-out pup made his way to his comfy dog mattress.

"Is it my turn?" Allie asked playfully. "Are you going to put me to bed next?"

He almost groaned and recalled the way her tiny whimper on the beach had flipped a switch on his libido. For now, he'd try to keep the sounds to a minimum so as not to send either of them over the cliff of desire too soon.

"That can be arranged, but I'm not sure either of us is ready for sleep just yet," he said and moved close enough to take her hand again.

He adored the feel of her skin against his. So far it had only been her hands in his, or his hands on her cheek, neck, or bare arms. But he wanted more. There was no doubt in his mind that he needed more from her. In this moment, though, just for right now, as she'd made perfectly clear.

"Not at all," she said and took the lead down the

narrow hallway as if she knew the way.

He followed because at this moment, he'd do anything she wanted. Skinny dip in the ocean, crawl on his knees, find that blasted matchmaker and tell them to stop messing things up between them. She hadn't said anything about it tonight, but he knew she still wanted to know. He understood that it was a part of the story she was trying to write, but it was also making her doubt what he was certain was naturally transpiring between them.

"Are you just guessing where to go?"

The way she tossed him a look over her shoulder was the sexiest thing he'd ever seen. "There's not much of an option. The kitchen and a bathroom are in the other direction."

That was true, even though he really wasn't thinking about the floorplan to his house right now. He was thinking of the moment he'd get to put his hands on every inch of her body. The second they could both succumb to this attraction that had been blazing between them for the past week.

Had he ever slept with a woman this soon before? He was almost positive that answer was no, but then she'd opened the door to his bedroom and stepped inside and he lost his train of thought. There'd never been another woman in this space, not one who wasn't related to him by blood. Any dates that he'd had he'd taken to the little boarding house at the end of Yardley Drive when the time was appropriate. The location of the boarding house had been inconspicuously close to the horseshoe of deserted land his high school buddies had dubbed "lucky lover's lane."

Allie released his hand then and walked farther

into the room. He stayed near the door and turned on the light switch.

"I like the moonlight," she said as she passed the bed and went over to the window.

There wasn't much tonight, as the clouds had rolled in fast between the time they'd closed the restaurant until now.

"I can turn it off again, but I didn't want you to trip over anything."

She turned to face him, his king-size bed separating them.

"Do you still love her?"

The words were a shock, but not so much as the earnestness of her gaze as it rested on him. His answer would no doubt determine where they went from here. As it should. No way did he ever want to be intimate with a woman if she had another man on her mind or if feelings for that other man were still an issue. So he understood the question; he'd just have to ignore that this was the second time tonight that he'd have to answer it.

"No. I haven't been in love with her for a very long time."

She gave a brief nod and then looked away.

"She wanted me to go with her, and I couldn't ask her to stay," he said. "The impasse was too big and we both made our choice. It's been over between us."

Her fingers touched the navy-blue comforter on his bed. He watched them moving up and down the material, until she spoke again.

"I've never been in love," she said, so softly he almost didn't hear her. "Never."

The pure honesty mixed with a sudden hint of

sadness squeezed his heart until he choked out a breath. There wasn't anything that was going to keep him away from her at that moment. Not a text message from some busybody matchmaker or the appearance of his ex. Ryan closed the bedroom door and switched off the light before moving around the bed to where she stood. The blinds in his room were always open, so there was a dull light dripping in from the moon. It touched her face like a kiss, and he reached out to push the tunic she wore off her shoulders.

His fingers brushed her bare arms as he eased the sleeves all the way free and tossed the material on the end of his bed. She stepped into him then, lacing her arms around his neck, and he pulled her into his arms. Their lips were fused in seconds, like they were magnets for each other and unable to stay apart.

The top she wore was so small, it covered all the important parts but left bare snatches of skin that had been tempting him since he'd seen her this morning. She broke the kiss and scraped her teeth along the line of his jaw. The groan came this time, and there was nothing he could do to stop it.

In a quick motion, he lifted her from the floor and laid her gently on the bed. When she reached for him, he grabbed each of her hands and kissed her palms. "I know," he whispered in response to her eager invitation. "I need you, too."

But he needed her naked first. Naked and waiting for him to take every ounce of her that she offered in this present time. If that's all he could have, he'd damn well make the best of it.

Her shoes went first, then he reached for the

button of her shorts, pushing them down her long legs. Her shirt and panties were next, and then he was standing there at the side of his bed, more aroused than he'd ever felt before.

"If you need help," she said and started to sit up.

"I got it," he replied. "You just stay right there." He swallowed at the way the moonlight danced over her naked body, touching all the best places, alluding to others. "Stay. Right. There."

His clothes practically flew off, and before she could offer any more assistance, he'd found a condom in his nightstand drawer, donned it, and joined her on the bed.

"Allie," he whispered her name as he pulled her into his arms.

"Now, Ryan. I want this right now."

And he gave it to her. He gave her everything she wanted and all the things he'd been dreaming of these last few days. From the moment he slipped inside her, to the exact second sometime later when she'd reached her pinnacle and cried out his name. She was wrapped around him so tightly, her arms and legs holding him in place, her whispers and moans cocooning him until he couldn't breathe, couldn't think, couldn't tell her that this moment was never going to be enough.

CHAPTER EIGHTEEN

Sarah Parker swung her legs out and tucked them back in, getting the porch swing to move with her rhythm. Beside her, the love of her life sat with his hands folded over the girth he'd acquired from years of tasting every piece of meat he prepared.

"Beautiful night," she said, looking up to the sky. "Remember a few months after I moved here with my family, and you used to come to my house just as the sun was going down?" She'd been sixteen and Vernon a year older.

"Mm-hmmm," Vernon replied without moving. "And your daddy would say you couldn't go any farther than the lamppost at the corner."

She chuckled. "Yeah, he was strict with me and my sisters. But you came that late on purpose so we could walk down the street out of his line of sight."

"Ole Bobby wasn't as smart as he thought," Vernon replied with a wide grin. "Got awfully dark between your parents' house and Mr. Greenbaum's two houses down."

"And you always held my hand in the dark. Said you didn't want me to be afraid."

"But really, I just wanted to touch you as much as possible without risking Ole Bobby's rifle at my temple."

She laughed louder then. "Daddy never had any bullets in that rifle. He just brought it out anytime he felt like scaring somebody. Usually, any boy that came to see me or Anna. He'd been that way when we were in North Carolina, too. Said just because this was a pretty little island didn't mean the boys weren't still slicksters."

"Yeah, but I was the only one slick enough to get a ring on your finger. Anna and Ruby are still single."

"That's by choice," she said. "And don't start talking about my sisters. They've got their own lives to lead."

"You right about that." Vernon shifted a bit, trying to get comfortable. The swing didn't like his movements and creaked in response.

"Our children have their own lives to lead, too." She'd eased into the conversation that she knew would get Vernon riled up. But there were some things she needed to say to her often obstinate and overbearing husband.

"You talkin' 'bout Ryan?"

She turned to him in shock. "You know about Kerry being back?"

"I do," Vernon replied with a nod. "Also know she's never gonna approve that investment money for him. Not after he told her to get gone."

"He didn't say it like that. At least I pray he didn't." Sarah had never known how that conversation had gone. And while she had a pretty good relationship with all her children, Ryan was the one she'd never been sure she was reaching all the time.

"He told me he told her he wasn't leaving Crescent. His family and his life were here, but if she needed to go, she should." Vernon scratched his stomach. "In other words, get gone."

She pushed his arm playfully. "You're a mess,

Vernon Parker."

"No, I don't take no mess," he said. "Which is why
I told Ryan not to worry over whatever Kerry decides to do. We'll find a way for his plan to work out."

"Really? You're gonna help him?"

Vernon lifted his head up then and turned to her.
"We don't have that kind of cash flow, Sarah. I told
y'all that before, and Sofia's confirmed it. I know
Ryan thinks I've just been acting like a hardhead
over this deal, but I knew we didn't have the money
to build that factory and warehouse and start distribution."

"But you do think it's a good deal, right? You
think it's something we should do?"

He nodded. "I do now. Had to let it all settle in my
mind. But I think it's a good move forward. And, if he
doesn't find a way to do this on his own, then we'll
just have to come together and help figure out how to
make it happen. I promise you."

Her nerves settled a little at his words. She'd been
worried from the moment she'd walked into the restaurant this morning and Nana had told her that
Reba had seen Kerry getting off the six o'clock ferry.
Of course, they hadn't gotten the news that she
worked for that big company in New York until after
noon when Willie came in to get his daily order of
hot wings for lunch. He'd seen Kerry as she was going
to visit her uncle who lived down the street from
Willie.

"I wish he'd find himself a nice girl to settle down
with, though," Sarah said thoughtfully.

"Now, Sarie…" Vernon had always called her
Sarie, and she'd always let him. "Don't go trying to

play matchmaker. This island's got enough of that foolishness running around."

"You think finding love is foolishness?"

"I think believing you can tell two people they're meant to be when you don't even know them is intrusive and, yes, foolish."

She kept on swinging on that swing until moments later Vernon reached for her hand, folding his beefy fingers around hers.

"If Ryan is falling in love with Allie, then that's his business, and if he's learned anything from his daddy, he'll get his ring on her finger just as I got mine on yours," he said.

He rubbed his finger over the pear-shaped diamond he'd bought last year for their anniversary, to replace the one she'd had before that. In their forty years of marriage, he'd replaced her rings every ten years.

"You know she's not home yet," Sarah said after another few moments of silence. "It's almost one in the morning."

Vernon let his head rest against the back of the swing again and squeezed Sarah's hand. "Mm-hmmm. I told you my boy learned from his daddy."

Sarah laughed heartily and continued to swing, hoping her wonderful husband was right this time.

• • •

The house was quiet. That's the first thing Allie noticed when she awoke on Sunday morning. There was always some sort of noise at the Big House. Dishes clanking in the kitchen, Brody's music playing, the sound of the waves coming through the window Allie always left open.

She didn't hear any of that right now. There was just silence.

And it smelled different here. She turned over so that she was now lying on her left side in a fetal position. She gathered up one of the pillows beside her and pressed it to her face.

It smelled like him.

A sandalwood scent mixed with the freshness of the sea. She closed her eyes and let the aroma permeate through every part of her, mind, body, and soul. This was all she'd have to remember him by, and she wanted to savor it.

She probably should've been bothered by the fact that he'd obviously left her alone, but she wasn't. This was what she needed right now. These moments to gather her thoughts, get her mind right, and then keep moving. Pulling the pillow slowly away from her face, she saw the morning light pouring in through the blinds to bounce off his unmade side of the bed.

It didn't take much to clear her mind of everything except for last night. Each time he'd touched her, whispered her name, kissed her. She pulled her lips between her teeth, savored that memory, then released them slowly. He was a great kisser, taking things up a notch with each stroke of his tongue. And when he'd moved over her, she'd wanted to weep with the expert precision. Everything he'd done and said had been perfect. Not that she had a lot to compare it to, mostly just the imaginings that often surfaced after she'd viewed one of her favorite romcoms.

She could admit, if only to herself, that part of the

joy in watching those movies for her rested in the fact that her only hope of finding any semblance of love was on the screen. Most times when she watched them at night, she'd curl up in her bed and imagine the man that would capture her heart. All the wonderfully romantic things he would do to win her, mixed with some normal stuff, too, because that's what separated her thoughts from being complete fiction. She didn't imagine a billionaire bumping into her on a busy street, or an NBA or NFL star spotting her across a crowded room at some party. No, she'd only thought of a regular man, handsome, caring, funny, and yeah, gainfully employed was always tossed in there. But most importantly, he would look at her as if she were the only woman he saw, the only woman who could ever fill his heart and she'd give him the same in return.

Last night, Ryan's desire-tinged eyes had gazed at her in that way. She'd felt like she was the only one he'd ever made love to like that—slow, intentional, mind-numbingly sensual. It had been a foolish thought, she knew. Yet a very small part of her—because she wouldn't allow it to be any more—had yearned to be the same sort of first for him that he was for her.

He was the first man she'd spent the entire night with. The first man she'd held on to throughout the night, afraid that the minute she let go would prove it had all been a dream. And he was the first she'd awakened in the morning thinking about.

It was like he'd known exactly what to do, how to make her sigh with contentment or soar with pleasure. She closed her eyes again and shivered as she imagined he was still here, still moving with her, still holding her.

He'd held her all night, and at some point, he'd turned over and she'd held him right back. She'd wanted to hold on tight to every moment, every breath and moan so she'd never forget. Because it quite possibly wouldn't happen again. That was if Ryan didn't want her to stay over for her remaining nights on the island. But that might be too much for both of them. While she'd been totally on board about doing this, she knew it was best not to overdo it. This wasn't one of her romantic imaginings or the start of a beautiful forever relationship, and if she stayed with him every night from now until she left, it might start to feel that way.

To be honest, there was a part of her that had already started on that path.

She despised that part. Wanted to push it into a closet and slam the door, because it was the weakest part of her. It was that miniscule section of her heart that whispered, "Maybe," when her mind screamed, "Hell no!"

Maybe she could fall in love with someone in real life instead of just her imaginings and maybe that someone would love her back the way they were supposed to. Not that cold and mechanical type of love her parents shared and had dished out to her and Bella as a reward for achievements only. And maybe, once she and this person she'd never actually believed existed, were together, they wouldn't mess everything up by not continuing as they began.

Not to mention if they had kids, how could she even begin to offer her children the love and support they deserved when she didn't know how it felt to receive any of that? It was an impossible situation, which was why she'd told herself a very long time ago that the small part of her that desired those things was foolish and needed an extended time out.

Her phone rang, and she jumped before rolling over until she was close enough to reach for it on the nightstand.

It was Renee calling.

Allie held the phone and sat up in bed. She cleared her throat and shook her head as if that was going to help her not sound like she was sitting in the center of a guy's bed. Considering she had no clue what that would possibly sound like anyway, she took a quick breath and answered, "Good morning."

"Well, hey there, Sunshine! Don't you sound much better after a week on a coastal island," Renee said. "Now, tell me you've got a fantastic story for me and we'll both be pleased."

Did she sound pleased? Her skin still felt ultra-sensitive, but that could've been because she'd just been recalling every place that Ryan had touched her. And yes, those thoughts did please her, almost as much as they worried her.

"I have a story," she said when she remembered she was on the phone. "It may not be exactly what you had in mind, but I think it'll have the 'heart' you seem to be looking for."

She could hear clapping in the background.

"Oh yippee! I can't wait to read it," Renee said and then sighed. "Listen, I know this is a shift for you and that you're not accustomed to change, but I promise, Allie, this is going to be good for the blog *and* for you personally."

"I wasn't aware that I needed to change what I was writing. It seemed like I was doing my job, giving people information they needed to make a good, informed decision." And she'd taken pride in doing that, had never once thought she might be doing it wrong.

"I didn't say you weren't doing your job," Renee continued. "It's just that the tone of your stories became more bitter."

"I'm not bitter!" The words rushed out as she took offense. "I'm honest."

"And like I mentioned before, honesty can be served in many different ways. Besides that, it just didn't appear that you could find the good in anything. And Allie, I'm speaking to you as a friend now and not your boss, that's a sure sign that something's off in your life."

Great, now she was going to make this personal. Allie frowned, glad that Renee couldn't see her because she prided herself on being as professional as possible at work. No way did she want Renee to know how badly she was reacting to this conversation. Especially after the fabulous night she'd had.

"My life is just fine."

"Is it? When's the last time you went out on a date?"

"Everyone does not need a partner, Renee," Allie clapped back, when she really wanted to say she *was* going on a date tonight. With Ryan.

"You're right," Renee responded quickly. "They don't. But you don't go out with any girlfriends, either. You don't socialize at all. You sit in your condo and write, or you travel the world and write. But when do you live, Allie? What do you do to feel alive and like you're an active part of this world?"

Ryan had made her feel alive last night. He'd awakened things in her she hadn't even known were there and this morning she'd allowed herself to think of all those things, to covet them in a way that, unfortunately, couldn't be good.

"You'll have the story by the end of next week," she said to Renee and ended the call.

There was nothing else to say. She held the phone in her hands and dropped her chin to her chest. There was also nothing else to do. Not here, anyway.

Ten minutes later, she was scribbling a note to Ryan on one of the napkins she'd grabbed from the holder in the center of the island in his kitchen.

Had to go and get ready for my beach day with Sofia. Will see you later tonight at Polk's!

She'd signed it and avoided using a heart to dot the "i" in her name like she was a twelve-year-old writing a letter to her crush. Even though that was kind of how she felt. Ryan was just like Aaron Moore who'd sat behind her in sixth-grade English class. He'd been everything her childish mind had dreamed she wanted in a boyfriend—cute, witty, and smart. Unfortunately, he'd also been off-limits because Allie wasn't allowed to date, nor did she have permission to participate in after-school activities, which Aaron and all the other kids at their private school normally did until their parents were off from work.

Ryan lived on this island with his family. His life and his job were here. Hadn't he sacrificed one relationship to prove that point? Yes, he'd let Kerry walk out of his life because he belonged here. She wouldn't be the reason he'd sacrifice another. No, Renee was right about one thing—Allie needed to write this story. Then she needed to get herself off this island before it did something she'd vowed to never let happen again—before this place and the people here could break her heart.

. . .

"What are you typing that has you so super focused? If it's a sex scene for your book, I wanna read it right now!"

Allie ignored Sofia and finished her thought:

She hadn't known this was what she wished for, hadn't believed that anything could ever answer the yearning that she'd buried deep within. But there was an answer and it came with the brilliant sunrise, falling over the morning tide like golden gems. It was in the air that sometimes came on a warm breeze. It floated on the laughter, his and everyone else's around him. It settled in her chest, blanketing her heart until she wanted to cry out in agony or rejoice in victory.

"Allie!"

She jumped at the sound of her name and glanced over at Sofia, who was leaning halfway off the lounge chair they'd set up on the beach earlier this afternoon.

"What? And are you trying to plant your face in the sand?" Allie asked with what she knew was a bewildered expression on her face.

"No," Sofia said, her arms flailing as she tried to right herself, but the leg with the clunky boot wasn't cooperating. "I was trying to get some action via my friend's secret story, but she's not being a friend right about now."

With a huff, Allie closed her laptop and set it on top of the laptop sleeve she'd put on the towel beside her. She swung her legs over the side of her lounge chair and stepped up to grab Sofia's arms, easing her back onto her chair in the proper position.

"Nobody's writing a secret story," she said, even though she sort of was writing something that she didn't want anyone to see. But that wasn't necessarily because she wanted to keep it a secret. She actually wanted to figure out what it was before she could decide if it was secret worthy or not.

The words had just begun flowing once she'd made it back to the Big House this morning. So much so that she'd almost forgotten that she'd returned to get ready for the day on the beach with Sofia. The decision to bring her laptop with her had been an impulsive one, and when Sofia had asked if she was working on this gorgeous Sunday, Allie had replied she was bringing the laptop in case they wanted to watch a movie. Which they hadn't done in the two hours since they'd been out here.

"Well, whatever it is, it's got your undivided attention. I've been chatting for a half hour and you haven't so much as grumbled a response," Sofia said before adjusting her sunglasses.

Her friend wore a daring hunter-green bikini, her long locks piled on top of her head in a big, messy bun. Allie wore a black two-piece, a cute floppy straw hat, and wide-framed sunglasses.

"Sorry. I'll put it away," she said. "You wanna try

to walk down to the water?"

Sofia turned to her. "Is that your way of telling me no I'm not getting a sex scene to read on the beach? Because you know that could be classified as a beach read and something to take my mind off the fact that Nana's still keeping me on lockdown."

Allie shook her head. "It wasn't a sex scene."

"But it's still something you don't want me to read."

"It's something I don't even know if *I'm* gonna read again." She sighed. "It's just words. They've been rattling around in my mind all day, and I'm just getting them out. That's all."

Sofia sat up and grinned at Allie. "I'm no author, but I think that's how a book starts."

"You're right," Allie replied with a half smile. "You're no author. And neither am I, at least not like that. So anyway, let's get in the water."

Moments later, after Sofia had removed the boot from her leg, Allie helped her. Sofia tenderly put weight on her ankle but for the most part leaned against Allie as they walked the short distance to the water. When the waves were lapping over their calves, Allie stopped.

"All those times you told me how beautiful it was here, I don't think I ever really believed you," she admitted.

"Why would I lie?"

Allie shrugged. "You know, people grow up someplace and they think that's the best place on earth. But I might be starting to believe at least part of the hype about this island."

"Not the part about the matchmaker, I know,"

Sofia said with a chuckle. "But there's more to Crescent than that. There's the people, the community, the slow pace that kind of soothes you every day."

"I'm not a slow-paced kind of girl."

Sofia shook her head. "Neither am I. At least there are times when I just want to run around the island. I mean, I've literally done just that. Anything to get my adrenaline going, to find that sense of adventure I used to have."

Allie looked over at Sofia. "You wanna leave Crescent? Go back to the city with me?"

Even though she couldn't see her eyes through the glasses, Allie knew when Sofia turned to her that their gazes had locked. "I don't know. And that scares me," she said. "I feel like I want to do something, to make some type of move or to make a difference. I just don't know what that is or how I'm supposed to do it."

Nodding and reaching an arm around Sofia again, Allie said, "I know what you mean. I'm wondering if there's something new on the horizon for me, too."

"Something new and perhaps something borrowed and something blue?" Sofia asked.

"What?"

"You know, wedding vows? You. Ryan. A beach-front wedding." Sofia grinned and Allie groaned.

"Have you been popping too many pain pills?" she asked. "I'm not marrying anybody, anywhere. That scenario couldn't be further from my horizon."

"Why?" Sofia asked.

Allie shrugged. "Because it's always been that way."

"There's no rule saying that things can't change."

No, there wasn't. And hadn't Renee mentioned something about Allie needing a change in her life, too? Allie wasn't opposed to change; she was, however, completely over wishing for the unobtainable. Her romcom-induced imaginings were one thing, but earnestly hoping for what she knew she could never have or had no idea how to sustain was a futile action she had no intention of indulging. No matter how pretty the sunrises were on this lovely island.

CHAPTER NINETEEN

At six thirty, Ryan slipped one leg into his khaki slacks and then the other. When he stood to pull them up, his mind drifted to early this morning. Predawn, the moment Allie's soft curls had brushed against his chin.

Half her body was sprawled over him, one leg over his, one arm across his lower abdomen, her cheek pressed against his chest. He'd inhaled deeply, letting the now-familiar sweet scent of her hair products sift through his nostrils. With his eyes closed, he wrapped his arms tightly around her, wondering if there were a way he could freeze time. Hold her here with him…for how long? A day? A week? Forever.

It was the oddest thing, her appearing on the island at a time in his life when all he'd wanted was to pursue his career goals. He hadn't thought about a relationship or starting a family in so long, he'd almost believed it was one of those wishes that stayed on the wish pile a person's entire life. For so long he'd told himself that work had to come first, that all he needed was to succeed in carrying his family's legacy into the next generation and then he'd feel complete. Finally, he'd feel like he'd done something real and meaningful.

But at this moment, holding Allie in his arms, the meaning of his life had shifted.

He'd eased away from her then, the magnitude of that realization hitting him like a ton of bricks so that his head had immediately begun to throb. Going through the dark house until he arrived in the kitchen, he switched on the light and rested his palms on the island, dropping his head in an effort to get his thoughts together. There were too many and they all revolved around her.

The surprised look on her face when Optimus had toppled her on the beach, the smile she'd given Sofia when he'd watched them at the restaurant together, the longing that had clouded her eyes the night she'd stood behind the screen to the back porch at the Big House, the utter joy that laced her smile and tinged the sound of her laughter the night of the carnival. How she'd sighed his name over and over last night as she'd wrapped her arms and legs around him, holding him tightly inside her as if she'd been just as afraid as he was that the night would end and in the morning the dream would be over.

Well, it was morning and she was still here. In his bed. Now what?

Optimus had come along then, sniffing around his bare feet and then finally sitting down to stare up at him. "Yeah, I know what time it is," he'd said and tipped back into the bedroom to pull on a pair of shorts and a T-shirt. Deciding against the black Crocs he normally wore when walking Optimus, he put on his tennis shoes instead, and when they headed out of the house, he went toward the Big House instead of the beach.

"Joining me this mornin'?" Trevor had asked minutes later when Ryan had met him at the three steps leading down from his parents' backyard to the beach.

Optimus danced around the older Parker until Trevor knelt down to scrub the top of his head and then beneath his neck.

"Yeah, I could use a run," Ryan had replied.

"Cool! How 'bout a race?" Brody said, jogging down the steps and skirting around both brothers. Optimus immediately followed the more boisterous Parker, barking and jumping up until Brody reached down to touch him, too.

"And I thought you were the competitive one," Ryan said, tossing a wry look at Trevor.

Trevor shrugged. "Guess I wore off on the goofball."

"All this talkin' and nobody's running," Brody told them. "First one to the pier buys beers at the Brew & Grub tomorrow night."

Brody had already turned and started running before Ryan or Trevor could respond. When Trevor broke into a sprint, Ryan followed, sucking in the early morning air, answering the call to push his legs and arms harder and faster.

This was exactly what he'd wanted, the reason he'd come to the Big House instead of going straight to the beach. Not racing his brothers at the crack of dawn, but the adrenaline rush of a run. Trevor ran for miles every morning. Had been doing so most of his life. When asked why he continued the running years after his football career had ended, his older brother had replied, "It clears my head of all the junk that threatens to break me."

Well, Ryan needed that type of clarity this morning. He needed it like he needed his next breath.

Trevor reached the pier first with Brody coming in

a close second and Optimus running around both of them trying to decide which one was going to offer him a treat for making the beach-long run with them. Ryan came in a few moments after he'd watched his brother stop. While Brody rested his hands on his knees and was bent over trying to catch his breath, Trevor had already begun dipping into leg lunges.

"So what's up with you?" the oldest Parker brother asked.

Ryan had just given Optimus one of the treats he'd stuck in his shorts pocket when he glanced up to see that Trevor was staring at him. "Me?"

Trevor smirked. "Yeah, you. Brody's never won a race among the three of us."

Standing up straight, Ryan frowned. "And he didn't win this one."

"Neither did you," Brody quipped, still trying to catch his breath. "Which is why he's asking you, what's up?"

Ryan didn't want to talk about what was up with him, especially not with his brothers. Or did he? He'd known that coming to the Big House would mean running into Trevor, who was always out on the beach before dawn. Brody was a wild card. There wasn't anything that Brody did by routine, unless you counted picking up women.

"Just trying to get my head right for dealing with Kerry again," he said, not telling the exact truth about what was bothering him.

"She wants you back," Brody said, and Ryan froze.

"Who told you that?" he asked.

"She did," Brody replied. "Last night at the party,

she said this business deal could be what brings you to the city with her."

"Not a chance," Ryan said.

"Hey, I don't blame you," Brody continued and shrugged. "She's a sneaky one. I could tell by the way she was looking at Allie last night. Like she was sizing up the competition and deciding she had the upper hand. I don't remember her being like that before, but then I didn't know her as well as you did."

Ryan had seen the way she'd looked at Allie, too. He hadn't realized she'd noticed Allie walking up to his place yesterday morning, but from the look in Kerry's eyes last night as she'd stood across from Allie and Brody, Ryan had noticed something familiar. In addition to being used to getting her way, Kerry had always been competitive and tenacious. But Ryan hadn't thought Kerry would consider Allie her competition, since he and Kerry had been over a long time ago.

"She's definitely barking up the wrong tree," Ryan stated. "I wouldn't go back to her if she were the last woman on earth." If that sounded bitter, so be it. He could be over their love affair and even wish her well in her life, but that sting of betrayal would stay with him forever because it had made him never trust his heart again.

"Besides that," Trevor added, "you've got another woman on your mind. And if there's one thing I know about my little brother, it's that he's a one-woman man."

On pure instinct, both Ryan and Trevor's gazes settled on Brody after that statement.

"Bite me," Brody snapped. "Both of you. I'm with

one woman at a time."

"You mean you're with one woman a week," Ryan added drily.

Brody folded his arms across his chest. "Yeah, well, we're not here to talk about me. We're talkin' about you and that pretty writer you insisted was off-limits because she's Sofia's friend."

"Sleeping over at your house doesn't sound off-limits to me," Trevor added.

With a frown, Ryan propped his hands on his hips. "Bite me," he snapped, mimicking Brody.

Trevor chuckled as Brody picked up a stick and tossed it a few feet away for Optimus to run after.

"Okay, okay. In all seriousness," Trevor began, "what's going on with you two that has you out here running before sunrise? I thought we already discussed how to handle this."

As the oldest, Trevor always thought his word was the last word. Since he could talk, he'd advised, guarded, and doted on his siblings. When their mother used to yell out, "Keep an eye on them," as they'd all run out into the yard on Sunday afternoons, Trevor had taken those words seriously. He would do anything for them, Ryan knew this, and his heart had ached at the knowledge that all these years Trevor had thought he'd somehow let them down. It wasn't something they talked about, but Ryan knew.

It was for that reason Ryan didn't bother beating around the bush or denying what was so obviously on his mind. He did need to talk about this, and who better than the two men he was closest to in this world?

Walking over to a bank of rocks that seemed to jut up from the sand and nestle against the pier, he leaned back on one. Trevor and Brody followed him over with Optimus in tow.

"She's not going to stay here, either." He said the words slowly, as if tasting them for the first time. Sure, he'd thought them, had hated the way they'd echoed in his mind soon after they'd both finished in the bathroom last night and climbed into his bed.

"Wow, so you like her enough to be thinking about whether you can keep her?" Brody asked.

It would be a hard concept for Brody to grasp, but for Ryan the only women he gave more than a passing thought were the ones—or rather Kerry, the only one before Allie—his feelings were entangled with.

"I liked her enough to let her sleep in my bed," he said and then shrugged. "What does that tell you?"

Trevor nodded. "That you really like her."

Lifting his arms, Ryan dragged his hands down the back of his head and then dropped them into his lap. He let out a big sigh. "Yeah, I do. And it's wild because I've known since day one that she doesn't belong here on the island. I knew, and I still walked into this like it didn't even matter."

"Wait a minute," Brody said, holding up a hand and shaking his head. "You're sayin' you're in this deep and this woman's only been here a week."

"Brody," Trevor said, but Brody continued.

"I'm just sayin', maybe this isn't as big a deal as you're thinking it is, man. You always want to look toward forever when sometimes, some things are temporary. And there's nothing wrong with temporary," Brody said.

"No," Trevor added before Ryan could speak again. "There's nothing wrong with temporary. But that's not how he's built. Is it, Ryan?"

There was an understanding tone to Trevor's words even though he knew Trevor wasn't the forever kind of guy, either. Sure, his brother had been with Taylor for a while now, and he was even staying at her house more nights than he stayed at the Big House, but Trevor was on this beach every morning for his run. He was at their family's dinner table more nights than he wasn't, and he was in the restaurant every day, sometimes twelve to fourteen hours a day.

Ryan shook his head. "No. It's not."

"But this is fast, man. You're standing here look-ing like you're about to lose your favorite socks and it's only been a week." Brody frowned.

"I can't explain it, either," Ryan said. "It has been only a week. Only one night with her in my bed. And hell, we're just going on our first date tonight, but I know what I feel. I know it, and I can't deny it. At least not to the two of you."

"So what are you gonna do?" Trevor asked. "Because I agree, she's not going to stay here. All she talks about is how this is her vacation and when she gets back to Miami. I even heard her and Sofia plan-ning a week when Sofia can go down there to visit her."

Ryan sighed again. "I'm going to enjoy the time we have," he told them.

And just about twelve hours later, as he sprayed on some cologne and slipped his phone into the front pocket of his khakis, he walked out of his bedroom with his mind set on doing just that.

• • •

"You didn't look like a total newbie," Ryan said a couple hours later after they'd left Polk's and walked along the dock.

The way she twisted her lips and looked up at him like she didn't believe a word he'd just said was nothing short of adorable. It was a look that tugged at his heart. No, scratch that, it was a look that held his heart in a vice, squeezing until it was hard for him to breathe.

"Okay, maybe you looked like a sort of newbie. You know, like it could've been your second or third time picking and eating steamed crabs," he said with a chuckle. But she wasn't buying it.

"First, you didn't warn me about the seasoning the crabs were steamed in."

"What? The Old Bay Seasoning? It's the best! Not too spicy, but just flavorful enough," he told her. "Lots of people throughout the state use different seasoning combos, but Polk's sticks with the classic, and we love him for it."

"No," she said with a shake of her head. "It wasn't too spicy, but I admit to almost choking a few times because I didn't realize so much of it had stuck to my fingers before I put them into my mouth."

He recalled her reaching for her glass of water a few times and then the one time she'd completely ignored the water and grabbed his beer instead. Watching her lips circle the bottle had him recalling those same lips on his, and he'd groaned inwardly. Now her hand was in his as they walked in the waning moonlight like lovers.

"Yeah, but you gotta admit they were delicious," he said. "There's nothing like steamed Chesapeake

Bay Blue crabs on a summer's night."

"With beer," she said. "Don't forget the beer."

He laughed. "How could I? I ended up ordering a pitcher after you finished my second bottle."

"Wait, you didn't want to share? I thought this was a date," she said, stopping so that he had no choice but to turn and face her.

"It is a date," he said, taking a step closer to her. "And I don't mind sharing anything with you. Not a beer, not the air we're breathing, and definitely not my bed."

She licked her lips slowly. "Is that an invitation?"

With his free hand, he cupped her face. "Stay with me," he said, and when she blinked in surprise, he continued. "For the rest of the week. Stay at my place with me."

For a moment that seemed like an eternity, she paused, and he thought for sure this was the part where she told him why they couldn't do this. Why it was pointless because she wasn't staying and he wasn't leaving. He'd run all the scenarios in his mind throughout the day and in the hours leading up to this date. It was an impossible situation, one he didn't know the solution to, but one that he couldn't get out of, not even if his life depended on it.

"Are you sure?" she asked finally. "I mean, is this what you really want? You know I—"

He touched a finger to her lips to silence her. "I know our situation as well as you do. I just want you, for as long as I can have you. Is that okay?"

She puckered her lips to place a kiss on his finger and then nodded. "That's okay."

CHAPTER TWENTY

Late Tuesday afternoon, Sofia sat in a booth at the restaurant. She'd wiped down all the menus with bleach wipes, had filled napkin holders, salt-and-pepper shakers, and bottles of house sauce. It had been two hours since Nana had led her to this booth and given her assignments like she was a ten-year-old, but at least she was back in the restaurant again.

She hadn't been here since Saturday when she'd MC'd game night, an activity which had really only consisted of announcing the event, then getting on the microphone every half hour to remind everyone that there were more games on the back table, more food in the kitchen, and more fun to be had. All of which she'd done from this same booth. With a sigh, she feared this might be her new designated spot.

There was an oyster-shucking contest down at the Docks today and a seashell hunt hosted by the Youth Ministry at the beach, so there wasn't a huge crowd at the restaurant, which was why she'd been assigned the refill duties. Music played softly in the background—the jazz station that Nana said Papa Teddy had loved—and a warm breeze came in through the open windows and patio doors.

When she looked up to see Kerry enter through the front door, Sofia frowned at what riffraff the breeze had obviously blown in.

Wearing blush-colored slacks and a white sleeveless blouse with ruffles down the front, she stood in the doorway for a few seconds, lifting a hand to re-move the blue, large-frame sunglasses from her eyes. She was looking for Ryan, no doubt, and Sofia was glad he was in his office dealing with some paper-work.

"Yoo-hoooo!" she yelled in an annoyingly high-pitched tone. "Yoo-hooo, Kerry. Over here." She added a wave when Kerry's gaze found her and even pasted on a fake smile.

Kerry gave her a brilliant smile in return, showing her many white teeth as she walked toward her. A bone-colored purse swayed at her side, matching the peep-toe sandals she wore. Her hair was left straight today, pulled over her left shoulder with a dramatic flourish. She looked like a city girl, or even the beau-ty queen she'd always pretended to be when she used to ride in the back of her father's convertible during the SummerFest parade.

"Hey, Sofia," Kerry said when she arrived at the table and slid onto the bench across from her. "It's so good to see you. I didn't get a chance to chat with you the other night."

Thank all that was holy. Sofia kept that to herself and continued with her fake smile. "I know. It was so crowded in here the other night. But I was surprised to see you back on the island at all. It's been years since you've been home."

"You sound like my daddy," Kerry said while pull-ing the strap of her purse from her arm and setting it on the bench beside her. "He acts like I don't have a whole job and a life in New York."

"Oh, I know very well that's what you have going on—after all, that's why you left my brother." She knew the smile had slipped, just as that light tone in her voice had quickly disappeared.

Kerry paused, taking a second to digest the new temperature of this conversation. To her credit, she didn't get up and leave—which Sofia hadn't thought she would—but instead squared her shoulders and made eye contact.

"I left this little island to pursue a bigger career goal. I see you kept your aspirations low and stayed here to work at this restaurant like it's the only food joint in the world," Kerry replied.

So she was up for this conversation, too. Well, she'd better buckle up because Sofia didn't plan to pull any punches.

"You don't have to try so hard to prove that loyalty doesn't run in your family. It shows," Sofia snapped.

"Loyalty doesn't always have to mean sacrifice." Kerry sighed. "You're just like your brother, believing that to prove your love to your family you have to sit in this restaurant for the rest of your days, cooking up the same food and smiling at the same people."

"We happen to love cooking up the same food and smiling at the same people, and for a few years you'd convinced Ryan that you did, too."

"I didn't convince Ryan of anything. I enjoyed the time we were together. I loved him."

"And yet you left him."

Kerry opened her mouth and then just as quickly clamped her lips shut again. "I made the decision that was best for my life."

Sofia had to admit that she really couldn't blame Kerry for that. Hadn't she been wishing she could do the same thing?

While part of her problem was that she wasn't sure what was the best decision for her life at the moment, she was certain that if there'd been anyone other than her family in her life right now, she'd at the very least consider how her decisions would affect them. It was the fair thing to do.

"And now?" she asked. "Why are you here now? Because I know you could've cited a conflict with this deal and handed it off to someone else. You didn't have to come back. Is it because of some half-hearted attempt at revenge? Your way of getting back at Ryan for not leaving with you?"

"I'm here to do my job," she stated adamantly.

"And to show Ryan what he missed out on, no doubt."

She touched the ends of her hair with one hand and sighed. "That would be so cliché, don't you think, Sofia? And I've never been anyone's cliché."

Sofia narrowed her eyes and leaned in closer. "This is a good deal, Kerry. A sound one that'll make triple your company's investment in our five-year plan. Tourism and business on Crescent are booming, and the barbecue circuit is its own machine; coming in on the ground floor of Parker Sauces is a sure bet. You'd be a fool if you advised your bosses any differently."

Kerry arched a brow. "I've never been anyone's fool, either, Sofia."

For a few moments, the women sat in silence, holding each other's gaze, until Sofia finally sat back. "Good," she said solemnly. "Don't start now."

"Don't start what now?" Ryan asked as he came

up to the table.

Sofia hadn't noticed him heading for them. If she had, she would've turned on her fake smile again and pretended to be talking about something a little more cheerful. Ryan wouldn't have believed it for one minute, but at least he wouldn't have caught her giving thinly veiled threats to his ex-girlfriend.

• • •

The minute he'd seen Sofia and Kerry sitting together, Ryan had known there was going to be trouble. Which was why, even though he'd been both anticipating and regretting his inevitable meeting with Kerry, he'd hurried over to their table as soon as he spotted them. From Sofia's sarcastic remark and Kerry's raised brow response, he'd known he'd gotten there at just the right time.

"Glad you could meet with me today," he said when he and Kerry were seated at another table outside a few minutes later.

Gwen appeared with two glasses of iced tea with lemon and asked, "Y'all want something to eat?"

"Nah, I'm good," Ryan replied.

"I'll have the evening sampler with baked beans and an extra side of potato salad. Oh, and I'd like a slice of Nana's apple pie for now and one of Ms. Annabelle's cinnamon rolls to go."

Nodding at Kerry, Gwen cast a quick glance at Ryan before turning to leave.

"Trying to taste everything on the menu, I see," he said when they were alone again. "I guess you do plan to do a thorough assessment of the restaurant."

She shrugged. "It's partially that and partially because I've missed your family's cooking. There's
nothing that compares to this place in the city." She
looked around then. "Not the ambiance, the salty sea
air, or the food."

"Don't forget the people," he stated. "Parker BBQ
wouldn't be anything without our customers. The
people of this town that've supported us since my
great-grandaddy first opened the doors."

She took a sip from her glass, then set it back on
the coaster shaped like a picnic basket with the
Parker BBQ logo scribbled across its center.

"Ernest Parker." She said his great-grandfather's
name with a nod. "I know the story, Ryan. Gael
Gibson brought him out here to the island and
Ernest turned the BBQ stand he had in Ohio into a
nationally renowned BBQ spot. You have every right
to be proud of that legacy."

"Which is why I'm trying to add to it, to expand
the Parker name in the BBQ industry," he said.

She'd been looking out toward the trees and then
past that, the water, before she turned her attention
back to him. "You could've ordered some lunch."

He shook his head. "I'd rather answer any questions you have about the deal. Do you want to see
the property where I plan to build the warehouse?"

"We used to have the big Halloween party in that
old shack Mr. Grambling owns. All the land surrounding it made for a great haunted maze," she said,
proving that she remembered the location well.

Not that he hadn't already known she knew the
location personally, besides the fact that he'd listed
the address in his proposal to her boss. He was just

trying like hell to keep this business-only. It's the way it needed to be handled.

"Remember when you and I went dressed as Michael Jackson and Iman from the *Remember the Time* video?" She grinned as she continued without waiting for his reply. "Everybody was so amazed by how authentic our costumes were, they couldn't stop talking about it. And when Mr. Grambling found his old Michael Jackson cassette tape, he'd put it in that boom box and blasted the song through the speakers. You started dancing the same sequence that was in the video, and Dyana Baldwin, who'd been carrying that digital camcorder around everywhere back then, started to record you."

He did remember that year he'd turned twenty and had come home from college for the holiday weekend. "The next day Dyana's parents called for an emergency island council meeting to do something about me, a Parker of course, behaving like a degenerate. I believe that's what her mother called me."

And, despite his father's objections, his mother had gone straight to Lois Baldwin's front door to tell her what she could do with her complaints about young people having innocent fun.

Kerry chuckled. "Yeah, that was such a fun night. And Dyana loved it, too, so I don't know why her mother was complaining."

Lois Baldwin was always complaining, especially about any- and everything anyone with the last name Parker did. It was in her nature since she believed the Parkers were several classes beneath her more influential family.

"It's a great location with lots of land. Plus, it's located close enough to the Docks that supplies won't have to be brought over on the ferry and then trucked across the island. Since, as you may recall, the town council is against too much traffic on Crescent."

"Oh, I recall all right. If you ask me, they're just trying to keep Eddie and that ridiculous Comet bus in business. This island could benefit from a public bus service with numerous buses moving on a schedule throughout the area. I know tourists would greatly appreciate that," she said.

"But what would the increase in traffic take away from the slow and relaxing pace of the island?" Kerry had always wanted things here to be bigger and better. He hadn't recalled that until this very moment, but now it made more sense. She'd never felt the way he did about Crescent, even after being born here. But none of that mattered now.

"This island can feel like time stood still," she told him and then inhaled a deep breath. She released the breath and continued, "Which is why trying to make this as a base for BBQ sauces we'd like to see go worldwide isn't exactly ideal."

Up until now, his hands had been in his lap. Before he replied to Kerry's statement, he needed a drink, so he reached for his glass and took a long, refreshing gulp. As he was putting his glass down on the table, Gwen arrived with Kerry's food.

"You don't think the sauces will sell if they're manufactured on this island?" he asked the moment they were alone again. "Have you even looked at the profit projections I sent with the proposal?"

She couldn't have. They boasted a steady profit

increase over the next five years, leaving a margin for the first year to build their momentum and get the marketing plan in place. But there was proof in black and white, across five sheets of paper and two graphs that Sofia had prepared for clarity if the stark numbers weren't readily understandable.

"I've reviewed the entire package, first with Phoebe and then with our analytical team." She used a fork and knife to cut the smoked sausage link that was included in the sampler. There was also a small scoop of pulled pork, pulled chicken, and three slices of brisket on the tray.

"So did you come here with suggestions or are you just ready to kill the deal because you've never liked this island?" He'd been trying valiantly to keep this purely professional, but there was so much personal in every word she'd spoken.

Instead of answering him right away, she forked a piece of sausage into her mouth and chewed. Then she ate a bit of the potato salad. Ryan wanted to leave her there to enjoy her meal, but he forced himself to sit still. At this point, she still held all the cards, but he couldn't deny that he was getting tired of letting her feel like she was the answer to his every prayer.

"Ms. Sarah's still got it. I swear she makes the best potato salad I've ever tasted," she said finally. "I don't know how Sofia's not a hundred pounds heavier sitting around this island all day every day eating this delicious food."

Considering Sofia was just as slim, save for being a bit curvier in the hip department, as Kerry was, Ryan didn't bother to reply to that dig at his sister.

"If you don't require a tour of the space for the warehouse, we can go over the financials again, take a hard look at the projections." He let his words trail off as he watched her fill the fork with pork she'd drenched in the house sauce. "Or I can leave you alone to enjoy the food that you've already admitted is better than anything you've had elsewhere."

When she finished chewing this time, she looked directly at him and smiled. "I like having lunch with you, Ryan. It brings back so many memories."

Memories that Ryan didn't want.

"I've got too much work that needs to be done to just have lunch with you, Kerry."

"But I'm here for you," she said and smiled sweetly. "I came all the way back to Crescent just to see you and to offer you my help. You *do* want my help, don't you, Ryan?"

He didn't want anything but for her to go back to where she'd been these past years. "I want to help you gather any information you need to make this deal come to fruition."

"Good," she said, an intriguingly cheerful grin spreading across her face before she speared a piece of brisket. She dipped the meat into the pool of Blazin' Blues sauce she'd requested on her plate and then stuck it into her mouth. She shook her shoulders and murmured, "Hmmmm," while Ryan continued to stare at her.

"Stop frowning, Ryan. I'm going to help you. I don't know why you thought I wouldn't."

He watched her eat another forkful of food and wondered why he'd thought Kerry wasn't here to help him, either. Or why her words and that happy little smile she'd kept plastered on her face wasn't convincing him the way it should've been.

• • •

Later that night, Ryan stared into a face with a smile that not only convinced him that this woman was good for him, but that she also held his heart captive.

"That yellow dress was just hideous," Allie said.

She sat on his couch next to him, her legs crossed with feet tucked, a bowl of candied walnuts and pretzels in her lap. Hours after his meeting with Kerry, Allie had come into the restaurant with Optimus trotting beside her obediently on his leash. They'd been sightseeing as Allie had told him, while she snapped pictures for her story. He hadn't bothered to ask her how the story or the hunt for the elusive Crescent Matchmaker was going because his mind had still been reeling with thoughts about this deal.

It'd been her idea to have a movie night and pizza, and the peace he'd felt the moment he'd seen her walk into the place that meant so much to him persuaded him to agree. She'd left the restaurant before him, and by the time he'd pulled up to his house, she was sitting on the front porch with the large veggie and extra cheese pizza she'd used Sofia's car to pick up from Island Slice, Natalia Bianchi's restaurant on Coastal Road.

"She could've just said no," he murmured for what he thought was the billionth time. Why this woman continued to agree to be in her friends' weddings, wearing these horrible dresses just because they asked, was a concept he just couldn't grasp.

"Not to her friends, I guess," Allie added. "I mean, I would've had to speak up about the dresses, but I'd definitely stand up for my friend."

"At over two dozen weddings?" The concept had boggled his mind. "I mean, really, how many friends can one person have?" He extended a hand and began to count off on his fingers. "Outside of my brothers, I've got Clay. He's the sheriff that I've known since pre-school. And Liam and Lucas, the Vereen twins who might actually count as friends of mine and Brody's since we all played on the baseball team together. That's it."

She was quiet for a moment, and he figured it was because she was chewing on another handful of that variation on party mix she'd bought from The Snack Shack, a food truck that parked down by the beach.

"If they asked you to be the best man or a groomsman at their wedding, would you do it?" she asked.

"Sure," he said. "But that's only five guys total, and I'm certain they wouldn't have me parading around in horrible colors and costumes." Not to mention he didn't think Brody would ever get married.

"I'd be Sofia's maid of honor in a heartbeat," she said, her tone almost wistful. "And I'd wear just about anything she asked me to wear, except for that scuba-diving thing." She shook her head. "I'm not big on the underwater idea. I mean, I guess it was kinda cute and original, but nah, that's a no for me."

Finally getting the change in her mood and kicking himself for not realizing where this was going, Ryan reached for her hand. "Is Sofia the only friend you have?"

She looked down as their fingers linked and nodded. "And Bella."

"Tell me about her," he said, rubbing his thumb over the back of her hand. "She's younger than you, right?" She hadn't spoken about her sister since that night at the carnival, but Bella, combined with Allie's parents, who he'd admitted only to himself that he didn't like very much, seemed to bring an almost unbearable sadness to Allie's eyes each time she mentioned them.

Tossing him a quick glance and a fleeting smile, she shrugged. "She got away," Allie said softly. "When we were young, we always talked about getting away from them, from the condo that felt like a prison and the never-ending expectations that threatened to choke us. But all I ever did was talk. Bella actually did it."

With her free hand, she set the bowl of nuts and pretzels on the other side of her and unfolded her legs so that they now dangled off the couch like his.

"We attended her graduation, watched her walk across the stage after receiving top honors. There was no other title we could carry, not if we wanted to avoid endless lectures and the threat of losing our only luxuries—the television in the family room and the radio/cassette player in our bedroom closet that we both loved."

She sighed. "They wouldn't take Bella's camera because she'd been careful not to show them how much it meant to her. And my writing in all those notebooks gave more of an intellectual optic to them, so I never mentioned that I'd been writing fiction for fear it would be frowned upon and subsequently taken away."

His heart broke for her as anger toward two people he'd never met vibrated through his veins. But he didn't speak, just moved closer to her so that his arm now brushed against hers. The warmth of her skin left bare from the sleeveless top she wore pressed against the parts of his skin exposed from the short sleeve of his polo shirt, their fingers still interlinked.

She huffed out a breath. "Anyway, Bella had always been the brave one. She'd had the guts to join that dance troop in high school even though she knew our parents would flip when they found out. And she'd had a boyfriend—Pete Francis—a basketball player she used to sneak off the campus with during lunch period to sit in his car." She chuckled and looked at him again. "I watched Bella walk across that stage. And then I never saw her again."

The light from the television made it possible to see the sheen of tears in her eyes, and Ryan gathered her up in his arms, rocking her as she released a tiny whimper. He didn't know how long he held her or how much of the movie they'd missed, but he hadn't wanted to let her go. Had needed to hold on as long as it took to make her feel she was wanted and cared for, something he doubted Allie had ever felt before. He couldn't snap his fingers and make her sister appear, which was something he sensed she wanted more than anything else, but he could give her this space in his life, his family, for as long as she wanted it.

That thought had him closing his eyes as she hugged him closer, her fingers gripping his shirt as if she needed to hold on.

Moments later when she eased out of his embrace, she did that stilted laugh again and shook her head. "Sorry. I've never had a mini meltdown while watching *27 Dresses* before."

She sat back against the couch, dropping her hands into her lap again.

"Don't apologize," he said, recognizing her physical and mental retreat. He would've held her all night, still prayed he would be able to, but knew that now he needed to allow her the space she craved. Space she'd probably built around herself in all these years she'd been living alone.

"Bella was my best friend, and then I met Sofia and she sort of filled that space that was like this big, gaping hole in my heart. I tried really hard not to cling to her that first semester when we were in New York, but Sofia's got a magnetic personality, and she's tenacious as hell." This time Allie's laughter was honest yet still piercing.

"You don't have to tell me," he said, trying to keep his tone as light as possible. "I'm the one who saved her from drowning when she was nine and insisted she was a good enough swimmer to come out to the deep end of the ocean with me and Brody."

"Oh no." She gasped.

"Oh yes," he continued. "And when I dragged her to shore, she swung and kicked at me, yelling for me to let her go so she could try it again."

"Yeah, that sounds like Sofia."

"She can be a menace, but I wouldn't trade her for the world," he said.

This time, Allie reached out and let her hand linger on top of his where it rested on his thigh. "I envy you and your siblings. You have so much here. Your parents, your grandmother, a community who knows and embraces you. There's so much kindness and encouragement. I've never experienced any of that before."

"I'm definitely blessed," he told her. "There's no doubt about that, and I appreciate all that I have. But I also know that if I really want them, I can try to obtain the things I don't have." The business deal wasn't at the forefront of his mind at this moment. The thing that he didn't have, the small part of his heart he'd locked away until he deemed it was safe enough to open, had just broken free.

"That's what I thought I'd done," she said softly. "I went to the college of my choice, selected my major when I knew my parents disagreed with both. I worked hard at my internships and then my first two jobs at magazines, living in small apartments until I started working at the blog and began making really good money. I bought a condo a good distance away from where my parents lived and tried to create a life of my own, one where I could do whatever I wanted without constant lectures and disappointed looks and sighs. I regulated my contact with them to protect my peace and yet—"

She still wasn't happy. She hadn't said that part, but the words floated through the air, and on some visceral level, he could totally relate to them.

"You say you envy me," he began. "But actually, Allie, I envy you."

Her eyes widened at his words.

"I may have left this island to go to college, but I came right back to what I knew."

"Because you love it here. It's so obvious that there's no other place you belong. The restaurant and the plans you have for its future, they're engrained in everything you do, and it's remarkable," she said.

"It's safe," he admitted. "Once, when I was in college, I thought about branching out on my own. Starting another business, perhaps consulting other restaurant owners or something like that. I even drafted a business plan. I told myself it was a school project, but there'd been some tiny seeds of hope within me that it could come to fruition. But then I changed my mind."

"Because of your family?"

He nodded. "Because the desire to build upon the Parker legacy, to add another brick to the fortress created by my great-grandfather—the son of a former enslaved stable hand who'd shined shoes on a corner until he could buy enough materials to make his first smoker and purchase the meats to put in it—was stronger than any other goal I could ever devise. You're right, my family has and always will be my foundation, but I don't think I've really allowed myself to think beyond that, to want other things outside of that."

To want love again.

But he couldn't say those words. They got stuck in his chest and wouldn't bubble up to the surface.

Music blared from the television, and she looked over at the screen and grinned.

"This is my favorite part," she said. "Well, except for Kevin's grand gesture at the end."

Ryan followed her gaze and couldn't stop a grin at the two main characters on the stage completely

butchering the lyrics to "Bennie and the Jets" in a
drunken karaoke performance. "Where I'm guessing
he wins Jane's heart after all."

She laced her fingers through his once more, but
this time when she settled back on the couch, she
leaned in closer to him and rested her head on his
shoulder as she sighed. "Yeah. That's always the best
part of these movies, when the main characters win
each other's hearts."

Ryan's heart swelled until warmth burst free like
the water rushing over the edge of earth down at the
Springs and filled him with a lightness he'd never felt
before. He wrapped an arm around Allie's shoulder
and pulled her even closer, resting his chin on the top
of her head as they watched the movie. And when
Kevin and Jane came together in that last scene on
the screen, he knew the woman sitting beside him
had already captured his heart.

He could only pray she'd be willing to give him
hers, too.

CHAPTER TWENTY-ONE

GM Allie. This is Nana. Can we talk? I'm at the Big House.

Allie read the text again, staring at the number that hadn't been stored in her phone. It had the island's area code, so she didn't immediately fear this was some type of spam message. But it suddenly occurred to her that she'd never given Nana her cell phone number.

There was no reason why she should've given the older woman her number. They weren't going to keep in touch after she left this island. Were they? Still, for six days, she'd slept in the same house with her, and for the past three days, she'd been sleeping with the woman's grandson. Facts which meant this text wasn't actually as strange as it could've been. Still, as she lay in Ryan's bed staring at the phone screen, a wave of uneasiness filled her.

"Bad news?" he asked.

She jumped because she hadn't known he was awake. The sun wasn't up yet, and Optimus hadn't made his appearance outside of Ryan's bedroom door, where he'd huff and whine until Ryan climbed out of the bed to take him out for the morning. The time on her phone read 5:27.

"Uh, no, not really," she replied and then cleared the screen. "Nana wants to talk to me."

He rolled over, wrapping his arm around her waist and pulling her back against his front. "She probably wants to know how you managed to seduce her focused and workaholic grandson."

Allie pushed her phone under the pillow and groaned. "No, please, don't say that. I do not want to have a conversation about you and me with your grandmother." Though she'd known it was no secret that they were together, not with the Parker family, that is.

At least she hadn't received another text since that first one about her and Ryan on the bench at the carnival, and after Sofia had denied being the matchmaker and they'd both questioned Lucy, Lindy, and the Sinclair sisters, Allie hadn't known where else to go with her search. Add to that Ryan's opinion that the matchmaker was harmless and Allie had decided to just go with the temporary interlude she and Ryan had going and not tie too many strings to this matchmaker's crown as a result.

So why was she now considering that Nana could've been the one sending the messages all along?

"Hey, baby, you okay?" Ryan was saying as he snuggled closer, kissing her shoulder.

She pulled her thoughts back to him, back to how good it felt to wake up next to him, how natural it felt to be in his arms and how much she loved his kisses no matter where they landed.

"Yeah, I'm good," she said.

"Nana probably just wants to give you an assignment for Friday night's Juneteenth celebration. Her and Mama were talking yesterday about all the things that needed to get done and who was going to do them. I wisely crept out of the kitchen before I received an assignment. But that's usually only a temporary reprieve."

His hand had moved up from her stomach to cup a breast, and she sighed as the now-familiar pulsing of desire beat in her veins. Yes, waking up beside Ryan had so many perks, all of which she was certain she would miss when it was time for her to leave.

"Well, since I failed the dough-making lessons your mother tried to give me last week and I'm much better at eating Nana's apple pie than mixing ingredients for the filling, I'll just volunteer to help set up the extra tables, chairs, and tents outside the restaurant."

In a couple of weeks, there was a huge bonfire and firework celebration planned to take place down at the beach for the July 4th festivities. But as this weekend marked the end of SummerFest and Juneteenth, the Parkers had decided to host their own independence celebration, which also coincided with Ernest Parker's birthday on June 20th.

"Nah, me, Brody, Clay, and the twins will handle all that setup," he said.

"Why? Because you're big, strapping men?" She'd meant her tone to be light, but it sounded snappy, and she wanted to cringe.

"Whoa," he replied instantly and moved so he could maneuver her onto her back as he propped his head up on one arm beside her. "I'm not giving off chauvinistic vibes, am I? Because that's not my intention. I'm just trying to find the easiest options for me and the guys."

There was a glint in his eyes, his lips curved into a simple smile, and his normally neatly shaved goatee was shadowed by this morning's new growth. He looked equal parts rugged and adorable, and those pesky pokes of desire threatened to consume her.

"I'm sorry. Nana's text is throwing me off. One good thing about staying here with you these past few days has been that I didn't have to do the walk of shame in front of everyone at the Big House. Now, it seems I've been given an early morning invitation to do just that."

He traced a finger over her forehead. "No frown lines before dawn," he said, continuing the soothing touch along her skin. "And believe me, it's not a big deal. My nana adores you."

"You don't know that."

"I do," he said with a nod. "Because if she didn't, she would've been making comments about you being in my bed without a ring on your finger every day this week."

She scrunched her nose up at that remark. "Really? Trevor spends the night with Taylor most of the time, and nobody says anything about that. I presumed because they're both consenting adults."

"Trevor's a touchy subject with my parents and Nana. And Nana's old school. She wants all her grandchildren married before having children."

"Hasn't she heard of birth control? Condoms?" She was feeling pretty punchy, and she hated that it was spurred by the incessant fear of facing this woman who so far had been very nice to her.

"I'm sure she has," he said, letting his fingers slide down to the line of her jaw. "And like I said, Trevor's a touchy subject with them. Me, on the other hand, I've always been the more discreet one with women, and I've never had a woman spend the night here."

"Because you haven't been serious about anyone since Kerry," she said quietly. This morning was not going in the blissful direction the previous ones had. She laced her fingers across her stomach and took a steadying breath.

Ryan nodded. "If Nana asks you about us, you can tell her to talk to me. I don't want her making you feel uncomfortable about what's essentially our business. That goes for anyone else in my family."

"And the Crescent Matchmaker?" she asked but then shook her head. "Sorry. I didn't mean to say that. Look, it's fine. I'll go talk to your grandmother, and I'll be okay with whatever the topic of discussion is. Her text just knocked me for a loop, and it's early, so I'm hungry."

He grinned then. "You're always hungry in the morning," he said and then leaned in to kiss her neck as his hand slid down to her breast again.

His touch, his lips, this moment, it all felt so good. "You're getting to know me pretty quickly, Mr. Parker," she said and wrapped her arms around his neck.

"I'm a fast learner," he replied and then lifted his head so he could touch his lips to hers.

• • •

Forty-five minutes later, Allie was headed back to the Big House. The day was warm but not as sunny as the others. In fact, it looked like they were definitely going to get rain. She entered the house via the kitchen because she could see that the patio doors were open through the screen surrounding the porch. On the walk over, she'd hoped that Nana had gotten tired of waiting for her and had headed to the restaurant instead, but when Allie stepped into the kitchen, she realized she wasn't that lucky.

"Good mornin'," Nana said the moment her gaze met Allie's.

She was sitting at the table in the breakfast nook, a newspaper spread out in front of her and a mug to her left.

"Got a minute for me?" Nana asked.

Well, she'd never done the walk of shame before and would've preferred it not to be in front of Ryan's grandmother, but sometimes you just didn't get what you wanted.

"Sure," Allie said and tried to act as nonchalantly as possible as she went to sit across from the woman whose grandson had been naked and spooned against Allie all night.

Okay, she definitely needed to erase that visual before she started talking because she drew the line at mistakenly giving Ryan accolades for his performance to his grandmother.

"You're reading the paper," Allie said in an effort to ease some of the nervousness bubbling around in her stomach. "I haven't seen them in so long, I'm always shocked they're still around."

"Really?" Nana arched a brow. "Oh, I guess people get all their news from the television and the internet now."

Allie nodded. "Yeah, most newspapers are online, too, so their readers have a choice."

"Well, my choice is to read the paper in the

mornings when I don't have to hurry over to the restaurant. And on Sundays." A wistful look covered her face. "I used to sit right out there on the back porch with my paper and coffee every Sunday morning. Teddy would sit out there, too, reading the sports section, of course. Then we'd go to church and come back here so I could cook dinner. Teddy would head back out to the porch while I cooked. Smoked that nasty cigar while he was out there, too."

Allie settled back in the chair, content to listen to Nana tell stories all day. As long as none of those stories circled around to her spending the night with Ryan.

"But that's not what I wanted to talk to you about," she said and carefully folded the paper on every crease.

"Okay," Allie replied.

"I wanted to know if Sofia had ever told you the history of our little island." When Nana was finished folding the paper, she put one hand on top of the other and stared at Allie.

"Um, not really. I mean, Sofia always said it was a beautiful place and I should visit. But before I came, I went to the town's website, and I did a little research on some of the information I got from there." She'd actually done a lot of research and thought she knew the story of the island's inception very well, but something told her it was best not to open that door with Nana. Because what if she asked Allie why she'd done all that research?

"Well, it's a very special story, and it started with a loving couple named Gael and Baleigh. They were both esteemed astrologists, and one of their hobbies was looking for any cosmic anomalies here on Earth. So, when they learned of this island shaped like a crescent moon, they knew they'd have to come and see it."

"There's more than one crescent-shaped island," Allie added, but Nana only shook her head.

"There's only one Crescent Island and don't you forget that." Satisfied that she'd shut Allie up on that subject, Nana continued.

Fifteen minutes passed while Nana talked, and Allie's stomach began to churn from hunger. She hadn't eaten a thing since last night's pizza, candied walnuts, and pretzels.

"Oh, my goodness," Nana suddenly exclaimed. "Well, I do tend to go on tangents every now and then."

"No, I wouldn't call it a tangent," she replied. "It's interesting to hear all this firsthand knowledge of the island. This is a wonderful place." She could easily admit that now, without all the cynicism she'd felt when she'd first arrived.

"There're so many stories I could tell you about me and my family's time here and why we love it so much, but I'd like to ask you a favor. That is, if you and my grandson don't have other plans for the day."

Allie tried to wrap her mind around the quick topic change and the actual topic that it'd been changed to.

Nana gave her a knowing smile that shouldn't have had heat rising in Allie's cheeks. Hadn't she mentioned something about consenting adults when she'd been talking to Ryan this morning? Yeah, well, that had been before she'd let this woman's very handsome grandson make sweet morning love to her. She groaned inwardly and squared her shoulders.

"Ryan and I," she started and then cleared her throat. But before she could continue, Nana tossed her head back and laughed. Now, Allie felt a mixture of embarrassment and confusion.

"Chile, don't you sit here and try to give me an explanation like I ain't never been with a man before."

Heat fused Allie's cheeks, and she wanted to crawl under this table and die. She'd thought she'd escaped having this conversation with Nana, but she'd been sadly mistaken.

Allie cleared her throat and sat up straighter. "I really like Ryan," she said instead of what she'd been planning to say. It would've sounded like an explanation that she didn't have a clue why she was going to give. Perhaps because she didn't want to lose this woman's favor.

For the past week it'd felt so good to have Nana and Ms. Sarah talk to her like not only a woman, but as someone with her own mind and opinions. Not one time had either woman talked down to her the way her mother usually did. And they listened; each of them had listened to whatever it was she'd said. She could tell by the way they'd casually reference something she'd said to them previously.

Nana reached across the table and put a hand over Allie's. "And he likes you, too," Nana said. "I know my grandson well, and he wouldn't have you in his house the way you've been if he didn't."

Waves of stress seemed to flow from her mind as she stared down at their hands. "I don't take that lightly," she said, more as a reminder to herself than an admission to Ryan's grandmother.

He'd told her a couple of times that no woman had been in that house or in his bed before her. That was a big thing, and initially it had been a very intimidating one. Ryan was putting her in a place she'd never intended to be with him or anyone else. He'd opened a door to her, and she'd walked in knowing that eventually she'd end up walking right back out. But he knew that, too. She'd made sure of it, so the tiny pricks of guilt that began to surface weren't warranted.

"That's good to hear," Nana continued and patted her hand. "You're both smart and beautiful people, so I trust you're going down your own path. But I'd like to ask you to do me a favor."

"Anything," Allie replied. This woman and her family had been so nice and accepting of her that there wasn't anything she wouldn't do for them in return.

"I just have this envelope over here that I need Annabelle to get. But since I didn't go into the restaurant early this morning, I'll have to head over there in another hour to get started on the seafood salad we're having as a special today." Nana reached up a hand to pat the tight curls of her hair. "Take my cart and ride on over to her house. It's the big blue one over on the bluffs. You can't miss it."

Allie knew which house she was talking about only because she'd seen it online. She'd never been there even though she'd wanted to visit the Gibson Museum before she left the island. So today would be that day, and afterward she'd head back to Ryan's to put the finishing touches on her story. She'd been working on it in the mornings after he'd left to go to the restaurant, she and Optimus sitting on his back porch while the sound of the rolling tide lulled her, spurring a creative voice inside her head that she hadn't heard from in far too long.

"Sure," she answered Nana. "That's no problem at all." And actually, if Nana had just put that request in her text earlier this morning, it would've saved Allie a ton of unwarranted tension. The thought had her chuckling to herself as Nana handed her the keys to the golf cart and went back to her bedroom to retrieve the envelope that needed to be delivered.

• • •

The Gibson Museum was like a blast from the past. Imagine if that infamous tornado from *The Wizard of Oz* had dropped a whole house designed in the 1800s onto this quaint little coastal island. It was a grand dwelling painted a stunning lake blue color with stark white columns, railings, steps, and window frames.

Allie put the golf cart in park at the curb in front of the house and for a few minutes just looked at it.

Tall, mature trees flanked the house but didn't overwhelm it. She didn't think anything could take from the antique stature of this place. The lawn surrounding the house was perfectly manicured, the brilliant green shade almost appearing fake, but for the few persistent dandelions that had decided to invade the space. Majestic stone pots were placed at the bottom of the steps at each end and were stuffed with bushes of brash white flowers.

The sun still hadn't appeared, and a cool breeze blew. She shivered against it, glad she'd decided on the heather gray T-shirt maxi dress and her quarter-sleeve dark denim jacket. Her white Converses were quiet as she walked up the brick sidewalk and took the stairs. The envelope Nana had given her was tucked into her purse that she'd crossed over her body when she'd gotten out of the cart.

Two knocks later and Ms. Annabelle appeared at the door. Allie's greeting smile was natural and hopefully hid her enchantment at the older women's attire.

Annabelle Gibson wore a floor-length purple-and-white tie-dyed dress. White bangles stretched up from her left wrist while silver charm bracelets bunched at her right one. Long silver earrings dangled from pierced ears, stars and moons that twinkled as she shook her head. Her hair was a bundle of curls similar to the way it'd been each time she'd seen her, only today there was a sparkling hair clip in the shape of a crescent moon tucked above her right ear.

Matte raisin lipstick coated her lips as she smiled at Allie in return. "Allison. It's so lovely to see you."

"Hi, Ms. Annabelle. I have this envelope that Nana wanted me to drop off to you." Allie reached down to her purse and was about to pull the envelope out when Ms. Annabelle took her by the hand.

"Come on in, Sweetie. Let's have some tea," she said.

Manners and curiosity had Allie stepping over the threshold into the cool air-conditioned foyer of the pretty blue house.

If Allie thought this place was majestic on the

outside, the inside left her totally speechless. Eggshell-painted walls, coffered ceilings, and wood floors glossed to perfection greeted her. A plush Aubusson rug of deep blues, green, and beige cushioned her feet as she followed Ms. Annabelle deeper into the house. They turned left into what seemed to be a sitting room. Here the walls shifted to a deep green hue, a fireplace on one end with an ivory marble mantlepiece and four emerald-green chairs positioned across from it on a rose-and-green-patterned rug.

There was a fresh scent in the air, like a mixture of honey and sea salt, and a tinkling sound drew her attention to the window where just outside windchimes in the shape of stars and moons—just like Ms. Annabelle's earrings—moved in the wind.

But if the vivid colors, the scents, and the sounds weren't enough to capture Allie's complete attention, the huge, shiny crystal ball sitting in the center of the table between the chairs closest to the fireplace certainly did.

CHAPTER TWENTY-TWO

"It's just for show," Ms. Annabelle said as they both sat in the green chairs. "People always come here hoping to see all the trinkets of psychic abilities or even magic." She shrugged. "Since I charge twenty-nine-ninety-five per person, I figure I should give them what they're looking for."

Allie sat back and let her elbows rest on the arm of the chair. "So this place isn't a museum for all things relating to the island?" She was confused. Several things were churning in her mind, things she recalled from her time on the island, mixed with things that just didn't make sense.

"Oh, yes, it certainly is. I can give you a full tour in a little bit. Just want to sip on my tea first before it goes cold."

On a silver-and-crystal cart beside her chair was a lovely china tea set, bordered in gold with pretty purple flowers all over.

"Here ya go," Ms. Annabelle said, offering Allie a cup on a saucer before lifting her own from the tray.

On another gaze around the room, she noted more crystal on the mantel, cannisters filled with colorful crystals and vases with fresh flowers tucked into the water inside. In front of one of the windows was a huge black telescope.

"You have questions," Ms. Annabelle said and took a sip from her cup. "I knew you would. When I first saw you, I knew you'd want to know the why and how before you believed."

Slowly, Allie brought the cup to her lips and took a sip. The tea was amazing, soft, light, full of sweetness and calm. "What flavor is this?" she asked.

"Oh, it's my secret brew," Ms. Annabelle whispered. "My granny taught me how to make it with just a pinch of the island's soul in each cup."

Well, that was extremely unhelpful. Allie certainly wasn't going to be able to find that on a shelf in her local supermarket. She didn't know why that thought had crept up so quickly and soundly in her mind but admitted to feeling more than a little uneasy here.

"You said you knew I'd want to know the how and why? How'd you know and when did you see me first?" She had a vague recollection of noticing Ms. Annabelle in the restaurant the day after she'd first arrived on the island.

"When you came into Wanda and Brenda's store," Ms. Annabelle said, staring at Allie over the rim of her cup.

Allie held the saucer in her hand but didn't take her eyes off Ms. Annabelle. She searched the woman's face, the thick brows, curly eyelashes, narrow nose, and deep purple lips. But it wasn't until Annabelle put down her saucer and cup and leaned forward to retrieve a stack of cards from beside the crystal ball that another spark of memory hit her.

"You were at the Emporium, in the corner doing tarot readings," Allie said and sighed. "Why didn't I remember that before now?"

"Oh, well, we see what we want when we want," Ms. Annabelle said.

Narrowing her gaze at her, Allie put her saucer

and cup on the table in front of her as well. "And what is it you want me to see right now, Ms. Annabelle? Because I feel like Nana's instructions to come here and drop off an envelope might've been a ruse."

She felt strongly about that now. Nana had been insistent on her coming here to drop off an envelope, but the older woman had plenty of time to drive here herself, drop off the envelope, and then get back to the restaurant in the hour she had available. Besides that, Ms. Annabelle stopped by the restaurant at least once every day. More often it was twice a day when she'd come back in the early evening to collect the profits from her cinnamon rolls. Nana could've given her the envelope then.

Instead of answering her, Ms. Annabelle held the cards in the palm of one hand and acted as if she were about to draw one from the top. "Interested?" she asked Allie with a raised brow.

"No!" Allie knew her response was quick, and she punctuated it by standing abruptly. "I don't want a tarot reading. I want to know why I'm here."

And she wanted to leave. For the first time since she'd arrived on Crescent Island, it felt weird being here. This house had seemed so pretty and welcoming from the outside, but now she was agitated, confused, and she wasn't totally sure why.

"You're here because it's where you're meant to be," Ms. Annabelle said cryptically. "At this place and time, it's exactly where you're supposed to be."

Allie shook her head and walked toward the window. It was going to rain soon. The sky was a dusky gray, clouds so heavy and low she wondered if she reached up, would she touch one? The trees closest to the house swayed as the breeze had picked up. If she were meant to be here at this moment, that must mean she was meant to get caught in this storm because Nana's golf cart had nothing but an overhead covering, and it wasn't going to keep her from getting drenched in the downpour.

"You don't use a crystal ball, but you use tarot cards," she said as she turned to face Ms. Annabelle again. "I don't know if you're purposely being peculiar or if you really are this eccentric."

The woman had put the cards on the table and now sat back in her chair, legs crossed at the ankles so that her white Crocs peeked from beneath the long dress. She looked like a character on television. A good witch in *The Wizard of Oz*, perhaps? No, definitely *The Wiz*. Annabelle Gibson would've starred in *The Wiz* with her cosmic persona and wide grin. Hadn't Motown music been playing in the Emporium that first time Allie had been in there? Come to think of it, more Motown tunes had been playing on her next two visits to the store. The days she returned to question the Sinclair sisters about their mailing list.

No, it couldn't be.

Ms. Annabelle's grin stayed fixed, her eyes widening as if she knew exactly what Allie had been thinking.

"You were at the Emporium the day I put my information on that mailing list," she said, crossing the room again and stopping right in front of Ms. Annabelle's chair.

"I was," the woman replied with a nod.

"Did you copy my cell phone number and birthdate down? And before you answer, you should know that's a crime." Ryan had warned about her making that statement to the residents of Crescent Island, but at this moment, Allie didn't care. "You're the matchmaker, aren't you?"

Ms. Annabelle stood from the chair slowly. She lifted her hands and fluffed her hair before pursing her lips. "Well, I think it's time," she said. "Follow me, Allison."

"How do you know my full name?" This was the second time she'd used it, but Allie had been too enamored by this place to wonder how she'd known it. Now that cynical Allie was definitely back on the scene, she had a question for everything.

They walked down a tight hallway, with more eggshell-colored walls covered with pictures, some of people but most of the stars, the moon, the sea. The woman who was a half a foot shorter than her and shuffled along in front of her wasn't answering any of her questions, a fact that was beginning to irritate Allie.

But not enough that she would turn and walk out of this house. No, if she didn't believe anything else Annabelle Gibson would possibly say to her today, Allie believed that she belonged here at this very moment. She sensed she was about to get the answers to the reason she'd come to this island in the first place, one way or another.

They went down four steps, and the rooms opened to a big space—like an open concept, but cluttered with stands and shelves, antique chairs that didn't look comfortable for anyone to sit on, glass and brass tables. This space had periwinkle-colored walls, more crystals, a ton of wind chimes and huge windows.

"When my great-great-grandparents found this island," Ms. Annabelle began as she walked throughout the space, switching on Tiffany lamps and adjusting knickknacks, "there wasn't a thing here," she continued. "Just the land, the nature, and the stars. My great-great-granddaddy loved the stars, said they led him here after all his many years studying them."

She stopped and touched a part of the wall that was full of maps. They'd been mounted in the crescent moon shape, pasted close together like a collage. "These were his maps," Annabelle said. "He kept so many maps of the constellations and the galaxy in his office on the first floor, his bedroom upstairs and at the lighthouse. He loved being at the lighthouse, and so did my mother."

There was a wistfulness to her tone and also a sincerity. Speaking about her family and their history wasn't part of the show; it was her truth. A part of Allie wanted to beg her to continue, to share more about the people who'd made her who she was, who'd made this island what it was today, but there were more pressing questions. More things she needed to know to complete the task she'd started.

"I read the story online," Allie said, clenching her fists so that her short nails dug into the palm of her hand. The nagging pain served as a reminder, a pinch that kept her in the present.

Ms. Annabelle turned, giving her a quick and fleeting smile. "My great-great-grandmother had a different story," the woman said.

That shut Allie up and had her following Ms. Annabelle over to a small table with two chairs behind it.

"Baleigh Gibson was smart and tenacious. My mama used to say I was a lot like her. Not only because she had a way of getting what she wanted, but also because she loved hard and steadfastly."

Annabelle looked away then, her hand moving to her neck where she fingered a green rock—maybe it was jade; Allie didn't know and wasn't sure it mattered. But the way she touched it and stared off at nothing in particular told Allie whatever the stone was actually called, it meant a lot to Annabelle.

More chiming started, and Allie looked around to see all of the windchimes hanging from hooks on the shelves and fish wire tacked to the top of the windowsills began to move. They sparkled, some with golden sun pieces, others with crescent moons in silver, white, a marble-like deep blue, stars in gold, gray, and a translucent peach.

Suddenly, Annabelle cleared her throat and dropped her hand to her side. "She was also one lucky lady, my GG Baleigh—that's what I used to call her. Not to her face, she'd been really sick by the time I was born, and when I was old enough to talk good, she'd already passed on to the heavens. Anyway," she continued with a shake of her head. "GG Baleigh won herself a whole island in a risky game of poker."

"What?" That hadn't been on the website, and Allie couldn't help but feel stunned at what Ms. Annabelle had just said.

The woman plopped down into a chair that looked far too dainty to hold her voluptuous figure, but the wrought-iron legs held firm as Ms. Annabelle extended a hand in invitation for Allie to sit on the other chair. Allie eased down, never taking her eyes off Ms. Annabelle. "Are you saying that the stars didn't lead Gael Gibson to this island? That Baileigh Gibson won the island instead?"

Ms. Annabelle nodded, and her cosmic earrings swished back and forth. "She won it but let my great-great-granddaddy believe he was making an important discovery. After all, they'd fallen for each other because of their love of the stars."

"Hmphf," was all Allie could say as she sat back in the chair. This was an odd twist to the story she'd been hearing non-stop since she arrived here.

"They built this island together. Got some other people to come and help them and lived here happily ever after. Loving each other and loving the idea of people building their life here under the stars," Ms. Annabelle continued. "Two years ago, I found some letters that my mother had apparently received before her death. Letters stating that taxes or fees of some sort hadn't been paid and that the island would revert back to the government if we didn't come up with the money."

"How much money?" Allie asked.

Ms. Annabelle shook her head. "A lot," she replied and then crossed her arms over her ample bosom. "I couldn't let that happen. So I did what I always did. I ran to my friends, the Diamonds. They'd helped me out of so many things before that I knew they'd be there for me again. But I'd already come up with a plan. I just needed them to help me put it into motion."

Allie stared at the woman across from her, piecing things together slowly but surely. "It was a marketing scheme all along. I knew it!" She slapped a hand on her thigh. "You're luring more tourists to this island, taking their money, and adding it to your fund to pay back those taxes so you can keep this island."

"Shirley said you were smart." Annabelle nodded. "I told her you were lonely and looking for a connection, for someone to unlock that door you'd built around your heart. But she insisted you were here for your job. Trying to get a story."

"I was," Allie said. "I mean, I am. That is why I'm here."

Annabelle pursed her lips again, narrowing her eyes as she stared at Allie. "You can keep telling yourself that if you want, but the stars don't lie." She held up a hand as Allie was about to speak. "Now, I know my great-great-grandmother wasn't exactly honest with her man, but that was because she loved him above all else. Her heart was in the right place. What about your heart, Allison? Is it in the right place? Right here and right now?"

There was a heaviness in her chest at the woman's question. The thumping of her heart perhaps, or was it something more?

Every place has a heart if you're open enough to see it.

That's what Renee told her the day she'd threatened to fire her. It's what Allie had told her boss she was coming here to look for. But that had been a lie, just as all that lovelorn advice Annabelle was dishing out on the Written in the Stars blog was.

Still, as much as Allie hadn't wanted to prove the

love advice and the blog was a lie, there'd been so
many conflicting signs. She hadn't been here a week
when Nana had told her the kitchen was the heart of
the house. That same kitchen was where she and
Ryan had almost had their first kiss.

Ryan. Optimus. Sofia.

Her heart hammered against her ribs until her
breathing became labored. Each of them had a place
in Allie's heart. She could give a logical explanation
for when she'd developed a connection to each of
them, but there was one common theme. Shaking her
head didn't rid her mind of all the conflicting
thoughts circling around, so she tried to focus on her
breathing instead.

In the next instant, she felt Ms. Annabelle's hand
on her shoulder before it slipped to her back where
she gently patted. "Just breathe," she told her. "I ain't
seen nobody die yet from figuring stuff out."

"There's nothing…to figure…out," Allie managed
to say. "I came here for work. To write an article."

"About this island, like those other articles you
wrote?"

She looked up at her and saw the woman arched a
brow.

"Yeah, I know about you, Allison Sparks, and
your articles on that travel blog. You thought you
were coming here to write an article tearing us to
shreds like you did all those other places, but really,
the stars had another idea."

Allie shook her head. "No. I don't believe in that
stuff."

"Do you believe in Ryan and what the two of you
have been doing since you been here?"

Standing, Allie shot back, "That's none of your business."

"Oh, now that's where you're wrong. The stars, the moons, it's all my business. I was born into it, and just like my great-great-grandparents believed in love, I do, too. And the charts don't lie. I saw it just as plain as I'm looking at you right now."

"I'm leaving," Allie said and started to walk away. "All of this is ridiculous, just like I knew it was. It's a ploy, a gimmick, and people have a right to know."

"People have a right to *believe*," Annabelle said from behind her. "Just like you believe that you're falling for Ryan and he's falling for you."

Allie spun around. "You didn't do that!" she insisted. "Ryan and I would've met eventually. I've known Sofia for years, and I'd always planned to come here."

"But look how long it took you to get here. Ever asked yourself why that was? The answer's in the stars, Allison. That's what your heart's been tryin' to tell you since you got here, but your mind's in a hellfire hurry to shoot it all down. To keep you in that box you've built around yourself."

"You don't know me," Allie said when she made it to the steps. "You stole some information off a mailing list—which you really need to stop doing before somebody has you arrested—and you twisted it around to create some fanciful story in your head. Why? I don't know, because I was already here on the island? And Ryan lives here. So it wasn't to get tourist dollars that you were already receiving."

She shook her head then because she still didn't understand all that was happening here. Like, who else, besides the Diamonds, knew about this? Because somebody had to be taking the tourist dollars and sending off tax payments for them to keep this island. And who was collecting that money? What government was Annabelle talking about?

It didn't matter. None of it did. She had her story now. The story she'd come here to get. All she had to do was write it.

Annabelle didn't speak again as Allie continued through the house and out the door. She jogged down the steps and the walkway until she could ease behind the wheel of the golf cart and pulled off.

When she finally arrived in front of the Big House, she hopped out and walked Nana's keys back into the house to drop on the kitchen table. Then she kept going out the back patio doors and across the grass until she arrived at Ryan's place. There, she found her laptop and headed straight out to the back porch.

That's where she was when the rain started. Huge drops that landed with a loud splatter, drenching the ground in seconds, plopping into the sea like a truckload of coins had been tossed out there. And in the midst of the storm Allie began to type:

The heart of Crescent Island rests in a big blue Victorian house where secrets are kept and love is presumed to be the answer.

CHAPTER TWENTY-THREE

Early Friday evening, Ryan watched Allie set a red velvet cake on the dessert table. The six-foot-long table covered in floor-length black linen was already crowded with half a dozen other cakes, five pies, trays of cookies, and bowls of banana pudding, peach cobbler, and strawberry trifle. She stepped back and pulled her phone from her pocket, aiming and snapping pictures at the spread before her.

He'd seen her doing that a lot these past couple of days. Taking pictures of the beach, the food as it was plated at the restaurant before being carried out to tables. When they'd gone out to dinner at the Brew & Grub last night, she'd snapped shots of the pictures that lined the walls. Ones of the fisherman who lived on the island, their boats, them bringing in a day's haul, the plate of chicken and waffles they'd ordered and she'd gawked over before eating every morsel.

He grinned at the memory. Her appetite no longer amazed him, because he loved to see her eat. Loved the sounds she made as she enjoyed each taste. And that satisfied look she always got when she was stuffed warmed his heart to see such unabashed joy. When she'd told him that she'd never felt the way she did when she was here on Crescent in any of the other places she'd traveled to, Ryan believed her. And he'd hoped that he was part of the reason she felt that way.

"Setup looks good," Sofia said, coming to stand

beside him.

He gave his sister a quick glance before turning his attention back to Allie. She'd moved on from the dessert table and was now taking pictures of the full outside setting.

"Yeah," Ryan replied absently.

There were eight long tables, four on each side with a path down the middle. Each table was covered in black linen, vases filled with red roses in the center. Ernest Parker loved the color red. Paper plates, utensils, napkins, and cups were red, yellow, and green, metal chairs tucked under each table. Balloons matching the color scheme hung outside the restaurant doors, inside the dining room, and along the railing on the back terrace.

"And there's enough food in the kitchen to feed three armies," Sofia continued.

Ryan nodded. "I brought six trays of fried chicken over from the Brew & Grub about an hour ago, and Clay said he had more coming when he picked up his mother to bring her here."

"We sure do know how to prepare for a celebration," she said.

He grinned. "Yeah, we do. It's gonna be a good night," he said.

"You mean the meal and fellowship or after, when you and Allie head back to your place?"

Turning, he stared at her now.

She smiled and shook her head. "When I told you to show her around, I just figured she'd be good company for you since you'd been walking around here so uptight for so long. But I never guessed there'd be a love match in the making."

"She doesn't believe in the matchmaker," he said, recalling his earlier conversations with Allie about the blogger and the sender of those text messages.

"I know, she told me," Sofia said. "And she showed me the two texts she received. I even went around with her, asking about who the matchmaker was."

"You did?" Allie hadn't mentioned that.

"Yeah, but I could've told her it wasn't Lucy or Lindy from the B&B. For one, Lindy is too young. Her attention is much more focused on Eric Seymour and his new position as the star forward on the high school basketball team. And Lucy keeps a smile on her face, but she's still indulging in a hate/loathe relationship with her ex, so matchmaking isn't something she'd be interested in right now."

"How do you know so much about people on this island when you barely like to socialize with any of them?" he couldn't help but ask. Sofia had been moving around a little better in the past few days, and she hadn't been balking as much about Nana's directives that she still take it easy, but Ryan wasn't fooled. He knew his sister was simply biding her time until she could break out of this recuperation stage altogether.

She elbowed him. "Hey, I socialize. A lot more than you do."

"You haven't been out with Ivy and the others you went to school with in months."

"I'm no longer a part of their club since I'm the only unmarried one," she replied. "And don't change the subject. We were discussing you and Allie."

"Nah, we weren't discussing that. You were making assumptions."

"Correct assumptions," she added. "Everybody on the island knows she's been staying with you."

Of course they did. Clay had even mentioned it this morning when he'd stopped by to drop off more chairs they'd borrowed from the community center for tonight. If Ryan hadn't given his friend a long, drawn-out explanation of what he and Allie were doing, he certainly wasn't about to give his sister one.

"She's perfect for you," Sofia said just as he'd turned back to see Allie fingering one of the roses in the vase on the table farthest from him.

Her phone was in her other hand, but she was focused on that flower, on the petal her fingers moved over. She'd been doing that a lot these past couple of days, too, staring off at something, thinking, he surmised, but not sharing her thoughts. He'd only asked her once what was on her mind, and when she'd declined to tell him, he'd decided that it was probably what had been on his mind, too.

Their time was winding down. Soon, she'd be leaving Crescent. Leaving him.

"She's perfect without me," he replied to Sofia. "Everything that she was before she came here was enough. This island, me, our time together, none of that changed who she's always been inside." He'd been telling himself that since late last night as he'd lay in the bed beside her, watching her sleep.

But her presence had definitely changed him.

These past two weeks had been the only time in the last three years that he hadn't been totally focused on the restaurant expansion every hour of every day.

"That's not true," Sofia said. "Both of you have changed."

It felt like she'd been reading his mind, but Ryan knew that wasn't possible.

"Allie's more relaxed. She's more open to happiness than I've ever seen her before," Sofia continued. "And look, I know that she wanted happiness above all else. I still remember the pain in her eyes each time she told me another story about her parents and the cruel way in which they'd treated her and her sister. I also recall how much she still yearned for their approval."

"Not anymore," he said with a shake of his head. "She's not trying to prove herself to them. She wanted to prove to herself that she could be okay without them. And she has."

"Yeah, she has," Sofia said. "And she's better with you."

He took a deep inhale, letting the breath out in a slow sigh. "I'm definitely better with her," he admitted.

"Have you told her that?"

"No."

"Chicken."

He frowned at his sister. "Anybody ever tell you that you're nosy and a smart-ass?"

She shrugged and leaned into him. "Only the people who aren't afraid I'll punch them for saying such a thing."

Ryan laughed. He wasn't afraid of Sofia, but he did love her for being nosy and a smart-ass and for suggesting he show Allie around the island. He'd forever be thankful to Sofia for that.

• • •

"We should all go sailing tomorrow," Liam said. He was sitting at the other end of the table.

Ryan and Allie sat side-by-side with Clay on his left. Sofia, Taylor, Trevor, and Brody were on the other side of the table.

"Lucas already said we have a light schedule down at the marina so we can take one of the boats out at dawn, see the sunrise, and then spend the day on the water," Liam continued. His older twin Lucas had gone inside to the bar to get another pitcher of beer.

They'd been sitting at this table drinking, eating, and talking ever since the festivities began two hours ago. Now, night had fallen, the air was balmy, and other guests walked about, ate, danced, played cards, and simply enjoyed the celebration. Allie rested a hand on his thigh and smiled over at him when he asked, "What do you think? You down for a day on the water?"

"Sunrise on the water sounds lovely," she replied. Sitting next to her like this had felt so right, so normal. When other islanders had come over to the table to chat with them, he'd happily introduced her to the ones she didn't already know, like his aunts Anna and Ruby, some of his cousins and their kids, and Mayor Nat, who'd stopped by a while ago.

If there was some tension while Nat had stood at the end of the table talking to everyone about the island and the remaining centennial celebrations for the year, nobody verbally acknowledged it. Especially not Taylor, who'd taken that time to lean in closer to Trevor. Or Trevor who'd looked everywhere but at Nat, or Taylor for that matter. That was a situation on a slow burn, but it was bound to boil over sooner rather than later.

"I'll pass," Sofia said suddenly. "I've got a book to get started on."

Beside him, Allie shook her head and looked away from Sofia, but Sofia laughed and Ryan felt like he was missing the joke. If Sofia was referring to what Allie had been writing for hours each day since earlier this week, then he wasn't going to be hurt that his sister was getting to read it first. After all, they were best friends. And what was he to Allie? Lover? Boyfriend? Summer affair?

Scrubbing a hand down his face to push those thoughts away, he focused his attention on Brody, who was finishing the last of his iced tea that he'd spiked with rum, and clapped. "We're sailing tomorrow! Who's gonna ask Nana to fix us a picnic lunch?"

"Oh yeah," Liam chimed in. "Ms. Shirley makes those overstuffed chicken salad sandwiches on that super-soft bread."

"We should go into the kitchen and claim a couple of those whole chickens we had out on the smokers now," Brody added. "I can get them all chopped up tonight so all she has to do is apply her special mix and spices."

"I'll go with you." Liam stood.

Sofia shook her head. "She's gonna fuss both of you out for waiting until the last minute. So I'll go with you. I hate to miss out on all the fun."

Ryan chuckled as Sofia was just about to stand. But when Kerry walked up to the table with her arm looped through Harlan Baldwin's, everybody went stone still.

"Well, hello," Kerry drawled, her saccharine laced smile in place as she glanced at everyone at the table. "Sorry we're a little late. I had some last-minute reports to finish and a couple of emails to send off."

"Hey, guys," Harlan said with a slow wave.

The Parker/Baldwin feud tended to run hot and cold where this generation was concerned. Ryan, who could care less what any of the Baldwins thought about him or his family, had always taken a cordial route with the five children who were around his age. Sofia and Brody leaned more on the hot side, as evidenced by the deep scowl they each now wore.

Trevor gave Harlan a nod and a "Hey man," before Ryan followed with his own, "Hey."

"You two dating now?" Liam asked, confusion etching his face. "I thought Kerry was only here for a visit to, you know, give Ryan an answer about his business."

If Ryan were closer, he'd have elbowed Liam in the ribs, hard. Clay took care of that for him, and Liam grunted.

"Oh, well, speaking of that," Kerry continued. "Ryan, you remember when I told you the other day that I was here to help you."

He wanted to groan or, better yet, to just tell her what she could do with her company's money, but Allie eased her hand over to link her fingers with his. He stared down at them and then up at her, giving her a small smile of thanks for keeping him steady. For being the peace he hadn't even thought he'd needed.

"As I was saying," Kerry continued by clearing her throat. "I saw a post on the See, Eat, Travel blog that a very special story on Crescent Island was coming tomorrow. There were some really great pictures of The Docks and Parker BBQ to give a little preview, I guess."

Allie stiffened beside him, and Ryan stared quizzically at Kerry.

Sofia frowned. "You are such a bi—"

"Oh, wait, save that," Kerry said, holding up a hand. "I suspect you might want to aim that animosity at your little friend here. You know, the one who's been here snuggling up to all of you only so she could write a scathing story about this island for her little blogger job."

"You're a day late and a dollar short," Ryan snapped. "Everybody here knows exactly what Allie does for a living."

Brody's hand raised slowly. "Ah, except for the part about writing a scathing review about the island."

Kerry's grin spread, her satisfied gaze finding Allie. "Oh, you didn't tell them that's your thing?" She looked back at the group seated and silent at the table. "Yeah, so Allison Sparks writes reviews for places she visits. Most of which are so horrific travelers stop visiting those places. She's like the authority on where not to go on your vacation. I can't wait to see how she rates Crescent and this place, of course. Since she sent a picture of the restaurant, I'm sure she's got plenty to say about your lovely family establishment."

Ryan frowned. "That's enough," he said. "You're barking up the wrong tree. Like I said, we all know what Allie does for a living."

Kerry raised a brow. "Then you should know that my company can't knowingly back a business that's about to take on a ton of negative press."

The sting of rejection didn't hit quite as fiercely as it had years ago, and Ryan only glared at Kerry. "So, you're advising Brownstone not to invest in Parker Sauces?"

"Thank your little girlfriend for that decision, Ryan," Kerry spat.

"That's a bunch of crap!" Sofia stood, and Trevor put a hand on her arm to both steady her and keep her from jumping on Kerry. "You had no intention of ever approving that investment. Especially not once you got here and saw that Ryan was happy with someone else. You're still the same selfish brat you were when you lived here."

"Maybe so, but I'm successful," Kerry said and leaned into Harlan. "And I'm happy. At least for to-night. You and the rest of your family can stay stuck here on this backward little island, running this same 'ole shack. I'll choose making money, living in my high-rise condo, and driving my fancy car every time."

"And I'll choose happiness and family," Ryan told her. "Every time."

• • •

Allie's chest hurt. Her legs felt like lead weights as she walked away from the table. Ms. Annabelle and Nana had appeared, and so had Mr. Vernon as Brody had asked, "So is it true? Did you write a scathing story about the island?"

Ms. Annabelle had shushed his question with a wave of her hand and a directive to, "Don't just sit there. Get up and play some music. Start one of those line dances y'all like to do."

Allie didn't know if Ryan had attempted to follow her or if the dancing had ever started. She opened her mouth as she walked quickly, sucking in deep gulps of air. The sweetest air she'd ever smelled, on this place that up until a few moments ago had brought her the most joy she'd ever experienced.

"That Kerry never did play well with others," Ms. Annabelle said from somewhere just behind her as Allie approached the beach.

In the next seconds, Nana came up to stand at her other side. Both of the older women stopping when Allie did the same and looked straight ahead.

"This is precisely what I didn't want to happen," she said quietly. "It's why I never tell people I'm a travel blogger. I just show up, observe, write the story, and go home." She talked as if she were alone, the words just tumbling from her mind and out of her mouth.

"People are gonna think what they wanna think no matter what you tell them," Nana had replied. "It's what you show them that counts."

"And even then, they still don't believe," Ms. Annabelle chimed in.

Allie hadn't spoken to Annabelle since she'd walked out of her house two days ago, but she'd thought a lot about her and her great-great-grandparents.

"I never intended to hurt anyone," she continued. "Not on this island or anywhere else. I just wanted to tell the truth."

"Some people don't like the truth." Ms. Annabelle seemed like she was gonna keep going with her little jabs, but Allie wasn't in the mood to engage with them.

"I always believed you'd do right by us," Nana said, looping an arm around Allie's shoulders. "Once I searched your name on the computer and read some of your other stories, I knew one thing for sure. That you were hurting. Looking for some peace in yourself that you were never gonna find as long as you kept your heart locked away."

"Yep, my momma always said hurt people will hurt other people," Ms. Annabelle added.

Allie didn't even look her way.

"I'm over being hurt by my parents and my dysfunctional relationship with them," she declared.

"Maybe so, but the remnants of that relationship have been guiding you every step of your adult life. You treated every place you visited just like your parents treated you," Nana said.

Allie didn't know how this woman had known so much about her. Had Sofia told her something? Ms. Sarah? At any rate, Nana's words had rung true, but none of that mattered now. What was done was done. She'd emailed her story to Renee this morning and had planned to show it to Ryan tonight.

Ryan.

She sighed at the thought of how he must be feeling at this moment. He wasn't going to get the funding he needed, and she knew he was disappointed right now. A part of her ached for him and the fact that she was partially responsible for his defeat. If she weren't here, Kerry wouldn't have had the ammunition to strike back at him. Then again, if Kerry's goal in coming back to this island was to either get Ryan back or make him pay for not leaving with her in the first place, she was going to do whatever she could to make that happen whether Allie was here or not.

"I should go back and see if Ryan's okay," she whispered.

"Ryan's got his family and his friends surrounding him," Nana said, lifting a hand to Allie's shoulders. "You need a moment to digest the situation and gather yourself. Take it."

A moment she probably could've taken alone, but for the first time in far too long, Allie was happy that wasn't the case. She didn't have to sit alone in her condo trying to atone for why she felt a certain way about her parents. Didn't have to carry the guilt and anguish inside for fear nobody would understand her. She didn't have to dwell on the fact that she'd once had a sister she could lean on. Nor did she have to blame herself for any of those things.

She could just breathe, as Nana had said.

But on her second breath, Allie's phone vibrated in the back pocket of her jeans. She let out a heavy sigh, thinking it was probably Sofia calling to see where she was, or perhaps Ryan checking on her. She was wrong. The number on the screen was familiar and only made her grimace.

"Let's give her some privacy," Nana said to Ms. Annabelle. "We'll head back to the restaurant and wait for you there."

Allie had nodded, just as both women hustled away, leaving her to stare at the phone while the waves peaked and crashed in the distance.

She could decline the call. It would be for the best. Her mother was the last person Allie needed to talk to right now. Or she could tough it out and deal with whatever complaints Claire had ready for her, like she always did.

Why haven't I heard from you? Are you away on that little job again? You need to communicate more. Allie had heard all those things before, and her temples throbbed as they replayed in her mind.

When the phone stopped ringing, she breathed a sigh of relief and let the arm holding it drop to her side. Her gaze resumed focus on the ocean, the dark and ominous look of the water, and the warm breeze that stirred tall grass in the distance. She was just about to replay the events that had taken place and remind herself that she needed to go back and check on Ryan when her phone began ringing once more.

The same number, she noted when she frowned down at it again. Her mother was being persistent tonight. Claire never called back-to-back. She'd leave a strongly toned message and then wait until Allie got up enough nerve to call her back. But, apparently, not this time.

"Hello?" Allie answered because she had no desire to keep this up for the duration of the night.

The voice on the other end of the phone wasn't her mother's, and after she'd managed to listen without collapsing to the ground, Allie turned and took off running toward Ryan's house.

CHAPTER TWENTY-FOUR

She was gone.

Those three words played in Ryan's mind like a scratched record.

She was gone. And he was alone in his house once again. Optimus jumped up, resting his beefy paws on Ryan's thigh as he sat on the back porch.

A raspy chuckle sounded as he rubbed a hand over the dog's head. "Okay, so maybe I'm not alone," he whispered. "But she's still gone."

With one hand, he scooped the dog up and set him on his lap, while the other hand still held his phone. He had no idea how long he'd been sitting out here, just felt like he had no other place to go. No, he actually felt closer to her here. Every day this past week Allie had sat in this same chair, feet up on the wicker ottoman that matched the two flower baskets Nana had brought over months ago. Instead of a dog on her lap, her laptop had taken that spot as her fingers breezed over the keyboard. He'd thought she was writing her book because whatever she was doing had seemed to be longer than a story for a blog post.

At any rate, he hadn't bothered her while she was writing. The sight played way too closely to the daydreams he'd begun having about their future. A future that had never been promised to them because Allie's home was in Miami. Still, he'd tried to hold on to the stems of hope that had wrapped around him every night along with Allie's arms as they lay in bed together.

They'd talked about so much in his dark bedroom late at night or in the early morning hours. She wanted to see Crescent at Christmas, had insisted he had to watch *Four Christmases* with her.

"You're gonna love it!" she'd squealed. "It has everything you like, comedy, family, and romance."

They'd been lying on their sides that night, face-to-face as they each rested their heads on the edges of a shared pillow. "Nah," he'd replied. "You love the romance."

She'd grinned, her cheekbones going high, teeth bared as a little giggle escaped. "Facts."

She'd looked amazing with her hair a wild mass of curls, face makeup free, and bare toes sliding along his leg. His heart had swelled so big he'd had to cough to keep from choking out the next breath.

Tonight, he felt like a stack of bricks had been piled on his chest and each inhale he took was a struggle. With his gaze toward the water, he replayed the events of the night. The moment he knew Kerry was about to wreak havoc and the seconds after Allie's hand had slipped out of his.

He'd stood as soon as she had, ready to go after her, when his mother had appeared out of nowhere, touching a hand to his arm. "Let her go," she'd said softly. "Nana's got her."

But he'd wanted to be with her. He'd wanted to assure her that he hadn't believed Kerry for one moment. Kerry had decided to deny the funding long before figuring out what Allie did for a living; he was sure of it.

And while he'd wanted this expansion for the restaurant more than he'd ever wanted anything else, the day he'd sat at the table across from Kerry listening to her reminisce about their past, he'd concluded that, just as his father had said, with or without Brownstone, the expansion would happen.

Some way, somehow, he'd make it happen, just like his great-grandfather had done.

Finding out what Allie did for a living was just the icing on the cake for Kerry. Something she could gloat about and make one last jab at him. He'd wanted to despise her for that, but really, he'd only been worried about Allie in those moments. Just as he was now.

"You gonna sit out here all night?" Brody asked as he came around the side of the house into Ryan's view.

"It's my porch," Ryan replied drily.

"But your girl's gone back to the city," Trevor, who was a couple steps behind Brody, said.

Frowning at both of them, Ryan asked, "What?"

He'd supposed that was a possibility, but he'd been more comfortable telling himself she'd simply returned to the B&B. He knew she wasn't at the Big House because Sofia had gone straight there when he'd called her seconds after walking into his house and finding Allie's stuff gone.

Sofia was last to come up onto the porch. "She called Eddie for a ride, and he rushed her down to the Docks just in time to get the last ferry out for the night," she said somberly.

Still clenching his phone in one hand, he tightened the other arm around his dog and let out a heavy sigh. "So, she's gone, gone." The permanence of that slammed into him like another boulder and threatened to take him down, if he weren't already sitting.

"You can go after her," Sofia said. "Go inside. Pack your bags and be at the Docks by six tomorrow morning to get the first ferry."

Ryan heard her words followed by the expectant silence his brothers dished out, but he couldn't respond. He only looked down at his phone, pressing the button on the side to awaken it.

"I read her blog posts," he said quietly. "When she told me she was here to write a story about the island, I looked her up online. Saw some of her stories, the comments." He let out a heavy sigh. "But she was enjoying herself here. I saw it. I…felt it." Clearing his throat, he continued. "So I knew she wouldn't find anything negative to write. It's Crescent after all." His lips tried to tilt into a smile, but it faltered.

"And you see how much she was hurting when she wrote them," Sofia added. "You notice that every word she wrote came from a place of pain and despair."

He glanced at his sister, emotion clogging his throat, so he nodded. "I don't know what to do."

It was the truth. The pain he felt now at knowing she was gone was more intense than anything he'd ever felt before, so stifling that he hadn't been able to move from this spot. Even when he'd tried to console himself with the thought that she just might be staying someplace else on the island, he hadn't been able to go to her. Hadn't known what to say or do.

"What do you want from her?" Trevor asked.

Ryan lifted his head and turned to see his brother leaning against the railing.

"Do you want to let her go and you continue to stay here and focus on how you're going to get that warehouse built?" Trevor continued.

"Or do you want to follow your heart?" Sofia added.

"I can stay here and keep your dog," Brody said and then grinned when all eyes turned to him. "If he goes to Miami, I can move in here and keep that little bullet he's cradling in his lap."

"You mean you can stay here and finally have a private place to take all your women without spending money for a room at the motel," Sofia chided.

Trevor nodded. "That sounds about right."

Ryan didn't speak, but he did grin at his siblings. They never let him down. Were always there when he needed them, saying the things that needed to be said whether he liked them or not.

He knew that whatever he decided to do, he'd always love them, always cherish the bond the Parkers had.

• • •

"Allison."

At the sound of her name, Allie bolted up in the chair so fast she almost fell over onto the bed. Her gaze darted around the room as she fought through the sleep still fogging her brain.

"Allison."

Her head jolted in the direction of the voice, eyes connecting with her mother's. "Yes, ma'am," she replied in a raspy tone.

Allie was in the hospital room they'd finally allowed her into in the early morning hours. She had raced to get here after the nurse's eerily calm call last night. A call that had shot a piercing fear through Allie's system. And by the time she'd finally arrived at the Miami hospital, her mother had been in surgery.

"I'm right here," Allie said, clearing her throat before standing and taking the two steps she was away from the bed.

Her mother looked weak amidst the stark white of the pillows and sheets. It took Allie a moment to adjust to that fact. Claire Sparks had always been a pillar of strength. Her shoulders always set, eyes keeping unbroken contact with whomever she was facing, voice clear as she enunciated each word, administered every demand.

"Water," Claire said before taking a long blink.

Allie hurriedly reached for one of the cups that had been left on the wheeled tray a short distance from the bed. Removing the half of wrapper still on the top of the straw, she went to the bed again, this time closer to where her mother's head lay. "Here you go," she said softly.

The top half of the bed was partially upright, so all Claire really had to do was turn her head toward where Allie held the cup. She did that with a slow roll of her eyes, and Allie inched the straw closer to her mother's lips. After two sips, Claire turned her head away from the cup and sighed.

"What did the doctors say?" Claire asked.

Allie turned away to set the cup back onto the

tray before facing her mother again. Claire's short cap of honey-blond hair perfectly highlighted her copper-toned complexion. Full, dark-brown brows were expertly arched, high cheekbones and full lips always ready for the cover of makeup her mother never left home without. Except this morning, Claire's face was scrubbed free and marred with half a dozen tiny cuts from the broken glass.

"Your car was T-boned by an SUV," Allie began, hating how the scene played out in her mind as she spoke. "You had the right of way; the other driver ran the red light." She paused and took a deep breath while her mother stared straight ahead. "When the police arrived, they called the fire department and the paramedics. They had to cut you out of the car, and they airlifted you here, to the trauma center."

Claire still didn't speak, and Allie fought back tears as she continued. "You have a concussion, three broken ribs from the airbag deploying, and…" Her voice hitched. "And your leg was broken in three places."

Her gaze wavered from her mother's face to see Claire's hands quickly grip the sheets before releasing them.

"The doctors repaired the breaks with rods and screws." Allie kept going because when Claire asked a question, she expected a complete answer. "You'll be in a cast for at least seven weeks, and once the orthopedic specialist confirms the break is healing satisfactorily, you'll begin intensive physical therapy."

Allie's hands were shaking now, and she clasped them together to keep from reaching out to touch her mother. If this were Nana or Ms. Sarah, there would've been no hesitation. Just as there hadn't been when Nana had touched Allie's shoulder last night. But that type of touch, of emotional freedom, had always been frowned upon in the Sparks home.

"Where is your father? Did he speak to the doctors as well?" Claire asked, still not looking in Allie's direction.

"Yes," Allie replied. "He was here when I arrived last night, but after you came out of surgery, he returned to the neuro center to finish out his shift. He'll be here when he's off." Because work always came first. Always.

A few moments passed, and Claire finally turned to look at Allie. "What are you wearing?"

For a second, Allie was startled by the totally off-topic question, but then she remembered where she was and whom she was speaking to. Her navy-blue-and-white-striped maxi dress was wrinkled after a night curled up in that uncomfortable chair, and she could only imagine the bushy mess her hair probably was after hours of travel. She cleared her throat. "I was attending a cookout on the beach when I got the call. I came directly here from the airport, so I haven't had a chance to shower and change."

Claire attempted to scowl, but pain must've interrupted the effort because instead she winced, and despite the slow rise of irritation, Allie moved closer to the bed. She rested a hand over her mother's and asked, "What is it? Do you need me to call the nurse?"

"No," Claire snapped. "She'll just pump me with more pain medications. I need my mind to be clear so I can have a conversation with these so-called specialists. I'm sure your father has compiled a list of all the best ones for me to consult."

As she spoke, Claire eased her hand from beneath Allie's. "You go home and get cleaned up. Then go to my place. I'll need some things from my home office, so call me when you get there. And don't take your time, Allison. I have very time-sensitive business that needs to be handled, and for the moment, you're the one I need to assist me."

Allie took a slow step away from the bed. When she didn't respond to her mother's instructions, Claire turned her head to look at her.

"I know you can hear and speak, Allison. If you have questions, ask them. If not, I need you to not delay."

The cold disdain in her mother's tone was painfully familiar. The exasperated look she was giving her daughter—the only one that she'd been able to have summoned here, the only one who'd graduated from college with honors as she'd been instructed, and the only one who'd attempted to give her the respect she barely deserved—was also one that Allie was acquainted with.

She took another step back, this time shaking her head. "Bella was right," she whispered finally.

In a flash, snatches of her time with the Parkers in the last two weeks moved through her mind like a movie trailer. Family laughing together on the back porch, working together in the restaurant, setting up for the Juneteenth cookout, and cooking in the kitchen. Not once had she heard anyone talk to anyone else in the tone her mother was now using. Not once had she been so coolly dismissed. And the

Parkers weren't even her blood relatives. They weren't supposed to love and respect her. They weren't supposed to care about her feelings.

But Claire Sparks was.

"Allison!" her mother yelled.

"What?" Allie snapped back.

"What is wrong with you? Why are you standing there looking like you didn't comprehend what I said to you?"

Allie was nodding this time, her chest rising and falling with the deep breaths she'd begun taking to keep her voice steady. "There's nothing wrong with me," she said evenly, letting her gaze lock with Claire's. "Nothing at all."

"Well, I can't tell. You're standing there like a statue when I expressly asked you to do something for me."

"What have you done for *me*, Mother?" Allie asked. "Besides put a roof over my head and feed me like you would've done a goldfish if you'd ever been inclined to have a pet. What have you done for me?" The last word came with a raise of Allie's voice, and Claire blinked in confusion.

"If you don't have an answer, that's fine. I have one for you," Allie continued. "You dismissed all of my hopes and dreams, criticized everything from the texture of my hair to my very slightly bowed legs. You've been displeased with me, it seems, since the day I was born, and nothing I've ever been able to do or say has changed that. And even still, I stayed." Her temples throbbed, and her fists clenched at her sides. "I stayed, just like Bella said, to continue to appease you because that was the least I could do since I didn't go to the school you wanted me to. And I didn't go into the career that you wanted for me. I stayed in Miami so that you wouldn't have to face the fact that neither of your daughters wanted to be near you and your husband."

The words fell into the silent room and settled there like a bitter, cold storm. Claire only blinked at her, and Allie held her stare.

"I came when they called because I was worried about you. You're my mother. I'm supposed to worry about your well-being. But you've never worried about mine."

"Allison, you're being ridiculous. And now is certainly not the time for these dramatics."

Allie shook her head. "Now is *exactly* the time," she countered. "Because it's the last time."

Those words were spoken with such unexpected finality, they left Allie trembling.

"I'm going to go home, shower, and change. I'll call to check on you, but you'll handle your own business. Have Dad go to the house to pick up your things."

And then what? Allie didn't know, but she turned to leave the room. Just as she came to the door and reached for the handle, her mother spoke.

"You're going to just leave me here when I need you, Allison?"

Allie turned to look at the woman she'd desperately wanted to love her all her life. She stared into the face she'd at one time wished she resembled more, replayed the sound of the voice that had echoed in her mind with harsh criticisms and ridiculous expectations for far too long.

"Yes," she said solemnly. "I'm going to leave you here because it's the best thing for my mental stability. It's the one change I've needed to make in all these years that duty, loyalty, and yes, fear have kept me from making. I'm going to leave you here so that I can save me."

CHAPTER TWENTY-FIVE

Allie had been right, there were plenty of beaches in Miami.

Ryan gave a wry chuckle at the thought and slipped his dark sunglasses back onto his face. A ride-share service had dropped him off at the sixteen-story oceanfront condominium development. The sky was a brilliant blue, white cotton candy puffed clouds drifting amidst the heavens. Palm trees swayed in the balmy breeze while the sound of cars whizzed by on the streets.

He inhaled deeply and released a slow breath, reminding himself that he was doing the right thing. He was doing the *only* thing that he could.

He hadn't needed time to consider his options, not after his siblings had given him the news that Allie had left the island last night. There were no options that didn't include her. Not for him, not ever again.

So he leaned against a pristine white column, hands stuffed into the pockets of his jeans, and waited for her to return.

A trip up to unit 1006 twenty minutes ago had told him she wasn't home, but he was going to wait for her to get here. He'd been waiting for her his whole life; he could wait a little longer.

And then, as if the stars had decided to align perfectly with his wishes, a gray compact car pulled up in front of the building and Allie stepped out of the back door. He sucked in a breath at the sight of her puffy curls held back from her face by a thick, dark-blue band, her arms bare from the sleeveless dress, and those orange-painted toenails on display via the flat natural-colored sandals on her feet.

She had her big tote on one shoulder and reached into the backseat of the car to pull out the duffel bag she'd had with her the first day they'd met. Instinctively, he crossed the few feet of space between him and the car and, when she turned to close the door, reached for the bag.

"Ryan?" she said, surprise evident in the widening of her eyes and high pitch of her voice.

"Hey," he replied. "Let me help you with that."

For an instant he thought she was going to refuse, like she had when they were on the island that first day. But she released the bag and cleared her throat.

With his free hand, he took hers and said, "C'mon, let's get out of the way so this car can get going."

They walked over to the column where he'd been standing and she stopped.

"What are you doing here?" Her brow furrowed, and she slipped her hand from his.

"You're here," he said. "So I am, too." Those words sounded so simple, but he knew that wasn't the case. Packing his bag to come here, to this huge city, to find Allie, had been one of the biggest steps he'd taken in a very long time.

She shook her head. "I don't understand."

"Me neither, Allie," he told her. "You left without saying a word to me or to anyone else. I've been calling and texting you all night. So has Sofia."

"What? Wait," she said and then dug into her bag.

Just once Ryan would like to see what she carried around all the time in that big bag, but then he'd have to wrap his mind around why she thought whatever was in there was so necessary to carry around all the time. The thought had him frowning.

When she had her phone in her hand, she stared down at it with a frown. Then she glanced up at him again and let out a heavy sigh. "I didn't have a signal when I was on the ferry and by the time I got to shore again, called to book a flight, and then called a ride-share to pick me up, the phone went dead. The portable charger I keep with me was also dead, so I had to wait until I got to the airport to plug every-thing up and re-charge. By then it was so late I didn't want to bother Sofia with a call, so I figured I'd wait until morning. But so much has happened that I just…" She paused finally and shrugged.

"You were only going to call Sofia?" he asked and then shook his head. "Wait, no, what happened? Is this the first time you've been home since last night?" Because it just occurred to him that she'd been wear-ing that dress last night at the cookout.

"Yes," she replied with another heavy sigh. "My mother was in a car accident, so I went straight to the hospital from the airport."

And now he felt like a total jerk for whining about her thinking to call Sofia first and for thinking she'd left because of what Kerry had said last night. "Whoa, is she all right?" he asked as he dropped her bag to sit on the ground beside his and took her by the shoulders.

"Yeah." She nodded. "I mean, her leg is badly broken and she's got some cracked ribs and bruising, but she's...she's the same. Unfortunately."

She lowered her head after that last word, and Ryan touched a finger to her chin, applying the gentlest pressure until she glanced up at him again. From her reaction, he sensed that something big had happened with her and her family, and while his heart ached for the pain this obviously caused her, he still asked, "You wanna talk about it?"

"No," she said quickly and took a step back until he had no choice but to drop his arms to his sides. "I didn't think to call you first because I knew you were already dealing with a lot after Kerry's announcement. I was going to show you my final story last night when we returned to your place." She was shaking her head again, the sun's brilliant beams landing on her deeply hued skin. Her eyes were wide, a sheen of moisture forming as she continued. "I wanted you to know..." Her voice cracked, and she looked away.

Ryan dug into his back pocket and pulled out his phone. He'd made a screen shot of the paragraph from today's story on the See, Eat, Travel blog he'd read repeatedly while on the plane this morning and then more times on the drive to this building.

"'The heart of Crescent Island doesn't rest in its elusive matchmaker's hands. Instead, it lives in every breath that's taken once you step off the ferry,'" he read from his phone. "'It's in every smile you're greeted with as you walk along the cobblestone path of the Docks. It's in the lovingly prepared food, along the sandy shores, in the sound of the rustling Springs, the laughter emanating from rides atop the Ferris wheel. It's in his smile when he walks along the beach at midnight with his lop-eared dog by his side.'"

He stopped reading and looked up at her then. "I was in line getting ready to board the plane when I read that last sentence. And I had to stop because it felt like something was piercing through my soul. Like something had been ripped out of me and if I didn't get it back, I'd never be able to take an easy breath again."

Tears brimmed her eyes now as she folded her arms across her chest, holding herself in the way Ryan desperately wanted to hold her.

He closed the distance between them again, tucking his phone back into his pocket before lifting a hand to cup her cheek. "So, if you're here in Miami, then I'm here, too, Allie." He swallowed the lump he hadn't realized had been in his throat since he'd learned she'd left the island last night and let the warmth of being close to her again spread throughout his chest. "It doesn't matter to me where we are, as long as we're together. I'm falling in love with you, Allison Sparks, and I'm not letting horoscopes, logistics, or anything else get in our way."

She chuckled just as a tear rolled down her cheek. "I don't believe in horoscopes," she said.

"What about matchmakers?" he asked, letting her smile pull him closer until he could wrap his other arm around her waist.

Another tear fell, and he moved his hand to thumb it away.

"They're growing on me," she replied. "Just like your dog."

He shook his head at that last part. "Nah, I kinda think he's more your dog now. You should've seen the pleading look he gave me when I left this morning."

"Awwwww," she crooned as more tears fell.

"What is it, baby? Why're you crying?"

"Because I'm happy and I'm sad," she replied.

"Sad? I thought you said your mother was going to be okay."

She shook her head and then brought her hands to her face to wipe her tears before sighing. "She is, and so am I," she told him. "I'm coming back to Crescent Island."

His grin had just begun to spread when she held up a hand to stop whatever he might say next.

"Not just because you and Optimus are the most adorable pair I've ever seen walking along the beach and I'm pretty sure I'm falling in love with both of you. But because it's where I need to be at this point in my life. I need to be around people who smile easily and joke abundantly. Who like being around each other and bake delicious cinnamon buns and cook succulent brisket. I need to not feel like I'm doing something wrong when I take off my shoes and walk through the sand or enjoy the sound of the waves that crest and fall nearby. I need to write all the words that are in my heart, not the ones that have filled my mind for so long. I need to breathe, Ryan." She sighed. "I need to sit with you on that back porch at night and just breathe."

He let out a breath then, a long, slow breath that he hadn't realized he'd been holding since she'd started to speak. "Then you should do all those things, Allie. You should do all of them…and maybe just one more."

She arched a brow. "One more?"

"Yeah." He nodded as he leaned in closer to whisper. "You should kiss me."

She grinned, and when his lips touched hers, she did as he said.

EPILOGUE

Nine Months Later
The Midnight Wedding

At twelve-oh-five a.m., Allison Sparks said, "I do," agreeing to love and cherish Ryan Parker—and Optimus—for the rest of her life.

Battery-operated lanterns made a pathway from the steps of the back porch of the Big House down to where the grassy earth dropped to the sandy beach. There, an archway of white calla lilies and bright twinkle lights surrounded them. Dressed in a strapless ivory-colored dress with a two-foot train that blew in the spring wind, Allie shifted from one foot to the other, the three-inch heels of her turquoise sandals digging into the earth. Ryan looked debonair in a black tuxedo and turquoise tie. Beside him, Optimus, all one hundred and fifty-two pounds of black-speckled cuteness, stood as if he were the official best man and not Trevor.

Brody, Clay, and the twins wore black as well, their ties a variety of jewel-toned colors—fuchsia, plum, citrine yellow, and mandarin orange respectively. On Allie's side, Sofia was her maid-of-honor and wore a gorgeous teal-colored, mermaid-style gown that hugged her every curve and matched Trevor's tie. Gwen, whom she'd become good friends with in the months they'd both worked as servers in the restaurant, matched Brody's tie. Three of Ryan's cousins made up her remaining bridesmaids, and they all looked amazing in dresses they'd personally selected in the colors Allie had designated.

As they turned away from the minister, he proudly announced, "Ladies and gentlemen, I now present to you Mr. and Mrs. Ryan Zacharius Parker." Optimus barked, and she and Ryan faced the crowd before them.

Nana and Ms. Annabelle, who sat on the front row next to Ms. Sarah and Mr. Vernon, stood up first, clapping wildly. Well, Ms. Annabelle put her fingers in her mouth and whistled, the star-shaped hairclips she wore glittering in the dark of night. Across from them, Claire and Douglas, Allie's parents, also stood, albeit stiffly. They clapped as well and attempted a smile.

It had been a few months, and many online group counseling sessions, since she'd invited her parents to Crescent to meet Ryan and the Parkers. The first two days they'd been there had been full of surprised looks, stilted conversation, and her mother complaining about the sand, but by the time they'd left, and after a private dinner with her and Ryan, the Sparkses had committed to visiting Allie and her new extended family more frequently.

And because Allie had talked about becoming more active in the day-to-day workings of Parker BBQ, her father had actually brought up the possibility of becoming another investor in Parker Sauces.

While Ryan had waited for Allie to answer his call or respond to his text messages the night of the Juneteenth cookout, he'd decided to email Phoebe at Brownstone to tell her about Kerry's connection to him and the island. As he'd suspected, Kerry hadn't told Phoebe that she used to live on Crescent Island or that she and Ryan had been romantically involved. A few weeks later, Phoebe had shown up on the island herself, and after several meetings with Ryan, Vernon, and Sofia, a new investment deal had been signed. And in three weeks—after Allie and Ryan returned from their honeymoon in Greece—the construction crews would break ground on the warehouse where Parker Sauces would be manufactured on Crescent Island.

So if Allie was beaming, it was because her life had changed so drastically in the past nine months. Her heart had been filled, her career expanded so that she would continue to travel and write for the blog—albeit much happier reviews now—but on a part-time basis. She'd received her first publishing contract for an island-themed romcom that would release next summer. She couldn't ask for anything more, couldn't dream of another thing to make this evening any better.

Until she saw *her* walking down the aisle.

Wearing a white linen pantsuit and high-heeled yellow sandals, her hair styled in blond goddess braids, Isabella Sparks had arrived at the wedding. Allie gasped and took a slow step forward before stopping. She had to breathe, to think and try to understand what was happening.

In August, she'd reached out to Guy the PI again, telling him if he didn't give her more details about the lead he'd been following that she wasn't making another payment. To that, Guy had replied that he'd had an address for Bella in Boston but that she

hadn't been seen at that residence in over a year. Guy
thought the trail was cold and he'd given Allie the
very cynical "sometimes people just don't want to be
found" advice. It had taken her weeks to decide she
would accept that because it made sense. Their parents hadn't moved, so if Bella had wanted to return
home or reach out to them, she knew where to find
them. Up until that point, Allie had lived in Miami,
where Bella could've also found her if she'd wanted
to.

"How did she—" she started to say when she felt
Ryan's hand slip around her waist.

"I sent her an invitation," he said, dipping his
head to kiss her bare shoulder. "I didn't tell you—"

"In case she didn't come," she finished his sentence and turned to him. When he looked up, she
kissed his lips. "I love you," she whispered.

"And I love you," he replied before touching his
lips to hers once more.

When Allie looked up again, Bella was standing
just a couple feet away from her. Bella, her younger
sister. Her first best friend. The part of Allie's heart
she'd thought long lost.

The two didn't speak. Allie closed the space. Bella
extended her arms. And they hugged for what
seemed like forever, right there under the stars.

"I'm so sorry," Bella whispered as they finally
pulled apart. "I should've called or written. I
shouldn't have stayed away so long. I should've—"

"No," Allie interrupted, taking both Bella's hands
in hers. "I'm no longer living in the past, and you
shouldn't, either. It's a new day, or rather a new
night," she said and then chuckled. "And I'm just

thrilled to have you here to start it all with me."

Bella shook her head as tears began to fall. "I'm glad to be here, too," she said. "I really am, Allie."

"Well, well, well. If it ain't another city beauty come to bless our little island with her presence," Cyrus interrupted, coming to stand beside them.

Bella hurried to swipe the tears from her eyes, and Allie chuckled at Cyrus, who was dressed in a freshly pressed mint-green leisure suit and a bone-colored Panama hat over his bald head.

As if they couldn't possibly travel separately—and hardly ever did—Barney came to stand at Bella's other side.

"Pretty ladies must run in the Sparks family," he said, grabbing the lapels of the jacket that matched his beige plaid pants.

"I already said she was a beauty, old man," Cyrus grumbled.

"Yeah, well, I said she was pretty. There's a difference," Barney continued.

"Ain't no difference in the two," Cyrus said with a shake of his head. "Unless you gonna say that my word sounds better."

"How could your word sound better? That don't even make sense, Cyrus."

"Does too make sense because I know things." Cyrus nodded. "Ain't that right, Allison?"

Allie could only grin, as she often did whenever these two were around. "Yes. Bella, I'd like to introduce you to Mr. Cyrus. He knows a little something about everything here on Crescent Island."

And when Barney mumbled under his breath, Allie continued, "And this is Mr. Barney. He also knows a lot about the island. So while you're here, you should definitely sit with them a while and let them tell you about all the sights you should see."

"Oh, is that right?" Bella asked, her red-painted lips spreading into a smile that warmed Allie's heart to see.

Barney nodded. "That's absolutely right. Now, first you've gotta start by calling Eddie for a ride."

Cyrus immediately chimed in, "No. You just get yourself on the Coaster and let it take you to the Emporium."

"They've got everything at the Emporium," Barney added.

Yes, they did, Allie thought, everything. Including an eccentric tarot card reader who called herself the Crescent Island Matchmaker. And she was just fine with that.

Fans of RaeAnne Thyane and Brenda Novak will adore this sparkling frenemies-to-lovers romance…

come what maybe

KERRI CARPENTER

Social media strategist Lauren Wallace plans everything. But when she returns to the charming—if not too small for comfort—town of Seaside Cove, it's only about a second before her tough-love Grams is already on her case. So when Grams tells her not to go to that bar, Lauren decides it's time for a temporary rebellion. Which is exactly when the trouble starts.

Grams was right. The bar was not a good plan. Because suddenly super-cute bar owner Ethan McAllister has gone from being Lauren's (kind of) high school nemesis to a very unexpected one-night stand. And worse, Lauren's attempts to resume her ultra-responsible life keep getting thwarted by more unwelcome spontaneity. And a pregnancy.

Now there's a baby on the way, Lauren's the talk of the entire town, and all her planning has gone right out the window. All that's missing is childbirth to make her pain complete. But it'll be nothing compared to Grams's reaction when she finds out that Lauren broke the biggest rule of all…falling for the wrong guy.

*Return to Blossom Glen, where two
opposites must put their differences aside
to help the small town they both love…*

the
SWEETHEART
FIX

MIRANDA LIASSON

Juliet Montgomery absolutely loves her small town of Blossom Glen, Indiana, and everyone loves her. Except for the fact that she's a couples counselor who suffered a *very* public breakup that *no one* can forget. And now her boss asks her to take a step back…which is exactly when the town's good-lookin' and unusually gruff mayor offers her an unexpected job.

Jack Monroe absolutely loves being the mayor of his small town. Except when he actually has to talk to people. Can't he just fix the community problems in peace? Like right now, he's mediating the silliest dispute two neighbors could possibly have. When the town sweetheart steps up and solves everyone's problems in five minutes flat, Jack realizes what this town really needs…is a therapist.

Juliet is able to soothe anyone—other than the surly mayor, it seems. But there's a reason they say opposites attract, because all of their verbal sparring leads to some serious attraction. Only, just like with fireworks, the view might appear beautiful—but she's already had one public explosion that's nearly ruined everything…how can she risk her heart again?

AMARA
an imprint of Entangled Publishing LLC